HOME TRUTHS

Freya gave up a PhD to write her first novel, *Sally*, in 1991. For four years she turned deaf ears to parents and friends who pleaded with her to 'get a proper job'. She went on the dole and did a succession of freelance and temping jobs to support her writing days. In 1995, throwing caution to the wind, Freya sent three chapters and a page of completely fabricated reviews to a top literary agent, and met with success: five publishers entered a bidding war for her books. In 1996 *Sally* was published to great acclaim and Freya was heralded as a fresh voice in fiction. Her next books, *Chloë*, *Polly*, *Cat*, *Fen*, *Pip* and *Love Rules* have all been bestsellers. She lives in London with her family.

For more information on Freya North, visit her website at www.freyanorth.co.uk.

Visit www.AuthorTracker.co.uk for exclusive updates on Freya North.

Praise for *Home Truths*:

'An eye-poppingly sexy start leads into a family reunion laced with secrets. Tangled mother/daughter relationships unravel and tantalising family riddles keep you glued to the end.'   *Cosmopolitan*

'An engrossing emotional drama that's sure to feature on bestseller lists.'   *Eve*

By the same author

Sally
Chloë
Polly
Cat
Fen
Pip
Love Rules

FREYA NORTH

Home Truths

HARPER

This novel is entirely a work of fiction.
The names, characters and incidents portrayed in it are
the work of the author's imagination. Any resemblance to
actual persons, living or dead, events or localities is
entirely coincidental.

Harper
An imprint of HarperCollins*Publishers*
77–85 Fulham Palace Road,
Hammersmith, London W6 8JB

www.harpercollins.co.uk

1

First published in Great Britain by
HarperCollins*Publishers* 2006

ISBN 978 0 00 780836 6

Set in Sabon by Palimpsest

Printed and bound in Great Britain by
Clays Ltd, St Ives plc

For Georgia
my beautiful, beautiful girl

Write your sister's weak points in the sand
and her strong points in stone.

Anon

Prologue

'How do you say goodbye to a mountain?'

From her vantage point, Cat York looked across to the three Flatirons, to Bear Peak and Green Mountain. She gazed down the skirts of Flagstaff, patting the snow around her and settling herself in as though she was sitting on the mountain's lap. 'It's like a giant, frozen wedding dress,' she said. 'It probably sounds daft, but for the last four years, I've privately thought of Flagstaff as *my* mountain.'

'There's a lot of folk round here who think that way,' Stacey said. 'You're allowed to. That's the beauty of living in Boulder.'

The sun shot through, glancing off the crystal-cracked snow on the trees, the sharp, flat slabs of rust-coloured rock of the Flatirons soaring through all the dazzling white at their awkward angle.

'When Ben and I first arrived and I was homesick and insecure, I'd walk to Chautauqua Meadow and just sit on my own. It felt like the mountains were a giant arm around my shoulders.' Cat looked around her with nostalgic gratitude. 'Then soon enough we met you lot, started hiking and biking the trails and suddenly the mountain showed me its other side. You could say it's been my therapist's couch and it's been my playground. It's now my most favourite place in the world.'

Stacey looked at Cat, watched her friend cup her gloved hands over her nose and mouth in a futile bid to make her nose look less red and her lips not so blue. 'This time next week, the only peaks I'll be seeing are Victorian rooftops,' Cat said, 'grimy pigeons will replace bald eagles and there'll just be puddles in place of Wonderland Lake. Next week will be a whole new year.'

'Tell me about Clapham,' Stacey asked, settling into their snow bunker.

'Well,' said Cat, 'it's a silent "h" for a start.'

They laughed.

'God,' Cat groaned, leaning forward and knocking her head against her knees, 'I'm still not sure we're doing the right thing – but don't tell Ben I said so. I can't tell you about Clapham, I don't think I've ever been.' She paused and then continued a little plaintively. 'God, Stacey, I have no job, my two closest friends don't even live in the city any more and I'm moving to an opposite side of London to where I used to live, where my sisters still live.'

'It's exciting,' Stacey said, 'and if you don't like it, you can always come back.' She tore into a pack of Reese's with her teeth, her chilled fingers unfit for the task. 'And there's some stuff that's really to look forward to.'

Placated and sustained by the pack of peanut butter, the comfort of chocolate, Cat agreed. 'I've missed my family – by the sound of it, my middle sister Fen is having a tough time at the moment. And it's going to be a big year for Django – he'll be seventy-five which will no doubt warrant a celebration of prodigious proportions.'

'I'd sure like to have met him,' Stacey said and she laughed a little. 'I remember when I first met you, I thought you were like, so exotic, because you came to Boulder with your English Rose looks and a history that Brontë couldn't have made up. You with the mother who ran off with a cowboy, you who were raised by a crazy uncle called Django, you and your sisters brought up in the wilds of Wherever.'

'Derbyshire's not wild,' Cat protested, 'not our part. Though there are wallabies.'

'What's a wallaby?'

'It's like a mini kangaroo,' said Cat. 'They were kept as pets by the posh folk in eighteenth-century Derbyshire – but some broke free, bred, and now bounce happily across the Dales.'

Stacey took a theatrical intake of breath. 'So we have you and your sisters, living in the countryside with your hippy dude uncle and a herd of mutant, aristocratic kangaroos because your mom eloped with J. R. Ewing?' She whistled. 'You could sell this to Hollywood.'

'Shut up, Stacey,' Cat laughed. 'We're just a normal family. Django is a very regular bloke – albeit with a colourful dress code and an adventurous take on cuisine. I'm starting to freeze. Let's go into town and get a hot chocolate. My bum's numb even in these salopettes.'

'Weird, though,' Stacey said thoughtfully.

'What is? My bottom?'

'Your butt is cute, honey,' Stacey assured her, as they hauled each other to their feet. 'I mean it's a little weird that your mom runs off with a cowboy from Denver when you were small, right?'

'Yup.'

'And you've been living pretty close to the Mile High City these last four years, right?'

'Yup.'

'But you never looked her up?'

'Nope.'

3

'Never even thought about it? Never went shopping in Denver and thought, Hey, I wonder if that lady over there is my mom?'

Throughout Cat's life, it had always been her friends who'd been far more intrigued by her family circumstances, her absent mother, than she. 'But I never knew her. I was a baby. I have no memories of her,' Cat explained. 'I'm not even curious. We had Django, my sisters and I – we wanted for nothing. Just because we didn't have a "conventional" mother or father didn't mean that we were denied a proper parent.'

Stacey linked arms with Cat. 'Conventional families are dull, honey – stick with your kooky one.'

'Oh I'm sticking with my kooky one all right!' Cat laughed. 'I love them with all my heart. And now that Ben and I want to start our own, it feels natural to want to be within that fold again.'

At the time, Cat and Ben York had argued about putting the set of three matching suitcases on their wedding list. Cat had denounced them as boring and unsexy and why couldn't they peruse the linen department one more time. Ben told her that some things in life were, by virtue, boring and unsexy and he pointed out there were only so many Egyptian cotton towels a couple could physically use in a lifetime. Three years later, Ben and Cat are contemplating the same three suitcases: frequently used, gaping open and empty, waiting to be fed the last remaining clothes and belongings. The process is proving to be far more irksome than the packing of the huge crates a few weeks ago, now currently making their passage by sea back to England.

'Weird to think that this time next week we'll be back in the UK,' Ben says.

'Weird that we both now refer to it as "the UK" rather than "England" or simply "home",' says Cat. 'Stacey and I went for a fantastic walk this morning.' She looks through their picture windows to the mountains, a huge cottonwood tree in its winter wear with stark, thick boughs boasting sprays of fine, finger-like branches, the big sky, the quality of air so clean it is almost visible. 'God, it's stunning here.'

'Hey,' says Ben, 'we'll have Clapham Common on our new doorstep.'

Cat hurls a pillow at him. He ducks.

'We can always come back,' Ben tells her, 'but for now, it is time to go. We have things to do. That was the point, remember. That's why we came here in the first place. It's the things we do now which provide a tangible future for our daydreams. That's why it's timely to return to the UK.'

'Do dreams come true in *Clapham*?'

Ben hurls the pillow back at Cat. She hugs it close and looks momentarily upset. 'I don't even have a job to go back to,' she says, 'and not from want of trying. And I'm not pregnant yet – not from want of trying. I feel like I'm just traipsing behind you.'

'We're a team,' Ben states, 'you and me. I've been given a great job which will be big enough for both of us. I've taken it – for the both of us – so you can take your time and think about you.'

'I know,' Cat smiles sheepishly. 'But what'll I do in Clapham all day? Are we packing the pillows?'

'I don't know – do furnished flats come with pillows?'

'I'm not sleeping on pillows used by God knows who,' Cat protests, though she calculates that three pillows will fill an entire suitcase.

'You do in hotels,' Ben reasons, with a frustrated ruffle through his short, silver-flecked hair. 'It's not as if we're going to some boarding house – I told you, the flat is really quite nice. And when I'm up and running, we'll look for somewhere to buy.'

'In *North* London,' Cat says and Ben decides not to react to the fact that this is emphatically not a question. 'Pip says she's worried about Fen.'

'Your eldest sister worries about everyone,' Ben says, remembering that, actually, these pillows came with this apartment. He doesn't comment.

'But she says that Fen and Matt aren't getting along. Since the baby.'

'You're not your sisters' keeper,' Ben says carefully.

'Oh but I am,' Cat says, as if she's offended, as if Ben's forgotten to understand the closeness between the McCabe girls, 'we all are. It's always been that way, it had to be.'

Ben decides to change the subject. He knows that when his wife is emotional, the legend of her family can be detrimentally overplayed. But he knows, too, that once she returns to their fold again, all the normal niggles and familial irritations will surface and Cat will no doubt be glad of Clapham. He wedges socks into spaces in the cases and then crosses to Cat. 'Your family won't recognize you,' he says. 'They'll be expecting that blonde girl with the pony-tail they saw last summer – not this auburn pixie. Mind you, they won't recognize me – you couldn't call my hair "salt and pepper" any more, it's just plain grey.'

'Makes you look very distinguished,' Cat says, brushing her hand tenderly through Ben's hair. She tufts at her elfin crop with a beguiling wail. 'Do you think mine's too short? I told them to cut it shorter than usual, and colour it stronger than normal because I wouldn't be coming back for a while. It's like I forgot that the UK basically *invented* places like Vidal Sassoon and John Frieda.'

'You look gorgeous,' Ben says, 'really sexy and cute and fuckable.' He's behind her, nuzzling the graceful sweep of her neck that her cropped hair has exposed. He fondles her breasts and then takes his hand down to her crotch and cups at it playfully.

'Dr York!' Cat says. 'I have packing to do.'

'And I want to fuck my wife,' Ben whispers, with a titillating nip at her ear lobe.

Cat resists theatrically but he catches her wrists and suddenly he's tonguing her hungrily. 'Come on, babe. Procreation is top of our list after all, remember.'

'Making babies is a very serious matter, Dr York,' says Cat with mock consternation though she is wriggling out of her clothing.

Ben plugs her mouth with a kiss and takes her hand down to his jeans where his hard-on wells at an awkward angle. 'Well then, we'd better commit ourselves to honing our technique.'

'You're the doctor,' Cat says, dispensing with her knickers. Ben's hands travel her body, he gorges on the sight of her. He loves her naked when he's still fully clothed, the tantalizing interference of fabric between him and his wife's silky skin. She squats down and unbuckles his belt, makes achingly slow progress with the flies of his trousers, easing down his boxer shorts as if it's the first time she's done so. She's on her knees. His cock springs to attention. Her mouth is moist but teasingly just beyond reach.

'Christ, Cat,' Ben says hoarsely, clutching her head and bucking his groin to meet her.

'Blow-jobs don't make babies,' Cat tells him artlessly, but she kisses the tip of his cock and follows this with swift, deep sucks that make him groan. She stands and looks up at him. His height has always turned her on and when he dips his face down to kiss hers it darkens his brown eyes. 'Isn't there some position that's meant to facilitate fertility, doctor?'

'Yes, Mrs York,' Ben confirms, turning her away from

him, running his hand gently up her back, pushing between her shoulder-blades so that she is bent forwards, 'there is. Just. Like. This.'

He takes her from behind. The sensation is so exquisite that, for a while, they are silent, motionless.

'Dr York? Are you sure doggy-style is medically proven to assist conception?'

'No,' Ben pants as he thrusts into her, his hands at her waist to haul himself in, 'but I'm quite certain that the sight of your immaculate peach of an arse improves the quality of my load.'

Django McCabe

Often, making light of the dark makes good sense. When Django McCabe was trekking in Nepal in the early 1960s, en route to some saffron-robed guru or other, he came across a man who had fallen down a screed slope along the mountain pass.

'Need a hand?' Django had offered.

'Actually, wouldn't mind a leg,' the man had responded. It was then that Django saw the man in fact had only the one leg, that his crutch had been flung some distance. Django learnt more from his co-traveller than from the guru: not to let hardship harden a person, to keep humour at the heart of the matter, to make light of the dark. A decade later, when Django found himself guardian to three girls under the age of four, the offspring of his late brother, he thought about his one-legged friend and decided that the circumstances uniting him with his nieces would never be recalled as anything other than rather eccentric, strangely fortunate and not that big a deal anyway. 'I know your mother ran off with a cowboy from Denver, but . . .' has since prefixed all manner of events throughout the McCabe girls' lives.

I know your mother ran off with a cowboy from Denver,

but crying because I accidentally taped over Dallas *is a little melodramatic.*

It was mid-morning and Django McCabe felt entitled to a little sit-down. But there wasn't time for forty winks. It was Monday and if the girls were coming home for the weekend then he needed the week to prepare for their visit; he couldn't be wasting time with a snooze. However, to sit in a chair and not nod off was as difficult, perhaps even as pointless, as going to the Rag and Thistle and not having a pint of bitter.

'I'll multi-task,' Django muttered. 'Apparently it's a very twenty-first-century thing to do.' And so he decided to combine his little sit-down with doing something constructive, in this instance scanning today's runners. After all, studying the form would stop him dozing off.

And there it was. Staring him in the face. 2.20 Pontefract. Cool Cat. Rank outsider – but what did they know.

'It's a sign,' he said, patting himself all over to locate his wallet which, after an extensive grope through the collection of jackets draped over most of the chairs in the kitchen, he finally found. 'I'll put a tenner on the horse. In honour of Cat. I need to pop into town anyway so either way, it won't be a wasted trip.'

Django would never place a bet by phone. He doesn't trust the telephone. He says, darkly, that you never know who may be listening. But his Citroën 2CV he trusts with his life and, along the lanes of Farleymoor and the roads around Chesterfield, the little car filled to bursting with Django is a familiar sight. At seventy-four, Django is physically robust. Tall and sturdy, affably portly around the girth and crowned by a mane of grey hair always pony-tailed. He toots and waves as he drives. He thinks fellow drivers are slowing down to let him pass, to wave back. Actually they're swerving to keep out of his way, holding up their hands in protest.

There are people in every continent who regard Django as their friend, though his travelling days ended with the arrival of his three small nieces some thirty years ago. He has rarely left Derbyshire since and it is the area around Farleymoor, on the Matlock side of Chesterfield, where his warmest clutch of friends are massed.

'Morning, Mary, and don't you look divine for a Monday,' Django says, entering the bookmakers.

'And don't you look colourful for January,' Mary says, wondering if he's warm enough in his paisley shirt and tapestry waistcoat.

'From Peru,' Django tells her, opening his waistcoat wide, like a flasher. 'I had to trade with bandits on a mountain pass.'

'And what did they get of you, duck?'

'My passport,' Django says and he roars with laughter. 'A tenner on Cool Cat, if you please.'

'Rank outsider,' Mary warns him.

'I know,' Django shrugs, 'but the odds were worse for Fenland Star yesterday and truly terrible for Pipistrelle last week and they both won.' He hands over a ten-pound note. 'She's flying home as we speak, you know. Cat. I have all three girls descending on me for the weekend.'

Mary knows Django's girls. They were at school with her daughters. 'No doubt you'll be cooking up a treat for them, then?'

'She's been in America for four years,' he says, leaning on the counter and beckoning Mary closer. 'That's an awful lot of McDonalds. Apparently her hair is now red.'

Mary can't see the connection between McDonalds and hair colour. If she remembers correctly, Cat is the sporty one who married the doctor of a professional cycling team.

'So I am indeed preparing a Spread to welcome her home and put back some nutrients,' Django is saying. 'Oh, and let's have a tenner on Three's Company at Fakenham. Good little horse, that.'

Django McCabe hasn't had a beard for over twenty years, yet still, in moments of contemplation, he strokes his chin with fingertips light and methodical as if his goatee still sits proud on his face. The habit is one that he uses for all manner of pontification, from selecting horses according to their names or the form given them by the *Racing Post*, to his choice of the next domino at the Rag and Thistle. Currently, he is toying with his chin while wondering what to cook. Laid out before him are all the foodstuffs from the fridge, most of those from the larder, and a few from the capacious chest freezer too. He doesn't believe in shopping according to a recipe, he cooks to accommodate available ingredients; he invented food combining in its most oblique sense. He fingers his invisible beard and begins to make his considered selection, as an artist might choose pigment for the day's palette. Indeed, Django feels at his most creative when cooking – he sees blending, mixing, combining, concocting, as art, not science. Thus he never measures or weighs and he believes cookery books are to cooking what painting-by-numbers kits are to painting.

Whenever his nieces visit from London, it warrants a Spread. And as the forthcoming weekend is to be not just an ordinary visit, but a homecoming celebration, it has to be a Monumental Spread. Django hasn't seen Cat since the summer. None of them has. Christmas was peculiar for her absence. She'd turned thirty-two years old in the autumn and he hadn't been able to make her a birthday cake. On top of that, Pip implied recently that Fen has been a little down. He knows of no way better to warm the heart and feed the

12

soul than to fill the stomach with all manner of home cooking first.

Django is at his happiest when cooking for his girls, even though they are all in their thirties, with homes of their own, and their health has never been of concern.

'It's habit,' he'll say when they say he needn't have, when they say a pub lunch or ready-meal supper would be fine by them, when they say they are too full for seconds let alone thirds. 'I'm old and stuck in my ways,' he'll declare. 'Humour me.' He'll say the same thing when presenting them with carrier bags bulging with Tupperware containers when they leave again for London.

Django McCabe is their family tree. The desertion of their mother, the death of their father gave him no choice – but ultimately gave him his greatest blessing. His arms, like great branches, have been the protective clasp, the loving embrace of mother, father, confidant and mentor to Cat, Fen and Pip. He provided the boughs in which their cradles were rocked. His are the roots which have always anchored them and kept them safe.

Tuesday

Fen McCabe used to enjoy looking in the mirror. Far from it being a vanity kick, she'd found it an affirming thing to do. In the scamper of a working day, to grasp a private moment to nod at her reflection was sustaining. Hullo you, she'd sometimes say, what a busy day. And in the heady period when Matt Holden had wined, dined, wooed and pursued her, she'd frequently nip to the loo in some restaurant or bar, for a little time out with herself. He likes me, she'd beam at her reflection, you go girl! She'd wink at herself, give herself the go-ahead to party and flirt and charm the man who, soon enough, wanted to be with her for life.

Since having a baby six months ago, Fen has hated looking in the mirror. Not because she finds the sight depressing but because she finds the sight so strange. She doesn't so much wince away from the sight of a few extra pounds, the limp hair, the sallow skin, the dark and puffy eyes, as glance bewildered and wonder who *is* that? How can this be my reflection when I don't actually recognize the person staring back? And mirror mirror on the wall, wasn't I once a damn sight fairer than *this*? So it's something of a relief not to have the time during the day and to be too tired in the evening to face the facts staring back from the looking glass.

The phone is ringing, the baby is crying. Fen is nearer to the phone and Matt is nearer to the baby. Matt knows that Fen can find little wrong with the way he answers the phone so he's happy to swap places here in the kitchen.

'Hullo?' he answers. 'Well hullo!' He looks over to Fen. She's wearing truly awful pyjamas. Even if they'd been a matching set they'd have little to commend them. The bottoms have polka dots on a sickly lilac background. The top is littered with cutesy cartoon animals, a strange hybrid love child of a dog and a rabbit and even some teddy bear chromosomes somewhere along the line. 'Hold on, I'll just pass you over.' He holds out the receiver.

'Who is it?' Fen mouths but Matt will only cock his eyebrow and grin. As Fen shuffles over to the phone, the placated baby at home on her hip, Matt notes her slippers. The grey, felted monstrosities he once termed 'eastern-bloc lesbian clogs'. He'd had her in stitches at the time, she'd done a bastardized folk dance in them and had him in hysterics, before she'd banished them under the bed. For good, so he'd thought, until just then.

'Hullo?' says Fen.

'Boo!' says the voice.

'Cat?'

'I'm back! We're in a cab, on the M4. Heading for Clapham.'

Matt watches the smile warm her face. He thinks how clichéd it sounds to say that the sun comes out when Fen smiles. But in his eyes, it does. And suddenly he forgives her the pyjamas and the clogs and he feels bad for having felt irritated with her and now he wants to go to her and put his arms around her and kiss the asymmetric dimples on her cheeks, brush her overlong fringe away from her forehead and kiss her there too, scoop her hair into a pony-tail and bury his nose in her neck. She's hanging up the phone and he thinks that, though he's now ready to leave for work perhaps there is time for a little spontaneity, for affection, for physical and emotional contact. The baby can stay on Fen's hip. They're a family after all. Group hug and all that. So he crosses the kitchen and he's about to reach for her when her nose wrinkles.

'Gracious,' she's saying to the baby, 'how can someone so little and cute make such a revolting smell.'

'I'll change her,' Matt offers.

Fen falters. 'It's OK,' she says, 'I'll do it. I want to check that her nappy rash has cleared.'

She may only be six months old but Cosima Holden-McCabe has decided, quite categorically, that she will not be eating anything unless it is orange in colour. Fen is fretting over whether puréed carrot and mashed sweet potato for the fourth day running – and currently for breakfast – might give her baby carotene poisoning. Or have caused the nappy rash. Or created the current extreme pungency of the nappies.

'Wouldn't you rather have a nice squidgy banana? Are you OK, pumpkin?' Keeping her eyes on her baby, waggling a spoon loaded with orange mush, Fen speaks to Matt. 'Does she look orange to you?'

'Pumpkins are orange – you're probably giving her this complex.'

Fen looks at him for a loaded moment.

'Joke?' Matt says with a sorry smile. 'She looks bonny – she has a lovely glow to her fat little cheeks.'

'She's not fat!' Fen protests.

'It was a compliment,' Matt assures her. 'I meant it affectionately.'

'But do you think the glow to her cheeks is a bit orange?'

'No, Fen, I don't.' Matt peers in close to his baby and kisses her cheek. 'She looks fine.' He glances at his girlfriend. 'I think Cosima is happy and healthy and that carrot-and-sweet-potato mush is her favourite food of the moment. I reckon it's because you look peaky in comparison, Fen.'

'If I do look peaky,' Fen says defensively, 'it's because I'm so bloody tired.'

'I know you are,' Matt says and it irritates him that Fen heard an insult instead of the concern intended. He wants to say, I'm tired too, you know; but he hasn't time for a petty dispute over who is the more exhausted. 'Why don't you ask your sister if she's around today? You can have a little time to yourself?'

'She's only just got off the plane!'

'I meant Pip.'

Somewhere, Fen knows Matt's intention is sweet. But lately, unbridled sensitivity has lain far closer to her surface than sense. 'You don't think I'm coping, do you?' she says.

'You're doing brilliantly,' Matt says, because the books and the magazines have instilled the sentence in him and advised him to ignore the ironing mountain, piles of toys and general debris. 'I'm late. What are you doing today? Is it Musical Minis?'

'No, that's Thursday.'

'TinyTumbles?'

'No, that's tomorrow. I may meet up with the baby-mums this afternoon.'

'That'll be nice.'

Fen shrugs. 'I always come away feeling a bit insecure,' she confides. 'Their babies apparently sleep through the night and most have at least one tooth. And I'm not really sure about the women – I can't find a connection apart from the babies being the same age. They're forever trying to out-purée each other with increasingly exotic organic recipes. But all my baby wants is orange stuff.'

'You're being unnecessarily hard on yourself,' Matt says, 'and on Cosima. And possibly on that bunch too. Stop being silly. You're wondermum and we love you.'

Fen can't hear the last sentence. Her ears are ringing with the fact that Matt says she's silly. She wants to say, Well fuck you. But they've made a pact not to swear in front of their child.

'I'm late.' He gulps his coffee. 'Work is mental at the moment – I'll try and leave early, cook us something nice.' He kisses the top of Fen's head and brushes his lips over the peach fuzz adorning Cosima's. 'Bye, girls. Have fun.'

*   *   *

Tom Holmes likes Tuesdays very much. He doesn't like the fact that at school Tuesdays mean dictation followed by football. Tom finds it difficult to coordinate hearing a word, then assessing its meaning in context and having to write it down, all in the space of about two seconds. It thus seems entirely logical that instructions for rigging a yacht could well be 'Pacific' instead of 'specific'. It frustrates him that he never does well in dictation and that there's no opportunity in dictation to saliently reason that 'Pacific', taken contextually, is just as appropriate as 'specific'. He's slightly taken aback that Miss Balcombe won't at least acknowledge that 'Pacific instructions for rigging' sounds fairly logical. He doesn't like it that there's no room for manoeuvre with meaning where dictation is concerned.

Football makes Tom miserable, more so because he's acutely aware that a nine-year-old should never admit to being miserable in the context of football. He supports Arsenal, which has won him friends at his North London prep school, but he hates playing the game. He hates playing because his limbs are often sore from eczema. Mud can actually sting but tracksuit trousers can catch and snag on chapped skin. Though his teammates are pals enough not to comment, Tom still catches them glancing at his body, unintentionally repelled. However, what makes dictation and football bearable is that, on Tuesdays, he stays with his dad and stepmum at their cool place in Hampstead.

They actually only live a mile or so from his home in Swiss Cottage and, though Tom spends every Tuesday, Wednesday and every other weekend with them, and any time in between that he fancies, the novelty value is still high. His dad's place is closer to school than his other home so instead of his mum slaloming her Renault through the school run (which has its plus points because she appears unaware how much she swears) Tom strolls down Hampstead High Street with his stepmum. And, without actually holding hands (he's nine now, someone might see), Tom can still subliminally tug her into a detour to Starbucks for hot chocolate.

Tom's had Pip for nearly four years. Her presence at the school gates continues to provide much intrigue. Being a clown by trade, Pip is well known to many of Tom's classmates from the birthday-party circuit of their younger years. She's also been to assembly to talk about the other work she does, as a clown at children's hospitals. She did the splits and a flikflak on the stage, bonked the headmaster on the head with a squeaky plastic hammer, made a motorbike from balloons in four seconds flat and Tom was the centre of attention all that day. His friends still make a point of saying hullo to her when she collects him. Invariably, she has rushed to school from the hospital, with her hair still in skew-whiff pigtails and traces of make-up on her face. Far more exotic than the widespread Whistles and ubiquitous Nicole Farhi worn by the other mums.

*

19

This Tuesday was no different. There was Pip, eye-catching in orange-and-purple stripy tights and clodhopping boots, chatting amiably with the other Hampstead mums.

'Hi, I'm starving. It was shepherd's pie for lunch. *Heinous*,' said Tom, keen to drag her away.

'Dear oh dear,' said Pip, 'heinous shepherd's pie? I'd turn vegetarian, if I were you.'

'No *way*, José,' Tom retched. 'The veggie option is always vomtastic.'

'Vom*tastic*,' Pip marvelled, planning to use the word in her clowning. 'How was football?'

Tom gave a small shrug. 'Cold.'

'Are you angling for a brownie and hot choc?' Pip nudged him.

'If you say so,' Tom said.

'Well, your dad won't be home till sevenish,' Pip reasoned with herself, as much as with Tom.

'It would be very good for my energy,' Tom said not entirely ingenuously. 'Starbucks would *really* help my homework.'

Pip laughed. 'Come on, tinker,' she said. They walked towards the High Street. 'I had a sad day at the hospital. It's lovely to see you.'

Tom slipped his hand into hers. Just for a few strides or so.

Pip looked at the kitchen table laden with the remains of supper later that evening, then she looked at her husband and his son embroiled in PlayStation. She put her hands on her hips and cleared her throat. They didn't look up.

'Hullo?' she called, as if testing whether anyone was there.

Zac glanced up briefly from the console, but not briefly enough to prevent Tom taking advantage.

'Dad!' Tom objected. 'Concentrate!'

And then Pip decided she'd just smile and ask if anyone

wanted a drink. She still found it difficult to gauge her boundaries as a stepmother. Her own standards, based on her childhood and her family's dynamic, said that a nine-year-old should help clear the table, or at least ask to be excused a chore. But she also acknowledged that this father and son hadn't seen each other for a week and Zac had been first down from the table challenging Tom to a PlayStation final-of-finals. So she tidied up and allowed them their quality time.

She glanced at the clock and felt relieved that it really was nearing Tom's bedtime. Zac had worked so late the last couple of nights she felt she hadn't seen him at all. 'I'll run your bath, Tom,' she said.

'One more game,' Zac called to her.

'I'll run it slowly,' Pip said.

Despite actually trying his damndest to win, Zac lost at PlayStation. Far from being wounded, his pride soared at Tom's skill and after a noisy bathtime, he cuddled up with his son for a lengthy dip into *James and the Giant Peach*. Pip could hear the soft timbre of Zac's reading voice. She poured two glasses of wine and organized Tom's school bag for the morning.

Zac appeared and made the fast-asleep gesture with his hands. 'He was tired,' he said.

'Well, it's late for him,' said Pip, offering a glass of wine.

Zac looked at his watch. 'I just have a little work to do,' he told Pip who looked instantly deflated, 'just an hour or so.' He took the wine, kissed Pip on the lips, squeezed her bottom and disappeared with his laptop. He's happy, Pip told herself. She looked on the bright side, which was very much her wont. At least it gave her the opportunity to phone Cat, as long as her youngest sister had been able to resist the jet lag on her first day back in the country.

*

Many would say that being a high-flying accountant would have its ups and downs: financial remuneration in return for long hours and often relatively dull work; a bulging pay packet to compensate for a dry grey image. How else would accountants have become such a clichéd race? But the only things grey about Zac Holmes are his eyes which are dark slate to the point of being navy anyway, and the only dry thing about Zac is his sense of humour. If Zac's looks and his personality had dictated a career, it would have been something on the funky side of creative. But Zac's brain, with its amazing propensity for figures, decreed accountancy from the outset. Anything else just wouldn't be logical. Zac likes logic, he likes straightforward solutions and simple answers to even the most complex of problems. Consequently, he never judges anything to be a dilemma because he knows intrinsically that there is always a way to work it all out. Zac believes that problems are merely perceived as such. If you just sit down and think carefully, there's nothing that can't be solved. Problems don't really exist at all, it comes down to attitude. That goes for his personal life as much as his professional. So, when ten years ago, his on-off girlfriend announced she was pregnant a few weeks after a forgettable drunken friendship fuck, Zac welcomed the news with a shrug and easily devised a formula that would suit them all.

$$2 \text{ firm friends} + 0 \text{ desire to marry/cohabit}$$
$$(+ \text{ never} \div \text{by } \pounds/\heartsuit \text{ issues})$$
$$= \text{great} + \text{modern parents}$$
$$= 1 \text{ lucky child.}$$

June, the mother of his child, can never be an ex-wife or ex-girlfriend because she was neither when Tom was conceived. She's Zac's friend and Zac is her friend and for Tom to have parents who are friends is a gift. Tom also has two step-parents. Everyone is friends. It might appear unconventional, but it works. A large family of friends.

Django McCabe may have trawled the sixties, trekking from ashram to commune, hiking from yurt to kibbutz, in search of the same. But he was happy to admit that his eldest niece had found its apotheosis in London NW3.

Pip is hovering. Zac's hour at his laptop has turned into two.

'Coffee?' she offers.

'No, ta,' says Zac, 'need to crack on.'

'Tea?' she suggests.

'Nope, I'm fine thanks, Mrs,' says Zac. 'I have to knock this on its head.'

'Whisky?'

'No, nothing – I'm good. Thanks.'

'Rampant sex?'

'Tempting – on any other night. I have to work. Seriously.'

'One of my very special blow-jobs?'

Zac looks at his screen. He has a very good head for figures. But if there's one figure that gives very good head, it's Pip. His eyes don't leave his laptop, his finger hovers above the mouse-pad. 'A special blow-job?' Zac asks, as if it's a deal-breaker. 'Not just a standard one?'

'Trust me,' Pip winks.

'Because,' says Zac, 'if it's just run-of-the-mill sucky-sucky, I'll pass. This audit is crucial.'

'I'm not capable of run-of-the-mill sucky-sucky,' Pip clarifies, hands on her hips, chin up.

'I mean, I'm talking *cosmic*, Pip,' Zac stipulates with a lasciviously raised eyebrow. 'It needs to be mind-blowing.'

'I assure you it's not just your mind I'll be blowing.'

Finally, Zac looks from his laptop to Pip, then back again. Contriving a sigh, as if he was doing her the favour, he logs off. 'I'm sure the powers that be will understand,' he says.

'I'll write your boss a note,' says Pip. 'I'll tell him the dog ate your homework.' She takes Zac by the hand and leads him to the bedroom. They undress silently and have rude sex as quietly as they can.

*　　*　　*

Matt had come back from work early, made sausages, mash and onion gravy. Perfect for a cold January night and essential for his girlfriend who'd told him she hadn't had time to eat more than toast and Marmite during the day. He'd bought a DVD too, which Fen managed to stay awake through despite snuggling up against the cosiness of Matt's chest. Now she's reading in bed and Matt is nuzzling the fragrant softness of his girlfriend's neck. His cock is surprisingly responsive. He'd only intended to kiss her goodnight. He didn't know he had the energy to feel horny.

'How did we make Cosima again?' Matt whispers, running his hand the length of Fen's thigh, spooning against her, the sensation of her buttocks against his erection causing his pelvis to rock automatically, his hands to travel up along her torso. He bypasses her breasts. They're Cosima's for the time being. He doesn't really mind, it's lucky he's always been a legs and bum man. And his hands sweep down to Fen's thighs again, and over them, and around. And he walks his fingers up through the fuzz of her sex then attempts to tiptoe them down in between.

Fen's hand joins his. 'I do want to,' she announces, a tinge of apology, a ring of reluctance, which stills Matt's hand immediately. 'I'm just really really tired. Sorry.'

'I bet I can have you in the mood; bet you I can have you hollering for mercy,' he tells her. He always used to be able to. He leans across her and kisses her, pulls her to face him, holds her against him. He rocks his groin gently against her, takes her hand down to his perky cock and works his hands over her body. He is not sure whether he's taken her breath away or whether she's holding it to pull her stomach in. But he feels her stiffen, and a glance at her face, where anxiety is mixed with reluctance, causes him to turn away from her, to stare at the ceiling with a sigh.

'Do I feel different to you?' she asks. 'I'm still so squidgy and unattractive.' And then she mutters that she shouldn't have had all that bangers and mash.

'You look gorgeous,' Matt says, 'I keep telling you. God. Wasn't my raging hard-on proof enough how much I fancy you?'

Fen shrugs and looks downcast. 'I know you do,' she says quietly, 'but I have to fancy myself, too, to feel horny.'

'Will you give yourself a break,' Matt says. He switches off the bedside light and kisses her lightly on the shoulder. 'Stop being silly.'

Fen lies in the dark, wide-eyed and confused and wishing they had a spare room she could withdraw to. She encourages a hot, oily tear to sting its way from the corner of her eye and slick down her cheek and onto the pillow. She knows it's bizarre, but rather than being bolstered by Matt's assurances that he loves and lusts for her however she feels she looks, she's cross that he appears to trivialize her concerns, her loss of confidence, her fragile self-image.

He called me silly. For the second time today. Silly is a stupid, insensitive word to use. He just doesn't understand.

God. It's gone midnight. Cosima will wake in a couple of hours. I have to get some sleep.

Django McCabe
and the Nit-Pickin' Chicks

Though only three years separated the oldest and youngest of the McCabe sisters, Cat had always been very much the baby of the family. She was a little shorter than Pip and Fen, her features more petite. She lacked Pip's aptitude for performing, to entertain, which gave her eldest sister her apparent sassy confidence. Nor did she have Fen's self-containment, her ability to seem so quietly self-possessed, so attractively serene. While Pip and Fen had encountered the various dramas in their lives head-on and for the most part single-handedly and discretely, Cat had always simply stood there and cried loudly for help. It wasn't that she was particularly feeble, nor was she excessively attention-seeking or spoilt; Cat was accustomed to being looked after because there was something about her that inspired others to care for her. Ben believed it was to do with the arrangement of her features; her large eyes set winsomely around the childlike upturn to her nose which led down to the natural pout to her lips. It compelled one to offer protection, even if it was not specifically needed or asked for. However, Cat's strength was that she was never too proud to ask. She'd grown up knowing that what made her feel

26

strong and able was the presence of her support network, her sisters in particular.

When Cat had gone to live in America with a relatively new boyfriend (as Ben was then) and brand new job, everyone anticipated floods of tears to wash her soon back again. But the anticipated plea to be rescued never came. Her letters and e-mails and phone calls attested to her happiness, and her occasional visits home confirmed this. Her apparent self-sufficiency was a source of joy and relief for her family and soon enough they were delighted for her that she'd gone. Not half so thrilled as they are now, four years later, that she has come back.

Being swept north by rail for their family reunion, the McCabe sisters were initially preoccupied with three-way inane grinning and quietly assessing physical details and changes.

'So.'

'So?'

'So!'

'You're back.'

'I am.'

'For good?'

'Indeed. For better, for worse.'

'I do love your hair,' Pip told Cat. 'When you e-mailed to say you'd gone short and red, I had visions of a ginger buzz-cut.'

'It's very gamine,' Fen said whilst hastily retying hers into a hopefully smoother pony-tail, 'very Audrey Hepburn. God I feel a dowdy frump.'

'You don't think it's too short?' Cat asked them. 'And you're sure you like the colour? Yours is so much longer,' she said to Fen, 'and darker.'

'That's probably because it's greasy,' Fen said. She took a

twist of her hair and scrutinized the ends. 'I can't remember the last time I went to the hairdresser.'

'Go this weekend,' Pip said. 'Django will know some-where.'

'When did he last go to a barber?' Cat interrupted. 'You're not telling me he's chopped off his pony-tail? I expected things to change while I've been abroad – but nothing that drastic.'

'It's still his crowning glory,' Pip assured her with a smile.

'How's he been?' Cat asked.

'Fine and dandy,' Pip said. 'Same as ever, really.'

'It's funny, initially I'd curse him for not having e-mail, but actually I loved receiving his letters and writing back,' Cat said. 'I've kept them all. They're hysterical. He'd send me the TV listings page every single week so I could keep up with *Corrie*.'

'Zac and I bought him an answering machine for his last birthday – but he took it back,' Pip said. 'I suggested a mobile phone – but you can imagine what he said.'

'Talking of birthdays, I wonder what we'll do for his,' Cat said brightly. 'Can you believe he'll be seventy-five this spring?'

'He'll either throw a huge party – or go on a retreat,' Pip said. 'In which case we'll make him a surprise party.'

'Yes!' said Cat. She gazed at the sleeping baby nustled up to Fen in a papoose. 'Cosima is so beautiful,' she said dreamily, watching Fen's fingers tap out a mother's instinctive, gentle rhythm against the baby's back. Absent-mindedly, Cat rolled her thumb against her wedding ring. 'Still no plans to wed then, Fen?' She felt Pip glance at her.

Fen balked. 'What an odd thing to say.'

'Sorry – I just mean, you know, since you now have a baby.'

'Shock, horror, an *illegitimate* child? Is that what you're implying?' Fen said.

'Blimey Fen, I was only teasing,' Cat said, because she had been. She glanced back at Pip who, ever the diplomat, decided it was a good idea to change the subject.

'I'm hungry,' said Pip.

'I'm hungry now too,' said Fen. 'Do you think Django's made a late lunch for us?'

'Followed almost immediately by an enormous tea with just time enough to burp before a Spread for supper?' Cat laughed.

'I'll go and buy sandwiches for us,' said Pip.

'And salt-and-vinegar crisps!' Cat called after her. Fen smiled at her. Cat turned her gaze out to the English countryside zipping by outside the train. So different to Colorado, where she had remained in awe of her surroundings. Here, the scale was comfortingly familiar, if a little tame by comparison, the colours darker, damper.

'Sorry about before,' Fen said. 'I've been horribly snappish, lately. I hate it and I can't help it. I'm just so tired. And – well – things at home have been a little strained.'

Cat watched Fen's gaze drop. She'd been shocked by the physical change in Fen, the wan complexion, the dark eyes, puffiness here and a general lankness there. Objectively, Fen had always been the true beauty of the three of them; her features and complexion adding refinement where Pip was just pretty, where Cat was simply cute. Today, though, Cat noticed a certain pallor now veiling this.

'Is it Matt?' Cat broached, though she'd intended to seek details from Pip later.

'I don't know, Cat,' Fen said, a tear clouding one eye, 'but I think it might be me. My love for my baby is so primal and complete that sometimes I feel like running away so it's just the two of us.'

'Don't do that,' Cat said and she reached across the melamine for her sister's wrist, 'please don't do that. I've just come thousands of miles to be back in my family fold. I want Cosima to get to know her Auntie Cat. And when I am pregnant, I'll need you within arm's reach to tell me how to do it all properly.'

Fen smiled. 'I'll need bloody long arms to stretch to Clapham from East Finchley,' she said.

'Clapham is not, I repeat *not*, permanent,' Cat said. 'You know I've always had a thing for Tufnell Park.'

'It's good to have you home,' Fen said, 'but it'll be even better to have you on the doorstep.'

Pip returned. 'Cardboard bread with rubber cheese in between,' she announced. 'Don't anyone tell Django what we're about to eat.'

Peeping through the window, it is a joy for Django to behold his three precious girls spill out of the taxi. Momentarily, he turns away from the sight and offers a prayer of sincere thanks to all the gods and spirits who have ever interested him at any stage during his life. He can hear their laughter and their excited chatter. Will you look at Cosima – how she has grown in the last month. How naturally Fen has the baby against her. See the sun spin gold through Pip's hair. And Cat, that can't be Cat! Cat was the little girl with the jaunty pony-tail. Who is this beautiful woman? And what's with the red hair!

Django had intended to position himself in the hallway, so that when the girls opened the door he'd be there; his arms flung wide, like a celebrity tenor on an album cover. In the event, he is as excited as they are and he strides out to meet them, booming his welcome. The only member of the family who does not cry is Cosima. She regards the grown-ups with her solemn unblinking eyes, absorbing all the facts and details as if logging the information that when you haven't seen your family for a long time, you leap about and sob and touch each other's hair a lot.

'I'm still stuffed from tea-time!' Cat whispered to Pip while Django tinkered in the kitchen. 'Those scones were like cannon balls. Never mind enough to feed an army – enough to sink the navy!'

'Shh,' Pip said.

'Has he been well?' Cat asked quietly. 'Hasn't had flu, or something? It's just that he looks a little tired to me, a bit peaky, since I last saw him.'

'I think he's been fine,' said Pip. 'He certainly hasn't said anything to the contrary. He's probably been slaving over the stove all week, preparing for our arrival.' She spied a copy of the *Racing Post*. 'Or else he's put all his money on some old nag and lost the lot.'

Cat walked around the living-room, fingering objects, lingering over framed photos, feeling the heavy brocade of the curtains, running her hands over the worn warm upholstery, filling her nostrils with the scent of home. It was like remaking her acquaintance with the essential elements of her personal history; reminding herself how everything looked and felt and smelt and should be, while at the same time reasserting her own presence in this sacred family space.

The Spread was simmering and sautéing and roasting and steaming. Elements of it were happily marinating, or being chilled, or else ripening at room temperature. All the pots and pans were in use and every utensil had served many a purpose. The various scents emanating from oven and hob joined forces to create an olfactory explosion that, to Django, was as contradictory yet ultimately pleasing as a jazz chord.

The point of cooking and the point of jazz are essentially one and the same, Django thought to himself as he ran a sink of water and half a jar of Bar Keeper's Friend to soak all the knives. *It's about an element of surprise, of revelation and re-education. Of experimentation. Like when the African pentatonic scale met the European diatonic scale and jazz was born; a sound that was initially bizarre, disconcertingly discordant. It simply required one to open one's ears and one's heart to the flattened third and seventh notes and suddenly the aural pleasure of the blue note coursed through one's veins. Likewise, one's initial concern that Tabasco and tuna may be odd accompaniments to duck with a celery stuffing, dissipates when one shrugs off preconceptions of convention and allows the tastes to speak for themselves.*

'Not too dissimilar to Kandinsky either,' Django mused as he left the kitchen in search of his nieces, 'seemingly an arbitrary cascade of colour and shape yet utterly grounded in structure and purpose. Jazz, Cookery, Abstraction. It's all art.'

He found them in the living-room and observed them unseen for a nostalgic moment. Just then, the girls could have been any age. The scene was immediately familiar and timeless and the continuity was poignant. 'By golly,' Django declared, 'sing hey for the return of the nit-pickin' chicks.'

The nit-pickin' chicks looked up at him. Fen stopped plaiting Pip's hair, Pip stilled her hands from massaging Cat's foot, Cat brought her head up from Fen's lap and ceased tracing patterns on her sister's legs.

'Django, you're not going all sentimental on us are you?' Pip asked, resuming her massage in a businesslike way. The girls laughed. Privately, they each felt suddenly very sentimental, in an affirming way. It had been years since Django had referred to them as the nit-pickin' chicks, because it had

32

been such a long time since they'd sat in their huddle with their hands almost absent-mindedly working on each other.

'Stop fiddling,' Django said. 'Let's eat.'

'I'll just check on Cosima,' Fen said.

'You were only up there half an hour ago,' said Cat, 'and she was quiet then.'

'You'll see,' Fen said, slightly defensively, feeling entitled to her knowing nod, 'you'll see.'

'It transpires that Cat hasn't just come home because she misses your cooking,' Pip told Django, slipping her arm around his waist, 'she's come home to breed.'

Django took a moment. 'Wonderful!' he then said, placing his hand on Cat's head as if blessing her. 'Another reason to celebrate. There's some champagne somewhere. It may well be in the bottom drawer in your room, Pip.'

'I could look in on Cosima for you while I check,' Pip suggested to Fen.

'No,' said Fen decisively, 'I'll go. I'll do both.'

'The meal is organic,' Django told her, 'mostly. Shall I purée a little for Cosima for tomorrow?'

'No, thanks,' Fen said, hoping she hid her alarm.

'The sauce is relatively orange,' Django elaborated.

'That'll be the Tabasco,' Fen said, 'which isn't really appropriate for a six-month-old baby.'

'It's never too early to prepare the palate,' Django said.

Despite the size of the scones, the aromas from the pots and pans were too tantalizing to resist and appetites magically expanded to meet the quality and quantity of food prepared. Though the menu was predictably unorthodox and though they started with dessert because Django didn't want to risk the lemon-and-rum soufflé collapsing, traditional manners had always been proudly upheld in the McCabe household. Don't hold your knife like a pencil, elbows off the table, don't talk with your mouth full. Between courses, after polite dabbing with napkins, news and plans were discussed.

'A toast to absent menfolk,' Django said, charging his glass, 'to the accountant, the publisher, the doctor.' He took a sip. 'There was plenty of food for them, you know, even if you lot want second helpings.'

'But we didn't actually want them here,' Pip said as if revealing a secret. 'We wanted you to ourselves.'

'And Ben's mum wanted him to herself,' Cat reasoned.

'Next time you come, you bring your boys,' Django said. 'This stew will be good for days – you're all to take a tub home.' He topped up his glass again. 'Well, another toast. To the clown.' Everyone chinked Pip's glass. Django cleared his throat: 'To the art historian.' They raised their glasses to Fen. And then they all looked at Cat. 'What shall we toast you as?' Django asked her. 'Sports journalist? Redhead?'

Cat looked concerned. 'I'm not sure.'

'But you so love the cycling world,' Pip said, 'and you had such respect as one of the few female reporters.'

'And you're married to the doctor of one of the world's top cycling teams,' Fen said.

'*Ex*-team doctor,' Cat pointed out.

'No more gallivanting around the globe with that circus of Lycra and bicycles then?' asked Django.

'No,' Cat laughed though she looked a little forlorn. 'I've fallen out of love.' Pip and Fen jerked with concern. 'With the sport,' Cat clarified. 'So has Ben. Too many drugs, too much cheating.'

'So, what'll you do?' Pip asked again.

'I'm not sure – maybe write more widely. Maybe not just yet.'

'And are you back for good?' Django asked. 'Or is this a pit stop?'

'This is home. This is where we want to start a family. Maybe I'll take a leaf out of Fen's book – and yours, Django – and make motherhood my career.'

'No finer, more noble job than that,' Django said, 'mark my words.'

'You forgot to add *knackering*,' Fen laughed. 'Academia was a breeze in comparison. Not that I have any desire to go back to it.'

'But you're so talented,' said Cat, 'you've had stuff published. You've lectured at the Tate. You're the authority on the sculpture of Julius Fetherstone. You have all those hard-earned letters after your name.'

'Art is still my great love – just because I choose not to work in that field doesn't negate that,' Fen shrugged and continued more defensively. 'I've gone for a change of career. Raising my baby is just as challenging, as stimulating – and far more time-consuming.'

'I suppose I'll have to see which comes first – a blue line on the dipstick, or a job offer,' said Cat.

'I'd like to propose a toast,' said Pip, 'to my sisters, to our Django. To family.'

Django makes his announcement over strong Turkish coffee and enormous petits fours. He clears his throat and asks for silence, please, ladies.

'No doubt my impending milestone birthday has been the cause for much speculation – and I hope you haven't already planned a surprise party.'

'You're not going on a retreat are you?' Cat asks.

'On my seventy-fifth birthday?' Django objects. 'Good Lord no. I have no intention of retreating anywhere. Quite the opposite. They'll be coming out of the woodwork, far and wide, because I'm going to throw a party.'

'Here?'

'Of course *here*,' Django says, 'a huge rollicking knees-up that will rewrite the significance of May 16th in history. I'm going to have a party that'll be totally, eye-openingly unsuitable for someone of such an age.'

Cat, Fen and Pip gawp at him.

'You're all invited,' he assures them earnestly, 'along with anyone who thinks they might ever have known me.'

The Rag and Thistle

Early the following evening, Django placed his hands on Fen's shoulders. 'Do it for me,' he said quietly.

'It's only the Rag and Thistle,' said Pip, 'it's only down the road.'

'And it's my welcome-home weekend,' Cat protested.

'I don't *feel* like it,' Fen said.

'Your sisters request your company and I'd like to have my granddaughter all to myself,' Django said but he could see that he hadn't dented her defence. 'You do have faith in my abilities, don't you? Did I not bring up you three single-handedly – and fabulously – when your mother ran off with a cowboy from Denver?' He paused carefully to assess the just perceptible upturn to the corners of Fen's mouth. 'And isn't Cosima already sound asleep and unlikely to waken anyway?'

'It's not that,' Fen said. 'Of course I have faith in you. It's just I don't really feel like going out.' She wanted to sound needy rather than defensive so that they'd sympathize.

'But it's *my* weekend!' Cat reiterated.

Fen looked deeply uncomfortable. 'I don't want to go to the Rag and Thistle because I don't want to leave Cosima,' she explained, looking at the semicircle of her family surrounding her. 'It's not something that I've done. Why can't we just stay here – open some dodgy home-made elderberry wine?'

Her sisters and uncle regarded her while she scrutinized a threadbare patch on the Persian rug. Was that newspaper beneath it? Probably. When from, Fen wondered. She'd known the rug all her life.

'You mean to say you haven't had any time apart from Cosima in six months?' Cat asked.

'No – yes,' Fen elaborated, 'not really. Matt has babysat a couple of times.'

'You mean you and Matt haven't been out *together* since she was born?' Cat asked, thinking it sounded preposterous.

'That's right,' said Fen, with a tightness that told her audience she thought they shouldn't be questioning.

'That's *not* right,' said Cat, 'that's terrible.'

'Fuck off, Cat,' Fen said sharply.

'Don't swear,' Django said.

'I have offered,' Pip said to Cat and Django, 'to babysit.'

'But Cosima was colicky,' Fen said.

'No one's likely to judge your mothering abilities on whether you occasionally have some me-time,' said Django.

'It's not that,' Fen sighed.

'It's good for you,' said Pip, 'it said so in that baby book you keep in the loo.'

'What's all this Fen-bashing?' Fen asked. 'God, you're my bloody family. Cosima is a tiny baby and I'm allowed to indulge my maternal instincts.'

'I simply want the treat, the *honour*, of looking after my first granddaughter, and your sisters just wanted a couple of hours down the local with you to themselves,' Django reasoned. 'As you say – we are a bloody family.'

'It's not a challenge,' Pip said, 'it's just a quick drink down the pub, silly.'

'Christ, why is *everyone* calling me silly these days?' Fen muttered to herself. 'And it *is* a challenge, actually, to me. Do you not think it doesn't disturb me that my self-confidence can leak away like breast milk? That I'd reject my sisters' invitation to go out for a couple of drinks? That a strange and terrible part of me doesn't even trust the man who raised me to look after my baby for two tiny hours?' Her eyes darted around her family from under knotted eyebrows.

'Look – I'm sorry, Fen,' said Cat, who looked it. 'Please come. I'm so excited to be back. I've missed you.'

For a moment, Fen thought she might cry. Then she wanted to stand her ground and refuse. 'I don't know,' she faltered.

'Leave me a long list,' Django said brightly, 'with illustrations.'

So, still a little reluctantly, Fen took him at his word and did just that. When she was quite sure Cosima really was fast asleep, she left with her sisters for the Rag and Thistle.

As pubs go, the Rag and Thistle was both lively yet homey. Having been in the Merifield family for four generations, it retained the charm and authenticity that many brewery-owned pubs never achieve despite trying so obviously to replicate. Thus there were no mass-produced sepia pictures of Street Scene Anywhere but photos instead of Merifields old and young, dead and alive, their various dogs and horses, adorning most of the wall space. The cast of *Peak Practice* had signed beer mats which David Merifield had framed in a jaunty pattern around a cast photo. There was a paper serviette, illegibly autographed by an actress whose name no one could remember and sometimes this was hung upside down in case it was meant to be so. There were no laminated menus with novelty meals and photos of the dishes. Just simple home cooking, available whenever required. The bell for last orders was usually rung when someone remembered to ring it. The Rag and Thistle was a mainstay of the community and its community cherished it. Though the McCabe girls left home over a decade ago, they still think of it as their local and the Merifields welcome them back as if they last served them a drink just the day before.

'G & T,' Pip ordered.

'Glass of house red,' said Cat. 'Fen?'

'Oh go on then,' Fen said guiltily, 'V.a.T. But loads of tonic and easy on the vodka. I'm still breast-feeding, remember.'

'We couldn't possibly forget,' Pip murmured to Cat though it landed her a harsh glance from Fen.

'I'll bring them over,' said the publican Mr Merifield, who always treated the girls like royalty on their visits home. 'You'll be wanting to nab that table that's just come free.'

'So Django's going to throw a birthday party,' Cat marvelled, making a beeline for the table in the corner bedecked with horse brasses. 'Is he serious about having it at home? He could have it here.'

'This place couldn't fit everyone in – they'll be coming from the four corners of the earth,' said Pip.

'Didn't you know the earth was round?' said Mr Merifield, setting down their drinks.

'We're talking about Django's birthday.'

'Ah,' said Mr Merifield, 'and the party. No point us opening the pub that night – everyone will be at yours, if memories of his sixtieth party serve me right.' The girls laughed and everyone buried their heads in their hands.

'Can you believe he's going to be seventy-five?' Fen said, arranging a beer mat in front of each of them and removing the ashtray to the window sill with a look of utter distaste.

'It sounds so old,' said Cat. '*Seventy-five*.'

'He *is* a grandpa,' Fen defined, 'though actually he likes to be called Gramps.'

'Tom calls him that,' Pip explained to Cat. 'Tom calls him Django Gramps which is weird really, because he's even less of a real grandfather, in the literal sense, to Tom than he is to Cosima.'

'I laughed when you told me in that e-mail that Django refers to Tom as his "step-grandsonthing-or-other",' Cat told her.

'I wonder if our children will be confused that they have a grandpa for an uncle, but a non-existent grandmother?' Fen mused.

'They have other grandmas,' Pip said. 'Matt and Zac's mums.'

'It's odd,' said Fen and then she stopped. 'Nothing.'

'What?'

'It's just that, having really thought of her so rarely, just recently I've thought of her more.'

'Who?'

'Our mother,' Fen shrugged. 'Now that I have my baby. I just can't figure out how a mother can leave.'

'That's why we'll all make grade A mummies,' Cat said. 'We'll be automatically compensating for the fact that our mother was sub-Z grade.'

'It struck me recently that the only person I've ever called "Mummy" is myself,' Fen said. It quietly struck her sisters that they hadn't called anyone 'Mummy' at all.

'I can't wait to be called Mummy,' Cat said dreamily. 'Do you realize I was pretty much Cosima's age when our mother left?'

'It's only since having Cosima that maternal instincts, in all their crazy hormonal cladding, have made sense,' Fen continued, 'and to be honest, though previously I never much cared about her, it now makes me shudder. A woman ran off with a cowboy from Denver and left behind three girls under the age of *four*? How could she do it? How can a mother not have maternal instincts? It's *criminal*. They're *chemical*.' Fen looked at her sisters. 'I gaze at my daughter and I think of us three. Three tiny little girls. How could she have walked out?'

'I reckon life would still have been better under Django than under her if she hadn't left,' Pip reasoned. 'His maternal instincts more than made up for her lack of them.'

'It never bothered me before, really, because there were never situations when we wished we had her,' Fen reiterated quietly, 'but now, recently, it's made me utterly bewildered. Indignant too. That's why I don't like to be separated from Cosima. That's why I hold her so tight.' Pip and Cat regarded her and felt bad about before. 'I don't like missing a minute with her – not because I'm a hormonal fruit cake, though you probably think I am. But because, in my book, there cannot be such a thing as an overprotective mother.'

'Do you want another?' Cat asked Fen.

'God no,' said Fen, 'this one's gone to my head already.'

Cat laughed. 'I meant another baby – not vodka.'

'That would necessitate Matt and me having sex,' Fen said glumly.

'Oh God, does all that really go down the nappy-bin?' Cat asked.

'Pretty much,' Fen admitted. 'To be completely honest, we prefer that extra hour's sleep to banging away for an orgasm.'

'The royal "we"?' Pip asked. 'Do you speak for Matt?'

Fen blinked a little. 'You know blokes,' she laughed it off but didn't elaborate. 'The weird thing is, it all seems a bit irrelevant. As if Cosima has shown us what life's all about. It's like, in retrospect, it was all a means to an end. Fancying Matt, falling in love with him, rampant sex, domestic daydreams – it's as if all that was a preamble, all a clever cloak to ensure the continuation of the species. Having

42

Cosima has shown us that life is about going forwards with her, rather than backwards trying to cling on to pre-baby days.'

'Us?' Pip questioned. 'The royal "us"? Do you speak for Matt too?'

Fen glanced at her with fleeting annoyance. 'Life is more meaningful now that I'm a mummy,' she said to Cat. 'I have a true function, a role. I'm a mummy. I don't feel any need to reclaim my sexuality. This is me now. This is what I was made for. This is the best thing I've ever done.'

Cat thought this sounded extreme, mad even. Pip thought it was sad and she immediately wondered how Matt was. He was going out with Zac for a pint that night. She'd probe. She was fond of Matt and, being the Great Looker-Afterer, she'd see to it that his relationship with her sister did not suffer.

'God,' said Cat with nostalgic admiration, 'and you used to be such a vamp, Fen.'

'What are you talking about?' Fen rubbished. 'Me? A vamp? Hardly.'

'You were a downright slapper,' Pip teased.

'Piss off,' Fen protested, suddenly knowing to what they alluded and not wanting to revisit the past.

'Don't tell me your nappy-addled memory doesn't stretch back four years when you were having to choose between two men?' Pip said.

They looked at Fen who was peering through a cage of her fingers as if shying away from a horror movie that turned out to be her history. 'Stop it you two,' she winced, 'it was ages ago. It was a different me.'

'It was right here in Derbyshire,' Pip said pointedly.

'He moved away,' Fen said, 'a while ago. You know that.'

'Regrets?' Cat asked.

'Don't be daft,' Fen said.

'Does Matt know?' Cat wondered. 'Did you ever tell him?'

'Are you mad?' said Fen. 'It had no bearing on my feelings for Matt. When it ended, it didn't release extra love for me to bestow on Matt. My feelings for Matt never changed – my feelings for the other man did.'

'I love Matt,' Pip said.

'Me too,' said Fen, 'me too. I'm very lucky.' Suddenly she felt overwhelmingly sad. Just then she longed for Matt even more than she longed for Cosima. 'I'm such a crotchety old bag at the moment,' she admitted and her sisters could see fear written across her brow. 'I'm tired and narky the whole time. I can't seem to help it. Who is this Fen who doesn't have the energy to make love to her boyfriend, who has lost the desire to be touched but doesn't really care? I can't remember when I last told Matt that I love him.'

'You should, you know,' Pip said sternly, 'according to that baby book you keep in your loo.'

'Do you and Zac plan to have proper babies?' Cat asked. Fen and Pip stared at their younger sister whose cheeks suddenly turned the colour of her hair and she buried her head in her hands. 'God that sounded awful. Poor Tom – I didn't mean—!'

'It's not in our game plan,' Pip laughed. 'We're a gang of three. I like being a stepmum. It suits me. I'm not really broody, I don't think.'

'You wouldn't have time anyway,' Cat said, 'because you're always so busy looking after everyone else.' Pip looked a little nonplussed. 'It's a compliment,' Cat assured her. 'Even Django calls you the Great Looker-Afterer. You're only three years my senior but you've always mothered me. Capably, too.'

'And me,' said Fen.

'Someone had to,' Pip shrugged.

'To us,' said Fen, now toasting with mineral water, 'to sisterhood and motherhood.'

Pip went to bed hoping everyone was all right. She was worried about Fen. If having a baby had brought such sense and sunshine into her life, as Fen claimed, why did she seem so out of sorts? Alternately under-confident and yet smug, defensive yet somehow needy too. Pip didn't doubt that it was normal and right to be so absorbed in her child, but she was concerned that Fen seemed so defiantly blasé about the other aspects of her life. As if being a mother had given her a superiority complex and inferiority issues in one fell swoop.

And what about Cat and Ben? Pip lay there anxious that her youngest sister had skipped back home hoping to play out a rather unrealistic daydream of easy baby-making and rosy domesticity.

She thought about Zac. And Tom. Just then Pip felt intensely grateful for Tom. Really, what a joy her gorgeous stepson was – what a privilege to have so many rewards without any of the hormonal rumpus apparently affecting her younger sister. She chastised herself sharply for certain occasions when she was irritated by Tom; when he hogged Zac or overran the flat, when Zac all but ignored her, when Tom appeared to think he needn't listen to what she said.

I'd hate anything to disrupt what I have with Zac. There's a safe harmony between us; I know when our tides come in and go out. Tom graces our lives but ultimately, by virtue of the living arrangements, lets them be as well. Zac and I are man and wife in the conventional sense but I still feel we're girlfriend and boyfriend too. Nothing is a chore, nothing is a bore. Everything is a treat. The sexual buzz I feel for him is as charged now as ever it has been. Our domestic set-up is perfect. Nothing can better it. As a couple, we have freedom and privacy and Tom.

As Cat lay in bed, she wondered whether she could still blame jet lag for making her feel suddenly so teary. She considered going downstairs – Django would be up for another hour or so, with his 'medicinal' brandy. Or whisky if he'd used all the brandy in the soup. Or she could knock out the special sequence on the wall dividing her room from Pip's. Pip would remember their childhood code, the tympanic lingo of knuckle against plaster. Long, short, short – Are you awake? Short, long, long – Come in here. Long, long, short, short – Can I come in?

It's just the jet lag. I'll let Pip sleep. I'll let Django relax over the day-before-yesterday's crossword. I won't disturb Fen. Actually, I don't really want to talk to her. I hope having a baby won't make me like her. That sounds awful. Fen's consuming passion for Cosima, her zeal for her role as mother, is beautiful on one level – lucky little Cosima. But where's my sister gone? Where's Matt's girl? Where's Trust Art's brilliant art historian and archivist? I've come home to find that Fen has only half an ear to lend us and half her personality available. That sounds harsh. Perhaps I don't understand. But I don't want it to be like that for me. Cosima has gained a brilliant mother but we've lost Fen. It will be different for Ben and me. A baby is for the two of us. At the end of the day, it will always be Ben and me and when baby makes three, we'll welcome it into our life. I can't wait.

Fen's daughter slept soundly in her pop-up travel cot, making occasional grunts and snuffles. Fen listened carefully, while gazing around her childhood bedroom which Django had lovingly preserved. Above her head, an Athena poster of a semi-nude faceless bloke in peculiar tones of lilac duelled for attention against pouting men with big hair and a penchant for frills who postured down from album covers drawing-pinned to the wall. Teenage angst novels crammed a shelf, flanked by two chunks of Derbyshire stone holding their skinny spines straight. Under the Formica dressing-table, over-sized tiger-feet slippers, padded with scrunches of *Racing Post* from 1989. In her bedside drawer, the jewels of her pocket-money days: a Mexican silver brooch in the shape of a cat, small 9ct gold hoop earrings with a single seed pearl, a silver-plated heart-shaped locket whose hinge broke when she opened it and found it empty, a three-band Russian wedding ring she'd bought for Pip's fifteenth birthday but decided to keep for herself yet never felt comfortable wearing. It was all tarnished, everything was a little bashed.

It felt strange to be in a single bed, strange that only two-thirds of her own little family were together that night, nicely strange to miss Matt. She smiled at the pin-ups of her teenage years and suddenly Matt's face loomed large in her mind's eye. She hoped she loved him as much as she used to. Again, she felt subsumed by a longing tinged with loneliness and she sent him a text message saying night night love your girls xxxx. She looked at it and worried over the lack of punctuation, that he might think she was nagging him to love his girls. Hopefully he'd be distracted by all the x's instead.

Her mind drifted back to a time before Cosima. Not so long ago, really, there was a girl called Fen for whom mother-hood had then been such a distant notion as to have had no realism. It was like recalling a best friend she hadn't seen for years, a soulmate who had gone so far away that their paths would never now cross. Just then, it made Fen wistfully sad. She reminisced that there had been fun in all that dangerous gallivanting. It had been liberating and energizing, being responsible for no one but herself.

She thought back to that heady time when she and Matt had just met at work and were embarking on the definitive office fling. She conjured again the feeling of exquisite anticipation, remembered so clearly sitting amongst the papers and pictures and boxes in the archives willing Matt to rudely interrupt her with a furtive snog and a grope. She relived the joy of racing down the corridor to delight Matt with her unbridled enthusiasm about some discovery or other amongst the dust and documents. She felt again the euphoric pride when their romance was exposed amongst their colleagues, when they were the centre of attention, the focus of gossip and approval, soon enough the benchmark for love and romance.

And then she thought back to those short, secret trips to Derbyshire around the same time, to those exhilarating afternoons of sex with another man; the urgency to have her desire sated but to make her home-bound train. It's really only now that she feels horror while she wonders what on earth all that was about, how bizarre it all was. At the time she'd divided her heart meticulously into two and coolly separated her body from her conscience. It had been intoxicatingly exciting for a while. It hadn't felt wrong. But then her sisters found out. And, in retrospect, thank God for Cat and Pip badgering her on the finer points of morality. Thank God she chose Matt and he never found out. And thank God she'd grown out of all of that. And grown up. And most of all, thank God for her beautiful beautiful baby.

As Fen lay thinking, her hands subconsciously assessed the changes in her body. Really, she knew she ought to adore her post-birth figure, her fuller breasts and becoming curves. But lying there, squidging more than an inch to the pinch, she did not. Instead, she tormented herself with clear images of how her body had been when it was the object of all that sexual attention. Pert and lithe and powerful in its energy and desirability. Ultimately, though, it did not come down to aesthetics. Her body was no longer her own now. It was as if, in nurturing a baby, she'd renounced sole ownership. Though she was slowly scaling down breast-feeding she knew she'd never have the same freedom with her body, she wouldn't be reclaiming it as her own.

Does Matt miss it? My body? Does he miss the way we were? I don't like to think that he might. I haven't asked him on purpose. I've just been hoping that his tolerant nature and all those ante-natal classes plus the magazines I leave lying around and the baby book that's in the loo will have filtered through, will have put paid to any resentment or disaffection.

Anyway, what was all that spontaneity actually worth? Was it really such a privilege to be able to do as we pleased whenever we liked? I suppose I'm on a crusade of sorts – that what we have now completely outweighs what we were then. Surely Matt feels the same?

Django pottered around downstairs. He couldn't find the crossword from the day before yesterday. He couldn't even find today's paper. Then he remembered he'd used one to wrap up the giblets. And he'd used another to wrap up the broken wine bottle which had tumbled onto the flagstone floor after he'd sloshed its contents into the stew with excessive flamboyance. Instead, with jazz playing softly, he tidied and swept and took lengthy breaks to sip a little whisky.

He had loved babysitting Cosima. She was an angel who hadn't woken once but still he'd taken his responsibility gravely and hadn't dared tidy or sweep or search for lost crosswords lest she should wake and he not hear her. Sipping whisky any earlier had been quite out of the question. He'd spent most of the evening intermittently creeping up the stairs to the point where he knew the treads would creak. He could sense the baby in the silence and he'd had a lovely evening, halfway up the stairs. He was pleased Cosima hadn't woken because he wanted to be able to reassure Fen on her return. He hoped the fact would bolster her, encourage her to breathe a little more deeply in fresh space of her own, or even breathe a little more lightly in other spaces.

I can reason it out. I can see why. Couldn't anybody? Her mother buggers off with a cowboy so Fen has decided she won't be leaving her baby at all. That's OK. That's OK. It's still relatively early days. But I hope all is well with Matt. I'll invite them for a weekend soon. I'll take him to the Rag. Or perhaps I'll babysit and send the two of them there for a little them-time.

How lovely to have our Cat back in the bag. A relief that her accent is unmodified by her time abroad. She's grown, she's bloomed, she's chopped off her hair and she's home. I must have her and Ben up for a weekend too. He's a good chap. I'll try and find an opportune moment to slip in my little query. I'm sure it's nothing but if he could just pop his doctor's hat on for a minute or two I could ask him a couple of questions and be done with it. I don't want to worry the girls, or waste my own GP's time. It's probably nothing. I'm probably daft for even noticing it. After all, I am growing old – I can hardly expect the rude health I used to enjoy.

Pip looks well. Whoever would have thought that the wilful girl who denounced any merit in love and money, found both in the good form of Zac? And a ready-made son too! Tom may officially be a stepson but that doesn't place him on any lower rung in my affection. He's my grandson-thing-or-other. And I'm most certainly his Gramps. I haven't seen him for far too long, though I wrote him a letter in rhyme last week which I'll try and remember to post when I'm in Bakewell next Tuesday.

Funny thing, blood ties. I don't think of Tom as any less

my grandchild than Cosima. Some pompous old genealogist wouldn't even consider me a grandfather. I'd be stuck out on a limb on a sub-branch of some silly conventional family tree. But the girls do and the children do and that's what counts. My nit-pickin' chicks, back together in the embrace of our funny family.

Penny Ericsson

On the other side of the Atlantic, it is still the day before and Penny Ericsson is wondering how to handle the hollow stretch of another evening alone. This is her twenty-fourth since Bob, her husband of thirty years, died. And though friends have ensured that she does not often spend long tracts of time on her own, Penny has felt utterly alone whether she has company or not.

Her house is immaculate. She is not hungry. She doesn't care for television. There's nothing to do but grieve. In some ways, it makes sense of her life. You love, you lose, you grieve for ever more.

Even the staircase feels longer and steeper now Bob's gone.

'Life's gonna be one long drag,' Penny murmurs as she ventures downstairs because she's been doing nothing upstairs for ages. She rotates all the scatter cushions from resting like squares on the two large sofas to perching like rhombs. She changes the angle of the many framed photographs on the mantelpiece so that they all seem to be standing in line to the right. She chooses two large art books from the shelves to replace the current photography books on the coffee table. She sits beside them and laughs hysterically. So many places to sit, so much time. Too much time. She decides the scatter cushions look ridiculous and they should live up to their name so she chucks them around the sofas until she feels they've found their natural grouping. Still she doesn't fancy sitting there. She gazes at Bob's chair and her laughter is stilled by a sigh that seems to start in the pit of her gut and expels every molecule of breath in her body.

'You know, I always thought you were ugly and nothing but,' she says. 'I mean, my cooker may be ugly but I like it. But you, you I never liked. If I'd had my way I'd've sent you back just as soon as you arrived.' She looks out of the window. More snow. 'Think what I could've had here without you taking up all the space. You're the ugliest chair in the world. With some things, you can appreciate that form simply follows function. My summer sandals for example. If they were pretty I'll bet you they wouldn't be comfortable. But look at you – you're ugly and you don't even look like you'd be comfortable.'

There's someone at the door. A rattle of friendly knocks followed by a ring of the bell.

'Penny? Penny honey – you home?'

It's Marcia and she's gonna let herself in anyway.

'Pen? It's me. I've brought soup. Snow's said to be bad tomorrow. You in here?'

'In *here*,' Penny's voice filters through to the kitchen where Marcia has put the soup on the stove. She goes through to the sitting-room to find Penny.

'Hey you.'

'Hullo, Marcia.'

'You sitting in the dark on the coffee table for a reason? You want me to get some lights on in here?'

'Sure. I didn't see it's gotten dark. I've been sitting here, Lord knows how long, cussing Bob's chair.'

'Cussing Bob's chair,' Marcia says sagely. 'Well, you never did like that thing.'

'If the first sign of madness is talking to oneself, then talking to a chair must make me insane. But hell, it's ugly.'

'Ah – but is it comfortable?'

Suddenly Penny finds she's laughing again. Marcia seems taken aback. 'You know something, I don't know! I never even sat on it! I never tried!'

Marcia's eyebrows, tweezered into supercilious arches, shoot heavenwards. 'In thirty years, you never sat on it *once*?'

'Not once.'

The notion is simultaneously idiotic and rather amazing. 'Was that out of pure stubbornness?'

'A little,' Penny smiles forlornly, 'but then you see, Bob was usually sitting there himself.'

Marcia sits down alongside Penny and places a hand gently on her arm. They gaze over to the chair, both trying to privately conjure Bob – any image of him, at any point over the years – sitting in his chair. Marcia finds she can do so with ease; for Penny it's impossible.

When is his face going to come back to me? Why can't I remember how tall he was? Which way did he position his legs when he sat in that chair?

'Did you ever see Bob sit anyplace other?' Penny remarks wistfully.

'You know what,' Marcia marvels gently, 'no I did not.'

'For thirty years I've been complaining about it – I told Bob over and again that it was a clumpy, ugly thing, out of keeping with all our other furniture. But he wouldn't consider looking at an alternative. He'd sit there, relaxed as you like, while I cussed.' Penny gives just a little laugh. 'I can throw it out now,' she says, with dull triumph, 'I can dump it outside. I can have it chopped up for the fire.'

'Oh don't chop it up, my dear,' Marcia takes Penny at her word. 'Perhaps the refuge – they might find a good home for it?'

'Perhaps,' says Penny. Then she frowns. 'You know something, crazy as it sounds, I couldn't bear to. All these years I've been hating it. But just now, this instant, I love it. It's just where it's always been. And here it shall stay. I'll give it a good home – right here. How insane is that?'

'Honey, are you doing OK?' Marcia asks tenderly, giving Penny's arm a squeeze of wordless sympathy and concern.

'No. I'm not,' Penny states confidently, sucking in her bottom lip so hard her face looks turtle-like and inappropriately comic.

'It's been less than a month,' Marcia almost doesn't want to remind her.

'Twenty-four days,' Penny shrugs.

'Honey,' Marcia tries to soothe though she feels impotent in the presence of such pain.

'What am I going to do without him?' Penny asks. 'What else do I have?'

Suddenly, Marcia is acutely aware of the fact that her own husband is just fine. Just down the street and just fine. It's almost embarrassing. She feels guilty. And she's horribly aware that next week, she'll be swanning off to their winter home in Florida. 'Why don't we all go to Boca for the winter?' she says. 'I mean, Mickey and I are planning to leave next week but there's so much room for you too. Oh say you'll come. Stay as long as you fancy. I'd love it. It would be good, Penny.'

'I'll be fine here,' Penny says, surprising herself at how decisive she sounds. 'This is my home.'

'You know you can just call whenever? Come whenever?' Marcia says. She looks out of the window. 'I'd better go – it's snowing hard now. You eat that soup. I'll call you later. I'll see myself out.'

'Thanks for stopping by,' Penny says and she's ready for Marcia to go. She wants to be on her own, free to grieve, free to drift into a space where just perhaps she might feel Bob still. A semi-dreamland.

She listens to the muffled sound of Marcia's car driving through the fresh snow and away. She turns the lights out in the sitting-room and stands in the darkness quietly. The snow sends silver glances into the room. The moonlight silhouettes the hills as a lumbering but benign presence. Penny wishes she hadn't rubbished clairvoyance and the concept of the Spirit. Because just say it is for real, say it really does exist – has she jinxed herself by being a cynic most of her life? Are you there? Can I sense you? Is that you I can hear? How was your day, honey? Can I fix you a drink? You sit yourself down in your chair. That goddam ugly chair. Let me fetch you a Scotch. Then you can tell me about your day.

'I never even sat in that chair.'

Penny goes to it and sits down. She has no idea whether the chair is comfortable or not. It is as close as she can now get to being with Bob again. She sleeps.

Home from Home

Cat sat at the table, in the furnished flat she and Ben were renting, tracing a pattern someone else had gouged into the wood at some point. Some previous tenant with little respect, she assumed with distaste. As she ran her finger over it, she considered perhaps it wasn't wilful carving, it might even be as old as the table – a slip of the original carpenter's chisel? It was a nice piece of old farmhouse pine. Ben watched Cat work her middle finger along the furrow as if she was gouging it anew.

'Are you OK, babe?' he asked, looking from one tub of fresh pasta sauce to another. He held them to Cat for final selection.

'Arabiata,' she said. 'I'm fine.'

'Liar,' said Ben. 'What's up?' He left the sauce to simmer and sat, cowboy style, astride the chair next to Cat. He brought his face to the level of hers. Cat looked at him, stuck out her bottom lip in an over-exaggerated pout that she knew would invite a kiss, and shrugged.

'How are your sisters?' he asked. 'How's Django? Everything was all right up there, wasn't it?'

'God, fine,' Cat assured him. 'I don't know. It's just that

it's all changed a little since we've been gone. I suppose I was expecting to find my life, my family, just as I left them. As if they'd been happily freeze-framed in anticipation of my return.'

'And?' Ben said.

'Now Django's going to be seventy-five,' Cat said quietly.

'You staying in the UK the last four years couldn't have prevented that,' Ben pointed out.

'And Pip is more sensible than she used to be,' Cat bemoaned. 'By that I mean she's all settled and content with her grown-up role as a school-run stepmum.'

'What's wrong with that?' Ben asked. 'And aren't you settled and content?'

'Of course I am, you know I am,' said Cat. 'But Pip's the one who should be doing cartwheels down the hallway, who makes teaspoons disappear and then reappear from behind my ear. She didn't do one handstand against the wall this weekend.'

'It was the weekend. She was off duty,' Ben pointed out. 'It's normal for people to not want to take their work home with them. Imagine if I came home with my stethoscope, or took the blood pressure of any visitors to our house.'

'But we don't own a house,' Cat mumbled, 'just this horrid rented flat.'

'Cat!' Ben remonstrated. 'We've been back in the UK two bloody minutes.'

Cat ignored him by changing the subject. 'Fen is in the throes of this immense love affair with her baby and she can talk of nothing else.'

'What's wrong with that?' Ben asked. Cat shrugged.

She wasn't prepared to say out loud that though her niece was utterly adorable, she had found Fen uptight, boring even.

'They're not who they were,' Cat said. 'Their identities have changed.' She could hear the plaintive edge to her voice.

'That's par for the course – growing up, growing old,' Ben said, though he saw his wife flinch from his cheeriness. 'Anyway, they probably find you different too. But that's no bad thing.'

'I don't like this place,' Cat said, irritated. 'I don't like other people's furniture. I don't like stupid Clapham. I want to be in our own place, with our stuff. Perhaps we should have rented unfurnished. Perhaps we should have stayed in the US. It's all going to take ages.'

Ben looked at her, suddenly serious. 'Nothing's going to happen overnight,' he said. 'It'll take a while to attain Pip's peace of mind and Fen's healthy baby. Nine months at the very least.'

Cat thought for a moment. Perhaps that was it – perhaps she didn't resent her sisters their changes, perhaps she aspired to what they had. Or there again maybe it was just jet lag.

'I'll tell you what was peculiar,' she said. 'Fen talked about how being a mother had made her really think about our own mother. It had me thinking too.' Her voice dropped to a whisper. 'But say. Just say.' She looked imploringly at Ben, as if he might know what without her having to just say.

'Just say what?' he asked.

Cat paused. 'Just say it's hereditary?'

'But you just said that Fen is a caring mother to the point of being obsessed,' Ben said carefully.

Cat glanced at him shyly. She shook her head. 'I don't mean Fen. Say it runs in the family. Say I'll be a crap mother? Maybe I should concentrate on my career for the time being.'

Ben thought for a moment, scratched his neck. 'Actually, genetics rarely play a part in such extreme behaviour,' he said. 'For all you know, your mother sucks in her bottom lip – like you do – and that's the only family trait you've inherited from her. Think of Fen – mother superior, however much she might irritate you. Think of Pip – her maternal connection with Tom is great and there's no blood there. You McCabe girls are all destined to be extraordinary mothers – by virtue of the fact that your own set such a poor example.'

He watched Cat start to thaw. He ruffled her hair and she ruffled his. Then they put their foreheads together for a moment.

'Being a mother is a state of mind, a condition of the heart, as much as it is biological,' Ben said. 'Christ, look at Django – he's the best mother you girls could have wished for. Stop worrying, Cat. You'll be a star.'

'Do you really think so?' Cat asked, a little bashful but privately delighted.

'I do,' said Ben, 'but we have to get you pregnant first.'

Cat propped her head, chin in her hand, and looked over to Ben. 'It's what I love about you,' she said in an intentionally dreamy tone, 'that you know me inside out but I never feel I'm getting on your nerves. You love me in spite of my foibles. You're so tolerant. That's what I so love about you – that you so love me.'

'Stop it,' Ben joshed, getting up and checking his pager, 'you make me sound a wuss. And anyway, I thought you loved me for my enormous dick.'

* * *

'I cannot believe that I'm going to spend my Saturday traipsing around Alexandra Palace at a convention of model railway nutters and their train sets!' Pip declared, only half joking, surveying the hall and its eccentric population.

Zac raised his eyebrows. 'Firstly, it's the Thames and District Society of Model Engineers. Secondly, if it wasn't for me, you'd have to spend *every* Saturday dressed ridiculously trying to entertain roomloads of sugar-crazed party children.'

Pip fanned out her fingers in front of her sulky expression, then furled them away to reveal a winsome look with much batting of doe eyes. Zac crossed his arms and regarded her sternly. She fanned and then furled her fingers once more, reinstating a natural grin to her face.

'Thirdly,' Zac continued, 'we haven't had Tom for two weekends in a row.'

Pip nodded. 'I know,' she said, 'I'm only joking.'

'Look at him,' Zac said softly, noting that his son had teamed up with a new-found posse of young rail boffins, 'he's in his element.'

Tom was a thoughtful child; not shy, popular at school, but thoughtful. Zac had a theory that boys were divided into two camps: football and fantasy. His nine-year-old son was firmly in the fantasy camp. It wasn't that the restrictions of his eczema ruled out football, it was that Tom's natural interests were dominated by trains and dinosaurs. *My son the trainspotter who knows his connector rods from his couplings,* Zac would say with pride. *My son who could spell pterodactyl before he could spell his own name,* Zac would beam.

Watching an animated Tom admiring the array of essential pieces of kit and name-dropping each model engine from at least fifty paces with his new pals, Pip was consumed by a totally unexpected pang. It was like an electric shock and she jolted physically.

'Are you OK?' Zac asked.

Pip nodded earnestly and went off at a tangent to dislodge the thought. 'Django called us lot the "nit-pickin' chicks" last weekend.'

'That's a fine Djangoism if ever I heard one,' Zac laughed, strolling on to the next stand.

'He hasn't called us that for ages. Mind you, it's been a while since the three of us sat like that,' Pip said wistfully. 'We always used to, when we were little – gravitate into a huddle, play

61

with each other's hair, trace patterns on each other's clothes, tickle each other's forearms. We do it absent-mindedly.'

'Nit-pickin' chicks,' Zac mused. 'I'd've called you a bunch of monkeys, I think. Did you ever actually *have* nits?'

Pip laughed. 'I do remember that we all had them at the same time – some epidemic at school. But of course Django couldn't be doing with those torture combs and vile chemical shampoos so he doused our hair in some bizarre concoction of mustard powder and bicarbonate of soda. Or something. Tabasco. I don't know.'

'Did it work?'

'The daft thing is, I can't remember,' Pip laughed. 'I can only remember feeling slightly miffed that not even a case of head lice was going to make Django conform to conventional methods. I do remember the three of us having pretty short haircuts soon after. Django appeased us by saying our hair was so glorious that he'd been able to sell the offcuts to a master upholsterer in London and we would each be paid £5. We believed him. Even though the salon junior was sweeping it all away.'

'And you were £5 richer?'

'We were,' Pip laughed, 'though of course, Django made a rod for his back because we expected payment for every haircut thereafter.'

'You must have done well, between the master upholsterer and the tooth fairy,' Zac said.

'The tooth fairy never paid cash,' Pip bemoaned.

'Can I have some money?' a flushed and rather breathless Tom jogged over to ask. 'I'd like to buy the guys a juice. They're 50p each. I need about £2.'

Pip looked over to where the other three boys were loitering by a spectacular G Scale display. 'They seem nice,' she said, 'nice guys.'

'They are,' said Tom proudly. 'They're coming again

tomorrow. It's the last day of the show. There's a prize draw. A model of Lampton Tank. Can we come again too?'

'Sure,' Zac told Tom, and Pip took a deep breath. Hadn't they planned to take Tom to Tate Modern and then have lunch with Cat and Ben? Yes, father and son hadn't had a whole weekend together for three weeks but Tom had met Cat only a handful of times over the last four years. However, watching Tom belt off to buy refreshments for his steam gang, Pip let her breath and the objection go. He was a sweet, sweet boy.

Again, the pang confronted Pip and she shuddered. Zac sensed it. 'Pip?'

'Do you think Tom minds?' she asked Zac. 'I mean, do you think he ever minds being an only child?'

Zac looked at Pip and frowned into thought. 'I don't think so,' he said at length, 'I mean, he's never mentioned it. He has plenty of pals and he's thick as thieves with his first cousin.'

'I know,' Pip rushed, 'I just meant. I was just thinking about my sisters. Our closeness. I read a lovely saying the other day – Vietnamese, I think. *Brothers and sisters are as close as hands and feet.*'

Zac kissed Pip. 'Well, worry no more,' he said, 'because Tom isn't to be an only child for much longer. I mean, he may be *our* only child, but he's soon to have a sibling. June is pregnant. She told me this morning when I picked Tom up. He doesn't know yet – June wants to wait till the tests are all-clear. Rob asked me if we'd mind having Tom an extra night now and then while June is feeling ropy.'

Pip was dumbstruck, felt flushed and suddenly light-headed.

'Are you sure you're OK?' Zac pressed. 'You look a little odd, Mrs.'

'I'm fine. Good for June. Great news. I'll call her later.

Odd, though,' Pip said, though she was aware that her thoughts were unreliably half-formed and should stay silent until worked through, 'odd that Tom's being was the result of two friends getting drunk, feeling horny and being careless – yet his half sibling has been meticulously planned. I wonder how he'll feel about that later on.'

Zac stopped. 'What a weird take on it all, Pip,' he murmured.

Pip shrugged. 'I used to wonder if I was planned, you see,' she said. 'I used to presume that I *wasn't* planned – because that meant my mother had some kind of excuse for buggering off.' Pip linked arms with Zac. 'But then I think of Fen and Cat and my theory goes out the window. No one could be that careless.'

Zac slipped his hand into the back pocket of Pip's jeans and gave her buttock a light feel. 'Well, I'm pleased for June and Rob. And I'm made up for Tom.'

'Me too,' Pip said, 'me too.' But she turned away from Zac to conceal the prickle of tears, feigning interest in a Hornby set-up, while trying to figure out the provenance of these tears. And whether they were happy or sad.

Cosima was fed orange food, entertained, fed more orange food, played with, bathed, given some bosom, sung to, cuddled, cuddled some more and placed gently in her cot where she'd promptly fallen into a blissful sleep with the revolving night light and an *Elvis for Babies* CD playing softly.

'Perfect *perfect* baby,' Fen thought to herself as she padded out of the room. 'Bloody awful day.'

She went to the bathroom and tidied up, catching sight of herself in the mirror.

'Yuk. You haggard old bag.'

With a rubber duck in one hand and a Miffy flannel in

the other, she peered closer at her reflection. Sallow and saggy, limp and lacklustre, hollow and haggard, she thought. Then she thought, poor old Matt. Fancy coming home to *this* every evening. Not much to fancy at all. So she rummaged around in her long-forsaken make-up bag and turned to her faithful Clarins mainstays for assistance. Just closing her eyes and slowly, properly, cleansing her face felt as heavenly as a spa facial. Exfoliate. Moisturize. A careful dab of concealer under the eyes, a swipe of mascara, a lick of lippy for the hell of it. Lastly, a few pinches to her cheeks which made her eyes smart a little but gave her cheek-bones a comely emphasis. Matt's key in the door. Hear Matt sigh. A dormant butterfly taking wing in her stomach. Here, Matt, this'll make you feel better.

'Hullo,' Fen said, walking downstairs, carefully tucking her hair behind her ears.

'Hiya,' Matt replied. 'You look – have you got make-up on?'

'Yup.'

'Why?'

Fen frowned and wondered which way to take this. She felt helpless not to opt for the wrong way. 'Because I feel a frump and I feel I look worse than I feel,' she snapped.

'Are you fishing for compliments and craving attention?' Matt teased her. Fen felt embarrassed.

'Well, I think you look very pretty,' said Matt, 'and it's a nice distraction from the baby puke on your top.'

Fen didn't know which to take off first, the make-up or her messy top.

By the end of a rerun episode of *Taggart*, Fen was chanting to herself, *I will instigate sex; I will, I will.* But by the end of *News at Ten* half an hour later, she was willing herself to simply stay awake.

'Tired?' Matt asked.

Ruefully, Fen nodded.

'Go to bed,' he suggested with a friendly pat to her knee. And therein lay the calamity. As much as Fen feared the platonic mundanity of Matt's knee-patting, she loved his suggestion that she go to bed. She still wanted Matt to desire her, she thought she wanted to desire him, but actually her strongest inclination at the moment was to go to sleep. She sat beside him, torn between what her body was shouting at her and what her conscience was whispering and what her partner was sweetly telling her.

'I was trying to be all vampy for you,' she confessed, 'like the girl you fell for. But I'm just a tired old frump.'

'Fen,' Matt said, 'don't worry about it. Just go to bed.'

Fen had looked nice. Matt thought about it as he zapped TV channels. The messy top didn't matter. He felt a little badly for her – she'd made an effort but an effort it had obviously been. There was nothing on television. Matt looked around the living-room. A soft towelling rabbit on the armchair, one tiny sock under it. A muslin square, scrunched up, on top of yesterday's *Evening Standard*. A glob of something orange just above the skirting board. The all-pervasive scent of laundry washed in hypo-allergenic powder. But suddenly, Matt didn't want to smell drying babygros. He snapped his eyes shut. He didn't want to see any of these accoutrements of fatherhood. Actually, all he wanted to see was tits and arse. Quietly, he tiptoed up to the bedroom. It was dark, Fen was sleeping. Could he wake her? Would she mind? Dare he risk it? But realistically, was there really much point trying? He went instead to the cupboard, eased open the door, waited a moment to see if she'd woken. She hadn't. By feel, he differentiated between the suits that were hanging there, found the Paul

Smith one according to its superior cloth. He slipped his hand into the pocket and tiptoed his fingers along the edges of some discs. One would do. It didn't matter which. Though Fen slept on oblivious, Matt still felt obliged to tuck the DVD up his jumper and hurry from the room as noiselessly as he'd entered.

Porn. Odd stuff, really. In reality, pneumatic women had never been Matt's type, let alone the stuff harboured in secret fantasies. He'd never pursued a situation of sharing a girl with another bloke, exotic underwear had never really turned him on and he could take or leave the thought of getting down with a pair of rampant twin sisters. But Matt had always enjoyed porn. He'd been sustained by top-shelf supplies as a teenager, even wondering if sex for real could ever match up to the thunderous wanks he indulged in. And then in his early twenties, purchasing hardcore videos by mail order became a rite of passage. Did he dare? Yes he did. Matt Holden became Mr M. Smith and Mr M. Smith shared his consignments amongst the lads with whom he lived. By his mid-twenties, Matt was a serial monogamist and there were rarely fallow periods long enough between girlfriends to warrant the purchase of new porn. But then his girlfriend had become the mother of his child, their sex life had dwindled and porn had progressed to DVD.

Tiptoeing back downstairs, he didn't check which disc he'd pulled out. He'd never been one for the stories; he never had to start a scene from the beginning. He wanted cunts and cocks to fill his screen just as soon as he pressed play; fast forward any kissing or slinky foreplay, just delve in deep to the fucking and sucking. Matt loaded a disc and, with the sitting-room door ajar and the TV volume low, skipped forward until a mêlée of bodies was having sex in his face. Fantastic, he commented under his breath, as a variously pierced woman with a shorn head and spiked dog-collar was simultaneously being double penetrated, wanked upon, and orally stuffed from an incongruously orderly queue of erections.

Matt masturbated frantically and synchronized his orgasm with a generalized spurting from the remainder of his on-screen cohorts who were not yet spent. Their spunk was gobbled up; Matt had to mop up his from his belly. He didn't realize until he'd done it that he'd used the muslin square his daughter nustled up to, not the sheets of kitchen paper he'd prepared in advance. He was aghast. He put the soiled muslin into a plastic bag, knotted it and then threw it away in the dustbin outside. He wouldn't even want it washed on the hottest cycle. He took his DVD and made his way quietly upstairs, putting it back in the pocket of his Paul Smith suit before going in to check on Cosima. He slipped into bed and lay in the dark, staring at an approximation of the ceiling. He felt utterly empty.

I've always thought a wank to porn is similar to a curry. The sort of thing one craves, one hungers for. You're absolutely in the mood, so looking forward to it, ravenous to the point of visible drool – poppadams or a smooth little blow-job scene to whet the appetite and get you started, then straight for the glut of hot and spicy. Stuff it in. Gorge. But like a curry, once you've had your fill you really don't want to look at what's left on your plate; so it is with hard-core – once you're done you just don't want to see any more.

I feel grubby and not nice. I wanked into my baby's muslin. Fen's asleep upstairs while downstairs I'm shooting my load with a bunch of blokes over some really quite ugly woman. Physically I'm relieved, sated. But I feel a bit, I don't know – sad.

He listened to Fen's breathing, soft and shallow. Turning

towards her he spooned lightly against her. The sleep-scent wafted from her neck. Matt closed his eyes.

My sexy girlfriend who I used to fuck became this amazing vessel who carried and bore my child. But I miss fucking my sexy girlfriend.

Winter Ice

'Perhaps I'll thaw when spring comes,' Penny muttered to herself, a gaze at the wide white world beyond her picture windows informing her that she could thus stay exactly as she was for a good couple of months still. Her solitude and grief felt cathartic, they were becoming a way of life though she quietly wondered if they risked becoming a habit that would soon be hard to break. Penny Ericsson may have lived in the States for most of her adult life and though her accent was commendable and she had not left the country for practically thirty years, she displayed a control when it came to expressing emotions that her friends fondly remarked was transparently English.

'Oh honey,' Marcia once laughed, 'you fool no one with your rhinestones and your blue jeans and your Chevy and all. You're still an English Rose at heart – and that's because you keep your heart all polite and proper.'

'You mean to say that English women are incapable of expressing their emotions?' Penny had retorted.

'Heavens no,' Marcia had said, 'it's just we *guys* gush, while you *chaps* are more, well, *sparing*. It's genetic, is all. Nothing any of us can do about it. We are who we are. Can't deny that.'

And yet just recently, Penny felt her all-American friends, with their gushing and their ability to frequently say *I love you*, now seemed to expect her grief to have lessened. That she ought to feel able to find closure, be ready to move on, and confront a host of other emotional achievements carrying the Oprah Winfrey seal of approval.

Noni had left her a message, inviting her to see a movie at the Mall.

'I'll not go,' Penny told herself and justified that it was because she didn't share Noni's taste in film. Really, she didn't want to have to act upbeat and lie that she was doing just fine. But what else to do? What might pass time, occupy a couple of hours of her day which would be otherwise devoted to the futility of missing Bob? Where could she go in her snowbound county on a bright February afternoon and not bump into a soul?

'I could go for an ice cream,' she said, and she found that the notion was sweet. In fact, she was nearly excited. She'd go in honour of Bob, who had always loved the stuff, and by venturing by herself back to their favourite parlour she'd be simultaneously closer to him while also laying just a little more of him to rest.

There was only the one road into the mountains, with three communities of decreasing scale placed along it. They'd developed organically but a town planner could not have done better. Nothing was duplicated. Everything was shared. Lester Falls, where Penny lived and the largest town, had the Mall and a cinema and a Pack'n'Save on the outskirts. The smaller Hubbardton's Spring, further along and higher up, had a great fish place, a lively pizzeria, a gallery and a hardware store amongst its amenities. The last village, smallest in population but servicing the wider community no less, was Ridge. There, on Main Street, cosy alongside the bookstore, a small theatre, art supplies and a cheese maker, was Bob's favourite ice-cream parlour, Fountains.

Supply and demand. Make superior ice cream from the finest ingredients and people will want it, whatever the weather. The parlour wasn't busy, but it was by no means empty and Penny was relieved to see it wasn't patronized solely by brave widows out for day-trips. Recently, when browsing at the Mall, or strolling the nature trail to the panorama, or visiting the library, Penny had passed other women who'd catch her eye and hold her gaze with a searching nod of recognition. Yes, I lost my husband too, you know, they seemed to say. Join the club.

But I don't want to join your club, Penny would divert her gaze quickly, *I'm not ready to be a widow. It's different for me. You wouldn't understand. I don't want to nod knowingly back at you. I don't want to learn to play bridge. I'm not going to buy a little dog to give me a reason to leave the house every day and join communal walks. I'm perfectly content to pop out for an ice cream. By myself.*

'You want a taste?'

Penny looked up. The waitress behind the counter was offering her a pink plastic spoon on which was a furl of ice cream the colour of butter and the texture of suede.

'It's a new flavour. Banudge-Nudge.'

'Banudge-Nudge,' Penny marvelled at the appetizing name, accepting the sample.

'Banana, double fudge – half fat. Delicious, hey? You want a scoop?'

Penny glanced swiftly along across the colourful tubs like a pianist travelling the length of a keyboard with a single finger. 'You know what,' she said, 'actually I think I'll sit and have a sundae.'

'You take a load off,' the woman encouraged her. 'Menus are on the tables. Juliette'll be right over.'

Aren't the staff great, Penny thought, they give you long enough with the menu so that you're truly salivating and desperate to order. 'I'll have Chippy Chippy Bang Bang, please,' she said, just as soon as she was aware that the waitress hovered, 'with hot chocolate sauce. And nuts. And Lucky Charms. Hell, why not.'

The waitress brought over the sundae, perfectly presented in a pretty frosted dish, oozing with sauce and smothered in extras.

'Enjoy,' she said.

'Oh, I will,' Penny assured her, 'thank you very much.' She sensed the waitress linger, so with the long elegant spoon she dug up a glut of sundae and held it aloft as if to say cheers. Penny experienced a sensory burst that was delicious and exquisitely sweet and intensely painful. She closed her eyes. She closed her eyes to appreciate the taste. She closed her eyes because it hurt, because she suffered from sensitive gums and always seemed to forget the fact where ice cream was concerned. She closed her eyes because she used to bring Bob here when ice cream was the only thing he found digestible and that didn't taste metallic from the chemotherapy. That was the sweetest thought, and that's what hurt the most.

When Penny left, leaving an empty dish and a grateful tip, the waitress Juliette who had served her turned to Gloria behind the counter.

'I recognize her – do you?'

'Not especially,' Gloria said.

'Sure you do – she used to come in, with her husband I guess. You *do* remember him. He was sick. They used to sit right there. Sometimes she'd spoon it for him, feed him. Like a child.'

'Hey, I do remember,' said Gloria, 'but that was a few months back.'

73

'Yes. But today she comes in on her own,' Juliette said.

'You think he died?'

'I guess,' said Juliette. 'Sad.'

Noni invited Penny to the cinema again the following week but Penny thanked her and declined, citing other plans. She took herself back to the ice-cream parlour, which was no less empty though the day was dull and the weather was now too cold to snow.

'Hi,' said the counter waitress, 'have a taste.' The pink spoon, today laden with an ice cream the colour of coal, was passed to Penny.

'Liquorice,' Penny said, having assessed it with the commitment of a sommelier.

'And?' said the waitress.

Penny tasted it again. 'I'm not sure – there's something. I can't—'

'Raspberry.'

'Raspberry,' Penny marvelled, 'and liquorice. Fancy that.' And she went to the same table she'd sat at the week before. The one in the window, furthest from the table in the corner she used to seat Bob at.

'Hi, I'm Juliette,' the younger waitress came over to take her order. 'How are we today? You set?'

'I'm good,' said Penny, 'and I'd like a scoop of that liquorice one.'

'You should get a sherbet with that – brings out the flavour.' Juliette was quite forthright about that. Penny looked up. The girl looked like a confection herself, in her uniform striped the colours of apricot and strawberry, her hair in a high pony-tail, a jaunty little pink-peaked thing on her head, her name in copperplate across it. 'I'd recommend lychee,' Juliette said and Penny nodded.

When Juliette brought the bowl over, Penny took a small

taste and nodded her approval. Her gums didn't seem so sensitive today. She didn't have to close her eyes so often. But there again, she'd abstained from hot chocolate sauce or candy toppings. And Bob had not liked liquorice at all. She felt relaxed, as though she needn't scurry away just as soon as she finished. So when the waitress suggested a cup of coffee, Penny accepted.

'Excuse me, ma'am,' the waitress said after placing the cup and turning the saucer so that the handle was correctly placed. Penny looked up and read the girl's name again. Juliette. Well, Juliette looked a little concerned. 'I don't mean to – well, Gloria and I, we just. We remember you from the summer, from the fall. You used to come in with the gentleman? He was – he was.'

How old? Penny thought. Early to mid-twenties, she guessed. Nice-looking in a plain way, perhaps nicer-looking on account of her politeness and her slightly shy sweetness.

'Is he?' Juliette was bending down a little, as if in a reverential curtsy. 'Was he?'

'He was my husband,' Penny told her. 'He died. Near enough two months ago.'

'Oh I'm so sorry,' said Juliette, instinctively clutching her heart for emphasis. It touched Penny. It was as if everyone, no matter how little they knew Bob, had been rooting for him to pull through.

'Thank you,' said Penny. 'He sure loved this place.'

Penny returned two days later. Not to avoid any social invitation, nor because she had a craving for ice cream, but because Fountains felt like a nice place and seemed a good space to be. Comfort and warmth. Lovely warm chocolate sauce. Beautiful, pastel-coloured candy. Ice creams whose names brought a smile. Everything sweet. If you licked the blossom-coloured walls or bit the backs of the chairs, you'd

75

probably discover they were made from candy. Everything there was sweet. The staff especially. They were like a personification of some of the ices. Pink Wink. Smile Sweetie.

When Juliette brought over Honey in Heaven, with chocolate sauce and marshmallows, Penny spooned into it but then spoke before tasting. 'We were married thirty years nearly,' she said. She looked up. Juliette didn't seem taken aback by the information, her expression invited Penny to continue. 'He called me dear. Always did, right from the start. Good morning, dear. Well dear, I'll be off to work now. I'm home, dear. What a nice supper, dear, shall I fix the coffee? It may have sounded formal, but I always heard it as charming and old-fashioned.' Penny tasted the ice cream. Heavenly indeed. She had two more spoonfuls but Juliette stood beside her, quietly attentive. 'I guess you wouldn't call us a lovey-dovey couple. But we were a good team.'

Juliette was shaking her head shyly. 'I watched you feed him,' she said very quietly. 'That's far more beautiful than lovey-dovey. It must be so hard – but I guess it's a blessing that his suffering should be over, that he is at peace.'

'I'm not a superstitious type,' Penny said, working her spoon busily against the sundae as she spoke, 'I don't believe in astro-mumbo-jumbo, I pooh-pooh voices from the dead, I don't do karma and yin-yang spirit guides; you know? But when Bob was fading I'd whisper to him, over and over, *Find a way, Bob, find a way to be with me. Stay in touch. Send a message. Show me a sign. Promise me?*'

'I *believe*,' Juliette confided with quiet earnestness, while Penny ate.

'Nothing,' Penny said gruffly as if disappointed by Juliette's response. 'I haven't seen *any* signs, I haven't felt warmth – nothing at all. Just the icy emptiness of being on my own.' Her hand formed a fist around the spoon, the skin so taut across her knuckles they looked like the snow-sharp mountains outside. 'There is no blessing,' she ridiculed. 'He shouldn't have suffered in the first place. Death is not a good thing. It's very cruel and it's a waste.' She didn't finish her ice cream and she didn't leave a tip. And she didn't go again the following week.

But she did return the week after that. And she felt her eyes smart at the bright sweetness of the welcome Juliette gave her. Fountains, she decided, was better than any support group. 'Hey stranger, you missed out on Chuckle Berry last week. Gloria will give you a taste. You sitting?'

Penny sat. She managed to make the sundae last an hour and at any opportunity, she passed the time with the waitresses about the weather, or about ice cream. Then she ordered coffee. And a refill. She was obviously lingering but no one, herself included, was quite sure for what.

'My father passed,' Juliette told her, when she accepted a second refill.

'I'm so sorry,' Penny said, genuinely shocked. She'd practically forgotten that grief could befall other people. 'Can you sit awhile?' Penny asked. Juliette glanced around the parlour, raised her eyebrow at Gloria who gave her a nod. 'When?'

'Coming up to a year and I need to tell you that I think death is a great thing. He was a rotten drunk and he hurt me and my mom. So I guess I envy you a little,' Juliette said with a reluctant smile. 'Not your pain, not the longing that must weave the minutes into the hours and drag your hours into these dark days right now. But I envy you the fact that your loss is so great because your love itself was so great. I never had that.'

Penny didn't know where to put herself. For the first time she experienced the guilt that she assumed her own friends were feeling. The guilt at one's own good fortune. She put

77

her hand over Juliette's wrist because she was lost for words. She didn't know what to say because recently Bob was all she really talked about. Just then, though, she wasn't actually thinking about him at all.

Road Kill

Pip butters toast, Zac is skim-reading the *Financial Times* and the *Today* programme drifts sedately through the kitchen; not loud enough to be an active part of breakfast but audible enough to be an integral component in their morning routine. Pip knows to savour these few minutes before Tom breaches the peace.

And here he is. Hastily dressed for school. His nine-year-old physique spurting in fits and starts; just recently his feet have apparently doubled in length yet the softness of his peachy cheeks remains unchanged from when he was a toddler. His fingernails exhibit the indelible grubbiness commensurate with a boy of his age but the pale pitch of his voice seems so pure and clean. His hair truly has an energy of its own and Tom is not yet of an age to exhibit much interest in styling or even basic control. Consequently, it tufts itself into increasingly haphazard configurations, caused as much by spasmodic keratin production as by the freedom of such deep sleep. Today, it resembles something that the forefathers of punk rock spent hours trying to achieve.

'Happy St David's Day,' Tom announces. 'We're doing it in school today.'

'Good Lord,' Pip declares, 'it's the mad March hair.'

Zac looks up from his paper. 'Or the mad March heir,' he quips though neither Pip nor Tom cotton on to the pun. It's too early to hear silent 'h's. It's too early to have to explain, thinks Zac, returning to the pink pages.

Pip attempts to smooth down Tom's hair with her hand. He shirks away and ruffles up Pip's meddling. 'Toast?' she asks.

'Yep,' Tom says. Zac glances over his paper. 'Please,' Tom adds with a sigh.

'Do you want to go through your piece?' Pip asks.

Tom looks alarmed. 'My piece?'

'For assembly this morning? On the patron saints of the British Isles. Aren't you St George?'

'Oh. That. I thought you meant my piece of toast,' says Tom. 'Digby says that the dragon is a metaphor. But he doesn't even know what a metaphor is.'

'And do you?'

'No,' says Tom, 'but it sounds boring, like something Miss Balcombe would go on about. And on and on. Yawns-ville.'

'Well, would you like to go through your piece about St George?' Pip asks.

'I know it off by heart,' Tom says proudly, and launches into a fast, monotone delivery. Pip can see the *Financial Times* quivering. She surreptitiously kicks Zac under the table. Tom finishes his recitation to applause from the table and the 8 a.m. GMT pips from the radio.

'If babies are such a great thing, if they're such a miracle and stuff – why do they make their mums so poorly and so mega grumpy?'

Pip wasn't prepared for this. Usually when she walked Tom to school she was entertained with a diatribe of the personal hygiene habits and physiognomic misfortunes of his teachers, which merely required tuts of her disapproval whilst she bit back laughter.

'Seems a bit stupid to me,' Tom continued darkly. Pip wasn't sure what to say. Was Tom about to probe for the facts of life? She felt uneasy, having not yet discussed with Zac the information and terminology he was prepared to give his son. 'Did I do that to her, to my mum, do you think? When she was having me, did I make her puke like mad and be a grumpy old moo?'

Tom was asking Pip about something on which she had actually no authority to answer. 'Perhaps,' she answered cautiously, having never actually discussed the vagaries of June's first pregnancy, 'but excuse me, young man, your mum is not an old moo.'

'But she *is* grumpy,' Tom muttered. 'I thought she would be chuffed about having a baby but all she does is grumble and puke.' He allowed Pip to take his wrist as they made to cross the road. 'There's going to be buckets of blood too, of course, when the baby comes. And do you think Mum'll scream her head off – like that woman on *Holby City* last week?'

Pip couldn't really answer that one, not knowing June's take on epidurals.

'I can see why *you* don't want all that madness,' Tom said darkly, with much sage nodding.

'Pardon?'

'You and Dad,' Tom shrugged. 'Don't tell my mum I said stuff like that about her and stuff.'

Pip and Tom were about to step off the kerb when they saw the squirrel. Tom was still young enough to point and declare 'Hey! Squirrel!' as it bolted into the road. And then came the car at the same time and they both foresaw the death of the squirrel by a second or so.

'Oh God,' Pip gasped, helpless not to be transfixed by the

81

spatter of guts, the barb of torn limbs, the stark stare of sudden death.

'Gross!' Tom said, not quite sure if he was thrilled or distraught.

'We'll cross the road further down,' Pip said.

'Do you think it's really dead?' asked Tom.

'Yes,' said Pip, 'I do.'

'Oh.'

'Poor little thing.'

'Poor little thing. Do you think it was a boy or a girl?'

They crossed the road and Pip began to gamely tell Tom that babies didn't cause their mums to feel poorly and be grumpy, all that was down to chemicals causing a lady's body to be able to grow and carry a baby. And anyway, mums and dads so want to have babies that a bit of yukkiness now and then didn't matter at all in the long run.

'Tom?'

Tom was quietly sobbing though the school gates were in sight.

'Your mum is fine – please don't you worry about her. She doesn't mean to be grumpy and she can't help feeling a bit yuk.' Pip gave Tom a hug. 'Do you want your dad to talk to her? I promise you she can't wait to give you a little baby brother or sister.'

'Not the baby,' Tom sniffed, 'the squirrel.'

happy st david's day!!! Pxxx

Fen stared at the text message Pip had sent her and wondered for a moment whether St David's Day was something she'd forgotten that they celebrated despite having no Welsh blood in the family. Funny old Pip, Fen smiled, texting back.

and to you. F + C xx

Fen knew Pip would start to text her at length but soon

tire of the thumb effort and phone her instead. The call came a couple of minutes later.

'Happy St David's Day.'

'Same to you, with bells on.'

'What are you up to today?'

'Oh, the usual – puréeing things, changing nappies, singing daft songs, spending the afternoon with women I have nothing in common with other than postcode and the fact that our babies were born in the same month.'

'Shall we meet up, then? I'm not clowning today – and I'd love to see Cosima. And you.'

Fen looked around her home. It was a tip. She ought to prioritize the chores and say no. 'OK,' she said, 'that'll be lovely.'

'Kenwood?' Pip suggested. 'It's equidistant. Let's have coffee and cake. See you in an hour or so?'

Fen looked at the clock. It was ten o'clock and though Cosima was dressed beautifully in Catimini, Fen was still in her dressing gown. She opened her wardrobe and perused her pre-pregnancy Agnès B skirts and John Smedley cardigans. It was a perverse, masochistic ritual she taunted herself with almost daily. She didn't dare hold them against herself, let alone try them on; scrambling instead into yesterday's cargo pants. Packing Cosima in a snowsuit that made the baby resemble the offspring of the Michelin Man and Laa-Laa the Teletubby, Fen crammed essentials and non-essentials into the changing bag and just about remembered to grab her own jacket before heading out of the house.

Big Red Bus, Cosima!

Look at that little fluffy doggie!

Can you see the blue car, baby girl? Yes, it is a blue car, a nice blue car. Blue, blue, blue car blue.

Walking through East Finchley, Fen and Cosima passed buses and dogs and cars of various descriptions. However, there was little to point out to Cosima about the Bishops Avenue other than Great Big Houses and Great Big Trees and Great Big Cars.

But then Fen saw the young man with the flowers.

She slowed her pace. He was some distance ahead, fixing a bunch of flowers – tulips, they looked like – around the trunk of a tree. Fen was captivated; how often had she passed by a tree, some railings, displaying a bunch of bedraggled flowers as a memorial to a life lost? But such flowers had simply been there and, usually by the look of them, for quite some time. Had she ever actually seen someone placing such flowers? No, she hadn't. Had she ever seen flowers tied to this tree-trunk? She didn't think so. Not until today. She was approaching him, the man now fixing a bunch of daffodils alongside the tulips. Fen was close enough to see that some had orange trumpets, others white; a cut above the bog-standard yellow for sure.

Should I cross the road? Should I treat him as the bereaved – give him space and peace so he can have his ritual as solemn as is fitting? He looks so young. Who did he lose?

And the young man was offering a daffodil with a broken stem to Cosima. 'Happy St David's Day,' he was saying.

'Oh!' Fen chirped. 'A lovely flower! A lovely daffodil. Are you Welsh?'

'No. Will she eat it if I give it to her?' the man asked.

'Probably,' said Fen.

'Here, you have it, then,' he said, worrying his hand through his already tousled jet black hair as if he was genuinely concerned. 'Put it in her room. Or something.'

'Oh. OK. Thank you.'

The man paused. 'My sister would like it.'

Fen looked at him. Christ, how awful. Suddenly she wanted to know details; how awful. She should say something. 'I'm sorry for your loss.'

'Thank you,' the man said, and he genuinely seemed touched. 'She was twenty and was killed three years ago. My mum lives in Manchester and I've promised her that I'll replenish the flowers each anniversary.'

'Was it a car?' Fen asked, cringing that this sounded both tactless and interfering.

'No, a motorbike,' the man said.

Fen regarded him. He was fresh-faced and slightly gawky, looked as though he should be putting up leaflets about drama soc at Oxford or Cambridge, rather than road-kill flowers in East Finchley. How old was he? Early twenties? Had he been a younger or older brother to his late sister? 'How long do the flowers last?'

'Longer than in a vase, bizarrely,' he replied, 'but I hate seeing commemorative flowers all withered and limp. I always come back and check. I take them down before they've passed their best. You could say my sister was in full bloom when she was cut down. So I don't think she should be remembered any other way.'

'What was her name?'

'Kay. What's your name?'

'Fen.'

'Short for Fenella?'

'Yes,' said Fen, charmed. 'Not many people know that.'

'I was at college with a Fenella.'

'What's yours?'

'Al.'

'Short for Alan?'

'No, Alistair.'

'Ah.'

'Know any Alistairs?'

'Nope, you're my first.'

'What's the baby's name?'

'Cosima.'

'That's pretty.'

'I think some people think it's a bit pretentious.'

'Is the mum a bit arty-farty then?'

'The mum?' Fen was simultaneously shocked and charmed again. 'I *am* the mummy.'

'No way! I thought you were the nanny.'

'No. I'm the mother all right.'

'Cool. I see. Wow.'

There followed a pause that was simultaneously awkward yet heightened as they both scrambled around for some other common ground, just something to say, to prolong conversation.

'Anyway, we'd better go – we're meeting my sister at Kenwood,' Fen said, as if she'd been miles away and had suddenly come to. 'It's been nice talking to you. And I'm sorry – about Kay.'

'Thanks. Thanks. Nice to meet you too – and Cosima. How old is she?'

'Eight months old,' said Fen, now really wanting to know how old Al was and whether he was younger or older than his late sister. They'd paused too long for her to ask now. 'Bye, then,' she said, a little reluctantly. And just a little coyly too.

Fen walked on. She stopped and turned. Al was looking after her. She waved and he raised his hand. She strolled onwards to Kenwood House, breaking into a sudden grin every now and then. Flattery. How good it felt. 'I don't know whether to be charmed or insulted,' she said to Cosima as she walked. 'I thought I had "Frumpy mum" written all over me.'

The unusual incident, the unexpected attention of a stranger, the break from the drag of just a normal day, served as a tonic that Fen wanted to keep private for utmost potency. So when Pip said how bright she looked, Fen didn't mention

Al. She didn't say that attraction is a peculiar, sly thing that can work wonders on the complexion. She pointed instead to a good night's sleep at last and that Cosima had gobbled up pear purée that morning that had no orange tinge to it whatsoever.

'It wouldn't be wise to tell Auntie Pip anyway,' Fen chattered at Cosima as they walked back. 'Auntie Pip would only give me her worried look – her "Motherhood has made my sister loopy" look.' Fen stopped at Al's flowers. Cosima was fast asleep. Fen tucked the fleece around the baby and stroked her cheek. 'I feel a bit ambivalent that I should feel just slightly flattered that Al thought I was the nanny, not your mother. He said "Wow" when I corrected him. What did that "Wow" mean exactly? That I look good for my age? That I'm a yummy mummy? That I'm the first person he's met with an eight-month-old baby? I can't remember the last time I wowed someone. Daddy just calls me silly.'

Waterworks

'Mr and Mrs York! Mr and Mrs Holmes and Master Holmes! Mr Holden, Ms McCabe, Miss Holden-McCabe! Welcome one and all.' Django genuflected flamboyantly throughout his roll-call, much to everyone's amusement. He was wearing the jeans he'd worn to Woodstock, tessellations of denim patchworked together, teamed with a shirt swirling brightly with paisley motifs. His belt was all buckle, in the bashed bronze form of a mounted Red Indian, bow and arrow poised. Pip had seen similar go for princely sums on ebay. 'Cuppa tea? Something to dunk?'

'Can I have squash?' Tom asked, but directed the question to his father. 'And something to dunk?' Although Django was certainly the most exotic adult he knew, Tom still passed all requests via his father first.

'You can, my boy, you can,' Django responded to Zac's nod, 'but you'll have to tell me how to squash it – I'm sure to have the ingredients.'

'You just untwist the bottle top, pour in about a centimetre and then top it up with water. Even water from a tap,' Tom explained helpfully despite being somewhat incredulous. It occurred to Django only then that they were talking different types of squash. He realized with some relief that he needn't attempt to juice the pumpkin. And he realized with some disappointment that he did not own the bottled cordial to which his step-grandson-thing-or-other alluded. Good job, really, because he hadn't a clue what a centimetre was anyway. A dash he knew intrinsically, a dollop too; he could do a smidgeon blindfolded and had always denounced the pinch as miserly. Feet and inches he was fine with, metric however was another matter; one he staunchly felt did not matter. 'I have some cherry syrup,' he said quietly to Zac. 'Do you think that might do?'

'I'm sure it will,' Zac said, laying an affectionate hand on Django's shoulder. 'But what on earth do you use cherry syrup for?' he asked as they walked on up the path and into the house.

Django stopped. 'Do you know, I don't think I've used it for anything. I think it's unopened. I've had it ages.'

In the event, Django couldn't find the cherry syrup but he did have cherry brandy and decided that a smidgeon watered down excessively with flat R White's lemonade wouldn't do the boy any harm at all. He was right. Tom acquired a liking for it and asked for more.

'I hope you left the beds for the blokes to do,' Pip said, all stern, 'like I suggested in my letter and on the phone.'

'Yes, I have,' Django sighed, 'but only because you're so bossy I didn't dare do otherwise.' He didn't confess to certain relief at Pip's directive; that he didn't actually feel like shunting and shifting divans about any more, didn't feel he could. 'There's a zed-bed out in the shed,' he added, 'though I've used its mattress to lag the water tank.'

'Can't I sleep in the shed?' Tom sighed, looking imploringly to Zac before winking beguilingly at Django.

'Have you been incorrigible?' Django asked him.

'No, actually, I've been *exemplary*,' Tom said. 'Miss

Balcombe told me that's what I am in some things – like maths. It's just that Pip told me all about the shed.'

Django's contrived haughty expression softened. 'In the summer,' he said, 'if you promise to be as incorrigible as Pip was when she was young, before she was bossy, I promise to banish you to the shed for a night. Now come along, troops, we have a party to plan. There's only two months to go.'

No one would hear of Django sleeping on the sofa; they were reluctant enough to let him give up his bed but the deal was settled on Django sleeping in Fen's bed and Tom sleeping in Fen's room on the zed-bed plumped up with two sun-lounger mattresses, Fen and Matt in Django's bed with Cosima in her pop-up travel cot, Zac and Pip in her old room with Cat's bed dragged through, Cat and Ben on various cushions and beanbags in her room. 'You're the youngsters,' Django had told them, 'you won't have the spinal issues of those over a certain age.'

'Shall I point out that I'm older than Matt?' Ben joshed.

'No, don't do that,' Django replied. 'You know how I enjoy my theories.'

At the crack of dawn, Django came across Fen boiling a kettle in the kitchen.

'Did Cosima wake you?' she asked, alarmed.

'No darling,' Django said, 'just the infernal need to pee. Not that you'd want to know the finer details of my water-works. It's an age thing.'

'And a pregnancy thing – I remember it well,' Fen groaned. She took the kettle from the hob. 'Can we buy you an electric kettle for your birthday?'

'No thank you,' Django said, 'far too dull.'

'I don't suppose you'd like a microwave then?'

'Absolutely not. What would a seventy-five-year-old want with one of those?' Django said.

Fen poured boiling water into a Pyrex jug and immersed a baby bottle to heat through. 'I'm trying to reclaim my boobs,' Fen explained, with a tone of regret and a look of guilt, 'not that you'd want to know the finer details of my lactation.'

'Quite,' said Django. He paused. 'Matt must love it – the bottle feeding – enables him to feel hands-on and useful.'

'Absolutely,' said Fen. 'I like watching him.'

'Watching or checking?' Django posed. 'It's good for him to feel *useful* – because, you see, you are so very *capable*, Fenella.' Fen was taken aback by the use of her name in full and she detected a subtle note of warning from Django. 'It must be easy for Matt to feel left out a little – on account of you being so very capable.'

Fen felt a little defensive but it was too early and she was too tired to express it with much vehemence. 'It's not that Matt does things wrong,' Fen attempted to explain, 'it's that he doesn't do things quite right. It's often easier for me just to do it in the first place. It saves time. And tears.' With that she took the warmed milk upstairs to feed a now grumbling Cosima.

Fen gazed down at her daughter, sucking contentedly on the bottle, locking eyes with her and sharing silent waves of intense love. She looked over to Matt who was sound asleep. How strange to feel simultaneously grateful but also resentful of the fact. Though nothing, not even a much-needed simple lie-in, was worth trading these silent waves of love, yet still Fen felt a little put upon that Matt never woke instinctively in advance of the baby stirring. However, though she knew that he'd be happy for her to boot him out of bed and be on early-morning bottle duty, she also knew she'd only lie there wondering if the bottle had been mixed correctly, whether it was the right temperature. She'd end up double-checking anyway. So what was the point in not doing it herself in the first place? There was no such thing as a lie-in. Did it slightly offend Matt? She rubbished the notion – he understood, didn't he? He understood that it's a mother's prerogative to be finicky. It's out of love for the baby anyway. No bad thing.

An hour later, swathed in his voluminous velvet dressing gown, his hair not yet pony-tailed and so fanning around his shoulders in silver skeins, Django sat in state, in the huge old Windsor chair in the kitchen. He looked like a Norse god, or straight from a William Blake painting, receiving his house guests one by one. First Tom, who scampered down, hair in hysterics, to see where his roommate was. Then Zac, to check his son hadn't actually woken Django. Then Pip, to check Zac and Tom were helping themselves to breakfast though of course she found Django busy rustling up his panffles, because he'd offered to make his highly complicated hybrid of pancake and waffle and Zac and Tom had readily accepted. Cat and Ben appeared because the scent of maple syrup warming over pancakes or waffles or some such, had drifted evocatively into their room and filled them with hungry memories of American breakfasts. Next came Fen and Cosima, the baby dressed immaculately down to the colour-coordinated tiny hair grip gathering together the few strands she had, while her mother wore mismatched socks. Finally, Matt emerged, still sleep-crumpled but characteristically cheerful.

'The morning is for Chatsworth, the afternoon is for lolling and party planning, and the evening is for the Rag and Thistle – for men who are over the limit,' Django announced.

'Over the limit?' Zac and Matt asked.

'Over the *age* limit,' Django said, with an apologetic ruffle to Tom's wayward hair.

'I see,' said Cat, hands on hips with consternation that wasn't wholly mock, 'while we womenfolk keep the home fire burning?'

'And do the washing-up,' Django added calmly. The men cheered. The baby cried. Let the day begin.

* * *

If Django was a perk of being married to, or partnered with, a McCabe girl, it was definitely a high point of a trip to Derbyshire to share an evening at the Rag and Thistle with their eccentric host. While Zac, Matt and Ben donned a change of shirts, Django certainly dressed for his big night out; watched by Tom fascinated with the provenance of each article of clothing. Django gathered this was a delaying tactic but it was his pleasure to spin yarns about his threads. Whether they were fact or fancy was of little relevance to Tom. He'd further embroider it all at school next week anyway. Tales of Django Gramps and his pink shirt with the gold buttons. Real gold. A gift from the King of Kathmandu.

To Matt, Ben and Zac's urbane, understated signatures of Ted Baker, Gap and Paul Smith, Django added a certain flamboyance with his Astrakhan waistcoat, his Pucci neckerchief, his peculiar multi-seamed corduroys and yet another great big fuck-off belt, this one with an amber-encrusted buckle. The only item no one had seen before was the excessively floral shirt.

'I knew a woman who worked at Liberty's,' Django explained nonchalantly. 'Her name was Maureen. The summer of 1970. She was *spectacular*.' And with that, the men left.

While Fen checked on Cosima, who was compliantly sound asleep, Pip served up the casserole Django had left simmering and Cat poured the wine.

'Come on, Fen,' Cat muttered to herself, 'I'm starving.'

'Cravings?' Pip probed.

'Unfortunately not,' Cat said, 'but not for want of trying.'

'Django's recipes would be perfect for pregnant women,' said Fen, who'd appeared and sat herself down in a chair with a great exhausted sigh, 'on account of all his bizarre combinations.'

'I've just found a walnut,' Cat said, chewing thoughtfully. She detested walnuts and was privately slightly irked that Django appeared to have forgotten this. 'God, I've only been away four years.'

'They're very good for you,' said Fen.

'Isn't there stuff one should eat if you want to have a boy, and other stuff if you want to have a girl?' Cat asked her.

'Apparently there is,' said Fen, 'but I couldn't tell you which was which. Would you like one more than the other?'

'No, no,' Cat said, 'but I would like just the one – I don't think I have the space for twins.'

Fen glanced at her sister's slender frame with gentle envy.

'You certainly wouldn't have the space in that Clapham place,' Pip remarked. 'What's happening with all that?'

Cat sighed. 'Apparently, we're under contract until June. I keep telling Ben it's never too early to scout around. There's no harm in planning. It's fun. I've always really loved Tufnell Park,' Cat enthused, 'and Parliament Hill. I know it can be expensive – but what an investment. Then we'd all be within a mile or so of each other. And I'd have Hampstead Heath on which to push my pram and have picnics. It's Nappy Valley, isn't it?'

'You need to conceive first,' Fen said.

Cat giggled. 'Each time we have sex, I hold my legs up for about five minutes. Ben thinks I'm daft.'

'It'll happen when it happens,' Fen tried to reason.

'I hope it happens soon,' Cat said wistfully. 'I'm doing everything right with the folic acid and the yoga and the magazines. Or watching repeats of *Location Location Location*. I've always had a thing for Shaker kitchens and tumbled mosaic tiles in bathrooms.'

'You need to find a job,' Pip interjected. 'You have a little too much time on your hands at the moment, methinks.'

'And expensive taste,' said Fen.

'That's easier said than done,' Cat muttered. 'I have looked. There's nothing. Not even freelance work.'

'Maybe you should think tangentially,' Pip suggested.

'You mean settle for less?' Cat said gloomily.

'No,' Pip said gently, 'but perhaps you have to consider the bigger picture rather than fixate on details.'

'You're so sensible,' Cat muttered with slight irritation.

'What do you expect me to say?' Pip said.

'It was something he said,' Fen interrupted.

'Who?' Cat was confused. Hadn't they been focusing on her?

'Django,' said Fen, 'about that flowery shirt. About a woman called Maureen.'

'Who was *spectacular*!' Pip mimicked.

'I wonder who she was,' Fen said. 'A spectacular woman called Maureen, who defined Django's summer of 1970.'

'We can ask him,' Cat suggested. 'He's bound to be fantastically verbose when he comes rolling home with the boys later.'

'Come to think of it, I do remember him in other floral shirts,' Pip said. 'They were probably all Liberty. Perhaps they were all from this Maureen.'

'When you have children, there's so much you leave by the wayside,' Fen said pensively.

Instinctively, it didn't seem right to Pip or to Cat to tease their sister just then for contradicting her previous conceit.

'Flowers by the wayside,' said Fen, her voice cracking. 'Sorry,' she mumbled, 'sorry.'

'Are you OK?' Pip asked. 'Is everything all right?'

'Are things no better with Matt?' Cat asked.

'I don't know,' said Fen, 'I don't know. I'm just tired, I suppose.'

Django's posse was the centre of attraction at the Rag and Thistle, especially when it became known that the main topic of discussion was the forthcoming infamous seventy-fifth birthday party to which, it seemed, all the clientele and staff of the Rag and Thistle, plus their pets, had already been invited.

'I was thinking of three marquees,' Django proclaimed, accepting a complimentary pint of Guinness with effusive thanks, 'the Good, the Bad and the Ugly.'

'But Django,' Zac pointed out, 'how will you decide which guest goes in which tent?'

'Marquee!' Django objected.

'Marquee,' said Zac. 'It's rather subjective. I mean, take Matt, he's bad *and* ugly.' Matt raised his pint.

'I didn't see it like that,' Django mused, as if he now found Zac's take rather interesting. 'I envisaged a natural progression from tent to tent—'

'Marquee,' chorused Ben, Matt and Zac.

'Mar-bloody-quee,' Django sighed. 'You know: a suitable, conducive environment to assist the three key stages of any good party. Conduct starts off good, behaviour then worsens until hopefully proceedings become downright shameful. Each marquee would have food to facilitate, cocktails to complement and soft furnishings to, well, accommodate.'

'McCabe,' said Mr Merifeld the landlord, with a grave shake of his head, 'sounds right costly to me.'

'Merifield,' said Django, 'what's money? I can't take it with me and I *am* well into my eighth decade.'

'Marquees don't come cheap,' said Mr Merifield.

'Tents it is then!' Django exclaimed, to much raucous approval.

By the time the four men made their somewhat unsteady passage up the garden path after a lock-in at the Rag and Thistle, Django's party had been planned to an imaginative degree; the minutiae mapped out down to the wording of the invites, the order of speeches and cleverly themed play-lists for each hour.

'The devil is in the details,' Matt justified, with drunken solemnity.

'Then the devil can come too!' Django proclaimed. 'Who's for a cup of tea or a nightcap?'

'Nightcap,' said Ben.

'Nightcap,' said Matt.

'Nightcap,' said Zac.

Ben gave Django a hand, while Zac checked on Tom and Matt tiptoed in on Cosima and Fen, who sleepily protested that he reeked of booze.

'Django,' Ben said cautiously, while he searched under the kitchen sink and found a bottle of cognac shoulder to shoulder with Domestos, 'are you happy with your health? Is all well?'

In the context of the lightness of the evening's conversation, Ben's question surprised Django. 'I'm in rude health, doctor,' he declared, placing four enormous brandy balloons on a tray.

'Any concerns?' Ben pressed. 'However minor?'

'I can't shift and shunt the beds about like I used to,' Django joked.

'It's my job to notice that you appear to go to the loo a lot,' said Ben. 'Have you noticed an increase in this? Pain? Discomfort? Any change in the old waterworks?'

'You cheeky whippersnapper,' Django protested, 'don't you go calling my waterworks old.'

'I'm just saying perhaps a check-up might be a good idea,' Ben said evenly.

Django didn't reveal that he'd thought the same himself. He didn't tell Ben he'd gone so far as keeping an appointment with the GP.

But the GP turned out to be a girl who looked no more than twelve. Don't doctors seem younger and younger these days? I'd really rather not discuss my waterworks with a young lady. I had to invent a sore throat as the purpose of my visit. She told me to go easy on the Tabasco. And she recommended Strepsils. Jolly nice they are too.

'Django?' Ben was saying. 'There are basic steps you can take – restrict fluid intake after 6 p.m., cut down alcohol and caffeine. Limit spicy food. Increase fish, carrots, broccoli. And exercise.'

Django nodded thoughtfully. 'Life would be a bit of a bore,' he said.

'Just cut down on some stuff and increase other things. Invent new stews,' Ben suggested.

Django was about to respond but then Matt and Zac were joining them again, switching the conversation back to party planning.

He's Not There

If the devil is in the details, if the pleasure is in the planning, then the fun is in the fantasy. Though Fen knew well enough how reality can let a daydream down, that Monday she made sure she forgot. Though she was aware that the planning might well be pointless, she happily indulged herself. Though she knew that her own guardian devil was guiding her, she turned deaf ears to her conscience. All her conscience wanted to say was *Think about it – what is the point?* But for Fen, just then, the point was that her imagination had been ignited and running with it was fun. And wasn't it refreshing to have the energy and the desire to spend a little time choosing what to wear? And didn't it seem entertainingly decadent to put mascara on in the daytime? And wasn't it fun to think about something other than baby food for a little while? And when it all seemed suddenly fanciful, questionable even, Fen simply justified that Cosima needed some nice fresh air. And wasn't a stroll up Bishops Avenue as good a route as any? And if further corroboration was needed, then a date with Cat at the café in Kenwood House provided it.

*

'He's not there,' Fen said to Cosima as they walked up the Bishops Avenue, 'but there again, why would he be?' She walked on, mulling theories on coincidence, unrealistic expectations and downright improbability. She stopped to pick up Cosima's teething rings. She looked back over her shoulder to the tree and the flowers. 'Shall we leave a little note?' she asked. 'There's no harm in that. It would be friendly, wouldn't it – might make his sad task a little less so.' She turned the buggy and retraced her steps.

> Hi Al!
> Cosima and I were passing.
> I noticed a couple of Kay's daffodils were looking peaky so I've removed them.
> Hope that's OK.
> Fen.

'Shall we leave Mummy's mobile number too? I mean, it's no big deal, is it, it's just a friendly gesture – communication being a global thing.' Fen added her number after her name.

She set off for Kenwood in earnest and thought to herself how she'd just done the right thing.

It's not like I'm hoping he'll call. It's not like I'm swept up in daft daydreams. She spent the rest of the route distinguishing between the Daydream and the Distraction.

There's a major distinction between the two. A daydream can be pointless, a distraction useful.

It was with a spring in her step that she crunched along the sweep of gravel driveway heralding Kenwood House.

Cat was already there, sitting in the converted coach house, caressing a cup of tea. Fen zoomed the buggy over to her, mimicking a screech of brakes with her voice. An elderly couple looked slightly alarmed, as if that was no way to handle a buggy, as if babies should be in nice coach-built prams, not bizarre three-wheeled monstrosities.

Though they'd spent all weekend together, Fen gave Cat a kiss and a hug. She took Cosima from her buggy.

'Here, you cuddle your Auntie Cat,' she told the baby. 'Mummy's going to get herself an enormous slice of cake.'

'You're chirpy,' Cat told Fen on her return, declining the gateaux that Fen had bought.

'And you look miserable,' Fen commented, giving Cosima an organic sugar-free rusk. 'Everything OK?'

'I feel glum,' Cat admitted, 'and I want to be allowed to feel glum. So thank God you're not Pip.'

'What's up?' Fen asked, spooning butter-cream from the cake's surface directly into her mouth.

'I'm not pregnant. I don't have a job. I don't like Clapham. Ben's never home and I wish I'd stayed in Colorado,' Cat declared.

'Cat,' Fen said, 'you've only been home two minutes.'

'It's been three months,' Cat corrected. 'I've had sex forty-two times and have sent out nineteen pre-emptive letters for jobs. Nothing.'

'Cat, you make the former sound like a chore and you're being unrealistic about the latter,' Fen admonished her lightly.

'And you sound like Pip,' said Cat, 'so stop it because I need you to be the one who there-theres me.'

Fen paused to consider this. It was true. Go to Pip for practical advice and accept her authority. Go to Fen for a hug and be assured of some plain sympathy. 'It takes time,' Fen soothed, 'both take time.'

'You got pregnant overnight!' Cat objected.

'It wasn't planned,' Fen said.

'Then it's not fair,' said Cat.

Fen looked at her younger sister apologetically and put

101

her hand over Cat's. 'Come back to mine this afternoon,' she said. 'Let's look at my books and magazines. There's sure to be Ten Top Tips For Tip Top Fertility or something.' Though Fen made it sound as though she was doing Cat the favour, privately she liked the idea of a way out of the mums-and-babies group.

'What's wrong with Clapham anyway?' Fen asked. 'I thought it was meant to be quite a happening place?'

'I stick out like a sore thumb,' Cat said. 'All the women bustle about with perfect children, or sit smug behind the wheels of their SUVs.'

'But that's your goal too,' Fen said, 'that's what you're hoping for. And actually, it doesn't sound dissimilar to this part of North London.'

'But while it's not happening for me, it makes me feel so isolated,' said Cat, 'and it's made me realize that I really want to be nearer to you. And Pip. I felt less far away when I was living in Colorado – how mad is that? I feel lonely stuck over the river. Ben's really upbeat about his job but he's working really long hours. I haven't made any friends. I miss Stacey and the gang in Boulder. And I miss my mountain.'

'Your what?' Fen asked.

'Flagstaff. Remember that hike we went on? That's my mountain. You saw where Ben and I lived, Fen. You saw the awesome wilderness right on our doorstep. You filled your lungs with that crystal-pure air. You stayed in our gorgeous apartment. You hung out with our mates. You saw how people drive SUVs out there because of the terrain, not fashion. You had a taste of our quality of life.'

'But you wanted to come back,' Fen pointed out. 'It was part of your game plan and you were adamant.'

'I know,' said Cat, 'it's true. We had a purpose. A goal. Hopes and dreams. Absolutely. But you see, it's March, it's been three long months and none of it has happened. And in that context it's really difficult to like Clapham. And it's bloody easy to wonder whether we've done the right thing. You know me – I love planning in my head but in reality I can't set the pace. I was so eager to return, I suppose I've been a bit deluded too – thinking nothing will have changed, like everything has been on hold for four years, awaiting my return.'

Fen nodded. She rubbed her sister's knee. She wondered what constructive advice she could give. But then she thought, that's Pip's job. What Cat wanted her to be was typical Fen just then. 'I understand,' she said, with a ruffle to Cat's hair. It was still short, but longer than that stunning elfin crop she'd arrived back in the UK with. 'It will happen, Cat. I promise you. Everything will be fine. Don't worry – that's the main thing. You'll make a wonderful mummy. We'll pick up brochures from estate agents on the way back to mine. Make some appointments for next week. There's a new kitchen design shop in Muswell Hill – we could go there after Cosima's nap.'

'Thanks, Fen,' Cat said, squeezing her sister's hand, 'that's just what I needed to hear.'

Walking back down Bishops Avenue, Fen considered crossing the road as they neared Al's flowers. It was as if they suddenly personified Al; that Cat might see something she shouldn't, make something out of nothing. While Fen didn't want Cat even to comment on the flowers, she knew she needed to bite her tongue herself. Must not make a bouquet out of a hasty posy. Must not read into this. Must not say anything out loud.

Her note had gone.

A piece of folded paper was tucked between the stems of a few daffodils and the trunk of the tree. As they passed by, Fen could see her name written on the paper. Neat and bold handwriting. There was no way she could take it just then and though she didn't resent Cat, she reprimanded herself for having invited her forlorn little sister back home with her.

I wonder what it says?

I suppose I'll have to wait until Matt's home before I can retrieve it.

But say that's too late? It's windy. It looks like it might rain.

It's exciting!

Of course Fen couldn't wait for Matt. Could you? She nipped out while Cosima slept, supposedly to the shops, leaving Cat snuggled up on the sofa with back issues of *Prima Baby* and the property section of the *Ham & High*.

The note just said 'Thanks, Fen. Alistair.' There wasn't much to read. Certainly, nothing could be read into it. But she quickly reconfigured a crashing disappointment into no big deal. It was nice, anyway, wasn't it? Nice of him to reply, and nice to have a tiny, harmless secret.

However, it was difficult not to feel a little glum when, a week later, Fen saw that the flowers had been taken down. That there'd been no phone call to her mobile phone. It made it difficult to know what to do with his note. She'd kept it folded and tucked into a book of stamps in her purse. She'd have to throw it away, and her silly fantasy with it. The note was only three words long, after all, and you could hardly read into those. It wasn't as if it was even long enough for there to be any lines to read between.

April Fool

Penny had specified no flowers at Bob's funeral. She didn't much like flowers – not cut ones. You cut flowers and then the natural process decrees that you witness them die. Why be reminded of death by things that are themselves dying? Much better to say '*No flowers. Donations to the Lance Armstrong Cancer Foundation*'. Lucky Lance – cancer hadn't killed him, like it had Bob. Perhaps if other mourners over recent years had boosted the funds of cancer charities, rather than the coffers of the funerary florists, then things might have been different for Bob. Wishful thinking, perhaps – but what else could she think about or wish for?

She didn't feel like going out. But she knew it wasn't sensible to mope around the house. Not at this time of day. It would make the wait until bedtime interminable. Marcia was back from Florida and Penny thought to phone her, but they already had an arrangement for the next day and she didn't want to come across as needy. Marcia would worry. And when Marcia worried, she would fuss. And Penny had never liked being fussed over. So she summoned up some sense and energy and went out for a drive. Just a drive, she told herself, no rush to be anywhere specific. It was a fine day, though there was a chill to the air – the sharp brilliance of April sunshine issued a defiant dismissal of winter. Just beyond Hubbardton's Spring, Penny stepped from the car to admire the herd of unusual red-and-white Holstein cattle peacefully chomping away at the lush spring grass. She gazed at the cows for a while and found she was often gazed back at. 'I'll see you in a moment, ladies,' she said, marvelling how beasts so lumbering and lugubrious could also be unequivocally female. She walked to the famous covered bridge a few yards ahead. She read from the plaque aloud because she didn't want to hear Bob's voice in her head. He'd loved this spot: postcard perfect yet untainted by commercialism. '1872. *Horsemen keep at a walk,*' Penny read. She glanced around her. 'If they went at a trot, the bridge would bounce,' she explained conversationally, though there was no one around. 'It was used as a boxing ring too, you know.' Suddenly, she found the sound of her voice a little embarrassing – talking to no one sounded worse than talking to cattle – so she walked briskly back to the car, nodding quickly to the cows on her way. Making much of the correlation between the rich Holstein milk and the ingredients for Vermont ice cream, Penny headed off for Ridge as if the idea to drive there for an ice cream had only then occurred to her.

'Hi Penny,' Juliette said casually, whilst taking the order of another customer. Penny nodded without checking if Juliette had seen. She didn't go to the counter where Gloria was already preparing her a taster of that week's special flavour but when Penny realized that someone sat at her table – a mother and toddler – she felt so discombobulated as to be tempted to walk straight out of the shop.

'Penny,' said Juliette kindly, guiding her to a table with no fuss. She came back a few minutes later with a pink plastic taster spoon, mounded high. 'It's a new flavour,' she told Penny. 'It's called Sing for Spring. It's pistachio and meringue – boss says it symbolizes the spring pasture peeping through the snow fields.'

Penny sucked the glob off the spoon. 'I'll have a banana split, thanks,' she said flatly.

'Banana split for Penny,' Juliette called and Penny detected excessive jollity and loud kindness in the girl's usually soft voice. Simultaneously, Penny felt her eyes smart and her toes curl.

'It's April Fool's Day,' Penny told her with a shrug. 'In Britain everyone plays pranks – practical or intellectual.'

'I knew it,' said Penny, triumphant. 'I says to Gloria, that Penny's not from around here. You're English? How cool is that?'

'A long time ago,' Penny confirmed.

'I'm sorry – I interrupted. You were saying about playing tricks?'

'I made an April Fool of Bob one year,' Penny shrugged. 'He took it well – but I know he was a little upset. I never said sorry for it.'

Juliette wasn't quite sure what to say. 'Bob won't have taken anything by that,' she mumbled.

'That stupid movie *Love Story* got it wrong,' Penny frowned. 'Love means you *must* say you're sorry. I never said, *Sorry Bob – that wasn't funny and I apologize*. I've been saying it over and over today. But it's too late.'

Juliette hovered. Penny had barely established eye contact with her this visit. Juliette glanced over at Gloria who used her eyebrows and vigorous tilting of her head to signify for her to sit down. She slid into the chair next to Penny. 'My dad used to tell me I was a fool the whole time – he didn't need April 1st,' she told Penny. 'He used to tell my mom she was a fool as well. Actually, he didn't use that word. He called us dumb. Dumb-ass bitches.'

Penny jerked and locked eyes with Juliette.

'When he said sorry, he never meant it so I stopped believing him quick,' Juliette said with a shrug. 'He'd even try tears, get down on his knees and holler that he was sorry. He was a better actor than Ryan O'Neal, I'll say that. It's a crap film anyway.'

'I left my husband on April Fool's Day,' Penny suddenly interrupted in a hoarse whisper. Juliette's eyes darted in confusion. 'Not Bob,' Penny hastened to add. 'I left this other man for Bob. I left this other man for Bob thirty-three years ago today.' She tucked into her banana split that was on the verge of being renamed banana spilt. 'I'm sorry,' she said to Juliette, 'I interrupted you. It's just I never told a soul about this until right now.'

Two weeks later, when Penny caught sight of Juliette at the Pack'n'Save, a world away from Fountains Ices, she wasn't sure what to do but she didn't think she wanted to be recognized. Fountains had become a sacred space for her, her visits there sacrosanct. She liked the anonymity, the sense of sharing but of confidentiality. She'd come to feel that it was as close to a support group as she would ever come by. And it was a comforting thought that wherever she was, whatever the time, the candy-coloured parlour where everything was sweet and pretty, existed. So, it didn't seem right to see Juliette in Pack'n'Save. But Juliette was apparently pleased to see Penny there as she'd made her way over, an older woman with her.

'Hi Penny.'

'Hi Juliette.'

'This is my mom, Cyn.'

'Hi Cyn.'

'Hi Penny.'

'You shopping?'

'I am. You too?'

'We are. My aunt's coming to stay.'

'That's nice.'

'Honey, I'm going to pick up some soda.'

'OK Mom, I'll be right there.'

Penny and Cyn nodded at each other, smiled cordially. Penny thought about the woman's deceased husband calling her a dumb-assed bitch. It chilled her. 'Well, you have a nice weekend,' Penny told Juliette.

'Thank you,' Juliette said, 'and you. You doing something?'

'Not especially,' Penny said.

'Oh. Oh. Well, see you next week, I guess.'

'Yes,' said Penny, 'goodbye.'

But Juliette loitered. 'Bob sure was special,' she said to Penny. 'I mean – for you to up sticks and leave like that. Your home, your country. When you were so young.'

Penny was taken aback. She couldn't possibly comment.

Juliette tipped her head to one side and regarded Penny. 'I know you can come across a little frosty and all,' she said with kindness, 'but I say it's a shame you never had kids of your own. You'd've been a good mom.'

Penny was so stunned she hadn't the self-possession not to let it show, scrambling around for her composure whilst scrabbling for something to say. However, her feelings of disarray obviously didn't offend Juliette who smiled sweetly and made to go.

'Don't you go thinking you and your mom aren't special just because your daddy didn't say so,' Penny suddenly said.

Juliette was visibly touched. 'See you next week, Penny,' she said.

'Actually, I won't be here next week,' Penny heard herself telling Juliette though she knew the thought was unformulated.

'Oh?'

'No. No. I'm going to be in England,' Penny told her, 'I haven't seen my family in many many years.'

Juliette smiled and placed her hand warmly on Penny's arm. 'You do that,' she enthused, 'you do just that.'

My Round

Predictably, it had been Pip's idea to encourage the menfolk to meet.

'You always say what a good bloke you think Ben is,' she said casually to Zac as they dressed for work: Pip braiding her hair tightly into pigtails and securing them both ends with polka-dot ribbons, Zac donning a sober navy blue suit enlivened by a Paul Smith tie emblazoned on the underside with a 1950s pin-up girl. 'You should get together more often with him and Matt. You're brothers-in-law.'

'That's stretching it,' Zac laughed, peering over Pip's head to check his reflection in the mirror.

She twisted around and looked up at him. 'Well, whatever you are officially, you are certainly family,' she said. Zac kissed the bridge of her nose as the tip of it was already painted red. 'Anyway, you three need to meet up to discuss the music for Django's party. It's less than a fortnight away. He'll be digging out the gramophone and all his scratchy old vinyl if you don't.'

'Good thinking, Mrs,' said Zac. 'Remember to pick Tom up later.'

What a stupid thing to say, Pip thought.

*

To meet at the Mariners was Zac's suggestion and it was a good one. Tucked away up a side street off the Embankment, it was a hop across the river from Ben's hospital, a walk through the City for Zac and a quick taxi ride for Matt, better locating him for the journey home anyway. The establishment itself, though categorically a pub, had the feel of a gentleman's club, with walls panelled in oak, tub chairs set around tables placed discreetly apart and booths upholstered in dark green leather along the back wall. There were no fruit machines, no television, no music, no menu. The landlord and bar staff were male and conservative, in their waistcoats and ties and neat moustaches and referring to their clients as Sir. There was no active misogynism in play, indeed the landlord was somewhat mystified that the various girls to whom he'd offered bar work had turned him down. His bar, it seemed, was simply not conducive to a female clientele.

'It's what the young people refer to as the "vibe", dear,' the landlord's wife defined. 'It doesn't have the right *vibe* for the ladies.' Even she preferred to take her occasional gin and tonic at the Kings Head in the parallel street.

'Bitter?' Zac asked.

'And twisted,' Ben quipped. 'Actually, I hate to say it but I'm a bit of a bottled lager man now – those years in the States lured me away from warm beer.'

'You drank pints at the Rag and Thistle when we were there the other week,' Matt commented.

'Country pubs are different,' Ben said, 'and the Rag and Thistle is in a league of its own.'

'Apparently they're providing the beer for Django's party,' Matt said, 'in barrels.'

'We must discuss the music, we only have this weekend to sort it out,' Zac reminded himself out loud of the reason for their meeting.

'I can't do Saturday,' said Ben, 'I have clinics all day.'

'How's work?' Matt asked him.

'Brilliant – but long hours, which pisses Cat off,' said Ben. 'But I'm in my element – I'm pleased we seem to be taking sports medicine seriously in this country at last. It's not so much about treatment – if you get to that stage, you're a little too late. It's about understanding and management – that's why I pressed for the department to be called Sports Medicine, not Sports Injury. If we look after our sportsmen – professional, school, club – we'll see less injury and better results.'

'Interesting,' said Matt. 'God, it's years since I put on a pair of trainers.'

'It's not years,' Zac corrected, 'you and I were playing a bit of tennis last summer – you mean it's since your baby came on the scene.'

'Christ you're right,' Matt chinked glasses with Zac. 'All those things I used to do BC.'

'BC?' said Ben.

'B C,' Matt said. 'Before Cosima.' Then he continued, theatrically *sotto voce*, 'Can you slip me a nice little tonic, doctor? Some va-va-voom?'

'Va-Va-Viagra?' Ben asked.

'Sod off,' Matt laughed, 'not for *me*. Something I can slip into Fen's Ovaltine?'

'Oh dear,' said Ben, 'not enough action?'

'None whatsoever,' rued Matt, 'and I'm so bored of furtive wanks in the shower I can't even be bothered to do that any more.'

'Christ,' muttered Ben and Zac sympathetically, grateful it wasn't them.

'Bad patch?' Zac asked, knowing Pip had said so but not wanting to offend Matt by revealing this.

Matt shrugged. 'I don't know,' he faltered. 'It's probably

113

fine.' He took a sip of his pint. 'Look – it's just I'd rather it didn't get back to Fen,' he said, 'and you know what those sisters are like.'

'Off the record,' Zac assured him while Ben pulled an imaginary zip across his lips.

Matt shrugged. 'To be honest, things aren't as good as they were – dare I say it – BC. I mean, I've read the mags, the books, I went to the ante-natal classes, I cut the cord and I change nappies. I *expect* to be tired beyond belief – I *understand* that tiredness plays havoc with the libido. But actually it's not just about sex. It's more.'

'It's about more sex?' Zac asked and they all laughed before Matt buried his head in his hands in exaggerated woe.

'I love the mother of my child,' Matt said, 'but where the fuck has my girlfriend gone? I feel surplus to requirements, you could say. It isn't in any of the books that when your child has a wonderful mother, you can't have your girlfriend back.'

'She's obsessed with the baby?' Ben said, being careful to turn it into a question though actually he was stating the obvious.

'Yes,' said Matt, 'and nonplussed by me. I must admit, initially I was delighted and relieved by Fen's almost fierce maternal instincts – she's certainly not following in her own mother's footsteps. But now it's frustrating me.'

'It will be temporary,' Ben told him. 'It's hormonal – motherhood is still partly chemical in these months.'

'But we're dangerously close to being in a rut. Don't either of you say "Give her time",' Matt warned them, 'seriously.'

'Have you talked about this?' Ben asked.

Matt looked embarrassed. 'When? How?' he said. 'I arrive home from work and Fen badgers me to have quality time with Cosima. Then we eat in front of the television. She goes to bed early and is out like a light. If I can't use all the tricks

114

of the frigging trade to arouse her for some sleepy shagging, I certainly can't rouse her for a heart-to-heart.'

'You two need time together,' Zac said, 'grown-up time away from home.'

Matt looked deflated. 'I know,' he said, 'but she doesn't trust babysitters.'

'We'll do it,' Zac offered.

'Us too,' said Ben.

'Thanks,' said Matt, 'thanks. The thing is, she doesn't seem interested. She just wants an early night. Every night.'

Ben took a long pull at his bottled beer. He shook his head with a sorry smile. 'I tell you, Matt,' he said, 'it's a cruel irony – but I'm having so much sex I'm rapidly going off it.'

'You total wanker,' Matt laughed, a little bitterly.

'It's no laughing matter,' Ben assured him. 'Cat's constantly analysing calendars and her temperature and demanding sex at scientific moments and weird angles. I'm seriously thinking of providing her with samples and a turkey baster. We've stopped making love, we're "trying for a baby". And I'm the sperm bank.'

Zac laughed. 'Not really Kama Sutra, then, Ben?'

'It's about as far from the Kama bloody Sutra as *A Nun's Story* is from *Debbie Does Dallas*. All this sex – it's not fucking or shagging or making love. It's purely mechanical. But of course she also wants me to gaze at her in a deep and meaningful way because we're baby-making.'

Zac had a contemplative sip of his pint. 'Much as I do love my two sisters-in-law, I thank heavens Pip doesn't want to procreate. I have my son and my wife and life is very very good.'

'You smug git,' Ben laughed.

'Isn't June pregnant?' Matt said with a sly edge to his voice.

'June?' said Ben. 'Remind me?'

'Tom's mother,' Zac said and Ben slapped his forehead and said, Of course. 'Yes,' Zac confirmed, 'she's due this summer.'

Ben and Matt exchanged glances and eyebrow-raises.

'What?' said Zac.

'It won't be long before Pip's going to want to keep up with the June-ses,' Matt said.

'Pip?' Zac was incredulous. 'Pip isn't remotely broody!'

'Have you asked her?'

'We discussed it before we got married,' Zac said.

'Tick-tock tick-tock,' said Ben, with a shrug. 'Biological clock, mate, biological clock.'

'We have Tom,' Zac exclaimed, 'our family is complete.'

'Talking about tick-tock,' said Matt, glancing at the old clock above the bar, 'one for the road? My round. We need to discuss the music for the party.'

'A soundtrack to Django's life?' Ben said.

'It's going to be a memorable night,' Zac said. 'Take tissues. You know how over-emotional the McCabes become en masse.'

'Has Django been all right?' Ben asked. 'His health? The last couple of years?'

'I think so,' said Zac and Matt nodded. 'He always has a comedy moan about gammy hips and old bones and such. Why do you ask?'

'It's probably nothing,' said Ben. 'I'm trained to notice things, I suppose. Age can creep up on a person in quite a sudden way.'

'Pip grills him about how he is on a weekly basis,' Zac said. 'She goes through a checklist which covers everything from the freezer to the hot water to his bones and brain.'

'The trouble is, though Django's such a big character and he appears so robust – he's seventy-five.'

'Or at least he will be next weekend,' said Matt.

'Here's to a great party,' said Zac, 'and to Django McCabe's very good health.'

'Here's to Fen,' Ben said, knocking his beer bottle against Matt's pint glass.

'And to Cat,' said Zac.

'And Pip,' said Matt. They drank.

'Swing Out Sister,' said Ben, 'remember them? Are they in your collection, Zac?'

'Sisters of Mercy,' said Matt.

'Sister Sledge,' said Zac.

'Scissor Sisters,' said Matt.

'As if having two older sisters wasn't enough,' Ben laughed, 'I have two sisters-in-law too.'

Zac thought about what Pip had said that morning and he realized how much he liked Matt and Ben. He chinked his glass against theirs. 'Brothers in Arms,' he said and called it a night.

Freeze a Jolly Good Fellow

The fact that Django McCabe's seventy-fifth birthday party happened at all was a feat of some engineering and community spirit. On the Monday he had to admit that to single-handedly cater for over a hundred people was a tall order for anyone, let alone a man of his advancing years; but to request outside assistance was such an affront to his pride and his culinary standards that temporarily he thought he'd rather cancel than do so. On the Tuesday, the Matlock Marquee Company went out of business and though Django left a message saying he'd buy the bloody tents for cash, no one replied. On the Wednesday, the storms came with such ferocity that only an extreme heatwave could prevent the lawn becoming a quagmire on the night. However, by the Thursday, the sun indeed blazed and by Friday morning, Babs Chorlton had already made the spiced-chicken-and-white-chocolate vol-au-vents to Django's stringent specifications. By lunch-time, Mrs Merifield was baking Bakewell tarts with the quince jam and crystallized ginger that Django provided, and the Blakes car dealership in Chesterfield were installing their marquee on Django's lawn. He didn't mind in the slightest the ubiquitous Vauxhall branding emblazoned all over it – it brought back very colourful memories of playing jazz with Vauxhall Vinnie and the Bebop Boys.

Cat and Ben arrived at tea-time on the Friday; Zac, Pip and Tom were in time for supper – a vast, misshapen pie using all leftover ingredients, from pickles to plums, chillies to cherries. The beds were shifted and shunted, Pip turned her hand to floral arrangements, and Tom painted an old sheet with '!!! go Django !!! go Django!!!'. Cat managed to persuade Django to put the heirloom canteen of cutlery back under his bed and let her buy plastic cutlery, rather than silver polish, at Morrison's tomorrow. Fen, Matt and Cosima arrived in time for the institution of After Eights with *News at Ten*, and the family were sleeping soundly by midnight.

The day of the party dawned fine and the family gathered for a civilized breakfast. 'Speeches,' Django announced as if he was requesting the jam, please.

'Before or after the food?' Zac asked, noticing that the sisters were motionless in shocked silence.

'There will be no *before* or *after*,' Django said, 'the food is to be a constant for the duration of the party.'

'After the savoury and before the sweet, then?' Matt asked.

'I never make such distinctions,' Django said. 'One must respect one's taste buds – if one fancies Bakewell tart *before* Scotch eggs, then there's probably a jolly good reason for it.'

'When would you like the speeches to happen?' Ben asked him.

'Before we're all too blotto,' Django reasoned.

'What time is kick-off?' Tom asked, already anticipating this party to be the highlight of his life so far.

'Seven thirty,' Django told him.

'Cool!' said Tom, looking forward to staying up well past his bedtime.

*

While the menfolk, accompanied by Cosima and a long list of Fen's handwritten notes taped to the buggy, spent the morning chuffing between Matlock and Rowsley on the Peak Rail steam train, the sisters took up position under the apple tree with notebooks and pens and adjectives scattered around them.

'I don't know what to say,' Cat wailed. 'I used to write for a living and I don't know what to say. I feel pretty emotional, I must admit.'

'Me too,' Fen said, 'and I've never written a speech – only dissertations and academic lectures which are easy compared with this.'

'And here's me, able to juggle, do flikflaks and balloon-modelling in front of an audience, but I shudder at the thought of an ode to Django in public,' Pip declared.

'He'd love it in rhyme,' Fen smiled.

'We haven't the time,' rued Cat.

They looked at each other and laughed.

'Barber's shop?'

'A cappella?'

'God, he'd love that!'

'No bloody way.'

When Django and the others arrived back, he requested a run-through of the speeches. 'Just to check your chronology,' he said, 'and to approve the length and breadth of superlatives. You only have a few hours to perfect it, you know.'

'Django,' said Pip, 'if it's a dress rehearsal you're after, you need to follow suit – literally. We'll read our speeches – if you give us a twirl in what you'll be wearing.'

Django looked outraged. 'And spoil the surprise? Philippa!'

Pip gave a triumphant shrug and rolled her piece of paper tightly into a scroll. Cat and Fen copied her.

'I do hope everyone will come,' Django said thoughtfully. 'I'm looking forward to it immensely.'

*

And they came; they came from all over the county, from up and down the country, from further afield too. Jim McKenzie came down from Glasgow in his kilt, and Bibi came from Paris swathed in the shawls and jangling with the bangles the girls remembered so vividly from their childhood. Gregor and Ferdy brought their banjos and strolled amongst the guests like minstrels. Landed gentry rubbed shoulders with rogues; lifelong friends mingled with folk of a more recent acquaintance; musicians and artists vied for eccentricity – it wasn't officially a fancy-dress party but the colourful flamboyance of many guests suggested otherwise. Pip, Fen and Cat were embraced constantly as faces they'd forgotten beamed back into their lives. People ate and ate and their eyes watered; they drank and they drank and their tears rolled, theatricality seamlessly blending with genuine emotion.

Django coasted around; resplendent in voluminous batik trousers from the Caribbean, a floral shirt that was alarmingly diaphanous, a suede waistcoat in colours of fire and a trademark neckerchief in incongruous toile de jouy. He kissed everyone regardless of their sex or age, how well he knew them and whether he'd kissed them already. He sang and he danced, he improvised impressively on Ferdy's banjo and the sound of his laughter became the underlying theme tune to the party. He could not pass Cat, Fen or Pip without hugging them – and if he hadn't seen them for a while, he searched them out.

'Where's your sister?' he asked Pip who was mopping a splodge of mayonnaise from the knee-skimming hem of her black shift dress.

'Which one?'

'The Fenella one,' he said, having already noted Cat jiving with Joe and Jack, still nimble on their feet at seventy-five.

'Checking on Cosima, probably,' said Pip, scanning the

throng and noting Bibi encircling an entranced Tom in one of her shawls like a wizard taking an apprentice.

'Fetch the girl,' Django said. 'I feel a speech coming on.'

Pip made her way through the marquee and over to the house. She called Fen softly from the hallway and made her way upstairs. She trod a careful path along the corridor, knowing which floorboards to avoid. From Django's bedroom, she could hear gentle music. The door was ajar and Pip tapped out a little rhythm on it.

'Shh!' came the response. Pip put her head around the door. 'Oh it's you,' Fen whispered.

'Do you always hiss at Matt?' Pip asked quietly.

Fen put her index finger to her lip. Pip looked over to the travel cot where Cosima was evidently sound asleep. 'Just changing the CD,' Fen whispered. Pip frowned and mimed that the baby was fast asleep. 'In case she wakes up,' Fen mouthed. Pip looked at the CD case of *Elvis for Babies*. To the sound of 'Love Me Tender' being played out on a glockenspiel, Pip raised her eyebrows and made the universal symbol of insanity; corkscrewing her finger against her temple. Fen stuck her tongue out at her, and gazed down at her baby for a long moment before tiptoeing from the room.

'What's wrong with "Baa Baa Black Sheep"?' Pip said as they went downstairs.

'Nothing,' Fen said, 'but a girl is never too young for Elvis. Django will back me on that one.'

'Talking of Django, he sent me to fetch you. It's time for the speeches.'

'God,' Fen groaned. 'Hang on, I'll just double-check the baby monitor. Stay here.' She placed a plastic egg-shaped receiver in Pip's hand. 'I won't be a moment.' She went back upstairs. Pip held the machine to her ear. She could hear heavenly angels la-la-ing to 'Suspicious Minds'. Then she heard Fen's whisper crackle through. 'Pip? Pip? Code word: Tabasco.'

'Tabasco,' Pip declared, as soon as Fen joined her again.

'Good,' said Fen, 'now I can relax.'

'No you can't,' Pip said. 'It's the speeches.'

Django's speech was surprisingly short but effusive with thanks and characteristically emotional. 'But enough from me,' he concluded, 'let's hear all about me instead! I hasten to add I've paid them proudly so I'm confident they'll be extravagant with the compliments. Ladies, gentlemen, troubadours and one important young man of nine years old – I give you my three exquisite girls, Pip, Fen and Cat.'

The sisters weaved their way to the head of the gathering, turned to face the guests and curtsied to much applause.

'As you all know, my sisters and I are famous for having the mother who buggered off with a cowboy from Denver when we were small,' started Pip, clutching her hands in front of her and then behind her and not really knowing what to do with them.

'And a father – Django's brother – who died not long after,' Fen said, nervously tying and retying her pony-tail.

'But far from being poor little orphans, or being remotely rootless or in any way scarred,' said Cat, fiddling furiously with the beads decorating her cardigan, 'our glory is that we had Django.' There followed much applause and whooping from those gathered and the three sisters felt each other relax. The smiles broadened, their confidence and showmanship blossomed and they started to enjoy themselves.

'Most of you know Django as a friend, a musician, an artiste, a culinary superpower,' said Pip. 'For my sisters and me, he's all of these – but he's also our parents. A good father makes you feel safe, he provides for you and protects you.

He teaches you about trust and explains fairness so clearly that you can understand it even if you don't agree. He teaches you to ride your bike without stabilizers, he makes you a sledge by adapting the old garden slide, he takes you out for your first driving lessons and doesn't protest when you crunch his gears or clip his wing-mirror. He gives you pocket money when you're young, bales out your overdraft when you're a student and helps you with your first mortgage when you're trying to afford to be a grown-up. A father instils your sense of right from wrong.' Pip smiled and winked at Cat and Fen. 'You grow up hoping the man you'll spend your life with might possess even half the qualities of your father. We three are true daddy's girls. Thank you, Django, for being Superdad.'

Pip stepped back to whistling and clapping, stamping and banjo-strumming. She saw Zac wink, watched Tom clap his hands high above his head and Django dab tears from his eyes with Ferdy's polka-dot handkerchief.

'Encore!' Django cried. 'Encore!'

'A good mother,' Fen began, 'nourishes you.' She let it hang and raised an eyebrow. Laughter was spontaneous, followed by a tide of applause, just as she'd hoped when she'd practised it silently in the bathroom mirror earlier. 'When it came to love and food, Django ensured we were fed like royalty. A mummy strokes your hair when you've had a nightmare and mops up after you when you're sick. A good mother soothes your heart when some cad or other has broken it. A mother hands down prized recipes – be they for beetroot crumble or fish pie with olivey hollandaise – and has a snack waiting for you when you get home from school. A mother takes in your jeans to drainpipe proportions, lets you borrow Pucci scarves for dressing up, and French-plaits your hair perfectly before you go to school. A mother makes curtains for your Wendy house and clothes for your dolls. A mother brings you hot chocolate when it's that time of the month. You should always feel that a mother loves you more than anything and anyone. A mother must make you believe you are the purpose of their very existence. A mother is a daughter's best friend.' Fen looked at her sisters and giggled involuntarily, shrugging helplessly as tears spiked her eyes and caught in her throat. 'I raise my glass to the best mother in the world.'

Fen grinned at Django who clasped his hands against his heart while coos and ahhs resonated through the marquee.

'Encore!' Django croaked. 'Encore.'

'A friend,' said Cat, as if she was about to recite a poem at school assembly, 'is there whether you need them or not.' She paused and looked imploringly at Fen and Pip, biting her lip. She scanned the crowd for Ben, who gave her an encouraging nod when she found him. She plucked at her cardigan and faltered. 'I can't remember what we wrote.' The crowd laughed soothingly. 'Something about it's our friends who make our world.' She winced. Fen whispered something to her. Cat shook her head adamantly. 'But the thing is, usually you choose your friends – but Django McCabe had no choice when we had no one else. He created our world for us. And what a world. How fucking amazing of him was that!'

'Language, Catriona!' Django called from the throng, cupping his hands over the ears of an obviously delighted Tom.

'Django – you always said we could swear when we really needed to, if a situation truly warranted it. Talking of situations – Christ, you had no choice, Django. You had *no choice*. But look at the life you made for us – our lives are a tribute to your devotion, your friendship, your parenting. And of course your home cooking. You, who are mother, father and friend, to me and my sisters. So you *are* fucking amazing, OK? We couldn't live without you. Does everyone realize that?' Cat looked out amongst the guests. 'Do you? Does everyone realize how great this man is?'

'Never let a McCabe girl near the punch,' Matt whispered to Ben. 'One sip and they're squiffy and hyper-emotional.'

'The sacrifices he made,' Cat continued, 'his generosity, his altruism and selflessness.'

'I've always thought tautology a good thing,' Django nudged Bibi proudly.

'He's always made us feel that we are *his* good fortune,' Cat declared, 'but of course he gave up so much for us.' Thoughts of Maureen and the summer of 1970 sprang to her mind and, momentarily, Cat was unsure whether she'd spoken aloud. 'He's our life-force,' she started to sob.

'Christ,' Ben whispered to Matt, 'never mind journalism, her natural career is Oscar speeches.'

'Django,' Cat declared, 'look around. Look who's here. From far and wide. From over the sea. From over the years. It's because you are so *fucking* amazing.'

Pip patted Cat's shoulder and interrupted. 'Could you all please raise your glasses and toast Django McCabe's seventy-fifth birthday before my sister swears any more and is sent to her bedroom.'

'To Django,' said Fen, tears making a mockery of her mascara. 'Happy, happy birthday.'

The adrenalin from speech-making, combined with the gin, vermouth and some strange green liqueur from Grenada in the punch, had a fast-acting intoxicating effect on the McCabe girls though their reactions differed. Fen became physically demonstrative, offering hugs and hand-holding to whomever was within arm's reach. Pip became affectionately animated. Cat was simply over-emotional.

'I do so love my family,' Cat declared to Pip who was trying to French kiss a bemused Zac much to Tom's jaw-dropped delight. 'Family is everything,' she said, looking desperately fondly at Ben. 'The family you have, the family you create.'

'Family is what matters,' Pip agreed. 'You're so right.'

'Oh God, not the waterworks,' Ben groaned passing Cat a serviette to mop her eyes.

'I can't believe you said "fucking" *three* times in front of *everyone*!' Tom marvelled.

'Fucking fucking fucking fucking,' Cat laughed. 'There, that's another four.'

'Cat!' Zac protested, shooting a glance to Pip for back-up.

'Cool!' Tom laughed, deciding Cat was definitely his favourite step-aunt-or-something.

Cat hugged him. 'I just can't wait to have a little Tom or a little Cosima of my very own,' she told him. 'Family is what matters most in life.'

'I agree,' Tom said earnestly. 'I've got loads.'

'That's what they should teach children in school,' Cat said. 'Are you excited about your new baby?'

'Mega excited,' Tom said. 'I don't even mind if it's a girl.'

Zac laughed. 'That's only because you think your train collection will be safe.'

Tom grinned and shrugged.

Cat and Fen are teaching Tom how to swear in German and French. Matt and Ben have snuck behind the marquee for a secret spliff. Pip's arms are about Zac's neck again. 'Why don't we do it?' she whispers, whilst nuzzling his ear lobe.

Zac regards her with a lascivious grin. 'Sneak away for a quick knee-trembler against the oak tree?'

Pip frowns fleetingly. 'I don't mean that,' she laughs, 'I didn't mean a shag. I meant why don't *we* do it, Zac. You and me. Us. Have a baby?'

What was previously but the hushest of whispers in the furthest recesses of her own mind, is suddenly out in the open. Though she has enunciated the question mark and made it sound like a request, her words are less a suggestion and more a proclamation of intent. And Zac must respond, he must answer, he must acknowledge her invitation. And for Pip, in an instant, it is irrelevant whether Zac's expression is specifically one of shock, one of bemusement, one of aversion or an amalgamation of all three. The significance is the absence of a smile. It's shocking. Zac's smile was what she'd first fallen in love with. It can't have gone.

'You're drunk,' he's saying, 'you're joking.'

'I'm not,' Pip protests. 'Well, maybe I am drunk. But I'm not joking.'

'Don't be daft,' Zac says and he plugs her mouth with an affectionate kiss. 'And stay off the punch, Mrs.' He looks around while Pip stares at his shoes and quashes a sudden desire to scuff their well-tended shine. 'Have you seen Tom?' he asks her. 'There he is. Can you keep an eye on him? I'm going to find Matt and Ben for a crafty puff.'

Pip weaves her way to Tom. She feels winded. She hadn't known she was to make her revelation so of course she couldn't reasonably anticipate his reaction. But the reaction, when it came, flummoxed her more than her revelation itself. She's embarrassed. And a little hurt. It's a sensation she does not like, one that she won't allow to show because she'd hate anyone to pry. She's always been very committed and particular in her role as the eldest; she's taken it to mean that she must appear infallible and in control. How would Cat and Fen cope if she wasn't? They depend on her. It's their family way.

And here they are, her little sisters, their arms around her stepson.

'Where's my dad?' Tom asks.

'I don't know,' Pip says, 'and you should be thinking bedtime.'

'But it's not ten o'clock,' Tom protests.

'It's five to,' says Pip.

'But Dad says I can stay up until ten,' Tom moans.

Pip bites her lip. Fine. Whatever. What does my opinion matter anyway? I'm not your mother. I have no natural authority.

'Pip?' Fen asks. 'Are you OK?'

'What? Fine,' Pip says and she walks away.

'Go after her,' Cat nudges Fen.

'You,' says Fen. 'I need to check on Cosima.'

'Come on, kiddo,' Cat says to Tom whom she's noticed has much the same hairstyle as her – though his here-and-there tufting is beyond his control while hers requires expensive products and much time. 'Let's go and find some crazy chums of Django's to chat to.'

'It's my bedtime,' Tom says gravely.

'Fuck bedtime,' Cat says with a wink and a nudge. 'Let's pretend we can't tell the time.'

'You're wicked,' says Tom, beaming, as Cat puts her hand on his bony little shoulder and guides him into the party.

'Sleeping peacefully?' Matt whispers.

Fen turns from the travel cot and puts her finger to her lips. She nods. Matt comes over. He doesn't glance in the cot. He has eyes only for Fen. She looks so pretty tonight and he's feeling so horny, a bit drunk and stoned too. He comes up to her, tucks a straying lock of hair behind her ears and cups her head in his hands. He winks suggestively. The gesture is partly comic but engaging too. Over her clothes, Matt's hands peruse her breasts while his mouth finds hers. To his surprise and delight, suddenly she's tonguing him greedily, grasping his buttocks and pulling his pelvis against hers. Privately, he salutes the punch and the green stuff from Grenada. He thinks he'll ply Fen with alcohol on a regular basis. She's wearing a soft skirt and all evening he's been noticing how it catches the curves of her bottom, the sides of her thighs. No panty line. No panties? He explores. A thong. God, when was the last time he saw her in a thong? His hands move over her bare buttocks, he slips his fingers under the fabric of the thong and starts tugging it gently, knowing it creates tantalizing friction for her.

Fen's hands are all over him. Sweeping over his torso, grabbing his neck to pull his face even closer to hers, fondling the bulge in his trousers. He fumbles with buttons while Fen drops to her knees and tugs down his boxers. There's no preamble. No inner-thigh massage or ball-licking or shaft-caressing. She takes the entire length of his tumescent cock in her mouth and sucks so ravenously that he has to desperately conjure an image of the mad old woman near work, to stop him coming right then. He pulls Fen up to him, pulls at her top and fiddles with her bra cup to release her breasts. Her nipples are hard between his fingers and his cock is now achingly erect. He'd love to spend time sucking her tits, fingering her sex, maybe go down on her, some reciprocal oral sex, perhaps some mutual masturbation but actually all he wants to do is fuck her, get his cock up inside her in some primal urgency to reclaim her as his own. They fall onto the bed, not bothering about what clothing is on or off, just as long as there's no fabric restricting entry. Fen pulls her G-string to one side, fleetingly Matt brushes through the fuzz of her mound, to confirm the ready ooze from her sex. Her legs are spread, their eyes are locked, their lips are parted and wet. He thrusts into her and they hump vigorously. Usually, Fen likes to go on top. Usually, she wants to go on top, to dictate the pace and the angle to facilitate her orgasm. Usually, she needs penetration interspersed with manual or oral stimulation to climax. Tonight, it is as if she has started to come as soon as Matt is inside her. The longest, most overdue, most body-racking orgasm. She gasps and bucks and scratches and yelps and she's pretty sure she's just come again instantaneously. Yet despite this fantastic vast throbbing wet pleasure zone electrifying her body, her mind tunes into her baby's cry the millisecond before the sound is made.

And then Fen's eyes are wide open and she's shoving and pushing Matt off her. He's a matter of thrusts away from his climax but the strength of a mother is no match for him. She's gone. She's gone away. He lies there, his balls aching with unspent sperm, his cock more flaccid by the second. He thinks it's an amazing but dreadful feat, the way she can flit between sex-greed and maternal obsession. It's really quite some skill. One to revere, but not necessarily like. What he doesn't like at all is a lurking sense that while he was compelled by passion for her just now, she was pursuing only her own physical gratification. I've come – you can go now. Matt feels used, really. As let down and deflated as his ignored, limp cock.

Once Cosima has settled again, Fen offers herself to Matt; caressing his wilted cock, taking it in her mouth. Though she performs a variety of usually fail-safe tricks and techniques, it is not possible to disguise her drive as one of desire rather than duty. She's not even half-hearted; her heart obviously isn't in it.

'Moment has passed,' Matt shrugs, tapping her head.

Fen looks up. His cock snuggles against his pubic hair like a little creature asleep in a nest. He thinks it looks pathetic. He closes his eyes.

'Don't I turn you on any more?' Fen says and he looks down at her pouting up at him.

He knows she's trying to be cute but he wants to tell her,

Actually, sometimes no you don't, especially not when you reject me to faff with the baby. But it's not worth it. It's Django's birthday party. Matt can't possibly instigate a confrontation, or even a heart-to-heart.

'You can owe me one,' he tells her as he rearranges his clothing.

She gives him a quick kiss on the cheek. 'Deal,' she says warmly, led by growing guilt. She's horribly aware that throughout the fuck she was abandoned to the fantasy that Matt was someone else. No one whom she knew. Just someone specifically not Matt. But now is not the time to worry and analyse it. There's a party out in the garden. She double-checks the baby monitor and returns to the mêlée.

Django is telling Tom somewhat fanciful stories about his time with the Beatles. Bibi is nodding earnestly, adding details of her own which she's pretty sure must be true. 'The thing about the sixties,' she confides to Zac, 'is I can't remember a bloody thing about the sixties! I think LSD may well have been a terrific trip – but the downside is I don't honestly know which memories are real and which are purely chemical.'

'Where's Ellisdy, Dad?' Tom asks Zac, wondering if such a trip might be something they could do over the summer holidays. Zac is momentarily thrown. Now does not seem an appropriate time for the 'just say no' lecture.

'Ghastly! Don't go there!' Django rues, which is good enough for Zac and good enough for Tom.

'Gracious me, look at the time – it's nearly midnight and I'll turn into a pumpkin. Or, rather, seventy-five years old officially.'

'I thought it was a birthday party?' Tom says, confused. 'You can only have a *birthday* party if it's on your actual birthday. Otherwise it has to be called a *party*.'

'My seventy-fifth birthday is actually tomorrow,' Django says. He looks at his watch and counts down the seconds with theatrical nods of his head. 'No. I tell a lie. It's now today. I'm now seventy-five years old.'

'So it *is* a birthday party,' says Tom, dreading his father hearing all this talk about what the time is.

'Whatever you'd like to call it, I had an absolute blast,' said Django. 'And now I'm going to bed.'

Derek

Often, a great party is defined less by the event itself, than by the calibre and longevity of subsequent reminiscences. A balmy May Sunday morning in the idyllic setting of the house and grounds at Farleymoor, provided a conducive carte blanche for lounging, lazing and recounting. Of course, this could not be done on an empty stomach, nor with a hangover, so Django had prepared his remedy for both – a vast breakfast of sausages, eggs, bacon, champ and beans, all flooded with Henderson's Relish and roofed over with slabs of toast plastered with marmalade. His family lolled about outside, turning their faces to the sun, chatting. Behind them, the Blakes of Chesterfield marquee seemed to breathe; its sides swelling rhythmically in the gentle breeze, as if still sleeping off the excesses of the night before.

'You said "fucking" *seven* times!' Tom whispered to Cat who winced, covered her eyes and apologized profusely.

'Did anyone video the speeches?' Fen wondered, hovering her hand an inch above Cosima's head so that the baby's downy hair caressed the palm of her hand.

'Video?' Django balked. 'Gracious no, though the Ravellas brought their Super8. Doubt whether it had film in it. They've taken that thing everywhere with them over the years, amassing a footage that runs into – well – *minutes* on account of their forgetfulness.'

'Bibi's dancing deserves to be documented for posterity,' Ben marvelled. 'She's more loose-limbed than Josephine Baker.'

'Actually, she really was a contortionist in her prime. That's how we met. It was some festival or other. She was doing frightfully bendy things whilst saluting the sun, or the moon, or something similarly yogic. However, she ended up making quite a few bob as many people presumed she was busking for tips.'

'What a character,' Pip said warmly. 'I hope she pops in sometime today, to say goodbye again.'

'Look, here are Ferdy and Gregor!' said Cat.

'No banjos,' Tom remarked sadly.

It took some time for the couple to kiss everyone on both cheeks. They then made much of how ghastly their headaches were and that the least Django could do was provide hair-of-the-dog by way of compensation. Zac's constitution was far too delicate just then, to withstand an explanation of the term to Tom, though Matt promised the boy he'd tell him later, when his own headache had subsided.

'Will you be having an eighty-fifth birthday party?' Tom enquired. 'In a decade?'

Django considered the question carefully. 'I can't see why not,' he reasoned, 'as long as I'm still relatively hale and hearty.'

'I'll be nearly *twenty* by then!' Tom said. 'How fucking amazing is that!'

'Tom!' everyone remonstrated, before levelling accusatory glares at Cat.

'Goodness me, I need a cup of tea,' Django declared.

'I'll make it,' offered Pip.

'You stay put, darling,' Django ordered. 'I may be old, but I'm not incapable.'

'Can we just have Darjeeling, please?' Fen requested as diplomatically as she could.

'She means not that weird purpley stuff that smells like stewed grasses,' Cat laughed.

'I didn't bring you up to be dull,' Django protested, though he had to privately agree with the stewed-grass analogy. 'Might you settle for Lapsang?' he asked. They'd have to.

'Do a flikflak, Pip!' Tom implored his stepmother. Pip looked at the lawn: soft, level and inviting. It was where she'd taught herself all manner of tumbling over the years, but she didn't much feel like demonstrations today. She had a hangover and what she wanted was to have a private moment with Zac so she could say *Did you mean what you said last night? Because, actually, I meant what I said.* But Zac had been infuriatingly cheerful all morning, tactile and attentive, thus allowing her no recourse to challenge him.

'Please do a flikflak?' Tom pleaded. 'It makes sense to do flikflaks *before* you have a cup of tea.'

'I wasn't actually considering doing any after,' Pip pointed out. And then she looked at Tom's disappointed little face and flikflaks suddenly seemed a tiny price to pay for his smile. 'I want applause,' Pip stipulated, 'cheering and whistling, if you please.' And off she went, executing a perfect line of four.

'I used to be able to walk on my hands,' said Ben. Rolling his head, giving his wrists and ankles an energetic shake, to gasps of admiration, he found he still could.

'I can cartwheel!' said Cat, scrambling to her feet and doing just that.

And when Penny Ericsson came through the garden gate,

that's the scene that greeted her: a laughing bunch performing amateur acrobatics in the early summer sunshine.

No one knew who she was. Why should they? But the appearance of a stranger didn't surprise them. People had been calling in all morning to thank Django for the party and wish him many happy returns. Some hadn't even been present the night before, but still they came with their birthday greetings. So the group on the lawn didn't bat an eyelid at the woman. She was just another friend of Django's, wasn't she? Someone from his dim and distant past, from some far-flung shore, no doubt. Relatively conservatively dressed for a friend of Django's. Silvering blonde hair cut close. Small tortoiseshell glasses. A tunic top and cropped trousers in the same honey-coloured linen. Sensible sandals. Interesting jewellery. She had stopped some distance away. She raised her hand. Fen raised hers.

'Hi,' the woman called.

'Hullo!' called Cat.

'Hi,' she said, coming nearer, 'hi.'

An American. Django had plenty of friends from the States. Perhaps this was the famous Toni from Squam? Or the infamous Rayner from Sausalito?

'Hi,' she said, once again, slightly breathless, squinting in the sunlight.

'Hullo,' said Fen. And Cat. And Pip. And the men. And Tom.

It is often a peculiar surprise to hear the sound of one's voice on a recording. The sound doesn't make sense. I don't sound anything like that. Sometimes, a mirror presents an image so far from one's perception of oneself that the reflection could well belong to a stranger. But that's not how I feel I look.

However, for Ben, Matt and Zac, a glimpse of the future,

137

of seeing how their partners might look in twenty-five years' time, was immediate. But that wasn't the shock of it. The fundamental shock was that this woman's resemblance to their girls was so striking that there could be but one explanation. And yet the girls obviously hadn't noticed a thing.

But what when they did?

What then?

The three men could do little more than glance at each other and feel their heart rates thud like the countdown to a detonation.

'So,' the lady said, 'where is the birthday boy?'

'He's making tea,' Cat said. 'He'll be out in a mo'.'

'He always makes plenty,' Fen assured her.

'Sorry – were you at the party last night?' asked Pip.

'No,' she said, 'no.' And she fingered the cord of silver around her neck while being smiled at.

Tom wondered whether this new lady might be interested that Cat had said 'fucking' seven times.

'Here he is,' Fen said, before Tom had a chance to find out.

Django was far too busy balancing the tray with all the cups and saucers and teapot and plates piled high with biscuits to notice his guest at first.

'Hi Derek,' the lady said, 'happy birthday.'

Derek?
  Who's Derek?
  I don't think we know a Derek.
  There's no Derek here.

In severe electric shocks, it is impossible to let go. Such shocks are, literally, riveting; they simultaneously root you to the spot while they decimate you. Django didn't drop the tray, he didn't faint or fall to his knees and he didn't wail or gasp. He couldn't. He couldn't make a sound, let alone say a word. He couldn't drop the tray. He couldn't move. He stood there, momentarily paralysed.

'This is *Django*,' Cat was saying to the lady, 'Django *McCabe*.'

'If you're lost, there are loads of Ordnance Survey maps in the house,' said Fen helpfully.

'I think they're in that trunk in the shed, actually,' added Pip.

'Girls,' said Django, and the pureness of his audible pain was not for himself, but for those he loved most on whom he was about to inflict it. 'Girls.' Carefully he put the tray down. He did not know in whose eyes he should look. So he looked at her. 'Girls. This is your mother.'

* * *

Where were you when Princess Diana died? What were you doing when the planes struck the World Trade Center on 9/11? Were you sitting down to Christmas Day leftovers when you learnt about the Asian Tsunami?

On Django's seventy-fifth birthday, Cat, Pip and Fen wouldn't have had a clue where they'd been on those landmark moments. For them, history ceased to be defined by such events. On Django's seventy-fifth birthday, history was retold.

Our mother ran off with a cowboy from Denver when we were small.

And then she came back.

Then What?

Then what? No one could actually say a thing. Time had stopped, the temperature had dropped and Pip, Cat and Fen were paralysed in a state of frozen panic. If the magnitude of the situation was beyond belief, it was certainly beyond words. They had never imagined this occurrence, never craved it, never dreaded it. Therefore, they had never bothered to prepare fanciful speeches in the event of their mother showing up. They'd never even wondered 'What if?' This sudden reality was so far from their expectation that they were utterly ill-equipped to deal with it. They could only sit and stare, with time suspended while their hearts thumped with disbelief. No one wanted to break it. In the silence, they were still safe. If anyone moved or any sound was made, time would have to resume. Nothing would be the same again. This they knew. And yet Cat, Fen and Pip hadn't ever wanted anything to change in the first place.

Penny stood there and deduced which daughter was Cat, though just then she didn't know Pip from Fen. It also occurred to her, with unexpected pleasure, that she appeared to be a grandmother too. The particulars of her gene-pool were immediately legible; her three daughters had paired up and had two offspring between them. The bare facts were pleasing. The girls appeared in good health. Their men looked nice. Everyone seemed happy. It was a soothing scene to behold but one she suddenly wished she was seeing as a fly on the wall. Home seemed very far away.

'Hi,' she said, focusing on the baby, 'and aren't you a cutey?' She stooped to Cosima who was gurgling and bashing her pudgy legs with her little fists. Penny offered the baby a finger. 'Hi, hi, cutey-pie.'

Fen grabbed her baby away before she could grasp her grandmother's finger. She staggered to her feet, the brittle rubber of one flip-flop ripping away from the sole as she did so. Her face glowering with mistrust and animosity. 'What the fuck?' she managed in a hoarse whisper.

Tom gave a delighted gasp. 'Fen said f—'

'Tom!' Zac hissed, now in no quandary over whom to protect. He took Tom away, to the tyre swing at the outer edge of the garden. He could only touch his wife gently between the shoulder-blades as he went.

'You're Fenella?' Penny deduced. 'And look, you have a daughter!'

Fen couldn't respond, she could only hold Cosima protectively. What did all this mean? What was going on? Matt rose and stood oak-like and silent behind his family.

'You're Philippa?' Penny asked Pip.

Pip was unable to give much more than a childlike shrug. Where was Zac? Where should she be? By her sisters? But they had their partners. No one was looking to her for help. They were each in a constrictive space of their own. Pip felt entirely alone. Zac was in another space, protecting his son. She was surrounded by a family in splinters and

141

for the first time she had no idea how to go about putting it all back together again. She felt very cold.

'And I guessed you were Catriona,' Penny gave a small smile. She turned to Django. 'She has your eyes, hey?'

1960s and All That Jazz

If ignorance had been the background to the bliss in the McCabe sisters' lives until that moment, knowledge was its polar opposite and it suffused them with panic and pain. In desperation, they tried to plead ignorance. If they pretended they didn't know what she meant, everything might be all right.

'What are you doing here?' said Pip.

'Who's Derek?' said Fen.

Say something Cat. Quickly. You need to say something naive and pedestrian. Why not tell that woman she simply has the wrong family. But Cat's voice was horribly noticeable for its silence. Her sisters turned to her. She looked back at them, imploringly. 'What does she mean about me having Django's eyes?' said Cat, capable of little more than a whisper. They turned to Django who was staring at Penny. They turned to Penny who was gazing at the three of them.

'I had to come,' Penny told them. 'I know it must be a shock and all. But could we talk? Might you listen?'

The sisters turned to Django but his head hung low and his eyes were fixed on the ground.

'If you're on some mission to appease your guilt, you've

wasted your journey,' said Pip flatly. 'It has nothing to do with *us*.'

'What are you doing here?' Fen said so icily that Cosima wriggled and began to cry. 'What are you implying about Cat? Why do you call our uncle "Derek"?'

'You did not know?' Penny appeared shocked. 'Did you God-honestly not *know*? Your whole lives – and you did not *know*?'

'Know what?' Cat asked, her voice barely audible.

The faintest of whispers coursed through Fen and Pip, but they blocked it out, not ready to listen.

If we did not know any of this, what else might we not know? The thought was trying to sidle.

Cat now had her hands clamped over her ears, her eyes screwed shut. She did not want to hear them and she did not want anyone looking at her eyes.

'I am *sorry*,' Penny said with a hand at her heart for emphasis, 'this must be a terrible shock. Derek – could you not help me out here?'

All eyes turned to the man in the candy-striped cheese-cloth smock, the man with the moccasins on his feet, wearing patched cords with fraying seams and a faded CND patch appliquéd under one knee. Whatever his name was. There had to be an explanation. He was the man who had always made everything all right. Who had made sense of every-thing. He had always told them, when they were hurt, that he was there to make them better. That it was his job to kiss that bruise. That he was the world expert in cuddling away tears. There there. There there. Django is here. Don't cry. Don't worry. Django's here.

Except he isn't.

Some bloke called Derek is standing in his moccasins.

*

144

He suddenly looks very old and tired, thought Pip.

He doesn't look well, thought Fen.

I hate him, thought Cat.

Christ, this is one crackpot family, thought Ben.

Bugger, Cosima needs changing, thought Matt.

'I,' Django said. 'She.' He paused. 'You,' he said, though he focused on no one. Silence fell and Django felt powerless to do anything about it.

She took off her glasses. 'My name is Penny Ericsson,' she told them, 'and I am your mother.' Her voice was gentle and clear, tinged with reflection but underscored with relief; a timbre that told everyone that the truth was being told. 'I was married to Nicholas McCabe when I was a very young girl. I was seventeen and pregnant – not with you, Philippa, with another child. I miscarried. I had you. I had Fenella. I had Catriona. And I left.'

The silence, no less heavy, was calmer.

'Why do you say that Cat has Django's eyes?' Pip asked finally, the reluctant spokesman for the sisters.

'You have Nicholas's chin, Philippa,' Penny said levelly, 'Fenella has Nicholas's eyes.' She stopped. 'And Catriona has Derek's eyes.'

'What are you *saying*?' Fen then turned to Django who finally met her gaze. 'What is she saying?'

Django looked around him. His home. His garden. His girls. His grandchildren. All that he loved. He was soaking up the sights, as if within seconds he'd be denied them for ever. All that he held sacred, all he had hoped to keep safe, was teetering on a precipice that was as much of his own making as of Penny Ericsson's. He wasn't sure if he'd be able to step in as protector or if he was about to push what he held most precious straight over the edge. He stumbled, grabbed the cold edge of the curlicue garden chair and sat down heavily. With a hand on each knee, and rocking gently, he spoke with audibly heart-heavy reluctance. 'My name is Derek McCabe – or at least that's what it says on my birth certificate.' Suddenly, it seemed like a good if desperate idea to fixate on the triviality of this particular revelation, to step outside the bigger picture and the graver question. A glance at his girls suggested they were almost glad of the diversion. 'Look at me, I hardly look like a Derek, do I?' he tried a meek smile. 'Derek was my given name – but Django is my true name. Can we settle on that?'

'*Django*?' Pip enunciated the word as if it sat awkward on her tongue, as if it were no longer a name. 'How the hell did you go from Derek to Django?'

Django looked hurt. 'Jazz,' he declared, as if to prompt, '*jazz*.' Fen and Pip nodded as if they thought they understood. 'When I heard the music of Django Reinhardt, the colour and spirit at my core leapt free,' he explained, 'and in the sixties, to be who you felt was the easiest thing in the world. You think Bibi's parents called her Bibi when she was born in 1939? They called her Doris, but what did they know? Can you imagine Bibi being called Doris, for goodness' sake? One day she said, Hey call me Bibi, so we said, Cool. And one day I said, Hey call me Django, and they said, Cool. Feel the vibe. Tune in. Dig it.'

Too many psychedelic drugs, Ben mused in a quick, private glance to Matt.

Good thing his hero was Django Reinhardt and not Bix Beiderbecke or Thelonious Monk, Matt thought as he raised his eyebrow to Ben.

But for the sisters, Django's eccentricity was suddenly baffling and irritating. Throughout their lives, in spite of his quirks, he'd been utterly reliable and had ensured consistency in their lives. Now they felt conned.

'But are you?' Cat's voice suddenly rang out, far stronger than Pip's, much calmer than Fen's. She locked eyes with Penny. 'Is he?'

'I am,' said Django.

'How long have you known?' Cat asked.

'I've always known,' Django said.

With that, there was now nothing else to misconstrue, nothing to cling to in the faint hope of a mistake. And in the here and now, the hear and now became far too onerous for Cat. Burying her head in Ben's chest was her only option because, just then, he was the closest she felt she had to proper, genuine family.

Penny cleared her throat, to invite all eyes back to her. She looked from Fen to Pip, gazed at the back of Cat's head, at Ben's hand holding it protectively against his chest, his wedding ring glinting in the sunshine. Then Penny glanced at Django. 'He's kinda right,' she said. 'I don't know.' She stopped. Attempted to speak again. Stopped. 'Nowadays there's Prozac,' she said, 'and therapy. But back then, there were magic mushrooms and acid and free love. Only it wasn't free. None of it was free or liberating. The cost was high.'

'But why are you here?' Pip asked.

'You're screwing up our lives a second time around,' Fen cried.

Penny looked crestfallen. She hadn't anticipated this and she certainly had not intended this. Privately, she cursed Grief for having centred her world around herself. 'If I could try to explain?' she asked them and continued before they could deny her. 'Despite the fog of my screwed-up 1960s state, I met the love of my life. The love of my life. The light in my life. A beautiful man called Bob Ericsson.' She looked around her. Their faces wouldn't be blank if they'd known him, she thought. 'He died, you see. He died five months ago. The

147

light in my life went out. And I am here because suddenly I don't want to be hated like Juliette hates her father.' Penny faltered. So much to explain. How could she have suddenly arrived at Fountains ice cream when there was over a quarter of a century's details to divulge? 'Juliette is this young woman I've met,' she said, a little meekly. 'She's about your age, Fen, I would imagine. I don't actually know.'

'Don't you even know how old I am?' Fen cried.

'Oh, I know *exactly* how old you are,' Penny said, her voice so hoarse it had no tone, 'to the day. The minute. I just don't know how old Juliette is, precisely.'

For the sisters, details were now irrelevant. Other people's sob stories were irrelevant. The quandary all three shared was who to feel most betrayed by. The mother who had abandoned them when they were small? Or the man who had lied to them, to a greater or lesser degree, throughout their lives? In their past, at tumultuous points in their lives, there had always been that one place to go to – home, Derbyshire, Django. Now it was the one place they wanted to run from. Their hearts were not here so how could it be home? Their hearts had been fractured into splinters and shards by the arrival of this woman saying she was their mother, and this man called Derek admitting he was Cat's father.

'I want to go,' Fen told Matt.

Pip looked over at the tyre swing. 'Zac?' she called. He looked up. *We're going*, she mouthed with an urgent beckon.

She and Fen looked at Cat, at the back of her head, Ben's chest keeping her face from view, her hands still protecting her ears. 'Us too,' Ben nodded, kissing the top of his wife's head again and again.

Where were you when you found out that Pip and Fen were only your half sisters? That your father was a man

148

called Derek McCabe whom you'd known your whole life but was now a complete stranger?

I was listening to Ben's heartbeat, sixty-two beats per minute. Strong and steady. Take me away from here, Ben. Quickly. Back to Clapham – that's fine. Wherever. As long as I'm with you. Home is where my heart is. And it won't ever be here in Derbyshire. Never again.

* * *

From standing stock still with time suspended, suddenly the emphasis was on movement, on going, on getting away and fast. There was no flouncing, no histrionics, just calm and purposeful organizing.

'Have you had a wee?' Pip asked Tom.

'I'll just change Cosima,' said Matt.

'It's OK, I'll do that,' said Fen. 'You pack the car.'

Finally, the sisters hugged each other and pointedly stayed beyond arm's reach and avoided eye contact when muttering goodbye to the approximate location of Django and their mother.

How can something planned to perfection go so horribly wrong? Though the thought had conflicting relevance in terms of timescale, both Django and Penny pondered as they stood in the garden transfixed by the space made by the girls' leaving.

'Oh dear,' Penny said, 'this I did not plan. How dumb am I?'

'Ditto,' said Django, 'still. Still.' He sighed and glanced at her. 'One can't expect to hoick secrets one's whole life. They're far too cumbersome.' He spoke for them both. She nodded and hung her head. 'Though I'd say I'm more deluded than dumb,' Django said. 'I've spent over thirty years keeping them from hurt. How conceited I must be to have assumed I could maintain this.'

149

He looked at her. Penny at fifty-three. She hadn't really changed. Physically, the years had apparently treated her relatively well but a good complexion could not mask a certain delineating sadness. And it was precisely this that he remembered, from thirty years ago; more than the colour of her eyes, the set of her mouth. Still the same sad, mixed-up girl, currently hiding behind a more weathered façade. 'Why on earth did you come back?'

Penny looked at her sandals, looked at Django's moccasins, made an oddly childish semicircle in the grass with her foot. 'I don't really know right now.'

'Well it can't have been to wish me happy birthday.'

'No,' Penny agreed, 'I'd already booked my flight when I remembered your birthday and realized it was your seventy-fifth.'

'Why come?' Django asked. 'Why now?'

'Because Bob died,' Penny shrugged, hastily blinking away tears and feigning that it was the sunlight bothering her.

'I am sorry for your loss,' Django said, his eyes and his voice softening a little.

'I tend to lose most things, don't I?' Penny remarked. 'But I really did try to take good care of Bob, you know.'

I've just lost the lot, Django thought sadly to himself.

The M1

Junction 27

Guns N' Roses was a very odd choice. Odd, because Ben had no idea that Cat particularly liked their music. Odd because they'd always favoured Moby for motorways. Odd because the thrash and slash of heavy rock should surely be utterly at odds with the fragile, solemn mood. Wouldn't Cat want to listen to something more ambient, something to soothe the scorch on her soul? Obviously not. Sweet child of mine.

At first, Ben thought she was singing silently. From the corner of his eye, he assumed Cat was miming along to Axl, imitating his physiognomic contortions. But a swift glance across at her and he realized she was hyperventilating, tears streaming, her face racked in torment.

'Oh babe,' he said, while thinking to himself that he was driving at eighty miles an hour and wondering if he could pull over to the hard shoulder. He placed his hand on her knee. 'It's OK. It's OK.'

'It's not!' she cried. 'Nothing's OK. And I can't breathe. Help me.'

'In through your nose, out through your mouth, in through

your nose, out through your mouth,' Ben chanted at her, calm but insistent. 'Cat, breathe into that paper bag. Down there – that the bananas came in.'

'It has rubbish in it.'

'Take the banana skin out. Throw it on the floor. Put the bag against your mouth and breathe into it. Come on Cat – in through your nose, out through your mouth, in through your nose, out through your mouth.'

With the music hammering and Cat sucking and blowing into the bag, Ben thought it ludicrously plausible that she should look like some solvent-abusing rock chick.

'I want to stop.'

'Babe, I can't stop on the hard shoulder. There's a services in a couple of miles. In through your nose and out through your mouth.'

'I need to stop,' Cat gasped. 'Stop the car.' Ben swerved the car to the hard shoulder. He flicked on the hazard lights, unclipped his seat-belt and leant across to hold his wife. However awkward and uncomfortable the angle for him, he knew it was nothing compared to the pain she was in. There were hundreds of questions he wanted to ask but of course he refrained. There'd be time for that. Way too much time. Just now, he knew there was not much he could say at all. His job was to hold her and fill her ears with comforting hushing, place the tender kisses on her forehead and keep her freezing cold hands warm within his. He promised her, over and over again, that everything would be all right though he hadn't the faintest idea how to fulfil such a pledge.

'I can't believe it. I don't know what happened. What does it all mean? I don't want anything to change. Life will never be the same again.'

No. Oh fuck no. Not the fucking police. Blue lights flashed up behind Ben's car and an officer walked over. Ben racked his mind for explanations, excuses, lies – anything would do. He wound down his window.

'Everything OK?' the policeman asked, peering in to the interior of the car and politely overlooking the state of Cat's tears-ravaged face for the time being.

'Yes,' said Ben, 'fine.'

'Your car OK, sir?' the officer asked. 'Broken down?'

Ben faltered. It was his wife who had broken down. Wasn't that glaringly obvious?

'Everything all right?' the officer asked again, now looking directly at the sobbing, shivering heap of Cat half in Ben's arms.

Ben didn't know what he ought to say. 'I. It's. She.' He shrugged. 'It's personal.'

Suddenly Cat looked up. 'Someone died,' she told the officer. 'I've only just heard. It's my uncle, who brought me up. He's now dead.'

The officer spoke quietly to Ben. 'You need to move along, sir. It is an offence to stop on the hard shoulder. There's a services a few miles on. Take her there.'

Back on the M1, Cat continued to sob, alternating sucks on the paper bag with great soul-crushed wails while Axl Rose still blared out about bad apples and dead horses.

'It hurts,' she cried. 'Christ the pain, Ben.'

'I know, babe, I know.'

'You don't! You can't possibly! No one does!'

Ben thought about this. It was true. 'I know. You're right. I can only begin to imagine. I'm sorry. But *they* know,' he said, 'your sisters.'

'It's not the same, I'm nothing like them. They're the ones who are sisters. They still have an uncle called Django.'

Ben drove on in contemplative silence, one hand on the wheel, the other on Cat's knee. Perfectly true. The mother's reappearance was to some extent irrelevant. Much more of a shock to discover at the age of thirty-two that your father is in fact alive and that half of each sister didn't actually exist.

'In through your nose, Cat, out through your mouth. Good girl. Good girl.'

'I don't know who I am,' Cat sobbed. 'I'm not who I grew up thinking I was.'

Junction 23a

Matt's eyes scanned a constant triangle: ahead to the motorway, sideways to Fen, to the back to Cosima and then forward to the motorway. The traffic was light and driving conditions were good. The baby was dozing contentedly – her thumb had fallen from her mouth but her sucking reflex continued regardless, her cheeks dimpling and the underside of her chin pulsating rhythmically. Fen's gaze was directed out of the window but it was obvious she wasn't admiring the view. She usually commented on the cooling towers near Nottingham but they'd passed them, solid and peaceful and elephantine, yet she'd said nothing. Nor had she remarked on the radio listening station outside Rugby, as she was wont to do; today the slightly alarming, sci-fi forest of antennae in the lie of the two motorways was spared Fen's customary comparison with a Ridley Scott film set.

Every few miles, Matt had placed his hand on her knee with a supportive stroke or squeeze and asked her if she was OK. Each time, she'd reply that she didn't know. And Matt would ask if she wanted to talk. And she'd shake her head and return her attention to the hard shoulder.

Matt scanned his triangle of interest again. The motorway and Cosima were doing as he wanted, Fen remained beyond reach. He put his hand over hers.

'You OK, Fen? Do you want to talk?'

Don't block it out, Fen. It's not healthy. Don't block me out, Fen. It's not good for us.

'Fen, you OK?'

'Life will never be the same again, Matt.'

That's what worries me, Fen, that's what worries me most.

Junction 16

Aren't grown-ups odd. It's not a question, it's a statement. We'd already been in the car for years and I was trying to ask what name I should call Django Gramps from now on. Dad gave me one of those looks with his eyebrows that told me to zip it. Then Pip suddenly starts talking about dandelions. But the thing is, she finished talking about dandelions ages ago and we are all still sitting in silence. It's boring. Motorways are for singing and 'I-Spy' and playing 'I-love-my-love-with-an-A' all through the alphabet. I'd even secretly practised in case I had 'q' or 'z'. For 'z' I found the name 'Zuleika'. Imagine that! You'd change it wouldn't you, change it to something like Zara or Zoe. Like if you were called Derek it would certainly be a good idea to change it to something like Django.

I couldn't even join in about the dandelion – I was going to ask Pip if it was a metaphor because I thought it probably was because Miss Balcombe was teaching us about metaphors in English last week. But just as I was about to, Dad gave me another 'zip it' look with his eyebrows. I wonder if it is a metaphor or whether it is a simile or something. I'll ask my mum. Anyway, Pip starts going on about how in an instant her family is suddenly scattered and flung far beyond reach. She says she and Fen and Cat were like the seed head of a dandelion, that Django was the stalk around whom they gathered and clung to. And then that woman comes along and blows them away and Pip doesn't know where they'll

155

all fall but that she does know it is now impossible for them to be the same dandelion ever again. Or something like that.

'Dad, I really really need a wee soon.'

'Can you hang on until the next service station – about ten minutes?'

'OK. Dad?'

'Yes?'

'Shall we play I-love-my-love-with-an-A?'

'Er. Not just now.'

'I'm bored.'

'For goodness' sake.'

'It's natural for a kid to be bored in a car – that's why they invented games like I-Spy and I-love-my-love. And now they've invented cars with DVD players in the seats for the kids – so I suggest you get one of those next time.'

'Could you please pipe down, Tom. I'm driving.'

'Tom, I'll play I-love-my-love with you.'

'Well, if you're going to do "u", I'll do "z" – we don't have to do it alphabetically, Pip. We can make it more complex.'

'I meant *you* not "u".'

'Oh. I'll start with "z" anyway. But can I just ask one very quick, small question first?'

'OK.'

'Am I still his grandsonthing-or-other?'

'I'm sure you are.'

'Phew. One other minute question – can I still call him Django Gramps or do I have to change it to Derek? I've been thinking about it and Derek Gramps doesn't sound right – but I was thinking Grandpa Derek sounds all right.'

'Tom, will you please just button it.'

'It's OK, Zac, it's OK. Tom – I don't know. It's very complicated and I can't tell you anything at the moment. I'm sorry.'

'I was just thinking that it would be as strange as having

to call you Philippa all of a sudden. I mean it *is* your name but it's *not* your name. You're Pip. Do you see?'

'Tom – last warning.'

'Zac – it's all right. Tom, listen, I need some grown-up time to come up with some answers for you.'

'Oh. OK. The very very last thing I was just going to ask – is Cat still your sister, though?'

'Tom!'

'It's OK, Zac. Of course she is, Tom. She'll always be my sister.'

London

In previous times of crisis, the siblings had always turned to each other, and of course Django, for support and advice. In the past, there had always been an easily accepted hierarchy of need because crises had never befallen them simultan-eously. They've always had each other to turn to, to consult. They've never had cause to crave attention; they've never had to shout to be heard. Never had to face fears alone or mop tears unaided. Long distance, middle of the night, intrusive, time-consuming, occasionally expensive, sometimes frustrating – but always there, always there. That's what families are for. Families matter. But until now, the McCabes have never confronted family matters. Nor have their crises collided.

They have not been shaken to the core. It's far worse – now their core has gone. Like a split atom: something previously so complete suddenly obliterated; propelling components so far flung that they are surely destined to remain beyond reach. The destruction unfathomable.

No one phones anyone that night. This is not denial but a heart-rending clutch at survival in a world they don't under-stand. The only way to cope with a world you don't understand is to do something completely different. Reinvent yourself anew.

Dovidels

There were some crude similarities with a hangover in that, the next morning, Cat awoke feeling wretched, with details of the previous day swarming over her in bilious waves. Like a hangover, the easiest way to react initially was to pull the duvet over her head and beg for a dreamless sleep to numb the pain and drive the memories away. Unlike a hangover, there was nothing that could combat her fuggy head and untold nausea when she finally awoke at noon. No hair-of-the-dog equivalent to settle the soul from the shock of meeting your long-absent mother and being told that your father is not dead but standing right in front of you. A mammoth fry-up might be a miracle cure for a body depleted by alcohol, but it doesn't work when a mind racing with hideous facts ties a stomach in knots. None of the painkillers in Cat's medicine cabinet would have the slightest effect on the anguish choking her.

She deleted the voicemail messages on her mobile phone from her sisters without listening to them and she left the envelope icons of their text messages unopened. She sensed their contact was one of love and support but just then she felt too raw and bewildered to receive it at all. She phoned

Ben though she had nothing to say and clung to the receiver, eyes closed to direct the sound of his voice straight to her heart.

You're all I have, she said to herself when she hung up, *you're all I really have.* When the phone rang again, she didn't answer it. If it was Ben, she'd only break down. If it was anyone else, she didn't want to speak to them anyway.

There was a loaded pause, followed by an uncertain 'Hullo?' It was Django, famously suspicious of answering machines, leaving a message for Cat nonetheless. 'Hullo? Is that Ben? Oh, it's the whatsit. Is there anyone— Hullo? Hullo. This is Django McCabe. I'm leaving a message for Catriona. This is Django. Just leaving a message to say— Blast these blessed machines. I'd like to leave a message to say I hope your journey was OK yesterday. That was Sunday. And I'm. Thinking.' He phoned again almost immediately afterwards just to say, 'Monday. It's now Monday.' For the first time, Django's trademark flummoxed messages brought no smile to Cat. She deleted the messages immediately and switched the answering machine off.

I'm Cat McCabe. I'm thirty-two years old. I never wanted to meet my mother. I thought I was brought up by my uncle. I thought I had two sisters, that I was one amongst equals, in the same boat, cut from the same cloth, sharing the same blood tie. This is the opposite of finding out you're adopted. There's no one out there for me to find and I can't bear the sight of those staring me in the face.

Roof upon roof upon roof. Obnoxious pigeons the colour of concrete. Where was a mountain when a girl needed one most? Flagstaff. The Flatirons. Bear Peak. Where was the exhilaration of feeling so tiny in the great wide open, the comfort of feeling so alive surrounded by vast natural wilderness? It was time zones away. A whole day on a plane away. In Boulder, there'd still be snow on the peaks but the pastures would be so lush they'd be positively luminescent. Nowhere had Cat seen colours in nature clash so cacophonously and yet so pleasingly as in Colorado. Nature's daytime fireworks. She looked out of the window. Rust-red roof tiles smudged with lichen here, dull grey mass-produced slate tiles there, ugly dormer windows, redundant chimney-pots, bird shit, the spike and clutter of too many aerials. She looked at her watch. Stacey would be awake. And even if she wasn't, she wouldn't mind Cat phoning her.

'Did I wake you?'

'No – I'm just back in from a run. Seven-miler – the killer loop. I wiped the ass off your best time, lady. How *are* you!'

'Miserable,' Cat said. 'Where are you? In your kitchen? By your fridge? Will you look out of the window and tell me what you see? Tell me everything.'

Stacey's description was soothingly detailed and Cat listened with her eyes fixed on the roof network outside.

'I hate it here, Stacey. I want to come back.'

'You serious?' The surprise in Stacey's voice was edged with excitement and it heartened Cat.

'Yes,' said Cat, 'desperately. For good.'

'You OK, hon? Ben OK?'

'He's fine,' Cat said.

'And you?' Stacey repeated, a soft insistence to her voice, a perceptiveness that Cat was so grateful to hear.

'No,' she said, 'I'm not doing so good. Life's gone pear-shaped. In fact, there's no shape at all. It feels like my world has imploded. Can you talk?'

'Sure,' Stacey said. 'What's happened?'

'I want to run away and start afresh,' said Cat.

'What's happened?' Stacey repeated.

'You'll never believe who I met yesterday,' Cat said and out the story tumbled.

*

Ben came home to find Cat curled up on the sofa in his towelling robe looking as though she had flu. He put his hand against her forehead and then stroked her cheek.

'How are you, babe?' he asked. 'Did you have much of a day?'

'I spoke to Stacey,' Cat told him, 'for over an hour. Sorry – I know it's long-distance.'

'Don't be daft,' said Ben. 'It was probably a good thing to do. Have you – Fen? Pip?'

Cat shook her head and scrunched her eyes. 'Can't do that just yet,' she said.

'Did you tell Stacey everything?'

'Of course,' said Cat, 'and that I wanted to go back to Boulder for ever.'

'Would you like that?' Ben asked thinking the timing was lousy but he loved his wife and would move mountains for her, or move back to the mountains with her.

Cat gave a forlorn smile. 'The thing I love most about Stacey is that she's so good at the caring sympathy but she's also brilliant at common sense. She has Fen's and Pip's qualities perfectly combined.'

'What did she say?'

'She said going back now would be running away. She said if I don't face facts head-on, they'll hunt me down and haunt me.'

'And how do you feel?'

'I don't care if I'd be running away,' Cat said thoughtfully, 'but I trust Stacey and I know what she says makes sense.'

Ben put his arms around her. 'Bloody hell, babe, what a total palaver.' Cat snuggled into the crook of his arm. 'For the first time, I actually give thanks for the dullness of my own family,' he told her.

'For the first time in my life, I wish my family weren't

161

who they are. For the first time ever, I curse all those eccentricities and unconventional quirkinesses that I used to feel so proud of.'

'You have me,' Ben said, tufting life into the flatness of her hair, 'and for me, you're just what this doctor ordered.'

Ben could not reach Cat on her mobile phone the next day and it unnerved him. He had considered going in late but there was a departmental meeting he could not miss. She'd assured him she felt fine, that she'd slept well, that she felt much better than she had the previous day. He'd studied her face carefully. Pale but not drawn; her eyes dull but not so desperate now; she'd washed her hair and styled it.

'I'll be fine,' she told him. 'I'm going to fanny around the flat for a bit, do some ironing then go through the jobs in yesterday's *Guardian*.'

'I'll phone you later,' he'd told her, with a glance at his watch and a tender kiss.

And he had been trying to. But her phone was off. Now he wasn't sure what to do. Nip home during his lunch-hour? Not practical, as the afternoon surgery was always a busy one. Phone her sisters? He didn't think she'd thank him for that, at the moment, though he felt they would. He tried both phones again and left messages on each. Over lunch by himself in the canteen, he wondered if Cat had found much demand for sports journalists in the job pages of yesterday's *Guardian*.

Ben tried her phone a final time, five minutes before his afternoon appointments were due to commence. She answered. Thank Christ.

'Hi, just me,' he said, feigning a casual tone.

'Oh. Hi.' She sounded odd.

'You OK, babe? I've been trying all morning.'

'I'm fine. I can't really talk right now.'

Was she whispering? Why was she whispering? Ben shook his phone. 'Hullo? Where are you? Are you all right?'

'I'm fine. I'm at work. I don't know their policy on personal calls.'

'At *work*? What work! Cat?'

'I'll tell you when I see you tonight. I finish at 6.30. I'm fine. See you later.'

At *work*? Cat had a *job*? What sort of job? How could she find one and start there and then? What was she doing? This time last week he would have been delighted for her to have been so proactive and successful in finding a job. Instead, he worried that her haste was indicative of some state of denial. It was only forty-eight hours after meeting her mother and father for the first time.

Ben's secretary was buzzing through the first patient. Ben glanced at the notes. Ah yes, the male ballet dancer with the tendonitis. Later, between patients, Ben sent Cat a text message; hopeful that she'd be able to respond, whatever her employers' take on mobile phones.

job wot job? DrB x

The answer came an hour later.

Dovidels!

There are eighteen branches of Dovidels, up and down the country, comfortingly uniform in their classic bookshop interiors, a brave and stubborn reaction to the cavernous bookstores found in city centres and commercial parks. In design, Dovidels shops are bright and stylish; burgundy-coloured shelves edged in maple, limestone floors, leather armchairs and sofas. For Cat that day, it was the lure of such a chair and the opportunity to flick through a new Lance Armstrong biography in an amenable environment. Over an hour later, she was still there and the friendly manager who'd said hullo to her earlier now remarked in passing that there was a job going.

'You look part of the furniture already,' he added.

'Have I outstayed my welcome?' Cat worried.

'Not at all,' he said.

'Are you serious about a job?' she asked.

'Yes. Do you love books?'

'God yes,' said Cat, 'but I don't have any experience – I was a journalist. A sports journalist.'

'Hey – you wrote words, now sell them. Are you interested?'

'I think I am. Yes. Yes I am.'

'When can you start?'

'Now?'

'There speaks a Dovidels girl. Welcome.'

Kate and Max and Merry Martha

Over the time that Cat had spent analysing the roofscapes, making long-distance phone calls and finding herself a job, Fen and Pip had been trying to find their feet too, seeking a balance of their own amongst the debris of their family trauma. They've left messages for Cat by phone and text and they've been in touch with each other to say, Hullo, how are you feeling, what should we do. But the truth is, they don't know how they're feeling or what they should or can do.

Like Cat, their initial and instinctive priority is to establish firm footing in their individual lives before they can tackle their wider roles as sisters, half sisters, nieces, daughters.

'Fen, well *hullo*! We haven't seen you in ages! Come on in, come on in. Just wait until you see Max – he has four teeth and another two breaking!'

Previously, Fen had found Kate somewhat overpowering, her house a little intimidating and little Max rather annoying. Kate's life was all so fastidious, so impeccably ordered, so terribly grown-up. Kate's life, it seemed, barred tiredness, fretting and mess. The walls and floors, an elegant chorus of ochre and taupe, were miraculously unscuffed and gunk-free. There must be rusks and rice cakes in places other than labelled Tupperware in the meticulously organized cupboards. Mashed into the rug, perhaps? Down the sides of the sofas, surely? Apparently not. Max's hand-crafted wooden toys were so tasteful and so amazingly unchewed. How could Kate's baby never be sticky? How had he managed to sleep through the night since ten weeks old? And have four teeth and another two breaking? How did Kate have a wardrobe free from stains and why did her hair always look so good? How on earth could a baby co-exist so happily with decorative pebbles placed on the side of the modernist fireplace?

Fen had been avoiding these mums-and-tots gatherings at Kate's because invariably she left feeling personally unkempt, grubby even, self-conscious about her surfeit of stained clothing and split ends. She also felt petulantly discomfited with her own home: shelves yet to be painted, cushion covers in need of a clean, gaudy plastic toys with tinny electronic jingles and indeterminate stickiness, beakers with mismatched lids, no ensuite utility room, an ooze of Johnson's baby shampoo treacherous on the bathroom floor. She tried to rationalize how, if Cosima was partial to the woodchips in the playground, what a meal she'd make of decorative pebbles at home. After gatherings at Kate's, Fen would return home convinced her organic food wasn't organic enough, her baby wasn't teething quickly enough and that somehow she as a mother wasn't doing anything quite well enough at all.

Fen didn't much connect with Kate, didn't care for her plasma TV, shared nothing in common with her birth story, was irritated by her success with broccoli and her smugness with Max's centile chart. But more than her hair, Fen envied Kate her composure; her ability to achieve so much with so little visible expenditure. How could Max have four teeth and two breaking yet his mother have no dark circles around her eyes? How was it possible for Kate to prepare such successful dishes utilizing organic vegetables of every colour when there was no evidence of it daubed on her kitchen walls? How did Kate get so much enjoyment out of these banal gatherings when Fen left them feeling inadequate and insecure yet bizarrely envious? How was Kate able to be constantly so gracious? It made Fen feel all the more frazzled and fractious.

However, the day after Fen discovered Derek and met her mother, she made a beeline for Kate's and was the last to leave. Suddenly she found all the tasteful, neutral loveliness utterly soothing. She coveted Kate's walls and rugs and home cinema system, the shiny Lexus jeepy vehicle parked outside. Fen now felt slightly in awe of it all, as if here was a proper and conventional grown-up environment to which to aspire. She found herself far more conversant with the group than she'd ever been, happily imparting her recipe for carrot-and-sweet-potato fritters to a cheerily receptive audience. She made plans with Beth to take their babies to SplashyKins at the local swimming pool the next day and even suggested to the group at large that they all meet at the café in Highgate Woods the day after that. She asked Joanne for her hairdresser's salon, she wrote out Susie's salmon pie recipe, she took down the number of Kate's decorators and made a note to phone Lexus for her nearest dealership.

Fen suddenly didn't mind that Cosima had fewer teeth than her contemporaries, nor was she remotely worried that her baby was happy to sit Buddha-like whilst the others were keenly attempting to crawl. Fen's overwhelming ambition, just then, was not to compete but to blend in, to fit the scene as evenly as Kate's walls ran from soft ochre to antique buff. To dull down elements of her sense of self in return for an environment of safety and belonging seemed no compromise to Fen. It wasn't too dissimilar to her first days at university, when she chattered to anyone even if she sensed little in common, let alone any potential for lasting friendship. Just having company was the key. Thus she joined practically every university club, from Cycling to Cluedo, Wine Soc. to Winnie-the-Pooh Soc. – £1 for a sense of belonging was a small price to pay. It all helped to pass the time in a new world and made it seem not such a hostile place. Over a decade later, Fen found herself a new club out of necessity; Yummy-Mummy Soc. (London North branch), with daily activities to tag along to. Blend, blend until all is refreshingly bland.

Pip McCabe's career was an odd one. There is little true structure to being a clown. Children have birthdays but once a year and being married to a well-off accountant had enabled Pip to cut right back on her weekend work. Tuesdays and Thursdays she worked as Dr Pippity, her clown-doctor alter ego, a vastly different form of clowning for which she was rigorously trained to bring an alternative form of therapy to the children's wards at St Bea's hospital. During school holidays, Pip was rushed off her stripy, clodhopping feet, performing as Merry Martha in Golders Hill Park, on Parliament Hill, at Brent Cross shopping centre and the KidsKorners in theme-pub gardens.

Often on a Monday, she'd visit Fen, or spend hours on the phone nattering with Cat, since her return. However, the day after Pip met her mother, lost half a sister and discovered Django was called Derek, her appointments diary was frustratingly bare. It wasn't as though she had an agent she could phone to ask, 'Any jobs going for today?' But Pip had to get out of the house because thoughts were starting to lurk around her soul, badgering her mind and hurting her heart, and once they took hold, she feared they'd never let go of her. Where better to hide than behind a slather of slap and motley.

So Pip undressed. She pinned back her hair with kirby-grips, laid out pots and palettes, sponges and brushes and slowly masked Pip McCabe from view. She pulled on a pair of lurid tights that she'd customized from two pairs – one leg green and sparkly, the other red and stripy. She put on a polka-dot ra-ra skirt and a lemon-yellow top bedecked with patches of orange material. She rejected the multi-coloured waistcoat because it was an old one of Django's and she did not feel like having him around her today. Finally she plaited her hair into pigtails so tight they stood out at right angles to her head as if she'd suffered a comedy electric shock or was the head of the Pippi Longstocking Appreciation Society. Before she left the house, she took the bucket from under the sink. She drove to Brent Cross shopping centre and spoke to management about loitering with intent to raise money for charity. They gave her the go-ahead, knowing her well.

Four hours later, Barnardo's was £193 richer. She took the loose change to the bank and sent the charity a cheque immediately. The next day she dressed as Dr Pippity and immersed herself into her ward rounds at St Bea's. The following day, Wednesday, she was back at Brent Cross as Merry Martha but raised a disappointing £109.56 for Barnardo's. She drove back to Hampstead, parked the car outside the flat and, still in full clown guise, walked up the High Street with her bucket of change. She queued at the bank before brandishing the bucket at the teller and being invited to take a seat whilst the money was counted.

It was a beautiful afternoon. Tom would be finishing school, just up the road, in an hour or so. But today was not a Dad and Pip day, it was a Mum and Rob day. So Merry Martha swung her bucket and headed off for a stroll on the Heath. She decided to walk to Kite Hill, overlooking Parliament Hill fields, because the Kenwood side was out of bounds on account of it being the space she traditionally shared with her sisters.

Preschool children pointed at her, delighted, and she happily performed impromptu tricks and mimes much to their delight. Finding a bench, Pip sat. She turned her face to the sun and attempted to smile at its warmth, despite the risk of make-up meltdown. A cloud came and her face chilled. She opened her eyes and tried to see. She couldn't see the view. She could stare right into the mess of it all but was unable to deflect her gaze. Tears started to well caustically in her throat, impervious to any attempt to swallow them down. They squeezed themselves out of her eyes, resistant to frantic blinking and the digging of nails into the palms of the hand. Attempting to stem the impending flow only provoked her nose to clog with snot that impaired breathing and crackled audibly. Pip realized she could no longer break it all down into objective physiology. She'd just have to break down. Her throat was aching and her nose was running and her eyes were streaming because she was crying. She swiped at her wet cheeks and itched her nose vigorously against her arm. Then she buried her head in her hands before rubbing and rubbing her tired, hot eyes.

'The clown is crying!' Pip heard a child's delighted whisper.

'It's all part of an act,' Pip heard a parent explain. 'It's called *miming*, darling.'

'Does she have a red nose?' the child continued. 'I can't see – her hand is in the way.'

'We'll have to wait and see,' the parent enthused.

Oh shit, thought Pip, *can't a clown sit in a public space and cry in private?*

Of course not.

And then Pip thought, *Oh shit, when I look up, my slap*

*will be smudged to gruesome effect and will surely frighten
the child.*

Well, you'd better make sure that isn't the case.

Slowly, Pip unfurled her crumpled form and lifted her head.
Her histrionic sigh, her expression of highly theatrical grief,
were so fabulously comic that parent and child were delighted
and the blurred make-up was an irrelevance. Pip stood and
clutched at her heart while contorting her face in the universal
mime language of 'Woe is me'. Then she stooped to the child
and pulled her most beseeching face. She pointed to her nose
and pressed it lightly. The child looked to his parent for guid-
ance.

'I think the clown wants you to press her nose,' the parent
whispered.

Gingerly at first, the child eventually did so. Suddenly,
there was a chorus of great honking from a small horn hidden
in Pip's pocket. Her face broadened into a smile of prodigious proportions and she outstretched her arms in triumph,
performing a jig of merriment on the spot.

'I did it! I did it – I did a happy spell on her nose!' the
child shrieked with delight, clapping and jumping. The parent
put £1.70 into the empty bucket, nodded gratefully at the
clown and led the child away in the direction of the ice-
cream van.

Pip walks home and finds Zac already there. He looks at
her askance.

'Merry Martha again?' he asks, privately thinking she
looks more like Miserable Molly.

'Yup,' says Pip.

'Blimey, £1.70,' Zac says.

'Plus £109.56,' Pip protests.

'Are you OK?' Zac asks her. She looks a fright.

'Fine,' says Pip.

'You look as if you've been – well – crying,' Zac pauses. 'Your slap is all over the place.'

'Oh,' says Pip, thankful she has her mask still on, however blotched and smeared it may be, 'it's all part of today's act.'

'Oh,' says Zac, unconvinced, 'do you want to talk? I want to give Tom a call and I have a little work to do – but I could crack on with it while you're in the shower.'

'I wasn't thinking of having a shower,' Pip mutters and she leaves the flat, silently cursing Zac for making her feel so low down his list.

Zac takes a beer out onto the balcony and dials Matt's mobile.

'Hiya mate,' he says, 'it's Zac.'

'How are you doing?' Matt greets the call.

'Fine, fine. Listen – I don't want to speak out of turn or anything, but I'm wondering how Fen is? You know, since all the drama.'

There's a long, loaded pause. Matt clears his throat. 'She's gone absolutely barking bloody mad, if you ask me. Not that she'll talk to me.'

'Thank God for that,' Zac says. 'What I mean is, Pip too. Bonkers. The only time she's not being a clown is when she's asleep. And I can't get anything out of her.'

'Fen keeps putting rocks and pebbles everywhere,' Matt says.

'Why?'

'I don't know why – but they're everywhere. On the side of the bath. By the fireplace. On the mantelpiece. That's not all – suddenly I'm being asked to pay a fortune for some interior designer to go all Laurence Llewelyn-Bowen on the flat. 'And she keeps baking all this – stuff. I think she's joined the Women's Institute or the Stepford Wives or something.

Have you spoken to Ben at all? Because if our two are like this, can you imagine how it is for Cat?'

'No, I haven't,' says Zac.

'I'll give him a call tomorrow,' says Matt.

'I'll give him a call now,' says Zac. 'Pip's stormed off somewhere. Looking like Smarty Arty on acid.'

Sweet is the Voice of a Sister in the Season of Sorrow

Fen overheard Matt's conversation with Zac and she was pissed off. It wasn't because Matt thought she'd gone mad which annoyed her, just then she was far more riled that he didn't like her pebble motifs. And couldn't he see that her grand designs for their house were much more Kevin McCloud than Laurence Llewelyn-Bowen? What did he know anyway? Pebbles weren't indicative of insanity and nor was Pip choosing to dress as her clown character. It occurred to Fen that no matter how deeply they were loved by their menfolk, she and her sisters were fundamentally misunderstood. She realized then that the only people who could possibly appreciate how she was feeling were those feeling just like her. Suddenly she longed for Pip and Cat and realized the last few days had been all the more lonely for lack of them.

Traditionally, Pip had always been the one to take the mature option and decide what to do, taking all matters onto her own shoulders and then dispensing constructive and logical advice. Cat had always simply cried out loud for assistance, inciting the others to rally round. But Fen had customarily kept herself to herself, until her sisters instinctively came looking and coaxed her out into the open.

Well, hadn't so much changed. She dialled Pip. Zac answered.

'Is Pip there?'

'Fen?'

'Yes?'

'Hi – how are you?'

'Very well, thanks Zac. Is Pip there?'

'She's in the shower.'

'Please could she call me once she's dry.'

She dialled Cat. Ben answered.

'Is Cat there?'

'Fen?'

'Yes?'

'How are you?'

'Well, you know. Anyway, is Cat around?'

'She's not back from work yet.'

'Work? She has a job?'

'Yes. In a bookshop.'

'Oh. Good for her. Will you ask her to call me when she's back?'

'No problem – good to hear you, Fen.'

While Fen waited for either sister to call, she played with the configuration of various pebbles and analysed the Farrow & Ball colour chart through slanted eyes. What gorgeous names: Clunch, Mouse's Back, Dimity, Cornforth White, Porphyry Pink, Sutcliffe Green, Cook's Blue. Names are everything. If Dulux or Crown also did these particular colours, Fen reckoned she'd still buy the Farrow & Ball version, even if they were more expensive, on account of them being so inspiringly named.

'Do you like the sound of Ringwold Ground?' she asked Matt.

'Shouldn't the question be do I like the look of it?' Matt said. Fen thrust the colour card at him. The shade looked like unpainted plaster to him, though he realized that was probably the point and chose therefore to nod and not comment.

'For our bedroom?' Fen furthered. Matt considered this. The bedroom looked fine to him. Though of course he wanted to make her happy, to see her smiling, this was becoming costly in a single-salary household. He was about to allude to this but wisely bit it back. After all, hadn't he actively encouraged her change of career, from art historian to mother? Realistically, her freelance wage would mostly cover just childcare; the amount she'd bring home would be paltry enough not to be worth the separation anxiety. He thought about asking if B & Q did their own version of Sugar Bag Light but was saved by the bell. Pip was returning Fen's phone call.

'Hullo. It's me.'

'Hullo, you,' said Fen. 'I think it's time – don't you?'

'Yes,' said Pip, 'we'll go in our car. I'll pick you up.'

'Thanks.'

From the first-floor window of the flat, Ben watched in disbelief but with great relief Pip and Fen walking up the street. He glanced across to Cat, engrossed in a copy of the *Bookseller*, and could not anticipate how she might react. Did he have a duty to tell her they approached? Or did he owe it to all of them not to interfere? His wife would be better off for the company of her sisters, of that he was sure, no matter how over-emotional the proceedings might be. It had been difficult enough to gauge her reaction when told that Fen had called. And now the doorbell was sounding. He looked over to Cat and she looked up.

'Shall I get it?' he asked and she looked at him with a

slow nod as if it was a pretty daft question as he was nearest and it was gone nine o'clock and who could it be.

Fen and Pip filled the room. Cat's heart heaved with relief. Here was Fen, and Pip too, the promise of their familiar smiles, side by side. And Cat hadn't even needed to cry out loud, she hadn't asked for help, she hadn't said a word. Still they'd come. How lovely to feel so second-guessed, to be known so well, to be loved so fully.

'We thought you probably wouldn't return Fen's call,' Pip explained, walking straight over to her little sister and kissing both cheeks.

'So we came to you,' said Fen, glancing around the flat and thinking it would be really quite nice if it was given a lick of Joa's White. She went to Cat and hugged her close. 'I hear you have a job,' Fen said, 'in a bookshop?' Cat gave a nod. 'Do you get a discount?' Fen asked slyly.

'Signed copies?' asked Pip.

'I think I'll just pop out. To Waitrose,' said Ben, but the girls hardly heard him. Fen was fussing at Cat's tears with a tissue and Pip was fiddling with mugs and the kettle.

'Our blokes think we've gone nuts,' Fen said indignantly once Ben had gone. 'I heard Matt and Zac discussing it.'

Cat still hadn't said a word but it didn't bother her sisters. Her tears, and the way she clung to them, told them enough.

'I mean, Fen and I are entitled to have flipped out,' Pip reasoned, 'but you're allowed to go loop-the-frigging-loop, my dear.'

'I think we'd be far madder if we were untouched by this,' Fen said.

'Anyway, we're not mad, we're not insane, and we're certainly not over-reacting,' Pip decreed. 'It was a huge shock. When you're a child, normal is whatever you know. We've suddenly had everything we've ever known stripped away from us.'

Cat regarded her. While she felt the official age gap between her and Fen had lessened as they'd become older, she still revered Pip as very much the eldest and wisest – her keeper, her protector. How she loved her. How safe she made her feel, safe enough to finally find her voice. 'Do you love me less?'

Pip and Fen could clearly hear the quiet fear beneath the plaintive timbre of Cat's voice and they could see right through her beguilingly mournful expression to the presence of panic. Cat might be dressing her question with a certain theatricality, but the question was no joke. Her sisters let her ask it because they knew she had to. They were well aware that she'd probably tortured herself with the possibility of the notion, since the revelation. Pip folded her arms and raised her eyebrow. Fen put her hands on her hips and looked at Cat. 'Stupid question,' Cat answered shyly, on their behalf.

'Do you need us to answer?' Fen said softly.

'Would you like us to answer?' Pip asked.

Cat shrugged. 'Yes, please. I think I would.'

'You're our baby sister,' Fen said, nudging her gently.

'Nothing can ever change that,' said Pip.

'I've been wanting to be a grown-up so desperately,' Cat croaked. 'All these thoughts of baby-making and house-hunting. But now I feel like a crazy mixed-up kid.' She stopped. The faces of her sisters were close to hers, their eyes large with love and concern. 'I feel I've lost what I had – and what I had I loved.' Cat continued. 'Django is a liar. I've been lied to my whole life.'

'This will not come between us,' Pip said sagely, unfurling her sister's clenched fists, 'between us three. It wouldn't matter to me if I shared no scrap of DNA with you.'

'But suddenly our stupid little family seems so dysfunctional,'

Cat said quietly, 'whereas before, I was proud – I felt it was joyously eccentric.'

'Wonderfully unconventional,' Fen mused sadly.

'I agree,' said Pip. 'It now seems messed up to the extreme. Remember how we'd vilify those prim mothers of some of our schoolmates for assuming that our family was somehow substandard, not real because of it being not proper? Well, now it's hard not to think that they were right. I can't help but feel it's all been a bit of a farce.'

'But what can Django have been thinking?' Fen asked, sitting heavily on a kitchen chair. 'Did he really believe we'd never find out? Part of me would hope that it was irrelevant to him that one of us was biologically his child. I certainly never felt his love for us wasn't utterly equal and uncondi- tional. But actually, it appals me that fatherhood didn't make a difference to him. Sorry Pip – but don't you feel he should've loved Cat more? Or differently? Or something? Sorry Cat – but you're his *daughter*. A parent's love for their offspring should be omnipotent, it should be chemically impossible for it not to be. So is he an amazing man for loving us the same, or is he downright neglectful for that very reason? I can't work it out. I can't.' She laid her head on her folded arms and focused on the grain of the kitchen table.

Pip wanted to argue that a stepmother's love for her stepchild could be just as true. But she was aware that this was not the forum for hypothetical discussion.

'I don't know how to handle any of it,' Cat said with a frantic shake of her head, 'and we haven't even spoken about *her*.' She began to pace the room.

'The odd thing is, I'm not so curious as to why *she's* returned, why *she* showed up on his birthday,' Pip said. 'Perhaps I would be, had the Django stuff not transpired. I just don't know what to do about him.'

Cat looked taken aback – how could Pip not know what

to do? She always knew what to do. Cat stomped around the room again.

'He's called *Derek*,' said Fen, lifting her head from her arms only temporarily. 'It's so *weird*.'

'Why didn't we ever wonder why he has an Italian gypsy name,' Pip said, 'when his family were from Sutton Coldfield?'

Cat stopped pacing and burst into tears. 'All these years I've wept for the father I never knew, now I'm presented with one I'd rather not have.'

'Don't cry,' Pip tried to soothe her.

'We're here,' said Fen, feeling desperately in need of being soothed herself.

'I never want to see my father again,' said Cat. 'I want Django back. I don't know. I really don't. It's what Ben would call a complete and utter headfuck.'

'How very medical that sounds,' Fen remarked.

'The thing is,' said Pip to Cat, with a glance at Fen, 'it's your call, Cat, in the first instance. We can cease all communication, if that makes life easier for you. Or we can roll up our sleeves and dig around the mystery.'

'But I can't make the call,' Cat said slowly. 'I can't. I can't.' She fingered Pip's wedding ring. 'But you can.'

Their gaze alighted on the telephone and Pip sensed her sisters look imploringly at her, of course.

Pip wants to duck out. She wants to protest, 'But what will I say?' but she can't. That wouldn't do at all. Pip has always had the answers for Cat and Fen. She's grown up knowing that even if she doesn't have the answers immediately, she has to find them for the sake of her sisters. But today she doesn't know what to say – and what she'd like to say is that she doesn't know what to do. There's been little opportunity for vulnerability in Pip McCabe's life; the occasions when she's felt fragile have been kept carefully out of sight and out of earshot. She's always liked being the Big Sister, she's found it preferable to be the solver of other people's problems, she's been flattered to be hailed as the Great Looker-Afterer. But just now she curses these roles. Actually, she wants someone's lap for herself to curl up into, to assure her that it'll be OK.

Zac?

But she's been distant with Zac since he rubbished her revelation at the party that she just might like to make a baby. She's hidden behind her slap and motley and let him have Merry Martha or Dr Pippity for company since then. The sad irony is that, traditionally, when issues have been just too heavy for her to shoulder herself, it has been Django to whom she has turned.

'Ah, my precious caryatid,' he would soothe, 'whose burden is too much to bear. Let me help. Offload, pet, offload.'

I can't, Django. You're the burden.

You have to, Pip. See how Fen and Cat are depending on you?

So Pip dials. She'll know what to say, she tells herself, when he answers. Please let him be out. Be out be out be out. Dominoes. Something. Fen and Cat crowd around the receiver. They hear the click as the phone is answered in Farleymoor.

'Hullo?'

But it isn't Django. It isn't Django. The voice is female and American.

Pip hangs up in a fluster. 'She's still there,' she tells them, incredulous. Now she's bemused, very bemused. 'I have to phone again,' she says already dialling though she has no idea what she'll say when the American woman claiming to be their mother answers Django's phone. But the phone is ringing. And now it is being answered.

'Hullo?'

It's Django.

'Hullo?'

Pip glances at Cat and Fen but their wide-eyed gazes seem to mirror back her own question. *What do I say next? What was I going to say in the first place?*

'Is this a trickster?' Django is asking. 'Hullo? This is Farleymoor 64920. If you are going to sell me something, you can bog off.' He hangs up.

'He's hung up on us,' Pip tells Cat and Fen who've heard every word anyway.

'Phone again,' they urge.

Pip dials. No one answers. She dials again.

'Great Gods!' Django barks. 'Who *is* this? I'll have the police track you! This is *trespass*. Now bloody bog right off.'

'It's us. It's me. It's Pip.'

Now no one knows what to say.

'Hullo?'

'Hullo?'

Pip is clutching the receiver tightly, Fen has grabbed her wrist and Cat's face is so close Pip can tell she's had milky coffee before they arrived.

'Pip?'

'Yes. We're all here.'

'I see.'

'What's *she* doing there?'

'She? Oh. Packing. She flies home tomorrow.'

The girls send each other thank-God-for-that but what-the-fuck-is-going-on glances. 'What's she doing there anyway?' hisses Fen. Pip repeats the question down the receiver.

'She needed a holiday,' Django says.

For Christ's bloody sake. 'There are too many secrets,' Pip says, the words oozing acidly from between clenched teeth, 'and true families don't have so many secrets.'

'Nothing is secret,' Django replies steadily. 'You have only to ask.'

'Maybe we shouldn't have to ask,' Pip says, while Fen and Cat nod earnestly.

'That's because you're not sure you want to hear,' Django says.

Pip shrugs. Fen and Cat shrug back. Django can sense them, in a huddle in a muddle, clutching at each other.

'When you're ready,' Django says, 'I am here. You can ask all you like. And I will tell.'

Coupling

Bizarrely, in times of extremis, there is always sex. Actually, it's not all that bizarre at all. It floods the body with feel-good endorphins and releases reassuring opiates in the brain. It feeds the soul and occupies the mind. It infuses the spirit with a sense of well-being, it enhances communication, it builds an appetite, it facilitates sleep. Not tonight, dear, I have a headache, is one of the greatest misnomers. An orgasm can alleviate a headache far more efficiently than paracetamol. Sex is good for mind, body and soul. Sex is both a leveller and a lift; it soothes as it soars. Sex is necessary. It's natural and base and when the fundamentals of life have been challenged, sex takes an instinctive, primal function. If life is under threat, then make more life. Regenerate. That was the point of sex in the first place: the survival of the species. The fact that it also felt so good was life's great added bonus. The fact that it felt so good inspired people to connect on a spiritual dimension in addition to the primary physical level. Sex ceased to have the sole role of procreation. Sex, it transpired, was extremely good for the heart. And so sex evolved into making love, the most sublime form of communication. Words can be so clumsy. Action can be far more productive.

'Are you OK?'

Hold me, Ben, hold me. My head is killing me. Envelop me and keep me safe. Now I am OK. Yes, kiss and kiss and kiss the top of my head. Oh, the smell of you. Heaven scent. I can close my eyes and melt into you. If I raise my face I find your mouth, your lips meet mine with so much more than a kiss: a whisper of tenderness, the taste of love. I hear all that you say, you needn't utter a word. The touch of your tongue causes my hands to move, to search and feel and squeeze and stroke. Now your hands too. Traverse my torso in a caress so fluent, the flow of your touch, the walk of your fingers, the feel of your skin – the softest, warmest substance I know. The smell of you. The taste of you. The strength of your limbs, your manliness alongside my femininity. My breasts the most perfect shape for the precise cup of your hands, my sex soft so that yours can be hard. The yin and the yang. The ebb and the flow. The up and the down. The ins and the outs. The peaks and the troughs. The thrill of the thrust. We fit and flow, we fit and flow. You and me into you into me.

I'm going to come. Oh God I'm going to come. And as I come I go, my soul floats into yours. The synergy of it all, the rhythm of Us.

'How did it go?'

Oh Zac – you waited up, you noodle. You needn't have. You have that conference call first thing. But thank you. It's so good to see you, to be home. I don't really want to talk about it. You talk to me. I'm happy to just listen to the mundanities of your day. Just keep talking facts and figures while I listen to the timbre of your voice. I don't know why

I'm shivering slightly. It's May. But I sense your warmth and you sense my chill and you are doing something about it – now I'm not cold at all.

I love it when you tiptoe your fingers along my arms. I love it when you absent-mindedly finger my nipple. So instinctive for you, so exciting for me. This is a position I like so much – you on your back, me on my side, the lolling of limbs. I rest my outer leg on top of you, I stretch my arm along your torso, have my hand cup your neck, my fingers playing with your ear lobe. And when you talk I touch your lips and I know that before long you'll be unable to resist kissing my fingertips. Then you'll flick your tongue tip over them and then my face will look up and your face will look down and our mouths will be magnetized. Your hands will search out the parts of me that excite you and thrill me. Secret pathways to electrifying pleasure. You found them – I never knew they were there. I find myself rubbing against you. And my hands will seek your beautiful hard cock. Pull me on top of you, then you can sweep your hands up and over my buttocks. You love them, don't you. Makes me love them too, makes me believe they're the most shapely pair on the planet.

I like being on top. There's no psychology to it, it's not a control thing or a domination thing, it doesn't make me feel empowered or emancipated. I just like the angle of you inside me. Instinctively I move, I undulate and rock against you. I hold myself up on my arms because it increases the intensity and it enables you to fondle my breasts, to reach for them with your mouth by raising your head – which serves to increase the intensity of the angle even more. Christ I could come right now. Or I can push you down and still my body so I can build for a more exquisitely potent orgasm alongside yours in a while. Let's do that.

Let's do doggy.

God, you're close. I can sense it in the fluidity of your thrusting, I can hear it in the rasp of your breathing. Wait. Missionary – and quickly! I love it that you sense I'm on the verge of orgasm. I love it that you know my body inside out, that you know to push in and up, your balls nustling against my buttocks, your cock suctioned into perfect position. And your gaze penetrates me one way as your cock penetrates me another and you stare and it's so intense and you let me rock and writhe as you see deep into my soul while I come.

And then you trace a tenderness of kisses all over my face as the throbs of my body subside. And I love you and I fold my arms around your back and I move against you, letting you pick your rhythm. I love feeling you come. I love hearing the abandon and the desire. Come on, Mr.

Oh. You're spurting on my stomach.

God, are you that risk averse, Zac?

I'm stuck for words and I feel like crying.

'Do you want to talk?'

I thought you were asleep, Matt. Did I wake you? I tried to be quiet. I tiptoed in to see Cosima and tripped over her plastic turtle but she didn't stir. I'm exhausted. I have a headache. But I can't possibly sleep. There's so much in my mind, running rings around me, too much to fathom. From the dishwasher to Django, from Cat to Cosima; from stupid meanderings to portentous thoughts. If I bury my face in your chest, can I pretend that everything is OK? Because the sound of your heartbeat can block out all the other stuff. I think sometimes – recently – I don't listen carefully enough to your heart. Are you tired, Matt? Because quite to my surprise, I feel rampant and horny. So actually, Matt, no I don't want to talk, I just want to fuck. If I imagine myself a porn star, can I forget that Fen is just a frazzled mum with a pile of washing she's forgotten to hang out and a heap of shit on her shoulders?

On the Phone

Fen was standing in the middle of her sitting-room, looking from a pile of laundry yet to be ironed, to a heap of toys, to a mound of papers and magazines that she'd half sorted into recycling or keeping sub-piles the day before yesterday. She looked at her watch. 10.30 a.m. Was it really worth tidying the toys at this end of the day? No. Was there any real chance she'd do any ironing during daylight hours? No. Was there any point saving papers to be recycled when the bin-men were due to come tomorrow and she'd already missed the recycling service for this week? No.

'Don't eat the pebble, Cosima – Mummy give you a rice cake instead.'

Fen looked from rice cake to pebble and thought there probably wasn't much in it, taste-wise. The phone was ringing.

'Hi Fen. It's me – Kate. How are things? How's little Cosima?'

Fen imagined Kate in her tidy house, her perfect shades of unstained neutral, her toothsome ten-month-old baby happily doing algebra. 'Oh, great,' Fen breezed, 'and you? And Max?'

'We're wonderful. Listen, I was wondering – do you fancy coming to the Chelsea Flower Show tomorrow?'

She may as well have said Australia. Or the moon. A lovely idea but somewhat implausible. 'I'd love to,' said Fen, 'but how baby-friendly is it?'

Kate laughed. 'It isn't. That's the point. Can you get babysitting? We can make a girls' afternoon of it.'

Fen thought for a moment. She and Matt didn't have much of a garden, let alone the time or inclination to work the little they did have. But there again, she didn't have much of a social life either so, though her interest in horticulture and her friendship with Kate were both limited, the notion of an away-day from toys, recycling issues and laundry taunts was certainly attractive. Fen was surprised to find that the thought of being apart from Cosima for more than an hour didn't seem so unthinkable. She'd phone Pip; wasn't her sister always offering to babysit after all?

'Fen?' Kate prompted.

'I'd love to,' Fen said. 'I'll phone my sister and let you know this afternoon. We're meeting at Anna's at three, aren't we?'

'Yes. But actually, can you text me as soon as you know? Because if you can't make it, I'd like to offer the ticket to Ruth.'

'Oh. OK. Of course.' It did then occur to Fen that she herself may not have been Kate's first choice. But she didn't dwell on it. She fancied the invitation at any cost, even if she'd been Kate's last resort. Anyway, she couldn't be – because apparently Ruth was lower down the rungs than she. It made Fen feel rather smug.

'Hullo Pip?'

'Hullo Fen. How's you? I spoke to Cat on her way to work. She sounded a little brighter.'

'Good, that's good.' Fen paused. 'Pip – any chance you could have Cosima tomorrow afternoon? It's just that one

190

of the mums in my group has tickets for the Chelsea Flower Show. And she's invited *me*.'

'Chelsea? Are you now doing a Charlie Dimmock outside, in addition to Sarah Beeny-fying inside?'

Fen laughed. 'It just sounded different and fun. And aren't you always telling me I don't get out much?'

Pip looked at her Filofax. 'No problem,' she told Fen. 'We have Tom tomorrow but Cosi can do the school run with me. Can you drop her off?'

'Of course,' said Fen, loving Pip's intimacy with her niece but hating the way she abridged her daughter's name. 'Thanks, Pip. There's a bunch of daffs in it for you.'

'Daffs,' Pip said, 'are out of season. You'd better gen up before you go or they'll make compost out of you.'

'Dovidels, can I help you!'

Cat had been manning the phone all morning. It was her shift on the information desk at the back of the shop. She was loving her job: the books, the customers, her colleagues. It was more than a distraction, it was a revelation. And she found that to immerse herself in this new world, this lovely space, afforded her hours and hours where she didn't have the time to think about anything else. No one asked her about herself, they just asked her about books. The information desk put her in good view of the entrance and each time a customer came in she'd fling over a smile, hoping to lure them over, promoting herself as a preferable alternative to shelf-browsing. She unpacked the special orders with enthusiasm, lovingly handling the books and taking much pleasure in announcing their arrival to the customers, as if the books were one-offs, written to order. *Mrs Cohen, I'm pleased to tell you that your Laurie Graham is here. Mr O'Connor, good news – your Tom Holt has arrived.* And when they came in to collect their copies, she'd hand them over in a most midwifely way. Enjoy, she'd tell them, as she embraced the cover, enjoy.

Jeremy, the manager, was charmed by Cat. He'd never had a writer who wanted to be a bookseller; it was far more usual to be the other way around. He loitered as the phone rang again.

'Dovidels! Can I help you!' Cat answered.

The great thing about Cat, thought Jeremy, was that there was never any question mark. Just enthusiasm and energy. She might as well be saying *Dovidels! I can help you!* and he was in no doubt that, subliminally, this was the way most of their customers heard it. He'd never caught her picking her nails or gazing into the middle distance or clock-watching. During quiet periods, she busied about tidying shelves, checking orders and asking him the secrets of successful bookselling. She was in early, back promptly from her breaks and often stayed late.

'One moment please,' she was saying to a caller, 'the computer says we have two copies – but let me do a shelf check.' She scurried away, soon racing back, triumphant. 'Sorry to keep you on hold but yes! We do! I have a copy right here. I'll put it on one side for you. Pardon? It's my pleasure! No, thank *you*.'

'Cat,' Jeremy said, 'head office are coming in this afternoon – I'm going to recommend you for assistant manager.'

Cat blushed and gawped but the phone was ringing and it was her duty to answer it.

'Dovidels! Can I help you!'

'You might as well be trilling *hi-de-hi*,' Ben's voice told her. 'I'm just between patients – thought I'd give you a bell. Your mobile is off, as per usual.'

'I can't talk now, Ben,' Cat scolded him. 'We're very busy. The phone hasn't stopped ringing and head office are coming in this afternoon.'

'I just wanted to ask—'

'I'll call you later, Ben,' Cat said sternly, hanging up with an irritated sigh she ensured Jeremy could hear, lest he felt she condoned or, worse, encouraged personal calls.

'Dovidels! Can I help you!'

When Ben's mobile phone rang a minute or two later, he assumed it was Cat returning his call from the sanctuary of a storeroom or somewhere.

'Babe, I'm just about to see a patient,' he said. 'I'll call you at lunch-time.'

'Actually it's not Babe,' said the voice, 'it's Django. McCabe.'

For a suspended moment, Ben found himself wondering why Django had emphasized 'McCabe'. He really did know just the one Django. And it would only make sense to stress McCabe if the man was now going to refer to himself as Derek. Which, obviously, he wasn't. Ben's receptionist was buzzing through the arrival of a patient.

'Django – good to hear from you,' Ben said, 'but I'm just about to see a patient – can I call you afterwards?'

When it came to returning the call, Ben wondered whether to phone Cat first. But no doubt she'd give him short shrift for not being a bona fide Dovidels caller. He dialled Derbyshire. The phone rang unanswered. Ben dialled again, intrigued but slightly uncomfortable. Regardless of his affection for the old man, his allegiance was to Cat and she might well disapprove of this exchange. He'd just see what Django wanted. No harm in that. Keep the call short. He could always press the buzzer himself and invent a patient if the call was lengthy or the subject contentious.

'Django? Hullo – it's Ben. Sorry about before.'

'Hullo Ben, thank you for calling back. I'm no good with these telephone things. I always seem to use them at an inconvenient time. That's why I don't trust the blighters.'

Ben smiled at Django's characteristically convoluted theory. 'Don't worry. It was just a slightly neurotic dancer anyway. Now, what's up?'

'I,' the line went very quiet. 'Well.' Django cleared his throat. 'Are you still there?'

'I'm still here,' said Ben continuing to hope that whatever it was that irked Django wasn't going to take too long to reveal, and would not compromise his loyalty to his wife.

'Well, I'm telephoning you at work because I appreciate it isn't appropriate to telephone you at your home,' Django said, 'on account of Cat's needs. I fear my tones would not be dulcet but despicable to her ears – you needn't comment. But actually, the main reason I'm telephoning you at work, is because this call is in fact a work call.'

'I see,' said Ben, who didn't, and whose stomach was telling him it was past lunch-time. 'Django?'

'Yes?'

'A work call, you say? Hullo?'

'It's my waterworks,' Django said, his anxiety transmitting straight through the receiver. 'And. Well. It's just.'

'Django,' Ben said, with bedside manner expertly employed in an instant, 'has there been a change in the situation?'

'Oh, just a very minor one,' said Django.

'And that would be?'

'Well, just a little bit of, you know, something a little like blood.'

'There is blood in your urine?'

'Possibly.'

'Discomfort?'

'No. Not really. Though I'm rather irked by having to spend so many bloody pennies. Especially at night.'

'When did you first see the blood?'

'A couple of visits ago.'

'And since? Is it still present?'

194

'A little. I suppose. But you know I am partial to beet-root – and that certainly discolours one's water. Almost gave me a heart attack, when *that* first happened. Far more alarming than the effect of asparagus.'

'Have you eaten beetroot, Django? In the last thirty-six hours?' Ben asked.

'No. No. But I am fond of it and have eaten a lot of it in my time.'

'Django, did you see your GP about your waterworks? After we had our chat?'

'Well. I did go to my GP. But it's all changed. Dr Sutton isn't there any more. In his place, just some lovely young doctor but she really is too young to be dealing with me, you know.'

'Django, I really do want you to go and see a doctor. It's probably nothing. But at your age, we need to check your prostate. It's very easy to do.'

'Is it? I see. But I don't think this very young lady doctor should be bothered by me because as you say it's probably nothing.'

'Is there another doctor at the practice you might prefer to see?'

'I don't know. It's all changed so much. In Dr Sutton's day, you knew them and they knew you. Now they don't even tick you off – you have to tap in your name on a computer screen yourself. You know how I hate newfangled technology.'

'Will you phone them?' Ben pressed. 'Request a male doctor, if you prefer?'

'I could do that, I suppose.'

'You do that, Django, you do that. It's a very simple thing to test PSA. It's just a quick blood test to measure levels of a particular antigen associated with prostate conditions. Plus, an examination.'

'An examination?' Django said vaguely. 'I don't know very much about my prostate, I'm afraid. Or prostates in general.'

'No, Django,' said Ben, 'not that sort of exam.'

'No. I didn't think so.'

'It's just a very quick digital exam.'

'Oh a *digital* exam. Well. Isn't that marvellous. All this technology. Computers to sign you in and computers to diagnose your prostate. Marvellous. They say we're living in the digital age, don't they!'

'Django, I'm sorry – I've misled you. Digital – as in finger.' Ben closed his eyes and pinched the bridge of his nose. 'It's the best way to check your prostate gland.'

'Oh. Oh dear. A *finger*.' There was a horrified pause. 'The doctor's?'

'The doctor's,' Ben confirmed. 'The doctor will need to insert a finger into your back passage to assess your prostate gland.'

'Oh.'

'Django, I know it sounds ghastly but it's fast, gentle and diagnostically efficient alongside the blood test. I really do want you to see a GP. Prostate conditions are common but some can be quite nasty if they're left too long. I think we'd like to rule out anything more untoward.'

'You know, I'm just thinking here – but actually, I *may* have had beetroot.'

'Django – would you like me to phone your practice? Make you an appointment?'

'No thank you.'

'But you will phone them directly?'

'Well, yes I will. If that's what you say, doctor.'

'It is. I'm sure it's probably nothing – it might just be a minor kidney infection. But combined with your increased bladder activity, I would really like you to have a prostate check-up.'

'Yes, I see.'

'So will you phone me when you have an appointment?'

'Well, OK then.'

'OK then. Good. And if there's anything that worries you or you don't understand in the consultation, will you please call me? Take notes – doctors don't mind.'

'Righty-ho.'

'OK. OK. Good. I'm glad we're agreed. But don't you worry – as I say, it's easy to diagnose and sort out.'

'OK, Dr York. Thank you.'

'I'm glad you phoned me, Django.'

'Yes.' There was a pause. 'Ben?'

'Yes?'

'And how is Cat?'

'How is Cat,' Ben had to think fast how to answer. 'She's up and down, Django. But she's working at a bookshop and she's enjoying that.'

'A bookshop you say?'

'Yes, she's really taken to it. Very busy and enthusiastic.'

'Good for her. Good for her. Is she also – well – OK?'

'She'll be OK, Django,' Ben said carefully. 'She's still very confused. We'll just bide with her, I think. You know how emotional she can be.'

'Yes. Yes I do. And the others? Might you know?'

'They're OK too, as far as I'm aware.'

'Good. Good.'

'It's all been a little – odd.'

'More than a little odd, dear Ben. On paper, it's down-right preposterous.'

'Well, you know those McCabe girls – they need to vent their emotions before they can settle down and consider hard facts.'

'Yes. But the facts are very hard, Ben, for them. Very hard.'

'I know. But rest assured we're looking after them. Zac and Matt and me.'

'Bless you all,' said Django, 'bless you all.'

'Django – will you call your surgery now?'

'I will.'

'And we'll speak later today?'

'We shall. Goodbye.'

Ben sat and stared at his mobile phone. Ought he to phone Cat? But would it alarm her? Perhaps he should phone Pip and ask her the best tack to take. But Pip would no doubt be struggling with her own reactions. He wondered what would alarm Cat most – that he was phoning her, again, at work? That he'd had the call from Django? Or that there was some concern for the man's health? Ben decided it might be prudent to wait until Cat had left work and he'd next spoken to Django.

Cosima and her pals were alternately gnawing on wooden spoons and bashing them, or their fat little hands, against a variety of Tupperware containers provided by Anna.

'We could call them the Rhythm Method,' Fen remarked, clicking her fingers as if the babies were jamming a catchy beat.

'Hardly,' Kate commented. 'It's a contradiction in terms. If us lot had kept up the tempo of our Rhythm Method, this little lot wouldn't be sucking our kitchen utensils.'

Momentarily, Fen thought this was slightly harsh. But then she told herself it was just Kate's manner. She was to let nothing detract from her excitement for tomorrow afternoon's excursion.

'We heard from Highgate School,' Ruth was saying. 'Josh is in in in!'

'Good for Josh, it'll suit him. We turned down Highgate, because Jacob's more of a UCS boy, we feel,' said Anna.

'Fen, have you put Cosima down for Channing?'

'Um. No. No,' Fen said.

'God – you must.'

'Oh?' Fen felt all the other women nodding at her.

'Where *have* you put her name down?'

'Well. Nowhere, actually. As yet.'

'You are *joking*! You must have her down for nursery places, surely. The Avenue? Rosemount?'

'I haven't – as yet. I might not send her to a nursery,' Fen said quietly.

They stared at her.

'You're mad!'

'Or a liberal. Don't tell us you're a home-education type?'

'Fen – *honestly*, you must start calling around. You owe it to Cosima!'

Fen looked down at her spoon-sucking daughter. 'I suppose – but she's only—'

'No she's not – she's *old*! Believe me! I was phoning schools as soon as the pregnancy-test dipstick went blue.'

'I've spent over two grand on deposits at various schools – but it's money well spent, I reckon.'

'Fen you really should – whose phone is that? Mobile alert! *Mission Impossible* ring tone!'

'It's mine,' said Fen, wondering if 'saved by the bell' had ever rung truer, 'it's mine.' It was a mobile number she didn't recognize. 'Hullo?' she answered.

'Hi,' it was a man's voice, 'is that Fen?'

'Yes?'

'Hi – it's Al.'

Who is Al? I don't know an Al.

Yes you do.

'Al – with the flowers. On Bishops Avenue.'

'Hi! Hi! Of course! Sorry – it's a bit noisy. Hold on.' Fen moved out of Anna's sitting-room and into the hallway, turning her back on a particularly vile arrangement of orange amaryllis, red gladioli and yellow something-or-others. 'Hullo? Al? Are you still there?'

'I am. How are you?'

Oh you know, my mother popped in to see me after thirty years, I found out my uncle fathered my sister, I've been told my daughter stands to be denied a decent education and my partner and I live parallel lives under the same roof which I'm madly redecorating in my misplaced desire to fit in with a group of people I have little in common with.

'I'm fine,' said Fen. 'How are you?'

'Cool. I'm cool. I've been meaning to call,' he said, 'say hi.'

'Hi.'

'Hi.'

Fen could see Cosima. She loved watching her baby, unseen. Who cared about waiting lists and sodding private schools.

'I was just wondering if you fancied a quick drink. Sometime,' Al said.

'A quick drink?' Fen was about to add 'What for?' but she stopped herself.

'Yeah – you know. If you were free.'

Free? Free from whom? Free for what? If there's no such thing as a free lunch, does the same apply to a quick drink?

'Oh,' Fen said, delighted, flustered, 'well – I think so.'

'Babysitting permitting, I guess.'

Now that's good. His invitation is above board. He's just being friendly, isn't he. And I'll accept because there's no harm in a quick drink. It'll be nice. I'd like to go out for a quick drink. I don't get out much – as I like to say.

'OK – thanks Al. That sounds great.'

'Cool! When are you free?'

'Actually,' said Fen, glancing through the glass door at Kate, in all her sumptuous beige and stain-free white, preening her lustrous hair, 'I'm free tomorrow, Al. I have babysitting – I'm going to the Chelsea Flower Show. We could meet afterwards, for a quick drink.'

'OK, you have my mobile number now. Let's touch base sometime tomorrow and take it from there. Hook up when you're done with the flowers.'

Fen was helpless not to giggle a little. The last time anyone had spoken to her about touching bases was her second boyfriend who sent her a postcard of the Venus de Milo and a stick of Bazooka bubble gum with the priceless message: 'Show us your bazookas! Second base? How about it!'

But it's not what Al meant of course. Gracious no. Just touching base to hook up for a quick drink with a sweet boy I met laying flowers for his late sister.

'OK,' said Fen, 'I'll call you tomorrow.'

She felt flushed. It was suddenly all rather thrilling to have a proper little secret. A tiny harmless one, but fun all the same.

'Everything OK?' Kate asked her.

'Fine!' Fen exclaimed. 'Just an old pal. Might meet up for a quick drink after the flower show tomorrow.' Kate glowered at her and in an instant Fen sensed the other mums look up, offended, but swiftly pretending not to have heard. Fen scooped up her baby and cuddled her whilst babbling sweet nothings.

'Come on, gorgeous girl,' she whispered, 'let's head home.'

Ben hadn't heard back from Django and he was about to leave work. Cat was working late as the honchos from head office were in the shop and there was an after-hours team-bonding or book-binding or something. Ben felt irritated. With all aspects of the situation. He loved the responsibilities of his job, but not when they compromised his family life. Had Django even made the call to his GPs? Ben doubted it. This irritated him. And at what point would he be telling Cat of the call? This irked him. And the cause? This worried him. And how could the cause be any clearer if the old man won't visit his GP? But what could Ben do about any of it at this precise moment? If he called Derbyshire, would Django even answer? Six o'clock. He'd probably be cooking. Ben didn't want to make the call from home. Or from his mobile. It felt slightly disloyal to Cat to do so. But he wanted to go home; it had been a long day. It was that time of day when he sensed the smell of the hospital seep through to the fibres of his clothes.

Cat's phone was switched off. Dovidels' phone rang through to a chirpy message with opening times and website details. The phone at Farelymoor rang and rang. Ben persevered.

'Hullo – this is Farleymoor 64920.'

'Hullo Django, it's Ben.'

'Ben! And how are you?'

'I'm fine. And how are you?'

'I feel much much better, thank you.'

'Did you phone your surgery? Django?'

'I said – I feel much much better.'

'Right,' said Ben, rubbing his temples, pinching the bridge of his nose. You daft old man. 'Right. Oh, Django – can I call you back in two minutes? There's someone to see me.' There wasn't. But there was someone Ben wanted to see.

A few minutes later, the phone rang again at Farleymoor. That will be young Ben, thought Django. And though he really would rather not answer it, it was impossible not to. Ben knew he was there. And Django knew the wretched phone would just ring and ring until he picked up.

'Farleymoor 64920?'

'Hullo Django – sorry about that. It's Ben.'

'Hullo Ben. I'm cooking a stew. Pots of it. *Sans* beetroot.'

'Good, good. That's very good. Look, Django – I know how awkward all of this is for you. And I don't know your GP but I respect that you do. But I do know an excellent chappy down here. And he was just passing by my rooms while we were on the phone before. And I nabbed him and he'd be delighted to see you. He's a *he*,' said Ben. 'He's in his late fifties, I'd say. And he sees chaps like you all the time. He's a dab hand, a first-class doctor.'

'I see.'

'He really is,' said Ben, 'he's a specialist. A very nice man. I like him. You would, too.'

'I would?'

'Yes,' Ben said, 'you would. He's what you'd class a "proper" doctor. You'd feel comfortable with him. Confident too.'

'I would?'

'Will you come, Django?' Ben asked very gently, the tone of his voice full of the same soothing care and concern he'd invested the carefully chosen word 'chappy' with.

'To London?'

'To see my Mr Pisani,' said Ben. 'A quick consultation.'

'Is he foreign?'

'He's Scottish,' said Ben, 'he's excellent.'

'I see. But he's only a "Mr" not a "Dr"?'

'He's a consultant. Mr is far superior to Dr.'

'I see.'

'A day-trip,' Ben said, 'that's all. The trains are marvellous. Frequent and fast.'

'I haven't been to London in years,' Django said. 'The girls have always come to me.'

'I think you should come. I'm happy to accompany you to the consultation,' said Ben, 'or not. As you wish.'

'You won't tell anyone, will you?' said Django after a while.

'You have come to me in my capacity as a doctor,' Ben said evenly. 'I am bound by the Hippocratic oath.'

'Perhaps I will come,' said Django.

'I think so,' said Ben.

'All right,' said Django.

'I will make an appointment and telephone you tomorrow. I'll telephone you at this time. Then you'll know it's me.'

'Yes. OK, Ben.'

'Good. That's settled.'

'And Ben?'

'Yes?'

'Well – thank you.'

'Don't mention it, Django,' he said, 'it's nothing.' And Ben sincerely hoped that it was.

Seeds Sown

It wasn't so much a case of Fen not being able to see the wood for the trees, more that she couldn't see the flowers for the florid meanderings of her overactive imagination. It was a waste of a ticket, really. From the moment she arrived, Fen was planning her escape. She walked around the Chelsea Flower Show, her head nodding like a fritillary, while she pretended to listen to Kate's ostentatious commentary. Scandalously, Fen barely noticed the displays. She was aware of the scale of it all, of a certain cacophony of colour and fragrance, but ultimately her senses were set aside, held in abeyance, until later. She didn't actually have time to marvel at all this horticulture haute couture; she was too busy preparing for her next appointment. She'd been musing scenarios in her mind's eye of the various ways to sashay into a bar, finally favouring her version of a classic Western – stranger enters the saloon and all fall silent. It was compulsive to envisage being the centre of attention, to imagine Al give a double take, bowled over, greeting her with an appreciative 'Wow! I didn't realize it was you!' Fen couldn't actually remember what Al looked like and she was rather hoping he couldn't remember what she looked like either. After all, when they'd first met she'd been head to toe in frumpy mummy guise. Today, hopefully, she'd appear a vision in floaty bias-cut and dainty kitten heels.

God – hi, Fen. You look great. Let me buy you a drink.

She'd carefully blow-dried her hair and had spent as much time as Cosima had allowed her, to blend and blend the Mac and Bobbie Brown mainstays of her neglected make-up bag.

Fen? Blimey! I didn't recognize you. What are you drinking?

While Kate went into paroxysms of wonderment for the Great Pavilion, Fen convinced herself that Al would be currently awaiting her call. She was to let him know when she was free, and he was to tell her where they were to meet; that was the plan. As she was pushed along by the throng, Fen was too busy musing over the best way to touch base with Al to notice the gardens, or that she was being vigorously poked and shoved by all those green fingers. Fen suspected Kate was well able to appreciate the displays *and* eagerly eavesdrop her call, but Fen thought she'd be far more conspicuous standing stock still frantically texting in the midst of all this magnificent flora. A man next to her sneezed. And sneezed again. And suddenly Fen had her motive. She began to rub her nose, to feign a look of discomfort entailing much blinking and nose-twitching.

'Isn't it stunning? Who'd've thought to bind akebia quinata through actinidia? Inspired!' Kate gushed.

Fen realized she couldn't even pronounce let alone identify the majority of the exhibits. 'Kate,' she sighed, 'I hate to say this – but I think my hay fever is about to take hold with a vengeance.'

'At Chelsea Flower Show?' Kate looked at her, horrified, as if the salubriousness of the event surely counteracted such a vulgar affliction.

'I can't bloody believe it,' Fen bemoaned after an impressive chain of sneezes. She blinked and rubbed her nose. 'I'm going to have to go,' she apologized, with a woeful expression.

'OK,' said Kate glumly, 'OK. Come on then, let's go.'

'Kate – you needn't!' Fen rushed. 'Please stay – I'll be fine. My bloody hay fever shouldn't spoil the day for you too.'

'Are you sure?'

'Very.'

Both women quietly considered just then how Ruth would have been a far more worthy recipient of this spare, precious ticket.

As Fen fought her way out, she thought about flowers and gardening and pomp.

Give me a wild-flower meadow over formal planting any day; give me a thatch of heather on a moorside over topiary and edging. I've never been one for bouquets. I'm more of a daisy-chain girl. Pip and I once made one with daisies and buttercups that was almost two yards long. Django pressed the entire thing, between volumes of Encyclopaedia Britannica *set out for weeks in a long line down the hallway. He even contacted the* Guinness Book of Records *about it. I bet he has it still.*

For a while, Matt and I couldn't decide between Cosima and Daisy as names.

I do not want to think of family today.

Fen aimed to come across as imperturbably casual to the point of downright cool when she phoned Al from a side street and said yeah, wine bar coffee shop whatever. However, her stomach was flipping, her conscience was goading and her handwriting was scrawled with adrenalin as she attempted to jot down the location of the bar Al suggested. And then she stood there, palms clammy, heart pounding, wondering how to kill time for the next hour.

You are on the King's Road, Fen. Window-shop? Impulse buy? Full-on Retail Therapy?

Look, Daisy & Tom – their kids' stuff is adorable.

But today isn't about babies.

At first, she was tentative; nipping in and out of L.K. Bennett as if she was being monitored on CCTV beamed straight to all who knew her. She settled into browse mode after circum-navigating the collection at Jigsaw, and in Karen Millen she relaxed a little more, gently running her fingertips along the racks of garments like a pianist from one end of the keyboard to another. Though nearly everything struck a chord with her, still she didn't try anything on. It wasn't the price tags, or the fact that all the pieces she fancied were in implausible shades of white, it was her perceived decadence of the situation that prevented it.

I shouldn't be trying on organza cream shift dresses with bugle beads under the bust; I should be hurrying home to mash sweet potato with organic crème fraîche.

However, Whistles seduced her away from all thoughts of domesticity, luring her into a luxurious world lined with wafts of chiffon and silk, floating with sequinned butterflies and populated by retro imagery woven with humour and imagination into lovely skirts, groovy tops, heavenly knitwear and divine undies. So absorbed was she in the gorgeousness of it all, it was with some consternation that she noticed time had flown and she had five minutes to find the bar and no time to try anything on.

It felt as though a stampede of butterflies, sequinned or other-wise, had suddenly taken flight in her stomach, causing havoc with her ability to walk without tripping and interfering with the demure smile she'd planned. And so, with a slightly twitching physiognomy, she hurried into the bar. The first thing she noticed was the smell. It was overpowering; at once nostalgic and now faintly intimidating. When on earth had she last smelt that wine-bar smell: alcohol, cigarettes, olives in garlicky marinade, leather slouchy sofas? When? *When?* It was evocative – but unnerving – to realize it was not since her pre-pregnancy days. The Rag and Thistle, with its aroma of stale beer and fags partly soaked up by carpet and beer mats, was somehow a warmer, more welcoming smell. Similarly, the sounds at the Rag and Thistle were more affable, as if the carpet and the beer mats absorbed some of the volume and infused the interior with a convivial resonance, a hubbub of cheer. In this bar, however, with the obligatory stripped floorboards, the volume was unmoderated and the clatter and chatter of the clientele were staccato, loud and slightly inhibiting.

Fen was desperate to come across Al without having to search him out; she didn't want to have to stand there, staring from clique to clique, strangers glancing back disinterested. She'd envisaged simply waltzing in, calm, confident and eye-catching, for Al's eyes to alight in delight before she saw him. It appeared, however, that he had yet to arrive. Fen scanned the crowd again. No. No Al. She might not be able to remember precisely how he looked but she was quite sure that no one here just now was him.

'Fen? Hi!'

Oh here he is. Of course. I remember now.

'Sorry I'm late. Drink?'

He hasn't said 'Wow' or anything. What shall I have? What's the time?

'Just a glass of white for me,' said Fen.

'Do you want to grab that table over there – with the two leather cubes?' Al said.

Fen sat a little gingerly on a leather cube, which looked more stable than it felt, but was probably more stable than she thought. She wondered how many people toppled off them on a nightly basis, once balance was compromised by a couple of drinks. She'd be having just the one glass, she wouldn't be wobbling anywhere. She wouldn't even teeter. She had an image to maintain. And a baby to get home to.

She looked over to the bar. She'd define Al as 'cute' – a term men detested but women understood. She hadn't remembered just how lanky, how boyish, he was. His jeans hung a little baggy, his hair was becomingly unkempt, his skin soft and young. Fresh-faced and cute. He was an attractive package and she really *really* mustn't assess him as such.

'Sauvignon, madam,' he announced, beer slicking over his fingers from his glass as he sat down. Fen saw that he wore chunky Mexican silver rings on two of his fingers and one of his thumbs. She didn't like jewellery on men; she didn't like thumb rings at all.

'Cheers,' said Fen, diverting her gaze as she sipped. Revolting wine. Not cold enough. Never mind. Maintain eye contact, slide him a coy smile and ask what he's been up to.

'Oh, this and that,' he replied. 'Busy at work. Moving house.'

'Where do you live?'

'Now? In Camden. We've just taken on a house, five of us plus the occasional surplus body kipping on the sofa. It's good – it's a laugh.'

It sounded slightly unsavoury to Fen and she conjured an image of batik wall hangings, dog-eared posters of Jim Morrison, a chaotic fridge, forgotten washing-up and contrasting music reverberating from each room. She shuddered at her thought of what the bathroom might be like.

'It's not studenty,' Al was saying, as if sensing Fen's reservations. 'We're all a bit obsessed with cleaning, actually. It's a gorgeous house – all polished floors and high ceilings. It belongs to Jed's parents. They're collectors. Anyway, what have you been up to? How's your kid?'

Fen detested children being referred to as kids. 'She's wonderful,' she smiled suddenly missing Cosima terribly. What was she meant to say now? What had she been up to? Was Al really remotely interested in her daily grind of cleaning and tidying, of wiping bottoms and shovelling organic mush into a little mouth, of stocking the fridge and socializing with people to keep herself from going mad? She doubted it. And she was hardly likely to tell him all about the Mother, the Uncle, their Affair and her Half Sister. In an instant Fen assessed that for this afternoon to work, for it to have the function she hoped for, truth and veracity were not essential. 'I've been bloody busy,' she heard herself saying. 'I'm planning to go back to work.'

You are?
No.

'Work?' asked Al. 'What do you do?'

Fen reckoned 'archivist' sounded dull but 'art historian' sounded pompous. 'I lecture,' she embellished, 'in art.'

'Wow! Where?'

'Oh, the Tate usually,' she said with nonchalance, 'the Courtauld.' Partly true. She'd studied at the Courtauld and had frequently given talks as a student to people visiting the Institute's collection.

'What do you lecture about?' Al seemed impressed and genuinely interested.

'The European *Rappel à l'Ordre* of the post-war years,' Fen announced elaborately, simply repeating the title of one of her undergraduate courses, 'and Fetherstone too.'

'Who's Fetherstone?' Al asked, endearingly sheepish.

'A student of Rodin. Late nineteenth, early twentieth

century,' Fen discoursed. 'Famous – or notorious – for his exquisite feel for form, his intensely erotic subject matter.'

'Cool!' Al marvelled, his pupils dilating as he hung on Fen's words and gazed at her lips. 'I'll have to come along to a lecture, then.' Fen tossed her head and laughed and told herself to go easy with the exaggeration and embellishment. Instead, she turned to questioning him, flattering him, expressing great interest in all he said. And she took to touching his arm at times when he made her laugh. And laughed in excess of the cause. And licked her lips becomingly every time she sipped her wine. And lowered her eyes at opportune moments. And pouted now and then.

'Do you have to get back?' Al asked her eventually. 'To your kid?'

'Yes,' said Fen, with a shrug.

'Who's looking after her? Do you have a nanny?'

'No,' said Fen, 'my sister is.'

Al drained his beer glass. 'Is it tough? Being a single parent?'

Something Fen couldn't pinpoint, and hadn't the time to analyse, made her not jump to Matt's defence. It occurred to her only then that Al had never asked about the father of her child. But there again, she didn't wear a wedding ring and she'd never mentioned Cosima's father. Why wouldn't he suppose she was a single mother? Fundamentally, why would a mother in a relationship take up an invitation for afternoon wine, flirting and flattery in a bar? She wondered what to do. To whom did she have the greater duty to set the record straight – Al? Matt? Herself? Cosima?

But can't I just play a while longer? I'm not ready to go home. It's fun, liberating. It's just harmless acting. It's not like I'm telling lies. Or doing anything wrong.

'No, it's not tough,' Fen finally answered Al. 'I'm very close with my sisters. I have two.'

Al nodded. 'Shall we meet again?' he said.

Fen looked at him. It was all appealing and a little dangerous and all the more tempting for it. 'But I'm a frumpy old mum!' she protested with a winsome pout and a flutter of her eyelashes. 'I'm almost thirty-four!'

Al shrugged. His eyes sparkled. 'I think you're cool,' he said. 'I think it's sexy that you're a mum.'

'I'll call you – when I'm not so madly busy,' Fen all but purred, standing, leaning to kiss him on the cheek and making sure her lips just caught the side of his mouth in the process.

Al didn't say anything in response. But his eyes followed her as she left the bar.

He's looking at my bottom, she thought, unsure whether to enhance her wiggle or screen it with her handbag. He gave her a wry, desirous smile when she turned to wave before she sashayed away.

No one has called me sexy for ages. I can't even tell if I actually fancy Al – but I am turned on by the fact that he fancies me.

With a spring to her step, a sexy sway to her stride, she grinned her way along the King's Road, tossing her head and tempering her smile into a pout every now and then. She felt like pouting, she felt coquettish. Someone found her sexy. How thrilling! She enjoyed catching sight of herself in the shop windows. Oh look, here's Whistles. And look at that divine dress.

Did she dare?

Yes she did.

She didn't have to spend money to waste time, or spend time to waste money. She could just try something on, take window-shopping one logical stage further. Flushed with anticipation, Fen headed to the changing cubicles.

She was crestfallen. How stupid had she been? It was as if her trip away from home to an area far from her stamping ground, her shrug from responsibilities, had falsely invested her self-image with extra inches in height and fewer pounds in weight.

Nothing bloody fitted.

She denounced herself for being too round of figure and too square of image. She felt she looked ridiculous. The confines of the clothing made her feel saggy and squidgy and unrefined. And so she stood; horror-stuck in the cubicle, clammy and depressed, confronting all the bumps she could see and a fair few she imagined.

'I'm fine!' she all but yelled to the sales assistant hovering.

What Fen couldn't see was that if she tried a larger size, just one size up, she'd look wonderful. She couldn't see that the dress suited a fuller figure anyway. Designers don't want bagginess in a forties-style tea dress; the cut craves curves and the material needs undulations to flow to its best advantage. But Fen was defiant that once a size 10, always a size 10. And if she didn't fit a size 10, she simply wouldn't be able to have the bloody dress.

If nurturing a foetus required padding to the hips, surely running around after a baby should take it off again? If hormones had encouraged her ribcage to expand during pregnancy, then why hadn't hormones shrunk it back to normal after the birth? Ten and a half sodding months after the birth. Standing there, she scowled at her reflection, rounding her shoulders and relaxing her belly to compound her fears and loathe herself more. She felt resentful and out of sorts and dreaded leaving the changing room, the sparkle of the shop, the clear light of day.

I'm not sure it should be the fit of frock that makes you loathe yourself, Fen.

Seeds Not Sown

'Give us a hug,' Pip cooed and clucked. She scooped up her niece and pretended to gobble her cheeks. The baby giggled. Pip gobbled some more. 'You are scrumptious,' she said, 'but we'd better think of something to do before I eat you up.' Pip and the baby regarded one another, as if considering various options. 'I know,' said Pip, 'how about we pop over to Auntie June and save her the journey here?' Cosima didn't appear to object. 'She left a message to say Tom had left his cricket stuff there, which he'll need for tomorrow.'

For June and Pip, Zac had swiftly ceased to become part of their equation. June didn't think of Pip as the wife of her ex who was the father of her child; Pip had no issue with June being the woman with whom Zac had a baby. Not for June or Pip the dropping-off of Tom with cordiality. Sharing Tom was easy because the women liked each other; to some extent, Tom was both central and yet oddly irrelevant to their friendship.

June cooed over Cosima, marvelled at how much the baby had grown, in much the same way as Pip fussed over June's bump. 'It's not so much a bump,' Pip said, 'it's a perfect medicine ball. So neat!'

'I'm enormous,' June remonstrated, 'and I still have eight weeks to go.'

'You're gorgeous,' said Pip wistfully.

'I think I'm practically due on Cosima's first birthday,' June said.

'Well, we'll cancel the clown if needs be,' Pip said, 'and relocate the party to the labour ward.'

'Or I could just set up my birthing pool in Fen's back bedroom,' June said.

'Are you going for a water birth?' Pip asked.

'You must be joking,' June said. 'I'm going private this time so I can have all the fancy drugs available. I don't do pain.'

'Listen to you,' Pip chided in jest.

'Believe me,' June said, 'Tom's birth was a nightmare. This time, I don't want plinky plinky music, whale song and yoga – I just want drugs.'

Pip glanced from June's bulge to Cosima and back again. *I wonder what sort of birth I'd go for?*

'Do you ever think about it?' June asked.

'About?' Pip busied herself fussing over Cosima.

'About having a baby,' June said.

'Zac loves having just Tom,' Pip said.

'But that's not what I meant,' June persisted.

Pip wasn't sure if she wanted to answer fully or not. 'Sometimes,' she said. June said nothing. 'Recently?'

June clapped her hands and grinned. 'And?'

'Zac loves having just Tom,' Pip reiterated.

'Have you asked Zac?' June asked.

Pip shrugged. 'Sort of,' she said. June looked confused. 'I think he thought I was joking. And then I think he thought I was drunk. And ultimately I think he thinks I'm barking.'

'Well, he sounds complacent,' said June. 'You should keep the pressure on – you'll make a great mum.'

'I hate confrontation,' Pip said, 'and anyway, it's probably just a hormonal thing.'

'You know what,' said June, 'you're right it's probably hormonal but I for one think it'll be a shame if you let it pass.'

Pip wanted to cry. This was the first she'd said out in the open and it was being met with such tender but unswerving support it was rather overwhelming. 'The thing is,' she said tentatively, 'since the woman who is my mother barged back in, I've had something of a confidence crisis. Am I fit to be a mother? Say there's some rogue part of our DNA that dictates otherwise.'

'Rubbish, Pip,' June said, not intending to sound so sharp but she was beginning to feel a little tired. 'Look at Fen – she's a fabulous mum. Your mother – literally – has nothing to do with you. I think you should go for it. And I think when that stuffy old accountant comes home all hassled from work tonight, you meet him in an outrageous negligee and you demand that he impregnate you with his finest.'

Pip looked utterly disconcerted.

'Believe me,' June continued, 'and it's not because I'm an over-heating, hyper-hormoned pregnant woman. Well, perhaps it is – but that's no bad thing. But what I want to say is this – that urge to breed is one you *must* heed. Breeding is your *raison d'être*, Pip, it's your right.'

Pip pushed Cosima's buggy along Hampstead High Street. It was a glorious day and she'd toyed with the notion of taking the picnic blanket and lolling about on the Heath. But what swung it for the High Street were the shops. The shops provided one thing that the Heath didn't. Windows. And reflections. And every shop she passed boasted back an image of Pip pushing a buggy. It was visible proof, as if it was needed, that it suited her. She proudly told the first admirer that Cosima was her niece. But when the sales assistant in BabyGap cooed over Cosima and asked Pip how old her daughter was, Pip told her ten months and agreed with the assistant that she was quite the most beautiful baby girl in the world.

And Cosima ate everything Pip offered her, even if it wasn't orange.

And Pip could soothe the baby's tears quickly.

And Cosima needed minimal lulling to drift off to a lovely afternoon nap. She didn't need her *Elvis for Babies* CD which Fen had packed, nor flopsy bunny. A personalized rendition of 'I Had a Little Nut Tree' from Pip was all it took.

Pip let the answering machine take the call because she and Cosima were engrossed in *Teletubbies* and something extraordinary with the Tubby Custard machine was about to befall Po.

'Shall I pick it up?' Tom asked, looking up from his maths homework.

'That's OK,' said Pip. 'You crack on with your work, young man.'

It was Fen leaving a message to say she was running late and how sorry she was but she'd had a lovely day and would be there soon.

'Never mind,' said Pip to Cosima, 'you can have tea with Tom.'

'Am I her big cousin?' Tom asked because he was stuck with his maths but knew that Pip was no use to him whatsoever. 'Am I her big cousin officially? Or am I a step-cousin twice removed or something?'

Pip paused. 'Well, let's work this out. I think you're her step first cousin.'

'Will my new brother or sister be her step second cousin, then?' Tom asked.

'No, I don't think they'll be cousins at all.'

Tom looked perplexed. This was becoming more compli-cated than the maths homework. 'Of course they will!' he declared. 'It's all about family.'

'If I had a baby, then the baby and Cosima would be full cousins. I have you which makes you half a full first cousin. Step.' Pip and Tom looked at each other, brows furrowed. 'Or something!' Pip said and they laughed.

'Why do babies like eating such weird things?' Tom asked.

Pip looked over to Cosima who was sucking the remote control. 'Shit – that's Bang & Olufsen.'

'You said "Shit"!' Tom whispered, impressed.

'Don't tell your father,' Pip warned him.

'If you had a baby, I'd have two half brothers or sisters, wouldn't I?' Tom mused. 'I'd have brothers and sisters from all directions. That would be funny.'

Pip couldn't think how to respond.

'Why don't you have one, then? With my dad,' asked Tom.

Pip couldn't think how to respond, but Tom seemed happy to wait. 'Well,' she said, 'because he hasn't asked me.'

'Why don't you ask him?' asked Tom.

'I half have,' Pip admitted and wondered if she should now backtrack.

'I'm getting confused with all these halfs,' Tom laughed.

'Me too,' agreed Pip.

Fen appeared slightly flustered when she arrived to collect Cosima, mumbling something about wanting to die in Whistles.

'But how were the flowers?' Pip asked. 'Can you now tell your larkspur from your delphinium?'

'What? Oh. The show. Was – great,' said Fen, 'huge. Amazing.'

'Are you OK?' Pip asked. 'Want a cuppa?'

'I'm just a bit – stressed,' said Fen, looking very discomfited. 'You know – Tubes and rush hour and escalators that aren't working.'

'Welcome back to the real world,' Pip laughed.

'To think I did the rush-hour thing every day,' Fen remembered. 'Madness.'

'Would you like that cuppa?'

'We'd better go – Cosima needs her supper.'

'We fed her!' Tom announced, triumphant. 'She had scrambled eggs just like me!'

'Scrambled eggs?' Fen looked at Pip.

'Was that OK? The eggs are free range.'

'Well – yes. But did she eat?'

'The lot!' Pip said.

Momentarily, Fen felt put out, having had limited success with scrambled eggs. 'Organic milk?' she asked shyly.

'Of course,' said Pip.

'You're a star,' said Fen looking at her sister with affection and at her baby with pride.

'Any time,' said Pip.

'You're a super star,' Fen said, wondering if Pip really meant it when she'd said, 'Any time.'

Zac returned to find his wife and son embroiled in a backgammon tournament; a pile of pennies at Tom's side and a fraught expression etched on Pip's face.

'Hullo,' he said, scanning his son's impressive defence and two of Pip's counters desperate for access.

'Six, two,' Pip muttered at the roll of the dice. 'Blast and double blast, I can't bloody move!'

'That's her fourth "bloody", Dad!' Tom informed Zac, Pip's language obviously giving him far more pleasure than his victories or winnings.

'I'd say a "bloody" is worth 10p, Tom,' Zac said, taking

off his jacket, loosening his tie, opening his post. 'How's your mum?'

'She's like a great big beached whale,' said Tom, rather proudly.

'Tom!' Pip and Zac remonstrated.

'But she says so,' Tom protested, as if it were a standard description of her particular stage of gestation.

'June looks wonderful,' Pip told Zac. 'I babysat Cosima today and we met up. She's absolutely blooming.'

Zac regarded Pip. 'Oh Christ,' he said, with mock consternation, 'you're not going to go all broody on me, are you?' He winked at Tom, planted an affectionate kiss on Pip's forehead, bypassing her mortified expression, before heading to the kitchen to make coffee.

'What does "broody" mean, exactly?' Tom asked and Pip wished he hadn't because she didn't want to hear Zac's reply.

'Broody?' mused Zac. 'Broody is when hormones and BabyGap turn women into mad things.'

'What exactly are hormones?' Tom asked, knowing precisely where BabyGap was but not hormones.

'You'll learn about them in science, soon enough,' Zac assured him.

'Have you gone broody on my dad, then?' Tom asked Pip though he was still unsure to what it precisely alluded.

Pip wanted to cry out, Yes! yes I have – I am seriously broody. But she did not. She assessed that the circumstances were inappropriate. And though part of her resented Tom's presence, felt that it prevented her confronting Zac, she put the child's best interests first.

What I want to say is, For fuck's sake, Zac. I'm thirty-five years old and maybe my sodding hormones are hounding me. Most of the people I know have children. I would like to increase our family – a brother or sister for Tom, a baby for us. What the fuck is wrong with that? Why won't you take me seriously? All you say is 'Oh Christ you're not going all broody on me?'

So why don't you talk to him, Pip? You who are so adept at being a shoulder, an ear, an embrace for the needs of others; you who can listen so well, mediate so constructively when it comes to the strife in other people's lives. You've spent your life arbitrating other people's discord, sorting out the ways forward from their crises, dispensing wisdom, advice, support and affection. You can gently coax others down off their high horse, you can enable them to see clearly without their rose-tinted glasses. But you have no faith in your ability to stand your own corner and proclaim what you feel. You have self-awareness in that you know what you want; but you lack the self-confidence to express it.

She can't concentrate on her game. She thinks the right thing to do is to hide her hurt from Tom. It's much easier to put Tom at the centre of her equation than herself.

'I won!' Tom proclaims. 'Pip is such a complete walkover,' he says to his dad and the two of them disappear to play PlayStation, leaving Pip on her own.

Seeds in a Packet

'You're hot and you smell of – toast?' Ben remarked with pleasure, in bed, spooning up against Cat, nuzzling her neck.

'But I haven't eaten toast,' she said.

Ben took her hand to his nose. 'Toast,' he declared. He kissed the palm of her hand and flicked his tongue tip at the centre. Then he kissed her fingertips and sucked softly on her middle finger.

'I've got a sackful of seed,' he murmured, pressing up against her. 'I've been saving it up for the last – Christ – *week*.' Cat giggled. She travelled her hand down to Ben's hard cock, experiencing a buzz of excitement between her legs which caused her to turn towards him and find his mouth immediately. His hands caressed her breasts and she began to moan softly as his finger nudged at her clitoris, dabbing her with her own expectant moistness.

'What do you say, babe,' he whispered, 'want to mate?' He grazed at the side of her neck, dipped his head down to tease her nipple with his tongue tip. 'Want to mate?'

But Cat didn't writhe in reply. She didn't gasp the affirmative. His words had stilled her and his actions ceased to elicit a response.

And then she sighed. 'I do feel horny,' she whispered back, 'but I don't want to *mate*. I'd rather fornicate.'

'What you're saying is that you want me to give you a good seeing to? You don't want to make love – you want me to shag you senseless?' Ben gave a dirty laugh, his hands resuming a dexterous exploration of her erogenous zones. He rolled on top of her, his pelvis rocking as his cock probed its way between the lips of her sex. 'You want me to fuck you, then?'

Yes, that was precisely what Cat wanted and when Ben talked crudely to her, she wanted it all the more. And harder.

'Shall I fuck you?' Ben asked, desirous and gruff, doing precisely that with eager, ravenous thrusts.

'With strings attached,' she whispered, gasping as he powered into her. She bucked against him instinctively.

'Strings, hey?' Ben said. 'Tie you up? A little light S & M on a warm June evening?'

That's not what she meant at all.

I meant, yes fuck me – but with conditions. But I'm so close. I'm so fucking close and my body is tingling with the anticipation of orgasm. It's welling. Fuck. God. Ben. Oh Christ.

Ben felt Cat's sex close around his cock, every pulsation pulling him deeper inside her, luring his sperm, starting to suck it from his balls up his shaft; nearing the point of no return.

'Christ Cat,' he panted as his thrusts automatically increased in pace, 'Christ.'

But then Cat did something with her hips. And her knees. She'd never done it before and it took Ben by surprise, weakened as he was by being in thrall to his imminent orgasm. She levered him away and all of a sudden he was coming in the open, nowhere near her dark, damp gorgeous pussy. Instead he was spurting his load God knows where. In between her and him. Instantly, the orgasm became purely perfunctory. Not even as good as a wank. Simply as physical as a wet dream. A waste. He switched the light on, blinking, pissed off. He pulled the duvet off and regarded the sticky mess in Cat's pubic hair, caught too in the fuzz of his stomach.

'What was that all about?' he asked, flushed and frustrated.

'It's not safe to come inside me,' Cat said, disconcerted that Ben looked so displeased. She felt a nag of guilt over the greed for the quality of her own orgasm at the expense of his and it was spoiling the post-coital moment.

'What the fuck do you mean, Cat?' Ben objected. 'What are you on about? Our sex life has been ruled by your charts and temperature.'

'I'm not ready,' Cat said gruffly, 'not any more. Not without a condom.'

'Cat,' said Ben, sitting up, reaching for tissues, mopping at his belly, 'I thought *we* wanted to start a family. Our game plan. We make decisions *together*.'

'Bloody hell, Ben,' she protested, 'are you thick? In the light of recent events, why would I want to be pregnant?' He stared at her, shocked by her aggression. 'Parenting is a dangerous thing. Can't you see that?' she shouted. 'Believe me. It's not worth it. I should know.'

Ben waited a moment and spoke calmly. 'Cat, that's not an informed view – you're very tired and too emotional.'

'You cold bastard!' Cat hissed. 'Can't you see what I'm going through?'

'Of course I bloody can,' Ben said calmly, 'but now you're being a drama queen. Christ if ever there was a time to take the "sins of the fathers" and make something good from them, then this is it.'

'Fuck off.' She turned away from him abruptly. 'You don't understand.'

That last comment hurt Ben the most. He had no desire to spoon against her or nuzzle up to see if she still smelt of toast. If only this sodding rented flat had a spare room. He switched off the light, plumped his pillow and made an irritated grab at the duvet. And when all was still, he sighed emphatically.

'For fuck's sake,' he said, as if to himself, but loudly enough for Cat to hear. He sensed she was only pretending to be asleep.

They didn't speak when they woke up. Ben didn't wake Cat with his customary 'Rise and shine, sleepy head'. He went to have a shower and didn't pour her a cup of coffee, leaving the cafetière and its tepid contents on the table instead. Get your own mug.

'See you,' he said, already on his way out. Cat didn't look up from the newspaper. She continued to read, continued to sip her lukewarm coffee long after Ben had gone. The newsprint was illegible because the bruise of tears impeded her sight and the coffee caught harshly on the lump in her throat. She struggled with her tears as she walked to work, biting hard on the inside of her lip during the managers' meeting. She didn't want to be on the information desk. Couldn't she unpack deliveries instead? It wasn't beneath an assistant manageress to unpack deliveries in the back, you know. But Jeremy wanted her up front and the customers did too. Cat muddled through the morning, hauling a weak smile to her face and disappearing to the toilet on her break for a private cry.

Pip would know what to do. She'd know what I should say. She'll be able to tell me if I'm in the wrong, or a little right. She's my big sister. I'll listen to her. She's the wisest person I know. She can tell me what to do.

*

226

In her lunch break, Cat phoned Pip. Privately, it rankled Pip to hear about loving husbands actively wanting to make babies. But she had to listen because it was her job and her youngest sister was sobbing at the end of the phone, pleading with her to tell her what to do. Over the years, she'd conditioned herself to stop what she was doing, put thoughts of herself to one side, whenever she received those calls from her sisters that said, Pip? Pip? I need you. Can you help?

'I thought I was ready,' Cat cried, 'but I'm not. I don't even feel broody any more. I can't figure out this whole mother–father business. I'm scared, Pip, and confused.'

Quietly, Pip considered her sister's predicament. 'I understand, I do,' she soothed, because on an academic level, she did, 'but how I see it is that you've been gravely let down by a total lack of communication within our family – and the only history about to repeat itself is precisely this.' She paused. Why couldn't she herself boldly practise what she so gamely preached?

This isn't about me. It's about Cat.

'Don't let that happen, Cat. No secrets. We were kept in the dark – we weren't even lied to. We were ill-informed and misled. But Cat, don't take that with you into your life. Don't let that same lack of communication decimate what you have with Ben. It sounds clichéd, but *talk* to him.' She paused again.

That's what June told me.

'Tell him how you feel. He's your man, Cat. He's your future. You can turn to him. You must.'

'But he's not speaking to me,' said Cat, now smarting about the lack of coffee that morning. 'He's mad at me. We never row. It was horrible. I feel sick. Suddenly Ben and I want different things, Pip. We're totally incompatible.'

'It's not about how compatible you are, Cat – it's about

how you deal with incompatibility,' said Pip. 'When did you last tell him you loved him?'

When did Zac last tell me?

'I don't honestly know,' Cat was saying, 'but how do I start talking? And what do you think I should say?'

On the other end of the phone, Pip was pinching the bridge of her nose and trying to strip her mind of Zac so she could concentrate on Cat.

'You have to do the right thing,' she heard herself say. 'You have to open up and lay yourself bare – if you can't do this in front of your husband, then you are in serious breach of the trust and honesty you promised him when you married him.'

Which makes me a fucking hypocrite.

'Shall I phone him at work?' Cat pressed. 'Shall I ask my manager for a break?'

'Yes,' said Pip, 'do.'

'And tell Ben how I feel – even though some of it sounds daft?'

'Yes,' said Pip, 'you must.'

'Say he disagrees? Say he objects?'

'Say he doesn't?'

'Say he's cross?' said Cat.

'Say he isn't?'

Cat paused. The notion of Ben's love being just at the end of the phone, of his support and understanding being just a phone call away, of her being just moments from the comfort of his companionship, was thrilling. Suddenly, she wanted Pip off the phone.

'Thanks,' Cat said cheerfully. 'I'll phone him right now. Can I phone you again, though?'

'You know you can,' said Pip.

Pip hated herself for hoping that Cat wouldn't phone her again. She didn't want to listen to how the heart-to-heart had gone and she didn't have the energy for further counselling. But Pip hated herself more for her intrinsic inability to take her own sound advice. How easy it was to see the right thing to do. Crystal bloody clear. Talk it through. Lay yourself bare. Show your soul and open your heart to the person closest to you, the person who transcends a need for blood ties to create a bond. How pathetic, she felt, to be fundamentally incapable of doing this herself.

Behind the information desk, Cat contrived to look important and busy. She wasn't. She was utterly absorbed in the pleasure of planning the reconciliation. She hadn't asked for a break because it was premature. She had to know exactly what she'd be saying before she phoned Ben. She had to be word perfect and her words needed to be honed for ultimate poetic and meaningful impact. He'd be in afternoon surgery. She couldn't phone now, she needed the best forum and no time restraints for her soliloquy to resound. But say he was still pissed off and went to the pub instead of coming home? And say he was pissed when he then came home? She couldn't endure another cold-shouldered night. She had to let him know that she was sorry, and soon. That there was an explanation. A text message could work – something sweet and slushy. But texts were somehow too easy to send. Who hasn't used a text message to avoid having to talk to someone?

As she hung up from telling a customer's answering machine that their books were awaiting collection, Cat thought about message services. About telegrams and messengers and couriers. She phoned Ben's hospital and asked for the Sports Medicine department and when a female voice answered, Cat put on her most friendly, conniving voice.

'Hullo? Is that Marjorie?'

'Yes? Sports Medicine clinic – how can I help?'

'This is Cat – Ben's wife. We haven't met but he speaks highly of you.'

'Oh!'

'Can you help me, Marjorie? I did one of those silly things – those over-emotional daft-cow things.'

'Ah,' said Marjorie, who had been no stranger to the syndrome in her younger days.

'Ben has speaker phone, doesn't he – is that how you announce his patients?'

'Yes, that's right, dear.'

'Before the next patient can you tell him that his wife loves him and she's sorry for being a madwoman and that she can't wait to see him later?'

'I can,' Marjorie said with slight reluctance.

'Oh,' said Cat, forlorn, 'is it something to do with hospital policy?'

'No, dear,' said Marjorie, 'but can I reword it? I think I should say— In fact, he's ready to see his next patient. You can listen in.'

Cat pressed the receiver hard against her ear, giving Jeremy who was loitering an irritated 'Shh!' before turning her back on him.

'Dr York,' Marjorie could be heard to say, 'before I send in Miss Drew, I have been entrusted with the following announcement.'

Cat's heart raced. Marjorie's pitch changed, as if she was having to be heard across a football pitch. 'Your wife wishes you to know that she loves you truly, and that she is extremely sorry for her behaviour. She would like you to know that she looks forward to your homecoming tonight – and that she would be pleased to talk through the circumstances.'

Cat couldn't hear Ben's response, but she fully approved Marjorie's handling of the situation. 'You're a genius,

Marjorie,' she said, and she planned to send her some books in gratitude.

'Cat!'

Cat turned to see Jeremy looking put out.

'We do not, as a rule, take personal calls – let alone make them.'

'I know,' Cat beamed, 'I'm sorry – there was a family crisis. It's all sorted now. It won't happen again.'

The manager thought she spoke of the personal calls.

Cat stopped beaming on her journey home. It struck her that nothing was actually solved. All she'd done, hopefully, was give Ben an inducement to come home, pacify his anger and open a door to communication. They still had to talk. And reach an understanding, an agreement.

But he wasn't home and her confidence was instantly sapped. She started to allow herself to feel the wounded party. Why hadn't he figured out why she might now be reluctant to start a family? Why hadn't he been instinctively more supportive? Her mobile phone buzzed through a message.

U ok? Here 4 u. P xx.

Good old Pip, coming to the rescue. At least someone knows me inside out and understands.

'He's not home yet,' Cat phoned Pip in a whisper, in case Ben should be just about to come in. She told Pip of Marjorie. She could sense her sister's smile, her approval. 'But suddenly I don't know what to say when he does come home. Say he's still cross. Say he didn't like my message? Say we can't sort this out?'

'If you look out your window, will you see him walk up the street?'

'Yes,' said Cat.

'So, the sight of him will incite an emotional reaction in you. Act on it.'

I speak from experience. I could hardly bear to look at

Zac when he came home half an hour ago. So I invented
some urgent shopping. And I'm now advising my sister from
the canned-goods aisle in Sainsbury's.

'You're a genius,' Cat told her. 'Thank you. God, thank
you, Pip.'

'Call if you need me,' Pip said, by rote. But Cat had already
hung up.

Cat has been gazing out of the first-floor window for almost
half an hour. She's elaborately decided that if three red cars
pass in succession, Ben will be the next pedestrian to walk
down the street. But blue cars and white vans and the occasional candy-coloured scooter keep interrupting and there's
no sign of Ben. What a gorgeous evening. How lovely to see
a couple of children playing hopscotch on the pavement.
Clapham doesn't seem so unattractive today and Boulder
doesn't seem so far away. The world seems smaller, more
friendly, more manageable. Listen! That evocative jingle – an
ice-cream van! When had she last had a gloriously synthetic
whippy with a Flake? She can't remember. But she heads out
of the flat and down to the street. She's second in the queue.
She's first. She's being served.

'A medium 99, please,' she says.

And Cat sees Ben.

He's turned the corner.

He's only a hundred yards away.

'Two!' Cat says. 'Make that two!'

Can Ben see me? Has he seen me yet?

He has.

But is he smiling?

He is.

Cat walks fast towards Ben who is strolling along the street
with his shirtsleeves rolled up, his jacket slung over his

shoulder. All her words have gone, her memory stripped of the soliloquies she's spent the day perfecting. All she can do, within yards of Ben, is brandish the ice cream she's bought for him.

'Look!' she declares holding out the ice cream. Ben thinks she looks like the Statue of Liberty in jeans and a T-shirt. 'I didn't even take a bite of your Flake.'

'Well,' says Ben, 'if that's not a sign of your true love, then what is?'

Cat blushes and doesn't know what to say and Ben thinks it's funny so he dabs the tip of his ice cream against her nose. Then he kisses it off. 'Thanks for your message,' he says. 'You're a madwoman. But I've given Marjorie a promotion.'

They sit, busy licking, on the low wall outside their flat. Cat bites the bottom of her cornet, looks at Ben and then sucks until her cheeks pucker and the ice cream scoots down the cone. Her daft face makes Ben laugh.

'I can't believe you save your Flake until last,' Cat says, knowing she'd never have the self-restraint to push the chocolate down the centre of the cornet and studiously eat around it.

'I don't think I have a system,' Ben says, 'but I'm doing it because I know it'll wind you up.'

'Bastard!' Cat says softly. She's finished her ice cream now and she lays her head against Ben's shoulder. 'I'm sorry,' she says.

'Me too,' says Ben. 'I hate falling out with you.'

'Me too,' says Cat.

'It's not what we're about,' says Ben. He offers his cornet to her, he's nibbled down so the Flake, somewhat phallic, stands proud. Cat takes a bite. It's a beautiful evening. If they go inside, there'll be the television to flick on, supper to discuss, post to open. If they walk on, they'll hit that long patch of shade as the street bends right. So they decide to stay put, to sit on the wall and wonder what to say and who will speak first.

'Do you not want to have a baby?' Ben asks outright, because actually that's the basic question he needs answered.

Cat looks uneasy. 'No,' she admits quietly, 'I don't. Not now.'

'Not now, not *never*?' Ben probes gently.

It strikes Cat she hasn't actually thought about it to this extent. 'I'm so caught up in the mess of the moment,' she admits, 'I can't see beyond the immediate future.'

Ben nods. 'I know how awful all these revelations have been for you,' he says. 'Actually, I don't – I can only begin to imagine.'

'It's thrown into turmoil all my plans, all my previous beliefs,' Cat explains.

Ben nods.

'I'm not ready to be a mummy,' Cat says sadly.

'Because you're not ready to accept your own parents?' Ben suggests. 'In retrospect, your childhood may not have been perfect, but it is over.'

Cat shrugs. 'It's all been so – shocking.'

'I know. But you need to confront it all,' Ben advises, 'somehow. Stacey said the same, didn't she? I don't know if that's by soul-searching or full-on confrontation. You need to decide. But being in this vortex of bewilderment isn't good, Cat. If you're stuck in a downward spiral, it figures you can't move forward.'

Cat nods. Ben wonders whether to tell her about Django's call. But he can't really, the call was in confidence.

'You have all these strands of your life, flailing around,' he says. 'You need to either tie them up, or cut them off.'

'I know,' says Cat, 'but that's terrifying.'

'You need to face facts – quite literally,' Ben says. 'You should go and see Django – just you. Without me. No sisters to hide behind. Talk. Shout. Cry. I don't know. But you must have a million things to ask and he probably has a million things to tell.'

'I can't believe my father is alive,' Cat tells him. 'I can't believe I am Django's daughter. I don't want to see him, Ben. Should I have known? Shouldn't I have wondered at least?' Ben shrugs and places his hand over hers. 'Now that I know where I come from, I don't quite know where I'm going.' She pauses and rests her head on his shoulder. 'That's why I feel ambivalent about starting a family.'

'I understand you may feel this is not the right time to have a baby just now,' Ben sighs, because actually he'd truly love to have his family under way soon. He's thirty-four years old, he feels it's right, logical, that he should feel broody himself. 'But I also need to know that you are open to change. And most of all, I need to know that, theoretically, I'm still the bloke you'd want to have a baby with.'

Cat jerks her head up from his shoulder and looks at him, shocked. How could big strong Ben doubt this?

Ben shrugs. 'You have to hug me back, sometimes, you know,' he explains.

She looks at him again and despite his strong physique, his handsome face, his silvering hair, just now he looks like a little boy. Cat stares at her knees, ashamed. Regards a smudge of ice cream on her jeans. 'Of course there's only you,' she whispers. 'My family begins with you.'

They sit on the wall and like the words.

'But listen,' says Ben, 'I hate condoms. And pulling out is grim – and not sodding fair. Messy too.'

'Blow-job?' Cat says with meek coyness.

'Swallow?'

She giggles.

'The pill?' Ben asks.

'But I put on weight and got spotty last time,' Cat says.

'I still fancied you,' says Ben.

And Cat knows that he did.

'Perhaps,' she says.

'For the time being, hey?' says Ben.

Cat gives a small nod and slips her hand into his. It's a good enough answer for Ben.

Bad Seed

And where is *she*? The mother who ran off with the cowboy from Denver when her daughters were small, who reappeared with bombshells to drop thirty years later, has since returned to the United States. It's now June and Penny has been home for a couple of weeks and though the weather is glorious, Penny hasn't once been for ice cream. Not even a pink taster spoon. Though she'd love a sundae, nowhere but Fountains will do. Once tasted, never forsaken. However, she hasn't felt like going there but she'd rather go without ice cream than compromise with a tub from her local store. And she'd rather go without than confront sweet Juliette and her hopes of hearing that closure was a magical thing.

The house was sparkling, the fridge was full, the washing was done and the garden was so tidy that short of untangling blades of grass with a toothcomb, there was nothing more for Penny to do. The silence in the house was deafening but a coffee morning with Marcia and Noni would be more so. So she drove. All the way to the state line. Then she drove back and sat in the drive and berated the lawn for still looking so manicured and thus unmowable. She sat in the car with the engine running calculating the hours and hours until bedtime. A beautiful home, spick and span, empty and soulless. She phoned her home number from her cell phone and listened to Bob's voice on the answering machine. She phoned her home number again and cursed technology, denounced it as trickery that she could hear Bob's voice so clearly when the man no longer existed. She knew she ought to re-record the message. Some might think it macabre to hear a dead man's voice on it. And there was new information to record. She'd have to reword the message in the first person. No more 'we'. But how could she wipe Bob's voice away?

Penny started the car and headed out of town. She arrived at the intersection and turned right with a bit of a sigh and soon enough turned onto the mountain road. She wasn't heading for ice cream, or Ridge, she'd just stop at the first village, Hubbardton's Spring. There was an easy trail there that would take her to one of the most gorgeous panoramas in the vicinity. She drove through the village and along a no-through-route, parking up soon after the road petered out into an unsurfaced one. Her eyes were filled with the lushness of early summer; sumac trees and maples cloaked in such verdant hues it was difficult to imagine them ablaze in gold and scarlet and amber in a few months' time. Her sensible summer sandals were soon filled with powdery earth and the occasional small stone, viciously sharp despite its size. She headed for the vantage point high over the river, the land then surging and swooping to the mountains. It was one of Bob's favourite paths. Maybe he'd meet her there. She walked with hope though she chided herself an idiot for doing so. Wasn't she done with retracing old footsteps? After all, wherever she went now, she could look behind and see the unmistakable truth: there would only ever be one set of footprints.

There was nobody there. Of course there was nobody there.

Penny scrambled down to the cluster of flat rocks and took a seat. The purity of the air, the vividness of the view, the reality of the chill and scuff of the rock on which she sat, infused her with the clarity she needed.

I guess there's no point in mourning him any longer, because he's not coming back. There's only photographs and memories. I can close my eyes and try to recall the sight and sound and smell of him but I can't hope to conjure him.

I need to draw the proverbial line under it all. Re-record the answering machine. Find different trails to walk. I need to keep on going. Move on. I guess that's a positive thing to do – even if at the moment there seems to be a futility and finality to it which seems negative. If I can't hope for Bob – if I admit he's dead – will it somehow kill him off entirely? Death might be ultimately the simplest, truest thing we'll ever know – but it's way too complicated for the living.

People are coming. I can hear them. I want to curse them for stealing my moment. I want to tell them they're tres-passing. This is mine – take your picnic and your laughter some place else! But Bob and I often shared this hike with other people – friends and strangers – so I can't expect Bob's death to bequest it sacred, private land. I'll go. I'll nod at these people. Maybe I'll even say, Hi, enjoy the view, it sure is pretty today. Perhaps I can smile at them too.

Penny could have gone home. Hubbardton's Spring was pretty much equidistant from Ridge where Fountains was, and Lester Falls where she lived. But it was a fine afternoon. And there was nothing to do at home. And still there were hours until bedtime. Anyway, perhaps Juliette didn't work Sundays. And with the trails now fully open, the parlour would be fuller anyway. Though there were more cars parked along the way, people were obviously out and about on the trails because Fountains was no busier than when Penny had last been in.

'Well look who it is,' said Juliette, rushing to the counter to have Gloria load a taster spoon with Coffeebanoffee. 'So good to see you!' she told Penny. 'Sit! How was your trip?' Juliette's mousy little face, with her generous smile and button-black eyes, was alert with anticipation and affection. Penny fixed a beatific smile to her face which she hoped would tell the girl all she could possibly want to know. And shut her up. She sat at the table and chided herself for not ordering her ice cream to go; for coming here in the first place.

Juliette returned with the sundae and loitered, waiting for Penny to engage her in conversation or even invite her to sit. But Penny appeared not to notice her, so engrossed was she in a leaflet she'd picked up outside the gallery in Hubbardton's Spring. When Penny noticed that Gloria was busy serving at the counter and Juliette had gone through to collect orders, she left the parlour and her uneaten sundae.

'Hey – Penny? Wait up.'

Penny turns to see Juliette hurrying down the street, with her sweet smile and a warm wave and something held aloft in her other hand.

'Hey Penny,' says Juliette, a little breathless, 'here. You hardly ate a bite.' She hands Penny a polystyrene block encasing the tubbed-up leftovers of her sundae. Juliette regards her, tilts her head, frowns a little whilst smiling. A contradiction in terms, Penny thinks to herself, like so much of life.

Love blossoming from a bad seed.

'You crying?' Juliette seems perturbed.

Penny touches her cheeks and swipes away the tears.

'I don't know whether our relationship was blessed or doomed,' Penny announces and is helpless to stem the flow of words streaming out. 'I try and defend my actions, I try to justify that I was young, that it was the 1960s, that I was a crazy mixed-up kid, that I wasn't in love with Nicholas anyway. But actually, what Bob and I did was *wrong*. Love blossomed from a bad seed – it screwed with the lives of others.' She stops abruptly, gasping a little.

'I think you have it wrong, Penny,' Juliette says with a caring tilt to her head. 'It's not your fault Bob died – and it's not your fault that you guys fell in love,' and she touches Penny's arm tenderly.

Penny feels surprisingly irritated. How bizarre to feel the need to defend the bad in herself. 'But my dear, you really don't know me,' she protests in an accent more English than at any time over the last three decades.

'Sure I don't know the ins and outs – who does? But I'm a good judge of character,' Juliette says, a little defensively, 'and I sense you and Bob shared something beautiful.'

'We did,' Penny says flatly, 'but at a high price. And I'm sorry, Juliette, but you are *not* a particularly good judge of character – you have me all wrong.'

'Great love isn't given to those not worthy of it,' Juliette says. Then she quickly regards her feet and looks a little bashful. 'That's a song lyric by my favourite band, actually. But it says what I believe. You *were* lucky, you and Bob. You were blessed.' She looks up and gives Penny, who is glowering, a little grin.

'But those around us weren't,' Penny says stonily. 'Juliette honey, I'm tired and I just want to drive home.'

'Sure, sure,' says Juliette, but still she loiters. 'It's just I didn't like to hear you say you were a bad seed – you're not, you're what me and my mom call a *good egg*.'

Suddenly, Penny is disconcerted that her words have been listened to so earnestly but that the impression they've given is erroneous. And that this sweet young girl, troubled by the death of a useless alcoholic father, should have Penny so wrong too. Penny might once have been wryly amused at being glorified, but just now it seems immoral.

'You draw a picture only from what you've heard,' Penny tells Juliette. 'Believe me there's a whole bunch of stuff you wouldn't want to know.'

Juliette looks a little taken aback. 'But I like you.'

'Juliette,' Penny says, scrunching her eyes shut against the headache of it all, 'if I told you I had three daughters – whom I *abandoned* when the youngest was just a baby, would you believe me? Would you like me then?'

Juliette balks. What a weird question. 'Of course I wouldn't believe you,' she says.

'Well, I did,' Penny declares hoarsely. 'I did the unbeliev-able, OK? I walked out on three little girls. And you know something, I actually never regretted it. Now you stand there and tell me that the love I had with Bob was a good thing. You stand there and tell me I'm not a bad seed. You tell me you like me now.'

'But—'

'I'm no better than your father – in fact I'm worse. He treated you bad when he was drunk and in some ways not accountable for his behaviour. I walked out on my children when I was stone cold sober.'

Juliette stares; disbelief and hurt and horror striating her face. Penny perversely welcomes the scorch of shame which cuts through her. 'You know what,' Penny mutters, 'I have to go.' And though Juliette stands there motionless, dumb-struck and bereft, Penny walks the short distance to her car, dumps the polystyrene container in a trash-can on the way and drives off without a backward glance.

What is one more person hating her? What is one more person to have let down? Join the queue, Juliette, join the queue.

*

Penny is still awake in the early hours of the next morning. She's sitting in the dark, in Bob's chair, wondering why. In the last twelve hours, she's said goodbye to Bob at the vantage point near Hubbardton's, she's revealed the ugly truth of her life to Juliette and she's re-recorded the answering-machine message. So why does she feel so anxious and fretful? Why is there no sense of peace, of relief, of lightness, of that oft-bandied term *closure*?

Penny knows why. She can't achieve closure because the door cannot yet be shut. It is jammed with issues she must confront and own, see in black-and-white in the clear light of day, acknowledge out loud. Where she'd gone that previous afternoon, what she'd spoken of to Juliette, what she'd recorded into the answering machine, were single strands in a knot of loose ends which need to be untied.

Stray Cat Blue

Ben hadn't asked Cat what she was going to do on her day off which, this week, fell on a Wednesday. He hadn't asked and she hadn't mentioned it because he seemed a little distracted anyway, somewhat stressed. He was sitting at the kitchen table, flicking through the newspaper as if every item of news irked him.

'Everything OK, doctor?' she asked, handing him a mug of coffee and then giving his neck a quick rub.

'What? Oh, fine,' said Ben. 'It's probably going to be a bit of a full-on day, babe. I may be home late.'

'I'll have your pipe and slippers waiting,' she laughed, stroking his closely cropped hair; the flecks of grey catching glints of silver as she did so.

'That's my girl,' he said.

'Although you may have to fetch your slippers yourself – I might be late home too,' Cat said.

'Oh? Staff meeting or something?' said Ben.

Cat shook her head. 'It's my day off,' she said. She took a seat beside him, pulled the chair close so their knees touched. He looked at her: her cheeks were a little flushed, her eyes flitted with whatever she was on the verge of saying. She

244

gave a quick shrug. 'I'm going to go to Derbyshire. Just a day-trip.'

Ben stared at her, fighting hard to keep horror from his face. He must not let his dismay show. He must say nothing. He must smile and nod and instead say, Wow, babe, wow. He must fight the urge to say, Don't! You can't! Not today, Cat! He can't warn her that today's not a good day for a round trip to Derbyshire. Because then she'd ask why. And he couldn't say, Because Django's coming to see me. Because, as a doctor, he was bound by the Hippocratic oath. And anyway, just look at her, all flushed with the supreme effort of arriving at such a proactive and possibly tough course of action. How much late-night thinking had she done to come to this decision? How much soul-searching had she accomplished to be ready to go home and face her father? Ben loved her so much for her courage and her reckoning, but as full as his heart was for her, it bled for her too. Ben had been so anxious that Django might not make this trip – but suddenly he was hoping this would be the case precisely. Ben felt torn and compromised. He'd made the appointment on Django's behalf and without Cat's knowledge because he was worried about Django. Because he had thought it was the right thing to do. Just now, though, he wondered what right he had at all. He felt quite sick.

'What?' Cat said, her eyes darkening to khaki as her brow furrowed and she regarded Ben anxiously. 'Don't you think it's a good idea?' She looked crestfallen, her lips pouting inadvertently.

'It's an amazing idea,' Ben assured her, though his instincts goaded him otherwise. 'I'm so proud of you. Sorry – I've just got stuff on my mind. Sodding politics with the Trust and the NHS. Budgets. Funding. Targets. Sorry.'

'That's OK,' said Cat, 'but you do think I should go, don't you? It's not so much a gut instinct I'm acting on – my gut is in a knot right now – it's a carefully considered decision. The timing seems good to me. It feels like it's the right thing to do.'

'Have you told your sisters?' Ben asked. 'Are you going alone?'

'I am going alone,' Cat said, with slow, awkward nods. 'I haven't asked them along. I haven't actually told them I'm going.' She looked a little unnerved, trying to find twists of hair to bind around her finger though mostly it was too short and quickly sprung free. 'Do you think I should have told them? Or asked them along?'

'Not if you don't want to,' Ben told her while his mind sped through a variety of plausible suggestions to dissuade her from going. But it was too complicated. He needed more time to figure it all out. But Cat needed his advice. Now. 'This particular side of the story is yours,' he told her. 'You need to act on what feels right.'

'It's a rare old thing for me not to feel I have to analyse such a momentous decision with Pip and Fen first,' Cat said. 'I was proud of myself for having arrived at it on my own.'

'I'm proud of you, too,' Ben repeated. 'You'll be even more proud of yourself when you step down from the train at Chesterfield station.' And he wondered whether he should be phoning Django and alerting him. Ben's sense of duty, always hailed as one of his key qualities, was today giving him a headache. He rubbed his eyes. Not a good sign to feel this knackered at only breakfast-time. He suddenly loved his own family for being so conventional and dull. He must phone his mother, it was a good couple of weeks since he'd done so. He wouldn't phone Django. He couldn't. Ultimately, it wouldn't be fair on Cat. He rapidly justified that his duty to Cat was partly to ensure that Django kept the appointment he'd made for him.

'I don't know what I'm going to say,' Cat was saying, 'but

I feel ready to talk. To listen. I just need to make sense of my past, Ben. I feel in limbo until I do.'

Ben put his hand around the back of her neck and pulled her face close for a kiss. 'I hope you have a good day, babe,' he said. 'I hope it feels good to go back there, whatever you hear or don't.'

'Thanks,' said Cat. 'If you wait, I'll walk to the Tube with you.'

We know Django won't be there. But Cat spent the train journey alternately smiling and frowning as various scenarios came into her mind's eye. She even laughed out loud at a fanciful scene in slo-mo, she and Django running down the platform into each other's arms. Daft. She hadn't even tried the Farleymoor number from her mobile phone, let alone announced her visit to him in advance. She didn't want to give him a shock though she knew he'd be taken off guard. She anticipated his initial concern would be that he hadn't prepared anything special for lunch. What was she going to ask him? What did she hope to learn? She gazed out of the window and watched the landscape rush past, slip seamlessly from one landscape into another. The flatness of the South-East, the uniformity of the Midlands, soon enough the rolling promise of the Derbyshire Dales.

She thought about phoning from the station. Then she thought about phoning from the cab. But soon enough she was within ten minutes of the house and if she phoned now, the adrenalin coursing through her would surely give her voice little more than a whisper. The house came into view, sitting solid and squat in the grounds, as indigenous to the locality and as comfortable in the landscape as the moorland ponies or hardy little sheep.

'Just here is fine,' she told the cab-driver. She needed the walk up the drive to take deep breaths, plucking at the ivy which clustered along the drystone wall. If Django wasn't looking out of the window, she'd have the chance to stand awhile on the doorstep and collect her thoughts. As she walked up the path to the front door, she could only fix her sight on her feet. Her teeth chattered. *It's June!* she told herself, *and it's only Django.*

No Django.

No one at home.

She's been sitting on the great grey flagstone doorstep for some time, hugging her arms around herself. She'd envisaged a bear-hug from Django. It had been one of the driving thoughts that had got her here. She'd thought that no matter what she might say, or hear, that hug was a given. Only it wasn't. Because Django is not here.

The courage Cat had summoned to make this journey, the pride and excitement she'd felt in a huge affirmative surge when she'd stepped from the train at Chesterfield station, have now dwindled into disbelief and deep loneliness and despondency. Where could he be? Cat circumnavigates the house, peering into all the downstairs windows. Were there no clues? A pot of jam is on top of the *Racing Post* on the kitchen table. Not much to read into that. The living-room is extremely tidy. The flip-flops that Fen was wearing on Django's birthday, one broken, are on the bench in the utility room with other variously sized footwear neatly laid out to either side. The opaque window to the downstairs toilet is fixed ajar but though Cat squints inside, she can't really see anything, certainly no pointers to the whereabouts of the master of the house.

I don't believe this. Where can he be? Where does he go on a Wednesday? Dominoes is Thursday afternoon and he usually shops on a Tuesday and a Friday.

She taps on all the windows as she makes her way back

round to the front door. She raps on that and calls through the letter-box. She has a long look through, but the hallway is empty of details.

'Django!' she calls. 'Django!' She waits and listens. 'Where the fuck are you?' she mutters under her breath because she knows Django is not here to admonish her language. 'What am I going to do?' she sobs, sitting heavily on the doorstep.

You could go to the Rag and Thistle?

But I wanted Django to myself. And if he's not there, word will soon be out that I came looking. But that I didn't stay. Stupid man for not having a mobile phone!

Are you not going to wait awhile? Write a note?

And say what? 'Hi, Dad, I summoned every ounce of courage to come and see you. Oh well, never mind, I'll try again tomorrow?' No. I may as well just call a cab to take me back to the station. My gesture was meant to be momentous. But all that's happened is that the moment has passed. It's all been spoilt. It's no good. I just want to go home to Ben.

If only Django had said yes to the answering machine Pip wanted to buy him, hey?

Whatever. It was probably a stupid idea of mine anyway. Perhaps I should've run it by Pip first.

A Fish Out of Water

Django had always liked trains, but recently he liked them more so on account of Tom's fervent and endearing obsession with them. As he boarded at Chesterfield station early that morning, Django thought of Tom, thought how much he'd like to see him that day, to tell him about the Virgin train ferrying him to London and back. Wouldn't it be nice if Pip brought Tom to meet him at St Pancras? She might well have done so, had he not been Derek, the father of her youngest sister. Half sister. Anyway, they didn't know he was coming to town. Only Ben knew. He'd sent Django the ticket. Django felt uncomfortable about this. He would reimburse Ben the price of the ticket. He had the cash on him. Most, though, he felt uncomfortable about the trip itself; he didn't like London, he didn't like hospitals and he didn't like it that Ben felt it necessary to send him a ticket to ensure he'd keep the appointment.

As he settled into the seat, arranged the *Telegraph* and his Thermos flask in front of him, he tried to think of trains and tracks and north and south and not that he hadn't spoken to his girls since Pip's call to him over a fortnight ago. He curtailed the thought that told him he hadn't seen them for a month. Customarily, their visits home were every two months or so. But, devoid of all contact, this one month seemed the longest separation yet. Django thought about Cosima, wondered if she was crawling by now, imagined Fen dressing her in sweet, pink cotton creations. Did Cosima have more teeth? Did they make her grin look different? He smiled sadly but gazed out of the window as if he was particularly interested in the passengers alighting at Derby station. And was Cat perhaps pregnant, Django wondered, taking a long time to pour a cup of tea from his flask, trying to counteract the careen of the train. How wonderful that would be – although no more wonderful than Fen having Cosima or Pip having Tom of course – just a blessed situation for all three girls.

'The continuation of family,' Django said quietly, 'that's what it's all about.' And he felt appalled that his family were continuing without him. And he felt appalled that the purpose of this trip was not to visit family but to see Dr Mr Pisani. And he felt extremely disconcerted that the emotion this raised was fear.

I am seventy-five years old. I am frightened.

At Leicester, a young girl came and sat opposite Django, smiling politely before burying her nose in a novel with a candy-coloured cover festooned with illustrations of handbags, high heels and squiggly writing. So squiggly that Django had to squint hard to read the words, wondering which was the author, which was the title.

'Sandwiches, snacks, cold drinks, tea and coffee.'

The refreshments trolley was announced in robotic monotone by the stewardess, who was less trolley-dolly, more sturdy dinner-lady. Django had a good look at what was on offer because he could not believe that food could appear so unappetizing. The girl sitting opposite bought a can of fizzy something, tapping the ring-pull sharply before opening it.

'So it doesn't go insane,' she announced and Django realized he must have been staring. He felt a little awkward.
Does aluminium have sanity to lose? Is this a technique that
everyone knows about, instilled in all teenagers along with
the importance of condoms and just-say-no when it comes
to drugs? Why don't the manufacturers do something about
the design, if drinks go mad unless tapped sharply? Django
knew his thoughts were meandering excessively so that his
mind could be diverted from Dr Mr Pisani. He rummaged
around in his old canvas knapsack, the one that Pip, Fen
and Cat had each clamoured to use at some point or other
during burgeoning teenage trendiness. He took out a
Tupperware container and regarded the selection of sandwiches he had packed. The fizzy girl was looking too.

'Carrot, cheese and Marmite,' he told her, 'or tuna, piccalilli
and tomato.'

She looked at him as if he might be one of those dreaded
loonies that seem to inhabit every carriage of every train
journey one ever takes. Django showed her the sandwiches.
'Would you like one?' he offered. 'They're mostly organic.'
She shook her head though her gaze remained fixed on the
sandwiches, intrigued. 'Go on,' said Django, 'they're easy on
the calories and whatnots.' She smiled meekly and shrugged,
peering into the container and asking which were the carrot
and cheese. Django felt a sense of triumph that she took one
and, though she nibbled gingerly at first, finished the whole
thing, inch-thick crusts and all. She offered Django a Malteser
but he declined, saying forlornly he was watching his weight,
which made her giggle.

'I'm going to see my nan,' she told him, unprompted. 'She
lives near Luton.'

'I'm going to see my girls,' said Django, 'and their
offspring.'

'Are you a granddad then?' asked the girl.

Django nodded proudly.

'My granddad died when I was small and I don't remember him,' the girl said with regret, 'though I tell my nan that I do, of course.' Django didn't want to talk further on this. He was now worried he'd tempted Fate and tampered with Fortune with his white lies to the girl. But what was he meant to say – that he was going by himself to St John's Hospital so that Dr Mr Pisani could put a finger up his bottom?

'Your beads are cool,' the girl was saying.

Django touched the nibs of tiger's eye and turquoise, strung on leather around his neck. 'There's a story behind them,' he said. 'It starts in New Mexico.' And he set off on an extravagant elaboration of the truth which saved him from ruminating on whether or not he'd see his girls and their offspring ever again.

'Ta for the sarnie,' said the girl, as she disembarked at Luton, 'and have fun with your family.'

'Thank you,' said Django, 'you too.'

The train shuttled into St Pancras a quarter of an hour late. Django felt agitated; which was itself exacerbated by the unfamiliarity of the emotion. He observed people in his carriage, making calls on their mobile phones to alert whomever to the train's delay. Django would have liked to have warned Ben, but he didn't have a mobile phone. He thought of Pip offering him one as a birthday present and remembered denouncing them as preposterous, invasive and unnecessary. How his girls had laughed at him. Cat had said, Nonsense Django, you won't have one because you know you won't know how to make it work. And Fen had said, Yes yes, the apotheosis of mobile communication was via smoke signals at the reservation in North Dakota so do tell us the story featuring you and Chief Lone Hawk for the umpteenth time. And Pip had said, But Django, why don't you have one just for emergencies. And he'd been comically huffy while they teased him relentlessly and laughed. They all laughed. How they laughed. Always laughter when his girls were around.

Now he felt anxious. Leaving the train, stressed passengers bustled and shoved. Django did not like London, the pace of it all intimidated him. He felt apprehensive about taking the Tube to the hospital, with two changes of lines and escalators and people rushing and being underground. And he was already fifteen minutes late, at least, though Ben's ticket had afforded him plenty of time. He kept to his regular walking pace and attempted to wear an expression that said I know where I'm going, I'm savvy, don't shove me – and there's no need to stare.

When did buskers become beggars? I busked with Flint Maystone in Paris and we had a following. We made music. We were respected. I would go so far as to say we were the precursors of skiffle. But this isn't busking, it's begging and it's threatening and how can someone so unkempt and unsightly dare to stare at me?

But the chanting, ranting beggar wasn't the only person to stare at Django. Everyone who passed him gave him more than a passing, smileless glance. You'd've thought Django would have been more of a talking point, an eyesore even, in the calm backwaters of Derbyshire, than in the swirl of London where his physical eccentricities shouldn't raise an eyebrow or bat an eyelid. However, right from the start, when he moved to Derbyshire in 1969, hirsute and kaftan-clad, with beads clanking and pony-tail flowing, they welcomed him for bringing moccasins and Pucci neckerchiefs, Astrakhan waistcoats and voluminous, embroidered flared denims to their dale.

However, on the Victoria line decades later, people steered clear of Django, as if he might bark, in case he smelt. To his consternation, he realized they held him in the same regard as they held the ranting stinking beggar on the platform. He hardly felt that a Liberty shirt, suede waistcoat and green linen drawstring trousers warranted such suspicion. Yet it made him suddenly fret that perhaps protocol dictated the wearing of a suit to see a consultant. Soon enough he was embarrassed, ashamed even, of his apparel, denouncing himself a stupid bugger and feeling miserable. Would Ben be disappointed? Would Ben have to apologize on his behalf? If he had a mobile phone, Django supposed he could have forewarned Ben of his sartorial gaffe. Perhaps Dr Mr Pisani would decline to see him. And then he could go straight back home again.

But Ben is delighted to see Django, mainly because he'd been quite convinced that he would not appear. He's been loitering around the hospital's main entrance and silently praises Django's dress sense for holding him aloft from the crowd; a beacon of colour walking awkwardly amongst the drab bustle of everyone else.

'How was your journey?' Ben asks, guiding Django through hallways and corridors to his own office. 'Would you like a drink?'

'Scotch?' Django asks hopefully. Ben laughs. 'Is the tea plastic?' Django asks. 'Do you press a button for it?'

'No,' Ben assures him, 'Marjorie makes it in a teapot. She insists. It's why I gave her the job – that perfectionism.'

'I should like a cup of tea,' Django says and Ben calls through to Marjorie.

'How are you feeling?' Ben asks.

'Oh, you know – a little like a fish out of water,' Django confides. 'I don't like this town at all.'

'And how are you feeling otherwise,' Ben asks, 'in yourself?'

'Oh, you know,' Django dismisses any gravity, 'rather good for a gent of seventy-five. Can't complain about a rickety hip, gammy knee and mischievous waterworks.'

Ben nods and smiles. 'I didn't know you have a gammy

knee and rickety hip,' he says conversationally, though privately this concerns him.

'All that thigh-slapping to Lonnie Donegan,' Django says, 'all that toe-tapping to Namesake Reinhardt.'

'Ah,' says Ben. 'I made the appointment under *Django McCabe*.'

'Bless you,' Django says quietly.

'But do you know under what name your GP has you listed?' Ben asks.

'Well, Dr Sutton always called me *Mr* McCabe in the surgery and Django at the Rag and Thistle,' Django tells him, 'but that new young girl called me *D*. McCabe. So it could be the one, or the other.'

'OK,' says Ben, 'don't you worry. I'll handle it.' Ben looks at his watch. 'Do you have any questions? About the appointment? I'll come with you – all the way, if you like.'

'Yes, thank you, Ben,' Django says with a light laugh that belies the slight tremor of his hand when he raises the tea cup to take a sip. 'Will you tell Dr Mr Pisani that you are my personal physician and anything he says to me he can say to you too? I'm no good with medical jargon.'

Ben nods.

'Thank you,' Django nods back.

'Cat is well,' Ben tells him, 'but she doesn't know you are here.'

'Thank you,' says Django.

'And Fen and Pip are well too,' says Ben.

'Thank you,' says Django.

Ben glances at his watch. 'Well, I think we'll mosey on over now,' he says and Django is so thankful that he has Ben with him today.

Mr Pisani's appearance surprises Django who had envisaged an elongated Frankie Dettori. The consultant is in his late fifties, short and round with a very shiny pate ringed by a smile of neatly slicked grey curls. He's wearing a suit with an orange tie, has a wedding ring on his plump finger and looks like a bank manager. His accent is Scottish and his voice is quiet. Django likes him immediately though the imminence of the examination dampens much banter on his part.

Notes are taken. Information is given. Django tells Mr Pisani that Ben is his personal physician. Ben nods but also offers to leave the room, anticipating that Django might play down his symptoms if he is there. But Django says, Please stay, and he furnishes Mr Pisani with a host of details – apologizing intermittently about whether they are relevant or not. He admits that perhaps his hips and knees aren't so much rickety or gammy as really fairly painful. His lower back too. And he adds that he has steered clear of beetroot so yes, he's fairly sure it's blood in his urine.

'Prostate problems are common,' Mr Pisani smiles as if Django has something akin to a simple cold of the gland. 'Today, I'll be determining if your prostate is enlarged. And if it is – which I expect it is – what the reason may be. Most chaps over the age of fifty have an enlargement, you know, and mostly it's simply a benign condition. I'm going to take blood too. With those results – and the findings of the examination – we'll be able to see what's what and what to do.'

'Righty-ho,' says Django, looking to Ben for the nod and smile which he gives.

'I think Ben has alerted you to the procedure?' Mr Pisani asks with a sympathetic raise of his eyebrows. Suddenly, Django is concerned about the plumpness of Mr Pisani's fingers, and wishes for a tall thin Frankie Dettori. 'It may be uncomfortable – but it shouldn't be painful.'

'Django?' Ben asks, noting the colour has drained from his face.

'You will stay, won't you?' says Django.

Ben tells Django fascinating anecdotes about his time with the professional racing cyclists; he speaks quickly, jauntily and in great detail, maintaining eye contact with Django who is lying on his side. And, without asking, Ben takes his hand at the opportune moment, holding it firmly yet tenderly, talking at Django the whole time.

'Thank you, Mr McCabe,' Mr Pisani says eventually. 'I'm done. Do dress. There are tissues there. Take your time.'

'Can I help?' Ben asks Django.

'No, that's OK,' says Django. Ben sees he has a tear coursing its way down his nose.

'You did brilliantly,' Ben tells him as he pulls the curtain around to afford Django his privacy. 'Take your time.' Ben takes a seat and glances at Mr Pisani who raises his eyebrow and busies himself with his notes.

Oh Christ, thinks Ben.

'Now,' Mr Pisani says chattily when Django reappears and takes his seat, 'generally speaking – *generally* speaking – an enlarged prostate ought to feel firm and smooth. Yours feels rather hard and knobbly.'

'I see,' says Django, though he doesn't know quite what he's meant to be seeing, or what Mr Pisani was meant to be looking for.

'This may suggest something a little more serious than prostate problems,' Mr Pisani continues, 'which is why the blood test is important.'

'OK,' says Django. 'You can take an armful, if you like.'

Mr Pisani smiles and nods and says a test tube will be plenty. 'Now, you see the *symptoms* of both a benign enlargement and a malignant tumour are similar. And you have presented those symptoms. But a malignant tumour *feels* rather different to a benign enlargement.'

'A malignant tumour?'

'Most prostate cancers grow very slowly indeed, Mr McCabe.'

'*Cancer?*' Django stands up and looks at Ben in bewilderment. 'Who said anything about cancer? It's my waterworks. I'm just old.'

Al and the Girl from Purley

Despite all manner of skewed rationalization, Fen felt uncomfortable and at a loss. In the past, at such times, there was always Derbyshire to escape to – even if only in the realms of her imagination – but now not even that seemed an option. She was hardly likely to phone Django, nor did she consider the cause of her discomfort an appropriate topic of discussion between sisters. What was she meant to say? She told herself her sisters wouldn't understand – they'd go on about rocky patches and she didn't want to be judged or lectured.

Fen had long had an idiosyncrasy of looking from one hand to the other when weighing issues which irked her, to assist her in making a choice. Some saw it as an affectation, but it had proved a fail-safe method for her. For the second time in his life, Matt unknowingly was being held in Fen's left palm. Four years ago, a man called James Caulfield had been in her right palm. For a while she fought against having to choose, railed against her sisters' accusation of immorality, disputed their allegation of duplicity. She'd made her choice only when she realized the love she felt for Matt was more ordinary, thus somehow deeper and more true. And she has never looked back, never wondered *What if*, never doubted her decision. But now Matt is unwittingly back in one hand, and this time Al – whose surname she doesn't even know – is in the other; yet this time they weren't unsuspecting pawns competing for Fen's love. Love wasn't coming into it at all. On the one hand, Fen feared love was lost from her relationship. On the other hand, she feared the lure of lust. Left, right. Love, lust. Right, wrong. Her scale of values was unbalanced and tipping dangerously in favour of Al.

The easiest way to keep guilt at bay and to give her feelings for Al credibility, was to blame Matt for the irritation she felt increasingly towards him. She begrudged his freedom to go to work but also resented him for not being around more, for not helping enough, for not spending quality time with Cosima. Yet when he did, his ways got on her nerves, he got in her way and ultimately, she didn't trust him to be doing things quite right so she brushed him away, did whatever it was herself, felt put upon, then resented him. In Fen's eyes, Matt couldn't win, and she felt that this was his fault. She didn't like the sound of him eating and yet she'd never noticed it before. At night, she slept with a pillow half over her head because the incessant sound of Matt sleeping kept her awake. She didn't like the monotony of their communication; his daily question of 'And how are my girls?' set her teeth on edge – Fen didn't like it that he lumped her and Cosima together, that he only half listened to her answer anyway while he opened post or checked the television listings in the newspaper. He didn't seem to notice if Fen's hair needed a wash and she was wearing stained clothing, or there again if she'd made an effort with mascara and had changed before he arrived home. She was aware that her friends and sisters would proclaim her lucky indeed to have a man who never judged her on her looks but Fen interpreted it as Matt not really noticing her at all.

Left hand, right hand. Good, bad. Right, wrong. Harmless,

dangerous. Fen's scales appeared to be peculiarly calibrated at best; at worst downright faulty. On the one hand, the marks Fen placed against Matt became blacker, on the other hand the warning signs she'd seen in Al became fainter. Taken together, their collusion was dangerous and deluded, exacerbated by the fact that it had been almost a week since she'd seen Al and she'd heard nothing. Al's desirability increased the longer the message box on her mobile phone remained empty. The less he appeared to want her, the more she wanted to pursue him. These last few days, during which she'd consulted her phone with frustration and growing insecurity, and analysed the palms of her hands with increasing regularity, Fen had reinvented Al and invested him with much more bearing than his actual gaucherie. She reassessed his shared living arrangements in deepest darkest Camden as funky and intriguing, and in her mind's eye he'd become far more buff and beautiful. She had transposed her previous image of him as a fairly nondescript young bloke, into a vision of an arresting enigma. When Matt attempted to travel his hands over her body last night, she'd initially flinched but then an image of Al's hands came into view and even all the silver rings suddenly seemed achingly sexy. So she fucked Al while Matt made love to her. She squirmed away from Matt's post-coital cuddle and then she'd put the pillow over her head to block out the warning bells as much as Matt's breathing pattern.

Fen convinced herself that her self-esteem depended entirely on Al desiring her, that if she could just seduce him, her sense of her own femininity and self-worth would be restored. And, with her head under the pillow muffling any sound of chastisement or ridicule, she gamely justified that it would do her disintegrating relationship with Matt the power of good. She'd often read about stale relationships being rejuvenated by one or other partner having no-strings secret flings; heartening accounts of how people fell in love with their partners all over again in the aftermath of affairs. If she had a fling with Al, she'd see sense, wouldn't she? A fling with Al would prove what Matt truly meant to her, wouldn't it? A fling with Al would have a positive impact on her libido and this in turn would have a positive effect for Matt. Fen was convinced that if she had a fling with Al, she'd be doing everyone a favour.

But it had been three days since she'd seen him. And because it had been three whole days and because she'd heard nothing, Fen found it easy to transform Al from a bad idea best forgotten into an exciting challenge. She convinced herself that actually, hadn't *she* told *him* that she'd be in touch?

1.12 p.m.

`hey Al, ta 4 drinx. See u soon?`

7.56 p.m.

If Matt had at least forewarned me that he was going to be home late, I wouldn't be sitting here, feeling neglected.

8.00 p.m.

'Oh, hi – is that Al?'

'Yes?'

'It's Fen.'

'Oh – hi Fen.'

'I just thought I'd give you a quick call – I sent you a text earlier but I think I forgot to put my name to it.'

'Ah.'

'Anyway, just thought I'd give you a quick call. How are you doing?'

'Yes – good. And you?'

'Oh, you know, busy.'

'Cool. Cool.'

'Anyway – I'd better go, I suppose. I just thought – maybe meet up for a quick drink or something?'

'Cool – I'll give you a call.'

'Great.'

'OK, Fen – bye then.'

'Bye. Oh. When? Ish?'

'Sorry?'

'Us fusty old mums need time to organize babysitters – so I was just wondering if you had an idea of when? You know – when you'd be calling and when we'd meet up?'

'Oh. Soon. Next couple of days?'

'Great. Bye Al.'

'See you, Fen.'

That call was crap. Ought I to text him to rectify? Should I just compose one and see how it looks on the screen? Or should I sit on my hands and watch Grand Designs *and keep shtum?*

Who are you asking, Fen?

And by the way, where is Matt?

Matt is having an impromptu drink after work with an old mate, Jake, with whom he shared a flat and a certain level of rakishness in their twenties. Though their thirties have led them onto divergent paths, their friendship continues and they like to meet up every now and then and live vicariously through one another, just for the duration of an entertaining evening. Jake has taken to calling Matt 'Daddy', and Matt calls Jake 'Twat'. They are in Soho and the area is buzzing. Matt hates to admit even to himself how long it has been since he last had a night out in town; he hadn't thought he'd missed it, he wasn't aware of having craved it but it's reviving to be back here, heading through the colourful milling crowd to a bar, past shops specializing in everything from whisky to ship's chandlery, gay paraphernalia to hip and costly trainers, from sushi to sex. The bar is new to Matt though Jake informs him it's been open awhile, and is *the* place to drink and Where the fuck have you been, Daddy – it's where all manner of media scandal and celebrity debauchery are often chronicled. Shut up, Twat, and buy me a beer.

While Jake orders, Matt quietly wonders if he looks out of place, whether it's obvious that he's more accustomed to slouching in front of the television with a ready meal and being in bed by midnight. He scouts other people's clothing and footwear, feeling slightly faded and last-season in comparison; resolves to spend a lunch-time and a wage packet in Paul Smith the next day. Does he feel out of place? A little, just a little at the moment. But beer will help and make all equal.

'They only do bizarre beer in piss-pale shades from places like Latvia,' Jake apologizes, setting down two over-designed bottles in front of them. 'Cheers anyway.'

'Cheers mate,' says Matt. 'How's it going?'

'Madly busy at work,' Jake rues, 'and complicated as ever at play.'

Matt laughs. Jake lights a cigarette and offers one to Matt who falters for a moment and then takes one. He was only ever a social smoker but the arrival of Cosima stipulated a nicotine-free zone and now, the head rush he experiences after the first few drags is slightly disconcerting yet nostalgic and oddly liberating.

'There's this girl,' Jake is saying, clasping the cigarette between his lips as he describes her assets crudely with his hands. 'She's a total babe – Suze – pretty young but bloody bright. Anyway, I thought she was just after a good time, you know?'

Matt nods sagely as if he does.

'Suited me fine – absolutely. You know, finally a woman after my own heart – or rather, not after my heart but only my body. No-strings sex and the like. But the weird thing is,' Jake continues, *sotto voce*, 'increasingly I find myself wanting a bit more.' Jake slaps the table and roars with laughter. 'What the fuck is all that about then? Usually they harp on at *me* about mini-breaks and meeting my parents and bollocks, and here I am, toying with the idea of asking her to move in. Here's *me*, pissed off if *she* hasn't phoned all day!'

'Bloody hell!' Matt marvels, with a glug and a drag.

'Bloody hell is right,' Jake says darkly. 'Wedding bells and babies.'

'Have you talked to her?' Matt asks. Jake answers him with a look of ridicule.

'As I say, she hasn't phoned all day,' says Jake morosely, 'but I'm damned if I'm going to call her.'

'I meant,' says Matt, 'have you talked to her about – you know – how you feel? Longevity? The C word.'

'Cunt?' says Jake.

'*Commitment*,' says Matt. 'Twat.'

'Well. Almost. You see, what complicates it,' Jake says, 'is that Ellie is still on the scene – casually.' Matt covers his eyes in mock distaste. 'I mean, I never ring her, really. Well, not really,' says Jake. 'Sometimes I do – if I'm bored or drunk or both. And when she rings me – well, it's a bit mad to turn it down, isn't it?'

To Matt, Jake's life sounds dictionary-definition mad. Momentarily, it all seems a little unsavoury too, unnecessarily complicated and way too tiring. It's not a been-there, done-that derision Matt feels as he never quite subscribed to Jake's low-level ethics, more it's an uncomfortable feeling of what the allure can still be for Jake. Isn't he bored after well over a decade of bawdiness? Oughtn't he to have outgrown such philandering? Doesn't he aspire to a more grown-up way of life? A quiet side of Matt is slightly insulted that his own lifestyle, the developments and changes, the achievements and differences, appear to hold little attraction for Jake. Though Jake usually asks after Fen, after the baby, after the mortgage and the mundanity, Matt detects a perfunctory edge before Jake deviates to humorous accounts of his own ongoing hedonism. Jake is a great raconteur – and that's the point of such evenings. But Matt has to admit that the fact that their lives are now so disparate is also the reason that they now meet so infrequently.

However, alcohol is a great leveller. Once a certain level of inebriation has been reached, Matt finds he and Jake are blokes with equal charisma, wit and highly entertaining neuroses. So they drink and they smoke and they banter. They put the world to rights, they re-train the England soccer squad and they recite lengthy tracts from *The Office*. Jake confides that he had to be treated for chlamydia after a mad week in Aya Napa and Matt reveals that a baby and a sex life is a contradiction in terms.

'Do you not fancy Fen like you used to?' Jake asks, with slurred concern. 'I've heard about this – it's a syndrome, mate. Once you've seen what her vagina is really for, you can never see it as your playpen again.'

But Matt shakes his head.

'Oh!' Jake whispers. 'Oh.' He nods his head earnestly. 'I've heard about that too,' he says. 'It's another syndrome – that childbirth alters, well, the feel of the fuck. Like a familiar room with all the furniture moved around. Or, worse, *gone*.'

Matt laughs but shakes his head. Jake looks a little surprised that he's wrong again.

'Too tired?' he tries.

'Partly,' says Matt.

'Oh God – she's not up the duff again is she?'

'Hardly!' Matt snorts. He contemplates the cocoon of ash lying pristine on his knee. He flicks it away. 'I'm not getting it because Fen seems to have gone off me.'

'Maybe she's still – you know – *sore*?'

'What, ten months on?' Matt argues. 'Mate – it's like her opinion of herself has altered. She has this whole new identity. She loves being a mummy but she's not that into being my girlfriend.'

'She turns you down?' Jake is appalled.

'I guess,' says Matt, 'yes. And when we do have sex – I sense it's more like she just wants a simple shag. An orgasm – and quick.'

'Man,' sighs Jake, 'I've been searching my whole life for a simple shag.'

Matt shrugs. 'You know what I mean.'

Jake doesn't, but he nods anyway as he's not particularly interested in developing this strand of the conversation.

'You know something,' says Matt, 'I wonder if we hadn't had Cosima whether we'd have split up by now.' He picks at the label on the beer bottle. 'But I also wonder if our relationship would have been better without having a baby. Terrible thing to think, really.'

'Like you can't have the one without the other – or you can't have both? Or something?' Jake asks, his eyes drawn to three girls ordering at the bar.

'Something like that,' says Matt.

'Fantastic,' says Jake. Matt frowns until he realizes he's referring to the girls who are sending lascivious glances in their direction.

Usually, the point at which Jake starts to prowl is when Matt decides to bale out and go home. He tends to glance at his watch and calculate the maximum sleep he needs against the hours of sleep he's actually going to have. This is when Matt usually slaps Jake on the shoulder and tells the girl, or girls, to look after his mate. And this is the point when Jake says 'Goodnight, Daddy' and feels a slight sense of relief that he's free to continue the evening in his own inimitable way. This is when Matt goes home. As you'd expect. He's a father after all. It's not seemly to drink into the small hours; it's irresponsible. So go home, Matt.

But Matt sees little point in going home. Fen will just say he stinks of booze and fags and forbid him from going anywhere near the baby and then reproach him for the fact that it all amounts to her being the one who's always up at the crack of dawn despite her matchless tiredness. So Matt doesn't go home because just now he doesn't like who's at home; what he likes more is the upbeat revelry of his immediate milieu. And he likes the girls who have come, pouting and posturing over to him and Jake. He likes the way one of them licks her lips while he's speaking. She's hanging on his words and his arm because she's a little unsteady on her feet; not surprising, considering the combination of cocktail and the precarious height of her fuck-me shoes. Matt doesn't quite know what he's talking about but she seems to find him scintillating and hysterically funny. When she throws her head back like that, her throat looks so lickable. He likes her pierced navel, there's a sparkly dangly thing hanging from it. And look at the tantalizing wobble of her high, nubile – oh Christ – braless breasts.

What did you say her name was, Matt?

'Are you married?' she's asking him.

'Nope,' Matt says.

'Is your mate?' she asks, trying to focus on Jake who has an arm around each of her friends.

'God no,' Matt laughs.

'I'm so pissed,' she complains, lolling into Matt's chest.

'Me too,' Matt agrees, using it as an excuse to drape his

arm around her and flop his hand down to the small of her back. If she brings her face up, he knows they'll snog. In fact, he wants her to, so he strokes the small of her back and extends his fingertips beyond the unmistakable boundary to her buttocks. Up comes her face and in slips Matt's tongue. He can taste Bailey's and Marlboro Lights. For the first time in five years, he is sharing his mouth with a woman other than Fen.

'Hey! Daddy!' says Jake. 'Let's go to Eddie's.'

Matt takes his mouth away from the girl's though his hand keeps her clasped against him. 'Who's Eddie?' he asks, wondering why Jake isn't raising eyebrows at him, or looking remotely shocked, or even amused.

'It's this late-night drinking den in Dean Street,' Jake says with a glance around, as if embarrassed to be in the company of someone who's never heard of Eddie's.

'Why did he call you Daddy?' the girl is asking Matt, who ignores her.

'Nah!' Matt says to Jake. 'I'm going to head home.'

The girls with Jake look at their friend. 'You coming to Eddie's?' they ask her.

'Nah,' she says, just like Matt.

Jake and the girls shrug, say a brief goodbye and head off.

So, Matt, are you going to head home then?
Yeah, I'll just have one for the road first.
One what?

When it's very late and you're drunk and horny in a bar in Soho, where do you go? As Matt snogs the girl, he asks himself this question. They're still in the bar, but they've found an enclave with a curved leather banquette. He's bought them a drink which they haven't yet touched. They've been groping at each other while sucking face; there's a teenage randiness to it all which Matt is, literally, lapping up. He is sitting, legs spread, with a hard-on bulging shamelessly through his trousers. Every now and then, the girl sweeps her hand over it in a kind of maintenance check. Matt's been feeling her breasts through her top and because it's so skimpy and because she's not wearing anything underneath, she's as good as naked to his touch.

'Let's go back to yours,' she suggests.

Matt looks at her as if she's mad. But how's she to know his child and the mother of his child are there? He's told her Jake calls him Daddy because he's the eldest. He's told her he calls Jake Twat because he is one.

'Can't,' he replies to her, 'there are people there.'

She shrugs this off.

'Where do you live then?' he asks.

'Purley,' she says.

Even in his drunken state and despite his aching balls, Matt assesses that Purley is pointless. The taxis would cost a fortune. 'Purley,' he says. 'Oh.'

'There's the loos here,' she says. 'They're big and posh and this place turns a blind eye to people going in pairs.' She taps the side of her nose as if she knows a secret and it takes a while for Matt to realize she's alluding to cocaine.

'Have you got any?' he asks, actually feeling his desire for drugs is more iniquitous than the adulterous lust bulging in his trousers.

'Ruby's got the wrap,' she says forlornly, 'but I reckon your mate had most of it anyway.'

Matt thinks he's probably relieved. At the same time, he's slightly disconcerted that he didn't realize Jake had been doing drugs that evening. That Jake hadn't offered any to him. Though, in all probability, Matt would have refused. If this girl had in fact had some, would he? He's too drunk to debate it. She's winking at him, nodding her head in the direction of the toilets.

And off they go, hand in hand, no one is in the lead.

The cubicle is spacious; faux panelled with strangely subdued lighting. There's loo paper on the floor and a Vent-Axia whirring away, affording a contradictory soundproofing of sorts. As soon as they're in, with a giggle and a fast lock of the door, they're snogging and fumbling and grappling and groping again. Matt has pulled her top to one side so he can see her tits in the flesh. They're fabulous: sizeable but pert with keen dark nipples craving his attention. While he sucks, she ruffles his hair through her fingers, backs up against the wall and spreads her legs, guiding his hand up in between. He rubs his fingers ravenously against the gusset of her thong. She gyrates against him and his thumb probes under the material to the lips of her sex. She's shaven. He's aching, there's a sackload of spunk which has been cramped in the holding bay of his balls for what seems like hours.

'Have you got a condom, then?' she asks. Matt frowns. 'You've got to pull out then, all right?'

In spite of the alcohol, Matt's inner voice is suddenly sharply lucid. The harder the facts of the imminence of infidelity, the softer his cock becomes. Man's best friend. Warning balls. He's far more grateful for his flaccidness than he is embarrassed by it.

'Don't worry,' she says sweetly, glancing at Matt's limp penis and she sits on the toilet and takes a pee. 'Another time, maybe? Shall we go to Eddie's?' she says conversationally, while wiping herself with loo paper and righting her thong. 'See if Twat and the girls are there?'

'I'm going to head home,' Matt says.

'Will you see me into a cab, then?' she asks.

And he does. And he says that of course he'll call her though he's aware that she's not aware that she hasn't given him her number nor asked for his. He flags down a taxi for her and watches it go. He finds that he's now utterly sober. So sober that his mind is reeling with frantic theories on what constitutes infidelity. He doesn't want a cab, he wants to walk and think and fast. As he marches up Wardour Street, weaving his way through all the people, he wonders if he just cheated on Fen. He justifies that he was drunk. He reasons that it wasn't sex anyway, in the penetrative sense. When push was about to come to shove, he had not wanted it, regardless of the state of his cock. But had what he had done amounted to being unfaithful? Was it possible to rank degrees of infidelity and if so, how far down the scale had he just stooped? He'd snogged another woman, had a grope and a feel. So his heart hadn't been in it, his mind hadn't been on it, his dick hadn't been sucked and his conscience had remained firmly trothed to Fen. But the urge had been there and whose fault was that? Could he blame Fen? Or had he only himself to blame? Or should he marvel that his love for her had caused his inner voice to yell out, Stop? He crossed over Oxford Street and walked briskly along Tottenham Court Road, feeling slightly hostile towards the pockets of pissed-up people for whom a night out in town was still young and promising. Despite the crowds of people, no one but him had any thoughts of home so he flagged a taxi with ease.

'Good night out?' the cabbie asks him chirpily, having passed comment on the weather, the traffic conditions and Ken Livingstone.

'Crap,' Matt says, glowering at his reflection in the window.

'Coming home empty-handed are we?' the cabbie chuckles. 'Your powers of persuasion let you down tonight?'

Matt looks up, straight into the eyes of the cabbie staring back at him from the rear-view mirror. 'Quite the opposite,' Matt says. 'She was up for it. I wasn't.'

'Heart strings not plucked, then?'

Christ will he not just shut up!

'My heart's at home,' Matt says while wondering why he hadn't shut up, himself.

'Ah,' the cabbie sighs, 'so you knocked temptation back to touch. Good for you, mate.'

'I had a touch,' Matt mumbles, 'it didn't feel good at all.'

'Precisely,' says the cabbie, 'so it *was* good for you.'

Cat Out of the Bag

The last thing Matt felt like doing, two days later, was to go out again. However, the choke of guilt, the nauseated regret, became more severe in Fen's presence. When he was at work, he longed to be at home, as if he imagined Fen and, to a lesser extent Cosima, suddenly unprotected without him there. When he was apart from her, he desperately needed her in sight – even if this meant apologizing to her photograph which he carried in his wallet. He stroked the image with the tip of his little finger, proclaiming to her that he'd never drink again, that he'd see no more of Jake, that he'd re-focus his eyes for Fen alone. What had happened was nothing, just stupidity; it had felt vile, a lesson had been learnt. Or so he kept telling himself. Yet in Fen's company, he couldn't even meet her eye, so convinced was he that he wore his sin as a sandwich board, guilt writ large all over his face. All he could do was feign tiredness as the cause for his uncommunicativeness, close himself off by watching *The West Wing* on DVD, while Fen made much of doing all the tidying up, all the cooking and all the laundry. When Matt did glance at her, hoping to bestow a loving, affirming smile, he found himself flinching away, as if her top was emblazoned with You fucking bastard how could you. So, though a part of Matt felt he should go home directly, to silently beg her forgiveness and declare his utter steadfastness and enduring loyalty, when Ben phoned and suggested they meet at the Mariners, Matt embraced the opportunity to be distracted from both his atonement and culpability.

Ben had beers waiting for them.

'How's life?' Zac asked. 'Pip told me about Cat's non-trip up North. Is she OK?'

Ben took a visibly deep breath. 'She'll be fine,' he said, 'but I have to tell you both something and it's about Django.' Ben looked from Matt to Zac and saw the same look of surprise and enquiry. 'He's told me to tell you. It's not nice. The long and short of it is he came to the hospital for some tests and he has prostate cancer.'

'For fuck's sake,' said Matt, closing his hand over his eyes.

'Cancer?' said Zac. 'Jesus.' Ben let the news sit with them a moment. 'Hang on,' said Zac, 'he was down *here*? In London? When?'

'The day that Cat went up to Derbyshire,' Ben said, shaking his head. 'Last Wednesday. I made an appointment and sent him a train ticket. It was the only way I could be sure he'd have it looked into – he wouldn't go to his GP. And I'd noticed some signs a while ago – before all the Derek–Mother shit.'

'Does Cat know now?'

'No. He didn't want anyone to know. And now he wants me to tell you. And us to tell them.'

'Christ,' Zac and Matt said in unison.

'Poor sod,' Matt said sadly. 'What's the prognosis?'

'It's difficult to say at this stage,' said Ben. 'It's not uncommon and it's usually very slow growing – sometimes the effect of the treatment is much worse than the symptoms of the cancer itself. Often sufferers can live out a normal lifespan. However, he has pain in his hip, leg and back which suggests it may have spread to the bone. He's only had a physical exam and blood tests. Now he needs an ultrasound, then we're into the territory of biopsies and scans. The results will take a while but they'll show the grade and stage of the cancer.'

Matt and Zac sat silent and shocked. 'I can't believe this,' Matt said with audible alarm.

'What treatment will he have?' Zac said.

'It depends on what the tests reveal,' Ben said. 'It's not my area. But I know around one in twelve men are diagnosed with this illness. He may have had it for years – it tends to be without symptoms in the early stages.'

'I can't believe it,' Matt rued again. 'What are we going to do about the girls?'

'I have no sodding idea,' Ben sighed, 'which is why I thought we should meet. Cat is up and down at the moment.'

'Fen too,' said Matt.

'And Pip,' said Zac.

'Is he OK?' Zac asked. 'You know, psychologically?'

Ben smiled sadly. 'Beneath the neckerchief and dodgy trousers, there's an ill man of seventy-five. And unfortunately, the tests are pretty unpleasant.'

'Is he coming back down for the tests?' Zac asked. 'Perhaps we could arrange for him to see the girls then?'

'He's been referred to his local oncology department,' Ben said.

'He needs support,' Matt said, 'he needs his girls.'

'So what are we going to do about them?' Zac asked. 'I could tell Pip,' he offered, 'then she could tell the others? She's suggested to them that the three of them should go up to Derbyshire soon, anyway.'

Matt nodded but Ben shook his head. 'I don't know. I

know their traditional dynamic is to look to Pip for advice – but that dynamic was turned on its head by the mother showing up and the Derek business and the whole parentage thing. I speak for Cat, of course,' said Ben, 'because I think somewhere, deep down, she just can't help fearing that she's slightly less of a sister to your two than they are to each other.'

'Which is horse shit,' Matt assured him, backed up by Zac raising his glass.

'I know that,' said Ben. 'It's stupid, I know, but it's where her mind is at just now.'

'They should know at the same time,' Zac said. 'I could do a dinner gathering and we could tell them all together.'

'I don't know,' Matt said. 'It's going to be such a massive thing – we don't know how they'll react individually. And then there's Cosima – if we're round at yours, Fen will have half her mind on how the baby is.'

'Good point,' said Ben, 'and I think Cat might feel a bit compromised – like we've engineered a situation. She's very particular about her comfort zone at the moment – even if it is behind the closed doors of our rental place in Clapham.'

'The thing is, we *are* going to need to engineer it,' said Zac.

'Meticulously,' Matt agreed.

The three men sipped their beer contemplatively, half their thoughts directed to Django, half to their girls. 'I reckon we tell them separately but at the same time,' said Ben. 'We agree on a time, and specific information – perhaps down to the very wording.'

Matt and Zac nodded in agreement. 'I think we also let them know that we met to discuss this,' said Matt, 'that it's what Django wants. And that they're each hearing the news at the same time in the same way.'

'OK,' said Zac, 'this is good. We also need to decide which

order they'll phone each other. I know it sounds contrived but our McCabe girls have a tendency to leap on their emotional high horses and bolt. We can't have them all in a scatter – they're going to need each other.'

'Agreed,' said Matt and Ben.

'You find in traumatic situations, those involved need assistance in deciding what to do and how to do it,' said Ben. 'Cat is still insecure, somewhere, about the dynamic between her and her sisters. Perhaps she should make the first call. I'll have her phone Pip – and then Pip can phone Fen?'

Matt and Zac nod. They've gone off their beer.

'This is crap news,' Matt said forlornly. 'Really horrible.'

'It'll be the making or the breaking of them,' Zac agreed.

'As a family,' defined Ben, 'as well as individually.'

They dreaded being grilled by the girls when they arrived home because it had been settled that nothing would be said until 9 p.m. the following evening when the situation would be revealed according to the information advised by Ben, the precise wording honed by the three of them.

When Zac arrived home, Pip was watching a cable health channel about having babies, but she zapped over to E4 hurriedly.

'How was your evening?' she asked casually, reducing the volume.

'Fine,' Zac said, 'but you carry on. I have a little work to do.' And he disappeared with his laptop to sit on the edge of the bed, feeling winded and sad.

Matt came home to find Fen already asleep. He spooned up gently against her and mouthed 'Sorry' over and over again into her hair.

'You reek of booze,' she muttered sleepily, hitching her shoulder up a little to block him out.

Cat was full of beans when Ben returned because Jeremy was leaving to run the Basingstoke branch of Dovidels and had intimated to Cat that she should apply for his post.

'Everything's looking up,' Cat exclaimed, giving him a hug.

The Ten o'Clock News

Fen's morning started very well indeed. It was warm enough to dress Cosima in a broderie anglaise sundress with matching puffy knickers and frilled cloche hat which Matt's mother had bought her. The baby looked adorable and her matchless beauty in her mother's eyes made the day seem even more balmy. There were new gurgles, from which Fen could deduce a private language of sorts and she conversed with her daughter enthusiastically, not caring how daft she might sound. Cosima was also trying out a commando slither precrawl and Fen could not be more proud had her baby stood up and danced a jig. Strolling along to Musical Minis, chortling to Cosima in gobbledygook, pointing out the red letter-box, the nice mister postman and the big yellow truck, Fen felt her mobile phone vibrate through a message. She retrieved it from the back pocket of her jeans, the pair she'd been able finally to fit back into today, oh joyous day, for the first time, not minding that they felt comfortably snug.

Hi f - drinx 2nite? Al

Feeling comfortingly smug, Fen spent the next half-hour composing various answers whilst singing the tunes at Musical Minis by rote. Her walk home had her weigh up which order was best – phone Pip to check babysitting was possible, or text Al first to accept and then work through babysitting options later. Her sense of maternal duty was far stronger than her sense of adventure so she called Pip first.

'Shouldn't be a problem at all,' said Pip.

'Are you sure you don't mind coming to mine, though?' Fen double-checked. 'I'll be able to give Cosima her supper but then you'll be in charge of bath, bottle, bed.'

'No probs,' said Pip, 'we'll flood the house, drink the fridge dry and have a pillow fight. Who's this friend?'

'Oh, just Al – we meet up every now and then.'

'Have I met her?' Pip asked.

Fen realized that if she denied Al a gender, she could further avoid revealing her agenda to Pip. 'Probably,' she said casually. 'Thanks – you're the best auntie in the world.'

'You mean the best auntie north of the river,' Pip laughed. 'Have you spoken to Auntie Cat?'

'Yes, we had a chat yesterday when the boys were out,' said Fen.

'I think she sounds a bit brighter,' said Pip.

'I agree,' Fen agreed.

'We really should think about making a trip home,' said Pip, 'the three of us together.'

'You're right,' said Fen. 'Tell us when.'

The morning had not been going well for Matt and just before lunch-time, it became worse. The network at the office was still down, the art editor had thrown up in the corridor, the printers were breathing down Matt's neck and the news about Django was playing on his mind. So when he saw it was Fen bleeping through a text message, what he really hoped for was the tonic of sweet nothings. After all, it had been her speciality in their courtship days – daft e-mails and cute texts

282

and the occasional soppy card sent by snail-mail to work. Old-fashioned and romantic was the girl he'd fallen for. He had to admit, sadly, that since having Cosima, if texts came from Fen at all, they were usually asking what time he'd be back and could he detour via `Marx+Sparx`. What Matt needed just then was a `thnkng of u F xxx`. What he read was something else.

`havng drinx w/ old pal Al this pm - wont`
`b late. Pip bb-sittng - don't rush! F x`

Matt swivelled in his chair and racked his memory for an old pal called Al. Then he re-read the message and wondered why just the one kiss. Then he thought, Shit! she can't – not tonight, sorry Al – and he phoned Zac directly.

'Slight problem,' he said to Zac. 'Fen's organized a drink with some old friend and has roped Pip in to babysit until I'm back.'

'Damn,' pondered Zac. 'How can we prevent this without suspicions being raised?'

'I don't know,' said Matt. 'It's so rare for Fen to go out anyway. Any ideas?'

'I could call Pip,' Zac said, 'think of something that makes babysitting not possible – make her let Fen down?'

'Great,' said Matt. Then he paused. 'No it's not. We can't have anything come between the sisters today – and you know their potential to strop and sulk with each other.'

'God, you're right,' said Zac, who privately didn't want anything to come between him and his wife at the moment either. Recently she'd been not so much distracted as frosty.

'I'll phone Ben,' said Matt, 'and get back to you.'

'I was just about to call you,' Ben responded calmly to Matt's concern. 'Panic not – Cat called to say she's working a late shift to impress some honcho or other from head office – so let's just change mission time to 10 o'clock?'

'Twenty-two hundred hours,' Matt said through his fist to sound like a war film fighter-pilot, 'roger that.'

'Will Fen be back by then?' Ben asked. 'And sober?'

'Nowadays she is practically asleep by 9.30 and decrees more than two glasses of spritzer to be anathema to motherhood,' Matt said. 'You wait and see – Cat'll be the same.'

Privately, Ben hoped Cat wouldn't keep him waiting too long on that front. 'Listen,' he said to Matt, 'hope it goes well.'

'Yes,' said Matt, 'for you, too.'

'We'll touch base later,' Ben said.

'We will,' said Matt. He phoned Zac. 'Sorted. We have a later kick-off set for 10 o'clock.'

'Good,' said Zac, 'thanks for that.'

'Bizarre, isn't it,' Matt said darkly, 'to make light of it is the only way I can deal with it at the moment. Because actually, I'm fucking dreading it.'

'Me too,' Zac agreed. 'God – me too.'

'Speak later,' said Matt. 'Good luck.'

Matt and Zac and Ben sat there, in their offices, their working day stretching ahead replete with other people's problems. Ben had a wincing queue of twisted ankles and torn ligaments clamouring for his attention; Zac had corporate clients shirking millions of taxable pounds onto his shoulders; Matt had the irate printers and the hacking wafts of his art editor's vomit to deal with. But it all seemed like child's play in relation to the task and trauma of the evening to come.

'She's eaten loads,' Fen said proudly, delighting in her sister's obvious adoration of her daughter. Pip took Cosima from Fen and pulled what her family call her Guppy Face. Cosima glanced at her mother, as if to double-check this gurning lady was indeed funny, as if to seek parental go-ahead to chortle at this fish-faced auntie. Everything was making Fen laugh today and she and her baby squeaked with delight as Pip ran through her entire repertoire of animal impersonations, from chameleon to tortoise to two-toed sloth.

'She's so gorgeous,' Pip declared mistily, stroking Cosima's silk-fine hair.

'I know,' Fen cooed, 'she's the best little girl in the world.'

'You are *so* lucky,' Pip said while giving Cosima an affectionate squeeze.

'I made a list,' Fen said, with apologetic guilt, glancing towards the sheet of paper on the kitchen table. Pip raised her eyebrow. She could see it was densely written and awash with asterisks. 'Humour me?' Fen implored.

'If it says, Check milk temperature – I'll be offended,' Pip said.

'Of course it says, Check milk temperature,' Fen said, 'and the bath temperature too—'

'Use the inside of my wrist for the former, the outside of my elbow for the latter,' Pip mocked before Fen could say just that. 'Go and get yourself ready,' Pip chided, 'or you'll be late. I think I have met Al.'

'Yes?' Fen said vaguely. 'We're not that close – just fun to meet for a quick drink every now and then. We're hardly bosom buddies.' And suddenly an image of Al getting to know her bosoms simultaneously horrified yet thrilled her and she hurried away to change.

Pip couldn't decide whether to continue cuddling Cosima or to flop to the carpet and play with her. It was 5.30, just a precious hour and a half to fit in games, baths, bottles and bedtime cuddles. Fen was certainly indulging in a long shower. 'Hope she doesn't take all the hot water,' Pip said to Cosima, 'because I'm going to make you a great big bubbly bath.' She had to admit Cosima didn't seem remotely bothered and smelt good enough to eat anyway.

When Fen reappeared, Pip was quite taken aback. She hadn't seen her sister look like this for a long time. And she looked great. Her hair was glossy, having been blow-dried to perfection, and she'd eschewed her customary pony-tail to wear her hair loose and lovely. Her make-up was subtle but meticulous. She was in a dress Pip was sure she hadn't seen before though quite when Fen had taken herself shopping she didn't know. And wasn't it just a week or so ago that she'd endured that unsuccessful trip to Whistles?

'You look amazing,' Pip said. She frowned. Odd to make so much effort for someone who was hardly a bosom buddy. 'Is that dress new?'

Fen nodded guiltily. 'You can borrow it if you like.'

'Well, you look particularly gorgeous –' Pip said and though she'd intended to finish the sentence there, the niggle at the back of her mind made itself heard, '– for a quick drink with someone you only see once in a while.' Just then, Pip couldn't work out if her sister feigned not to hear or did not deign to comment but she did note that Fen did not want Cosima's dribbly kisses or sticky fingers anywhere near her frock. 'Doesn't your mummy look pretty!' Pip cooed to Cosima, trying to hand the baby over, but Fen busied herself with a glass of water. 'Where are you meeting?' Pip asked, because it was a reasonable question. She set Cosima down at Fen's feet.

'Some bar in Camden,' Fen replied, stooping awkwardly to stroke her baby's head whilst tucking the fabric beyond her touch.

'Why Camden?'

'Oh, Al suggested it,' said Fen casually, 'it's his stamping ground.'

'Well, that sounds like your cab,' Pip said airily though she was awash with the information confirming Al as male. 'Have a great time – and don't worry about Cosima.'

'Thanks,' said Fen, gazing reflectively, momentarily guiltily, at the baby in her sister's arms. 'Thanks. Nighty-night gorgeous girl.'

Pip marvelled that Cosima waved to her mummy all by herself. It seemed just the other day that her chubby little arm had to be held aloft on her behalf. It felt so nice to have the weight of the baby hitched on her hip. Once she closed the door, she went to the mirror, delighted that the sight looked as natural as it felt.

'So,' said Pip, taking the baby upstairs, 'so Al's a "he". If your mummy tried to hide the fact from me, what can she have told your daddy?'

Pip trusted the veracity of her vibes in the same way that Fen trusted the palms of her hands, and just then Pip's vibe was one of warning. Her instinct to protect kicked in, but she wasn't sure who warranted it first or the most. Cosima? Matt? Or in fact Fen? If she was to protect Cosima from a misbehaving mother, if she were to protect Matt from aban- donment, and both Cosima and Matt from potential heartache, she should reach out to Fen first. But Fen was being evasive, Fen was being deceitful, Fen wouldn't look her in the eye and give her a straight answer. Fen had every- thing to hide and thus nothing to confide. Though Pip felt very angry with her sister she felt impotent too; if her sister felt beyond reproach it was because she'd carefully taken herself out of sight and far from earshot, down to Camden for a secret rendezvous with some bloke called Al.

'She's made me an accessory to her crime – roping me in to babysit,' Pip said in a sing-song voice. She mounded bubbles on Cosima's head. 'Poor Cosi. Am I facilitating this – unwittingly or not – whatever it may be?' She sponged the baby gently. 'It's bad enough your mummy is using me – it's worse that she's consciously deceiving me too. But would I feel differently if she had asked outright, if she'd said, Cover for me, Pip? Would I have covered for her then?'

Pip smiled at the baby. One of a clown's skills is to multi-task, to juggle whilst singing, to converse solemnly whilst limbs veer off on an energetic mime of their own, to talk to the audience earnestly whilst concentrating on sleight of hand, to tell jokes with a straight face, to appear to be doing one thing yet enabling something else to be happening. So while Pip bathed the baby and sang about the AllyAllyOh, she thought about Fen. And Al. As much as she wanted to denounce her, she had to consider how lovely Fen had looked. It was so much more than the sum of a gorgeous frock, clean hair and careful make-up. She glowed on account of her demeanour. Pip had to concede that Fen appeared hearteningly, refreshingly ebullient.

'I remember that Fen,' Pip said nostalgically, 'but I'm worried about this one.'

Fen was right on time and momentarily she wondered whether to tell the cab-driver to go on a little, so she could walk back and not risk arriving before Al for a second time. But then she reasoned that if Al was there already she'd be denying herself his company. So she went in. And of course Al wasn't there yet.

She bought herself a tonic water because she wanted to pace herself and anyway, she could always say it was vodka and tonic. The bar was painted purple and, with the dark red plush booths and tea lights everywhere, the interior seemed far more convivial to a winter setting than the gorgeous June evening. Fen told herself that perhaps she'd simply brazenly suggest they have a quick one here and go on somewhere else.

I only want a little bit of fun; I hope to take home something I can call upon and remember when I'm feeling frumpy or weighed down by the drudge of the day – something to raise a private smile when it's most needed. Isn't everyone entitled to a small, risk-free escapade? Don't little secrets go a long way? I can feed my soul without hurting a soul.

She checked her phone. No messages. Al was now ten minutes late. And her tonic water was nearly finished.

Here he is.

'Shit – Fen, I'm so sorry,' Al flustered. 'I just completely – well, anyway, I'm sorry. How are you? Can I get you a drink? What's that?'

'Don't worry!' Fen implored him, dismissing his apologies as unnecessary. 'No problem! I was late myself! I'd love a drink – vodka and tonic, please.'

She snuck a glance at him while he ordered. He looked different to last week. Shorter, younger, plainer. That ghastly, cheap, tinny jewellery. Momentarily, Fen felt disappointed, as if all her efforts were somewhat unwarranted. But when he brought her drink over, set it down, kissed her cheek as he sat and commented on how nice she smelt, she called herself a daft cow and told herself to have fun because she was in control.

And she did have fun. She had fun because she could not afford for the evening to be anything but. She contrived to come across as lively and feisty and before long, she believed that she was. She ignored it when Al said things that were slightly puerile or rather dull and she tried not to waste time feeling irritated by him drumming along to music she didn't know, his index fingers chopping the table edge, his top teeth biting down on his bottom lip as if he were in torment. Her job was not to judge Al, but to present herself. So she tossed her hair and dipped her head coyly and licked her lips lasciviously and fluttered her eyelashes becomingly. It didn't really matter what she thought of him, just as long as she could weave some kind of spell that had him craving her. She knew to flatter him, to pout a little while he spoke, to laugh in excess. And to touch him. Every now and then she laid her hand on his arm, his wrist, nudged his knee. When he teased her about her not knowing some new band or other, she flicked his chin with her finger. And he caught her hand and while he held it for a suspended moment, she had the presence of mind to raise her eyebrow cockily and belie the welling adrenalin causing her stomach to flip.

'Shall we go on somewhere?' Fen asked because a football match was now being shown on the plasma screen and Al's eyes were drawn to it. He looked at her. 'Silly game,' she said.

'Go back to mine?' Al suggested, a little drunk by now. 'My place is just around the corner.' Fen stood up as her answer, smoothed her dress and jutted her bust just within the ambivalent side of perceptibly.

After the gloom of the purple interior, the bright evening was dazzling. A small voice told her to suggest a walk along the canal, a snack at an outside table, an ice cream from Marine Ices, but Al's hand around her waist led her away from such thoughts.

I won't stay if there are batik bedspreads as wall hangings.
There aren't.
I won't stay if there are lads lolling about.
There are lads lolling about, watching the football, but they appear not to notice Al come in. Or you.
I'll go if the kitchen is grimy.
It is surprisingly spruce.
I'll say I'm fine if he offers me a drink.
He's handing you a glass of wine whether you've asked for it or not.
Well, I won't drink it.
Al is rolling a joint.
And I won't be smoking that.
'Come on, let's go upstairs.'
Not if it's to your bedroom.

290

Well, you never know, Fen, perhaps the house has a delightful roof garden and that's where he's taking you.

But he isn't because it hasn't.

And remember, no batik bedspreads – I'll leave directly if he has one on his bed, let alone on the wall. Same goes for joss sticks. And Jim Morrison posters. Or Che Guevara. Or that Andy Warhol banana.

Where do you stand on mattresses-on-the-floor?

I hate those.

Al has one. But it is covered with a Conran bedspread.

That's different, then.

Be careful Fen.

She tinkers with his things, peers at photos of strangers she'll never meet but who grin alongside this man in whose bedroom she's mooching. Al is sitting on a pine trunk, having problems lighting the joint. She's planning to take a drag without inhaling. She never liked weed, it always made her feel discombobulated and queasy. She's intending to say something funny, like, I only do Class A drugs. But then she worries this might run the risk of him or his friends brandishing wraps of cocaine or handfuls of E.

'Fen?'

Al was looking at her in a dopey haze, offering the spliff. She saunters over but soon realizes that to puff without inhaling is harder than it seems. Oh well, one drag won't hurt. One drag and that's it. God it is strong.

She smiles and goes away to look at an abstract print. This is the wrong thing to do as the trompe l'oeil of prismatic colour exacerbates her headrush. She's pretending to look at old concert tickets, Blu-tacked to the wall, but actually she's staring at the white paint in between. She feels a little nauseous. Silently, she vows not to touch spliff from this day on if only the nausea would please just abate.

Al is behind her. He has slipped his hands either side of her waist. The surprise of him there, his lips at the back of her neck, have straightened her head and she finds she can close her eyes and concentrate on his touch without feeling dizzy. He's travelling his hands, down her hips, around the front of her thighs, inner thighs, oh God even inner more. He's missed out her stomach and gone straight for her breasts. He's now sucking and kissing at her neck and he's turning her to face him. Fen is suddenly terrified. Does she really want to kiss him? She hasn't time to figure it out because his tongue is in her mouth and she keeps her eyes closed and momentarily envisages Brad Pitt because she's not sure she wants the reality of kissing a bloke called Al whom she hardly knows. Luckily, the weed has fired Fen's naturally vivid imagination and she finds Brad is an excellent kisser. It's thrilling to feel his hands caressing, groping, being led by his excitement for her. With her eyes closed, she sucks Brad's ear lobe and grazes his neck with her mouth while he undoes the zip of her dress. The dress falls away and Fen keeps her eyes shut because she's conjured an airbrushed and idealized image of her figure in her mind's eye and she daren't open her eyes and find her physique causing anything other than awe and delight. But Brad is gorging on her breasts and searching for a way underneath her panties, so she needn't worry. Fen is wet and suddenly she wants to be fingered and sucked and fucked and she's so hot and turned on and slightly woozy that she no longer cares if it's Brad Pitt or Al.

And then a mobile phone rings and she knows that it's hers. She'll let it ring out. It does. They'll leave a message. No, they won't – they're ringing again. Sod off. They ring again.

'Shit, sorry, I'd better just see,' says Fen, opening her eyes, locating her bag, catching sight of Al's reflection in the mirror and feeling immediately shy. She goes over to retrieve her phone, holding her crumpled dress against her body.

'Hullo?'

'Fen – hi sorry, it's me.'

It's Pip.

And here's Al, slipping his hand down the front of her knickers and tugging cheekily at her pubic hair. Fen glowers at him in the mirror but he closes his eyes, bites her shoulder and works a finger through the lips of her sex.

'Can you hear me OK, Fen?'

'Yes.'

Fen is turned on by the sight of her body being ravished by this person. It doesn't matter that he's not Brad Pitt any more. What matters is that he's not Matt. He's secret. She spreads her legs, permits him easier access.

'Is everything OK, Pip?'

'Well,' Pip says, 'I wouldn't have phoned – but I can't seem to settle Cosima.'

Fen tries to still Al's hand, grabs at his wrist. She's doesn't want to be fingered in the same breath as talking about her daughter. She steps aside and is vaguely aware that he's now unbuttoning his trousers.

'What do you mean?' she asks Pip.

'Well she just seems restless, a little fretful.'

'Is she hot?'

'A little.'

'Shit. OK. I'm on my way.'

Fen shrugs apologetically to Al who is standing there with an impressive hard-on which she considers probably looks bigger because his body is so thin and hairless. Nothing like Brad Pitt. Or Matt Holden.

'My kid,' Fen shrugs and instantly detests herself for referring to Cosima as such, for all but blaming her baby for coital interruption. Al is absent-mindedly caressing his cock and Fen wonders, a little pathetically, whether he'll wank in her honour once she's left. 'I'm sorry,' she says, 'I'm really going to have to go.'

She dresses and as she does, she looks at a framed photo of a young woman.

'That's Kay,' he tells her. Al is still naked, his cock now at half mast. It seems disrespectful, really.

Fen looks at the photo. She was pretty, his sister. And as she sees herself out, she thinks how death distorts. She knows she was enamoured with the idea of Al because he was this brave boy who'd faced tragedy head-on. She loved the sight of him placing his flowers around the tree-trunk; his story. But she knows now he is rather immature, a bit boring actually, and a little too puny for her taste.

She heads out into the street, flags down a cab mercifully easily and phones Pip to tell her fifteen minutes. Fen gazes out, her head rests lightly against the window, being juddered; as if she needed physical discomfort to bring her to her senses. Yes, she feels guilty for the pleasure she's just had, the illicitness of it, the excitement and attention. She feels badly for Matt and she fears Cosima's unsettled state is directly attributable to her bad behaviour. But Fen's anxiety runs deeper too and it occurs to her that it is rooted in something far more ominous.

Is history repeating itself? Is this what my mother went through? Did her cowboy come riding by just when she was becoming stifled by the drudge of it all?

But did he lure her away or did she seek him out?

Pip tapped the phone against her lip. It was difficult to know what to do.

Should I wake Cosima in ten minutes or so? Or is that too cruel?

Because, in reality, Cosima had actually been sound

294

asleep since Pip laid her in her cot after her bottle two hours ago.

Matt came in half an hour after Fen. He'd left the bus early and taken a long walk to settle his nerves and ensure he was word perfect. He was dreading being the harbinger and he was dreading seeing Fen distressed, yet he hoped it might engender an opportunity to put his arms around her and hold her close. That she might feel safe. Protected. If she'd let him.

'You're back early,' he said.

Fen nodded. 'Pip couldn't settle Cosima.'

'Is she OK?'

'She's fine – she was fine by the time I arrived back. Probably tummy troubles or something.'

'Did you have fun with your friend?'

Fen looked at Matt and wondered if fun can only be fun if it's still fun in retrospect, in the aftermath. She nodded because she didn't want to say yes out loud. Because if she did she'd be saying to her partner's face, Yes it was fun to have some bloke I've met three times finger my vagina and fondle my boobs.

Matt looked at his watch, as if Fen's answer was a long time coming. 'Ten to ten,' he said. 'Do you want a cup of tea?'

'Please,' said Fen, 'thank you. I'll just pop upstairs and take off all this stupid make-up.'

'You look nice,' said Matt. 'I like your dress.' Shit – how long does make-up take to remove? More than ten minutes? Matt had no idea. 'Leave it on!' he exclaimed. 'You look nice.'

Fen found this touching. But she was desperate to remove the knickers tacky with the juice of infidelity. 'I'm just going to the loo,' she told him.

'You feeling OK?' Matt asked. Timing was everything but he really didn't want to ask her outright, Number One or Number Two.

'Just a bit tired,' said Fen.

When she came back downstairs, a cup of tea and a biscuit were waiting. And so was Matt.

When Pip arrived home from Fen's, Zac was already there, engrossed in some scintillating spreadsheet or other on his laptop.

'You're back early,' he commented, glancing up.

'Fen came back early,' Pip said tonelessly.

'How was Cosima?' Zac asked, squinting as he pulled the cursor around the screen.

'Cute as a button,' said Pip.

'Did it all go smoothly?' said Zac.

'Of course,' Pip said defensively.

'She is a poppet,' said Zac, 'a real little munchkin.'

Pip looked at her feet. 'I want one,' she said quietly.

Zac laughed a little. 'Oh God, one night's babysitting and you're all broody on me again!' he declared, returning his attention to his work.

'Oh will you just fuck off,' Pip stormed.

Zac looked up, startled. He'd been joking – hadn't that been obvious? Because hadn't she been joking too? It was some sort of shared joke, wasn't it? 'Pip!' he began to remonstrate.

'I'm sick of you not taking me seriously! I'm fed up of you demeaning how I *feel*,' Pip said and she flounced off to the bedroom with a slam to the door.

Zac was dumbstruck. He was amazed. He was worried – hadn't he discussed with Ben and Matt to keep the girls calm and enveloped with love and support? Most of all he was bewildered; Pip's words were in some ways irrelevant to the violence with which she'd expressed them. Pip rarely raised

296

her voice. She loathed arguing; even mundane bickering upset her. She avoided confrontation and was the person to whom others turned for assistance in deflecting situations. Pip was the least argumentative, least aggressive, most easygoing person he'd ever met. That's why he'd married her. She was also, in his eyes, so beautifully readable. That's why he loved her. But this he hadn't seen coming. And try as he might, it seemed illegible to him. But it was ten to ten and Django mattered most. Further discussion or shouting or whatever would just have to wait.

Cat floated in at quarter to ten. 'I've had the most brilliant day,' she beamed.

'Are you hungry?' Ben asked her.

'Nope.'

'Have you eaten?'

'Nope – I'm too excited to eat.'

'You ought to eat, babe.'

'Oh be quiet, you fussy old doctor.'

'Cup of tea, then?'

'That would be nice.'

'And then you can tell me all about it,' said Ben, glancing at the clock and hoping Cat could do so within ten minutes.

At 10 p.m. on 15 June, Ben put his finger over Cat's lip and said, 'That's wonderful news but you need to sit down. Babe, I need to tell you something.'

At 10 p.m. on 15 June, Matt switched off the TV and turned to Fen and said, 'Fen, I need to tell you something.'

At 10 p.m. on 15 June, Zac had to deny Pip her post-argument privacy. He went into the bedroom and sat along-side her. With tenderness and scorching regret, he put his arm gently around her. 'I need to tell you something, Mrs,' he said.

297

Where Were You When You Heard that Django McCabe Had Cancer?

In all his purple splendour, with his eternally optimistic smile fixed across his plastic face, Tinky Winky gazed kindly up at Fen. He was lying at her feet, she was sitting on the sofa, her hands clasped together tightly in automatic supplication. Matt was at her side, stroking her arm, her leg. It was ten past ten. Fen bent and picked up Tinky Winky, Cosima's favourite Teletubby, and hugged him tight. She pressed her nose to his head. He smelt of her baby. Just then, she gained more comfort from him than from Matt.

Is this my fault? In some horrible skewed scheme of things, I think it probably is. I feel sick. I shouldn't think of Django and Al in the same context but it all makes horrible sense if I do. Isn't this what they call karma? Or else, divine retribution? Of course I must have my comeuppance for all that stupid, stupid stuff with Al – but why does it have to be via Django?

'Is prostate cancer terminal? Where is the prostate exactly?' Fen turned to Matt, her eyes fixed warily at his groin. 'What does it do – can you live without one? Like an appendix or gall bladder? Is that what they'll do – chop it out? But they will be able to fix him, won't they?'

If I feel I am being punished, how must Django be feeling?

'He's on his own,' Fen continued, her voice cracking with emotion. 'He hates doctors and hospitals.' She looked at Matt, seeing worry and tenderness written all over his face. 'He'll be redefining cancer "a spot of the lurgy",' she said with a sad laugh. 'He'll tell us not to worry. What has he ever done to deserve this?' She stood and paced the room, clutching Tinky Winky to her breast like a prayer book. 'I think I know that he never meant to hurt anyone,' she said, 'so he changed his name from Derek and had a fling with his brother's wife. But he is a brilliant parent – he couldn't have been a better father to us, to Cat. His love was perfectly equal.'

'I know,' said Matt, 'I know. It seems so unjust, Fen. He's always looked after himself, what with his cooking and his love of Derbyshire air. He's one of the good guys.'

'Please don't let him die,' Fen pleaded, bursting into tears. 'I don't want this to be happening. I want Cosima to grow up knowing her Django Gramps. I can't believe we've been so horrible to him. We have to go up there, immediately. It's our turn to care for him.'

Matt went to her and pulled her into his embrace. She sobbed, knocking her forehead against his chest again and again. Snotty and tear-stained, she took deep breaths. 'If he could see me now he'd be saying, "Stop it with the sobbing, you'll ruin the carpets." Fuck, Matt, I'm terrified.'

Matt offered his arms to her but this time Fen stepped back and turned away, burying her face in Tinky Winky's tummy and sobbing anew.

I feel as if I don't deserve the comfort of Matt's arms, as if I've forfeited my place within his embrace because I've abused his trust and sullied our love for a pathetic fumble with that stupid Al. What sort of mother was I to Cosima earlier this evening? I have to change, for her sake. But actually, this isn't about me at all. It's about Django. And Django has to make it through, for her sake too.

'Pip's going to phone you,' Matt was saying, 'in a little while – once Cat has phoned her. We had to contrive it this way – it's why I met up with Ben and Zac yesterday.' And he told her about Django coming to London which made her cry; of Ben arranging for the consultation, that Django wanted the boys to tell his girls.

'He hates the city,' she cried. 'He must have been so anxious. He must be feeling so alone.'

I can't believe this is happening. And I can't believe it's still the same evening that I faffed around with Al. All that seems unreal, now; distant and past. Totally over and done with. Thank God Pip phoned me when she did. In some ways, she's always been there to pull me or Cat out of harm's way, to steer us clear of trouble.

'Pip will be phoning soon,' Matt said, and Fen shuddered at how close Matt seemed to her thoughts. 'Then you'll be able to decide what to do.'

'But even if we band together, can we help Django? Are we a match for cancer?' Fen whispered. 'Cancer happens to other families, Matt. Not ours.'

*   *   *

Pip was frowning so hard her head ached and the corner of her eyelids twitched.

Zac just said something like Django has cancer. I think I heard him right. But Django can't have cancer because I saw him a month ago and he looked as fine then as he has looked for the past however many years. And Django can't have cancer because he isn't the type. He's fantastically robust. You wouldn't believe he's seventy-five.

'But the most ill he's ever been is a head cold, which he cured overnight with his concoction of Caribbean Hot Sauce, brandy and an egg yolk whisked together and served in a

Babycham glass,' she said, a tone of protest to her voice. 'He made the concoction for me once – just before my A-levels. I swear my cold went before the glass even touched my lips. For Christ's sake, Zac – Django McCabe found the cure for the common cold. He can't have cancer.'

She looked at her husband, sitting beside her on their bed, and all the wariness and annoyance she'd harboured for him over the last month evaporated. Suddenly, she doubted she had the strength or the nous to fulfil her role as Great Looker-Afterer and she knew that, without having to be asked, her husband would take on that role. She knew that as soon as her tears came, Zac would be there, solid and close. She began to cry, lowered her head and crumpled into Zac who was there for her at once. She sobbed for a couple of minutes before physically pulling herself together.

'It's fine. It's fine,' she said loudly, sniffing away her fragility. 'If Django does have cancer or something, then he'll sail through it and no doubt discover some history-making, Nobel-prize-winning potion in the process It'll be the new penicillin It's all going to be OK.'

'Ben says that prostate cancer is not uncommon,' Zac said.

'Then it won't stand a chance in someone as rare as Django,' Pip said.

'Ben said often it is slow growing and the man can live out his normal lifespan in spite of it.' Zac matched her optimism because he sensed it was what she needed.

'And he certainly won't tolerate the ignominy of losing his trademark pony-tail during treatment,' Pip continued, almost brightly. 'I can just see him in a hospital gown, brandishing a Thermos of home-made soup, saying to the doctor, "Blast me with whatever but don't touch the hair, son." Can't you?'

Zac said yes he could, and he chuckled because he knew the sound of it would be a relief to Pip.

'He'll be fine,' Pip declared. 'Everything will be OK. It's a nasty, nasty shock. It's a terrible way to reunite us all, but reunite us it will.'

'Cat's going to give you a call, then you're to call Fen,' Zac explained because he deduced that facts and the opportunity to be proactive was what Pip wanted. 'We discussed it last night, Ben, Matt and I.'

They've thought it all through, the boys, bless them.

'Django McCabe will give cancer an unceremonious boot,' Pip said. 'Come on, Cat, ring me won't you? I think I'll make a cup of tea. Want one?'

'I'll make it, Mrs,' said Zac, kissing his wife's shoulder.

'We'll go up to Farleymoor at the weekend,' Pip said, 'and sort everything out.'

*　　*　　*

'Babe?' Ben looked at Cat who was standing as motionless and emotionless as a wax statue. She could hear him, but it sounded as though he was in a different room. She couldn't locate his voice or his presence and it felt safest to just keep standing still and staring straight ahead.

I'm sort of speechless and thoughtless. I can only compute facts at the moment.

I have been made manager at work.

Django has cancer.

'Babe – prostate cancer is not uncommon. It may have no great effect on Django's lifestyle or lifespan.'

Ben says prostate cancer is common.

'And I'm sorry, Cat, that I just couldn't tell you of his phone calls to me, of his trip down to St John's.'

Django came down to London on a train and went back home again.

My father is Derek McCabe.

302

The man who is my father has cancer.

I haven't seen Django for a month.

I thought I never wanted to see him again but just over a week ago I yearned to see him. Only he wasn't there because he was down here, with my husband, who helped him learn he has cancer.

'It broke my heart to know that you were going to Derbyshire, that he wouldn't be there. That there was nothing I could do about it.' Ben put his hands on Cat's shoulders and kissed the top of her head. She was stiff to his touch. 'Babe?'

'I have to be at work an hour early tomorrow,' Cat said.

'You need to phone Pip, when you're ready. Then she's going to phone Fen. We arranged it that way, the guys and I. With Django's approval.'

'OK,' she said, picking up her mobile phone and pressing the speed dial for Pip, whose number Cat currently had no chance of recalling otherwise.

Testing Time

The McCabe girls usually let BBC Radio Four pass the time when they made the journey to Derbyshire by car. That Saturday morning, though the radio was on and Ben was doing the driving, it was no more than a background sound to the lengthy loaded silences. What they wanted to tune into most were Ben's pragmatic facts about what Django was facing.

'So he may have had it for a long time?' Pip asked from the back of the car.

'Yes. Quite possibly,' said Ben, nodding at her from the rear-view mirror. 'Actually, a large percentage of men over eighty have a small area of prostate cancer.' She nodded back at him.

'But Django is only seventy-five,' Fen said. Ben looked at her too, but unlike Pip by whom she sat, Fen didn't meet his eyes. She was frowning intently at her hands.

'Many men can live out their normal lifespan without it causing any problems,' Ben said though he immediately regretted the joint sigh of relief from Pip and Fen. False hope could be a cruel thing. Also, despite being a level-headed scientist, Ben had always feared that Hope without Fact tempted Fate. 'But we are still unsure of what's what with Django,' he continued. 'He needs more tests. The results can take a couple of weeks to compute. There are all sorts of treatment possibilities, sometimes they even opt *not* to treat – and nothing drastic happens.' Ben had repeated the facts so often over the last few days he hoped his voice still sounded convincing.

'That's good, that's positive,' said Pip, leaning forward and nodding at him assertively. 'When can he have these tests? Can we bring him to your hospital? I suppose I'm asking if you can organize special privileges?'

'There are excellent urology and oncology departments local to Chesterfield,' he said. 'He's already been referred and tests have been set up. It's better for the patient to be closer to home.'

'Has he had them? These tests?' Fen asked quietly, disturbed by the thought of Django, on his own, being probed and scanned.

'I don't know – he was due to have some yesterday,' Ben said, trying again to encourage her with eye contact but she continued to look down, her hands now tight fists in her lap. 'I tried to phone a couple of times but he didn't answer.'

'Maybe now he'll buy a mobile phone,' Pip said, with a woeful laugh.

Ben was acutely aware that Cat had not reacted, let alone spoken and they were now just north of Junction 24, the eight mammoth cooling stations sighing out steam in slow motion. He glanced at his wife sitting beside him and wondered how much of the conversation she'd listened to. Though she appeared to be gazing out of the window, obviously it was not at the view. Much as Ben was fond of her sisters, and hoped they found comfort in his honest answers, so he also wished he had Cat to himself that journey. Over all others, his duty was to her. This he did not feel was an obligation of marriage, but a reason for it. In Cat he'd found a person other than himself, or anyone he had ever known, whom he wished always to put first. For Fen and Pip, cancer might well cure the situation between them and Django, and Ben understood that by genning up on details and prognosis, they might feel better equipped to make their reacquaintance. What could be more shocking than cancer of a loved one? In the scheme of things, didn't cancer cancel out all other ills?

For Cat, though, cancer had been thrown into a mix already clouded by complex fears, mistrust, hurt, shock and disbelief. Ben wondered whether, for Fen and Pip, Django's cancer in some way provided an easy way out, an excuse to move away from the disruptive revelations of the previous month; that cancer rewrote all scales of gravity. Django's cancer could also redefine their roles as nurses, and not accusers. In a bizarre twist, cancer might just make everything better. Ben felt that for Cat, however, cancer was confusing the ambivalence she was entitled to feel. If she wasn't yet ready to accept the shock of her parentage, the untruths she'd grown up believing, the hurt and the deception – then she certainly wasn't going to be prepared for the hard facts of cancer.

Suddenly, Ben resented her sisters for not being aware of this. Then he asked himself if he would still feel it was worse for Cat than for her sisters, was Cat not his wife? The truth was, he didn't want to talk about cancer any more because privately his concerns for Django were more grave than he was prepared to reveal before the tests were done. He was beginning to feel tired and irritated by the drive. Why couldn't Cat take the wheel?

Because she never did.

When the two of them were in the car, it was always

Ben who drove. A silly little quirk of marriage, of their dynamic, he'd never really thought about until just now. He didn't really mind. He was glad to be able to do something.

'He's going to die, isn't he?' suddenly Fen sobbed. 'Oh God, he's going to die.'

'Fen shut up and stop that,' Ben snapped. 'You're being hysterical and that kind of thinking is no good to anyone.'

'I'm sorry. I'm sorry,' Fen gasped, and she turned to Pip. 'Do you think everything will be OK? Pip?'

Pip had to gather her thoughts. It struck her that Fen was reacting in much the way she would have expected Cat to. Yet Cat, sitting in the front passenger seat, was currently doing the deeply thoughtful gazing out of the window more usual for Fen. It was as if the events of the past month had transposed her younger sisters' traits. It was Cat guarding her emotions now, and Fen spewing out hers. 'It'll be fine,' Pip told Fen in the tone of voice she'd often employed for her youngest sister. 'It's a nasty shock. Can you imagine Django as a cancer patient?' She waited for Fen to shake her head. 'Nor can I. It doesn't happen to people like him.'

'We were just this ordinary bunch, this normal family,' Fen said croakily, 'and in a matter of weeks, it's all fallen apart.' She thought of Matt and Cosima at home, suddenly praying hard that her other little family would never fall apart, shuddering violently at how close she'd come to ripping them asunder herself.

'We have to hold it together,' Pip said, misreading Fen's shaking. 'That's the point of family – one is duty-bound to hold it together to prevent it falling apart.'

I am duty-bound to hold it together to prevent it falling apart, Fen said to herself.

She gazed at the back of Cat's head, the soft auburn

307

spikes of her hair, the gold butterflies at the back of her ear lobes fixing her earrings. 'Is it harder for you, Cat?' Fen asked her gently, leaning forward between the front seats. 'You know – because of—' She paused. 'What we found out.'

'He's just my biological father,' Cat said quietly, her voice sounding new and emphatic after two hours of silence, 'and that can't mean much because Christ, we didn't even suspect, let alone know, until a few weeks ago.'

'Pit stop,' Ben announced, deciding to pull in to the services at the last minute. There was so much stress and emotion and anticipation in the car it was now making driving difficult. Part of him was dreading the weekend, part of him wanted to take Cat back to Boulder for good, far away from her first family so that he and she could settle down and make a new one of their own. He felt slightly burdened though it had been his decision to accompany the sisters, his advice to Zac and Matt that they stay at home with their children, his offer to be the chaperon, the doctor-on-call. He loitered behind the sisters as they made their way in to the services. He observed how Pip had put her arm around Cat's shoulder, that Fen's arm was around his wife's waist. And the sight released a surge of relief.

She'll be OK. They'll all be OK. Whatever happens, they have each other. They always will.

'Stop!' Cat suddenly said, anxiety riding high in her voice, as the car pulled along the one-in-ten drag to Farleymoor. Ben pulled over to the verge. The girls staggered from the car, allowing the sight of the dip and roll of the ancient and familiar dales to calm their nerves, the sweet soft air to fill their lungs and steady their minds; while goose grass, licked with flashes of silver as the sun and the wind played on it, whispered comfortingly against their legs.

'Why don't you three walk the last mile,' Ben suggested. 'I'll drive on. And pave the way.'

Django peered at length and with theatrical curiosity into Ben's car. He stroked at his non-existent goatee and frowned. 'Are they dieting?'

Ben laughed. 'They wanted to walk the last bit.'

'Dragging their heels?' Django asked.

'Steadying their nerves,' Ben said diplomatically.

'It's nice to see you,' Django told him, 'but I'm wondering whether you are here as intermediary or physician?'

'I have many caps to wear this weekend, Django,' Ben said. 'Chauffeur – currently.'

'You're very skilled,' Django told him, 'and you are of course most welcome, bless you. But your services as intermediary and physician won't be called upon. You see, I'm feeling dandy. Furthermore, I've made curried trout for supper And Eton Mess. It's their favourite. Guaranteed to break the ice and melt hardened hearts.'

From the garden, they could see the curve in the road as it started its long, meandering descent to Two Dales. And just then the sisters came into view as they mooched their way closer.

'It's funny how it never changes,' Django said. 'Whatever their age, wherever they've been, it's always Pip leading the way, Fen bringing up the rear and Cat, protected, between them.'

'Cat's extremely nervous,' Ben told Django, his wife's welfare his main consideration.

'I'm sure she is,' said Django, 'but there's so much ground to cover and most of it is a wasteland there seems little point in revisiting.'

'But they need to know,' Ben told him, a little irritated by Django's whimsy.

'If they ask,' Django said.

'They might not,' Ben said, polite but firm, 'but still they need to know. It's part of the point of this weekend – you must realize that.' He paused. 'How were the tests?'

'Tests?' said Django. 'I'm feeling dandy, my boy – and look, here come the girls.'

The girls were now walking up the drive. Pip. Fen. Cat lagging behind. The disruption to the familiar order perturbed Django. The pace was less their usual brisk walk, more a reluctant amble, and that vexed him too. And as he watched the girls approach in this awkward, unnatural arrangement and faltering gait, he sensed it was mostly down to him to realign it all. If only life could be like jazz. If only he could gather together these disparate components. If only he could make a sweet chord from discordance, a new melody from dissonance. Perhaps he could.

The girls stood before him.

'Hullo, chaps,' Django smiled. 'Cup of tea?'

It was incongruous; to drink tea so politely, in such silence, when the tea was so uncouthly strong and served in the great clunking stoneware mugs Django had made during his merci- fully brief foray into pottery in the late seventies. But they sipped away and smiled awkward half smiles while waiting for the scald on their tongues to subside.

'Well, I think I'll unpack,' said Ben but immediately the girls left the table too, which had not been his intention at all. He'd assumed he'd simply be on-call, in any capacity, but he had hoped this meant waiting in the wings, a step removed, while the action played out elsewhere. Django took the teapot and poured out the amber-coloured dregs into the curry sauce, desperately annoyed at the nag of his bladder. He dropped a mug on the floor, yet not even the flagstones could break it. Django wondered if he was allowed to read into this – that something rather old and odd-looking should be so strong and resilient. He'd made the mug himself. He looked at his hands, glanced around the kitchen to check he had no audience, and then he pressed his hands hard against his heart, his brow, his groin.

Cat watched Ben unpack. 'I wish I'd never come,' she whispered.

Ben nodded, shook the creases from a shirt and hung it on the back of the door. 'I'm sure, babe,' he said, 'but you need to stay open. Don't close yourself off, OK?'

'His birthday and all that – it seems a lifetime ago,' Cat said.

There was a gentle knock on the door and then Fen came in. 'You OK?' she asked Cat.

Cat shrugged. 'You?'

Fen shrugged back. 'I thought it would be easier, I thought there'd be tears and hugs and we'd all know what to say. It's all so formal. And awkward.'

'I wish I hadn't come,' Cat confessed. 'I thought everything would seem magically clearer, everything would be fine. But it's not.'

'We have to be here,' Pip, suddenly in the doorway, spoke strongly and a little irritated. 'Of course it's awkward. Come on. We need to go downstairs and help.'

'In a sec,' said Fen and she turned to Ben. 'Does your mobile have a signal? I want to phone home.' Ben handed his phone to Fen. There was no signal and she looked crestfallen.

'Come on,' Pip said to Fen, 'let's go downstairs. You can use the normal phone. But we'll lay the table first.'

'Isn't all of this freaking you out?' Cat asked her.

'Of course it is,' said Pip, 'but we have to do something about that. That's why we're here, remember.'

311

When Pip and Fen had left the room, Cat went over to Ben, laying her head against his chest. 'I don't even know where to look, let alone what to say,' she muttered. 'I can't seem to look him in the eye. It might make me cry and I don't want to. And I might see that I have his eyes and I don't think I want to see that either.'

'Yet,' Ben qualified gently.

Matching cutlery had never really been a priority in the McCabe household, nor had the resultant assortment ever been particularly noticeable. Food was the all-important element of mealtimes at Farleymoor, and though the laying of the table held some ritual, the lively clatter of crockery and cutlery was in anticipation of the repast itself. Cutlery was a means to an end, a way to expedite the passage of food from plate to palate. It was mostly irrelevant whether it was steel from Sheffield or silver from Harrods, ivory stems or antler handles; as long as the pieces could prong, scoop or cut.

That Saturday night, between silences as thick as Django's Christmas gravy, the cutlery provided a cacophonous and alien soundtrack. On account of each piece being unique, no two clinks or clatters were the same. No one had noticed this before, but they all tuned in to it now. The racket was irritating, so annoying that everyone tried to scrape and clang their cutlery the loudest to obscure the sound of the others and perhaps signify their own unrest as well.

'And how is little Cosima?' Django asked Fen who nodded her answer while making much of chewing concertedly. 'Good! Splendid. And how is young Tom?' Django asked Pip who, for some reason, smiled her answer to Ben. 'Super!' said Django, turning his attention to Cat. 'And I hear congratulations are in order, Cat.'

'I'm not bloody pregnant,' Cat retorted with her mouth

full, which in the first instance irked Django far more than the facts of her answer or the sentiment by which she expressed it. 'I meant your promotion,' he said. She shrugged, as if it were no big deal, as if he should expect her to be capable of such accolades.

The grating scrape of cutlery; the grate of non-communication anathema to this kitchen, this family. Ben asked for another helping, not because he was still hungry but just to break the awkward silence. In the most stinging indictment Django had yet been savaged by, each girl left part of her meal on her plate.

Django fetched the Eton Mess and placed it with justified pride in the centre of the table. Pip patted her stomach as if she were full, Fen burped politely into her napkin as if she didn't fancy it anyway and Cat wouldn't even bring her eyes to glance at Django's trademark triumph of a dessert. He sat down heavily and, with a great sigh, placed his head in his hands. And there they all sat, in a suspended moment of extreme unease. The silence was choking but with a cough, Django cleared his throat and let rip a roar the likes of which the girls had never heard and could never have imagined.

'Enough!' Django slammed his hand against the worn wood of the table. 'Enough. My name is Derek McCabe – it's a ghastly name and there should be a law against it. I have three daughters one of whom is biologically mine. I have cancer.' He rose. 'With regard to your blood lines, on my gravestone I want it said that I was a good father to my three girls,' he almost bellowed. 'You can punish me and condemn me for the details I withheld; put me in the prover-bial stocks and pelt me with how rotten you think me. It was naive of me to believe I could protect you – but then all parents wish to protect their offspring so the whole bloody lot of us must be fools.' He shoved his chair back. 'You tell me – any of you – that our life thus far was not better for turning a blind eye to the finer facts of biology and fore-names.' He smote the table. 'Pip – you dish up, I need the lavatory. Bugger the Eton Mess and bugger my blasted bladder.'

When Django came back after an infuriating and unsuccessful trip to the toilet, the Eton Mess was still intact, or as intact as a smash of meringue, gluts of fruit and great clods of cream defining this dessert can be. He looked around the table. Poor Ben, mortified, at the periphery of his comfort zone. The girls, looking glum, staring at their laps. Slowly, Pip stood up and Fen lifted her eyes and Cat raised her head a little. 'It's your job,' Pip said to Django with humility, 'you're head of our family.' And she held out the serving spoon. Before Django took it, he turned his attention to Fen, who could only mouth 'Sorry' on account of the choke of emotion tightening her throat. Then he looked to Cat, whose tears bounced on her plate like hail-stones.

'Don't do that, dear,' Django chided her softly, 'it's the best china. And the recipe does not call for salt. Just sweet things.' A glance back at Fen and Pip showed their tears had started to fall too.

'Dear God,' Django exclaimed softly, 'I'm about to do that ghastly Hollywood thing and tell you all how much I love you, how I never meant to hurt you.'

Oh Christ – mass hysterics, thought Ben, *we so don't do this in my family*.

Django went to Pip, took the serving spoon from her hand and embraced her tenderly; then went and stood behind Fen's chair and bent down to kiss her forehead over and again before pulling Cat to her feet and straight into the warmth of his bear-hug.

But nor do we do this, Ben thought enviously and he

moved quietly from the kitchen, taking his dessert into the garden, leaving the McCabes to their ways.

Bolstered by brandy and heartened by After Eights, the girls shyly gathered around Django's armchair in the drawing-room, as if he was about to read a story though it was the truth only that they craved and that finally he was prepared to give. With the apologies and declarations of love now fulfilled, a spew of questions surfaced, though it was only Fen and Pip who could voice them.

'Was it a shock, that *she* came back?' asked Pip.

'Yes and no,' Django told them. 'We've had no contact and yet I must admit to an inkling that at some point, she'd show up.'

'Did he know?' Pip pressed. 'Our father?' She glanced at Fen and then, apologetically, at Cat.

'No,' Django said emphatically, 'he did not.'

'So how can you be sure?' Fen asked abruptly, having slipped her hand into Cat's.

'Unlike me, my brother wasn't very good at maths,' Django said nostalgically. 'Perhaps I would have told him – when the dust had settled. When a little more time had passed. But life was back on an even keel – Battersea had been left, we were all happy here together. And within two years, he was gone.'

'Is it really *really* as you've always told it?' Fen asked, a little accusatorily.

'It really *really* is,' Django said.

'About everything?' Fen pressed. 'About all of you?'

Django nodded. 'Though with hindsight, I suppose one can see that she was on this mission to find herself and all that transcendental nonsense which, in the 1960s, we simply accepted as right-on and far-out. Nowadays I reckon one would call her a crazy mixed-up kid.' There was a pause as the girls tried to tag this description to the woman in her early fifties they'd met for the first time just over a month before.

'Did you actually have an affair with her?' Pip asked. 'A love affair?'

'No,' Django admitted, 'not technically.'

'Just a fling,' Cat commented sadly.

'But did you *love* her?' Fen asked, unnerved by the thought of a reckless one-night stand. She glanced at Cat but could not decipher the emotion that dulled her eyes.

'In a make-love-not-war zeitgeisty kind of way – yes, I suppose I did,' Django said and he could feel Cat's eyes burning into him. He looked at her and nodded again. 'There was a lot of love around,' he continued, 'between everyone in those days.'

'Did you think she'd come back?' Pip asked. 'At the time?'

Django looked upset. 'Of course I did!' he declared. 'Gracious, she had three beautiful *beautiful* babies.'

'Did you think she'd come back for *all* of us?' Fen pressed, squeezing Cat's hand and half hoping her sister would hear that she'd asked the question as much on her behalf as for herself.

'Of course I did!' Django said, a little impatiently. He paused and continued in a softer tone. 'I was mortified that she'd left – but soon enough I dreaded her returning. I didn't want to lose you three. Especially not after my brother passed away.'

'Was it a shock? When you realized about me?' Cat asked. They were her first questions and her voice rang out. Django, Fen and Pip looked at her, though just then she remained unable to establish eye contact with any of them.

'Well, yes it was. Goodness me, yes,' Django told them all. 'Although I didn't know until after she'd left. She told me in a letter. A letter that was unopened for days on end because I was so busy running around after you all.'

'But *why* did she leave?' Cat asked urgently. 'Why did she leave us? Did she say? Do you still have the letter? Why *didn't* she come back for us? All of us?'

What could Django do but shrug? What could he say but, 'I don't know, girls. I don't have that answer. You'd really have to ask her that.'

Time for Tests

After an exhausted sleep in which thoughts of their mother and thoughts of cancer were banished, the family reconvened at the breakfast table where the cutlery could no longer be heard, but could be seen making swift work of the stack of panffles and maple syrup. The C word was now horribly anticipated, but none of the girls could bring themselves to articulate it. Yet it was the news of Django's cancer that had facilitated this return home and they were leaving later that day.

Ben was acutely aware of this fact. And he was eager that the issue be broached with sufficient time to do it justice.

'How are you feeling, Django?' he asked, as conversationally as such a loaded question could possibly sound.

'I had the most dreadful procedure on Friday, truly ghastly,' Django replied in a similar tone, and he pointed his steak knife at Ben. 'You medical men are an imaginative and sadistic lot. Pass the syrup. Thank you, Fen. They trussed me up, Ben, they trussed me up.'

'A TRUSS?' Ben asked.

'Yes,' Django regarded the girls. They'd stopped eating. They looked terrified. 'As you know, I don't trust technology and I'm not one for all these new-fangled gizmos. It was a *camera*,' he muttered, shaking his head, 'at the end of a medical hosepipe.' Fen laid her hand over his wrist. He gave a little shrug. 'Not one for the family photo album,' he said robustly.

'You'll be fine,' Pip said.

'What's next?' Ben asked.

'Toast?' Django offered. 'Fresh tea?'

'I meant for you, at the hospital, test-wise,' Ben clarified.

'Let's see – tomorrow, it's something about "ice",' Django said.

'Isotope bone scan?' Ben asked.

'That's the one,' said Django benevolently, as if he'd been quizzing Ben on his med school revision. 'It all sounds increasingly Ridley Scott to me.'

The sisters stared at Ben intently.

'OK,' said Ben, 'OK. I'm the doctor so you can all listen to me. The bone is perhaps the most common place for prostate cancer to spread to. This scan can detect abnormal areas of bone. A mild radioactive liquid is injected into a vein in the arm and because abnormal bone absorbs more than normal bone, the radioactive stuff shows up as highlighted hot spots.'

'I could bag myself a role on *Doctor Who*,' Django said brightly, 'or audition as the new ReadyBrek boy.' But Fen had now begun to cry. The sudden sound of her distress rang out the truth about Django's alarming situation. 'Poppet,' he tried to protest but when he looked over to Pip for assistance, he saw that she hid her face behind her hands and a glance at Cat showed her tears falling steadily if silently.

'The scan is just diagnostic,' Ben told them, his arm around Cat.

'But what if it diagnoses horrible things?' Fen sobbed. 'We've only just got each other back. We want to rebuild our family, not have it taken away from us.'

'I've always worried that the more they look for the more they find,' Pip said, working hard not to let her voice crack.

'Girls,' said Django, 'it's probably just a spot of the lurgy. I have all my faculties. I just cannot take a pissing leak.' No one laughed. No one said, Language, Django.

'Did they warn you that after the injection you have to wait a good two or three hours before the scan can be taken?' Ben asked Django.

'No,' said Django, a little unnerved. 'I can't remember. Perhaps they did.'

'Nothing sinister,' Ben assured him, 'just a lengthy process – so take a book.'

'I'll stay,' Cat announced suddenly, decisively. 'I have a day off tomorrow. I'll come with you, Django.'

With the car packed and ready to leave later that day, Fen and Pip shuffled around and loitered, having final drinks of water and double-checking the rooms upstairs.

'I could stay too,' Pip offered.

'And me,' Fen added quietly though she was now desperate to see her baby.

'Thank you,' Django said, his hand at his heart, 'but much as I love the image of arriving at the hospital with my entourage, my bevy of beauties, I think you two should be back with your families tonight.' Pip asked him over and again if he was sure, and then she asked the same of Cat. Fen didn't want to ask if Cat and Django were sure because actually she was missing Cosima so much she felt sick.

'I'll call, as soon as there's anything to call about,' Cat told them, transformed into a capable nurse, currently in the arms of her doctor. 'I'll call you anyway.' While she hugged her husband, Fen and Pip said goodbye to Django.

'Oh Django,' Fen whispered, letting him make her feel better in his arms.

'Behave,' Pip told him, giving him the tight hug and brisk kiss to each cheek she gave to Tom when she took him to school. 'Do what the doctors say.'

'She's so bloody bossy,' Django said to Fen.

Fen suddenly felt great affection for her sister. 'And we love her for it,' she said. Pip looked a little embarrassed. Fen linked arms with her. 'Sit in the back with me?' she asked. 'Even though Cat won't be in the front.'

'I have dominoes tonight,' Django tells Cat as they wave the others off.

'*Big Brother* is on anyway,' she tells him, 'and you don't have a video recorder. Anyway, I'm all talked out for today.'

'Me too,' says Django, 'me too.'

They feel awkward but strangely excited to be in such close proximity, to have the opportunity to spend quality time, alone together. It is almost easy to forget the reason why Cat is staying on in Derbyshire.

When she first saw the hospital the next morning, Cat was pleased that Django was having the tests done there and not in London. In contrast to the vertical sprawl of the London hospitals, and the unfriendly busyness of Ben's in particular, this place was welcoming. Set amidst dunes of neatly tended lawns, a series of low buildings constructed in the buff-coloured local stone sat peacefully and spaciously, a little like the sheep that grazed the hills just beyond the perimeter fence. Cat wanted to say how she hated hospitals, hated the smell, that they made her feel nervous, but wisely she changed her perspective and wittered on about the landscaping and the architecture instead.

'Prince Charles opened it,' she marvelled, reading from a brass plaque.

'Well then!' Django declared, implying the Royal Family

wouldn't waste their time opening hospitals not at the cutting edge of medical excellence.

It still smelt like a hospital, though. And the sights and sounds were indisputable too. The rubbery squelch of the staff's sensible shoes against highly sheened linoleum; the rumble of trolleys and the clatter of wheelchairs; the whistle and cheeriness of the porters ferrying patients. The universally familiar typeface pointing out departments. Cat wondered whether an element of acting was an integral part of a nurse's training. Like barristers. As if facts and procedures could be dressed up or played down through their performance. But the kindness of the matronly nurse who led Django through, delivered in broad Derbyshire vernacular replete with affectionate monikers, was genuine in its down-to-earthiness. She might as well have been serving him chips in a café in Matlock as preparing his arm for radioactive fluid. And whether Django had been seventy-five, seventeen or seven, she'd still have addressed him as 'ducky'.

And Django was injected. And the wait began. Initially, Cat eyed him vigilantly, as if she'd be able to detect when the liquid came across something sinister, but soon enough the tedium kicked in and disparate topics of conversation were mused over in varying degrees of detail. After they had spent ages trying to remember the various teachers at the girls' school, there was a lengthy and loaded silence.

'Do you – did you ever – oh never mind,' Cat mumbled but she dragged her eyes to Django.

'Did I what?' he asked her gently.

'Doesn't matter. Nothing. Feel differently towards me than Fen and Pip?' Cat whispered. Django took a sharp intake of breath.

'It's just Fen says a parent's love for their child should, by definition, be supreme,' Cat explained in a small, guarded voice.

Django took time to answer. 'Well, I must be an exception to the rule because I have never distinguished between the three of you.' He paused. 'Would you say that makes me a bad parent?'

Cat twisted her fingers and wished she'd not veered from their mild and mundane nattering.

'Did I distinguish between you?' Django rephrased it. 'Do you think I should have?'

'I've always felt an equal,' Cat qualified, 'but it's difficult – it's difficult to wonder whether I shouldn't have. Whether I should have at least wondered.'

Django turned in his chair to face her head-on, wincing as he moved. 'Blasted ancient bones. Sometimes I've wondered, if your mother hadn't left, whether you'd have been told earlier.'

Cat thought about this. 'Would you have told me later, then – would you have told me *ever*, if she hadn't come back last month?' Then she gestured around her. 'With all of *this* now on the agenda?'

'I,' Django paused, 'actually, no – I don't suppose I would. I don't know, Cat. With this cancer business, might I have told you?' Django shook his head. 'I don't know. What's important in all of this? I don't know. I sway from thinking it matters not one jot, to it mattering a lot.'

Cat nodded but she didn't understand.

'I would hate Fen or Pip to think I ever loved them less,' Django said, sounding weighed down and tired, 'because the truth is, I simply couldn't have loved any of you more.'

Cat waited for the information to reach her brain, though she knew it might take a while longer, weeks, months even, for it to settle comfortably in her soul.

'I suppose you girls ought to think of it as you are my daughter and they are my adopted daughters.' Django paused. 'Take Tom – he's about to have a baby brother or sister made by his mother and her new husband but I don't think he'll ever doubt that he's loved equally. And if Zac and Pip ever have a child, I can't imagine that Tom would feel they had more love for their offspring.'

'I hear what you're saying,' said Cat, rubbing her forehead. Over the last month she found she could only spend limited time on the subject before a headache encroached. She felt like a soaked sponge; she'd absorbed so much that she was clogged; if she wasn't careful much of the cherished information would start to leak because she did not have the capacity to hold so much, as yet. 'So who was this Django Reinhardt?' she asked, needing to veer off at a tangent.

Django sighed, partly with relief, partly with pleasure, partly with comfort that this topic was one he could happily and knowledgeably discourse on for the duration of this radioactive trip.

'Django Reinhardt was the stuff of legend,' he began as if starting a biopic, his voice animated in contrast to the hush with which he'd previously spoken.

'When are we talking?' Cat asked.

'Well, he was born in 1910,' said Django, 'to a gypsy family. He was a banjo prodigy by the age of nine, horribly burnt and partially paralysed by a fire in his caravan when he was eighteen.' He checked to see that Cat looked suitably alarmed. 'Because of his handicap, he had to invent a technique to play at all – he'd use a whalebone collar-stiffener as a plectrum and a two-fingered method with sudden explosions of strumming.' Django gave a brief air-guitar demonstration, which made Cat laugh. 'His discovery of jazz – and his friendship with Stephane Grappelli, the great violinist, resulted in a musical marriage which gave birth to a new sound. He wouldn't play tunes *straight*. Gypsy music delights in improvisation and embellishment so Django and Stephane would take the melody of a dance or song as a starting point – "Sweet Georgia Brown", or "Jeepers Creepers", or "Ain't Misbehavin'"—'

'I know those!' Cat interrupted, feeling proud rather than embarrassed that other waiting patients appeared to be listening in now. 'The house used to ring out with them.'

'His guitar had a voice that was near-human,' Django said dreamily. 'Everyone wanted to play with him. From trumpeter Bill Coleman, to trombonist Dicky Wells, to harmonica player Larry Adler and, just before the war, the mighty Duke Ellington.'

'I've heard of him!' Cat said proudly, aware that an elderly man sitting opposite was nodding to himself.

'Of course you have,' said Django as if it was the most basic part of anyone's education. 'After the war, Dizzy Gillespie.'

'I've heard of him too!' Cat exclaimed.

'I would jolly well hope so,' said Django, sharing a raised eyebrow with the pensioner opposite. 'During the war, in occupied France, American jazz records were banned but the musicians set up a Resistance of their own – putting out hundreds of jazz records but with camouflaged titles. Silly Huns never cottoned on. After the war, Django and Stephane reunited in London and reformed their old quintet – at the BBC's request. Their apotheosis was to famously rerecord the *Marseillaise* – which had been banned from the airwaves for many years. Django Reinhardt's ultimate triumph, in his final recording, was to reconcile jazz with the electric guitar. And then he died.'

'When?' Cat asked, shocked at the bluntness of the end of the story, horribly aware that they were sitting in a hospital, desperate to be distracted away again.

'In 1953,' Django told her, 'on May 16th.'

'That's your birthday,' Cat noted sadly.

'He was only forty-three years old,' said Django McCabe even more sadly.

'Poor Django,' said Cat. Quietly, she sat and thought to herself that if her Django hadn't had his career cut short by the demands of three small girls, he'd probably still be living in Paris, a life as colourful and creative as his namesake. She glanced at him. She knew every whisker on his extravagant sideburns, every furl and kink of his pony-tail, every dint on his forehead. And she knew that Fen knew them too. As did Pip.

He gave himself to us, he did. Entirely. I don't know anyone as well as I know him. Not even Ben, I suppose. I've had a lifetime of knowing Django.

She linked her arm through his. 'Hum me your favourite Django Reinhardt tune,' she asked him, laying her head against his arm; closing her eyes as the vibration of his humming 'Georgia On My Mind' travelled through to her heart.

I can't believe you're my father. My real father. My own dad. My very own daddy. The thing is, you're so nice to share. Pip and Fen might never be able to say 'my real father' in connection with you – but they'll always be able to say 'our very own father'.

Say it out loud, Cat.

I can't seem to.

'All right petal, time for your photo shoot.' The nurse had appeared, accompanied by a porter with an empty wheel-chair. Momentarily, Cat thought she spoke to her. It seemed very odd to refer to Django as 'petal'.

'Your limo awaits,' said the porter, giving the wheelchair a twirl.

'I can walk,' Django objected.

'We'd rather you didn't, duck,' the nurse chided amicably.

'I pride myself on a smooth ride,' the porter protested, with a wink to Cat. 'You'll not find finer in the whole of Derbyshire.'

'Can I come?' Cat asked urgently, not wanting to leave him, or be without him.

'Only room for one,' the porter said, 'and I don't do pillion.'

'I meant—'

'I know,' the nurse said.

'Can she come?' Django asked.

'Of course she can,' said the nurse, 'as far as any of us can go. Come along ducky. How are you feeling, Mr McCabe?'

'Please,' he said, easing himself down into the wheelchair, 'call me Django.'

Cat insisted that she drove the 2CV back to Farleymoor though Django was a notoriously annoying passenger, stamping on imaginary brake pedals and gasping when corners were not taken at the angle he would have chosen.

'Mirror, signal, manoeuvre,' he muttered under his breath at regular intervals.

'It's a beautiful afternoon,' Cat said, when they arrived back in Farleymoor, 'shall we go for a walk?'

'I'm a little tired,' Django said.

'Are you feeling all right?' Cat asked. 'You look a little pale – not the Chernobyl glow we were expecting.'

'Just a little tired.'

'Sit in the garden,' Cat told him, repositioning the ancient Lloyd Loom chair. 'I'll make a pot of tea.'

By the time she came out, Django was fast asleep. She sat on the grass, listening to him breathing, the occasional extravagant, gruffled snore that always made the sisters laugh. Pip tape-recorded him once.

Cat looked at him. His mouth was slightly open, the deep laughter lines around his eyes a map of his life. 'Dad,' she said quietly.

'Daddy.

 Dadda.

  Pops.

   Da.

    Papa.

     Pa.'

None of them actually suited him. Tellingly, nor did he awaken.

'Derek,' she said softly. Certainly not. On he slept.

'Django,' she all but whispered.

'Yes?'

He could only ever be Django, really.

'Sorry – did I wake you?'

'Heavens, what's the time? How long have I been asleep?'

'About an hour,' Cat told him. 'I can make this into iced tea,' she said, tapping the teapot. 'My train leaves in a couple of hours.'

So iced tea it was.

'I've ordered a cab – I don't want you driving,' she said, 'but I can stay, Django, if you like. I'm sure work will give me dispensation.'

'I'll be fine,' Django said. 'What's a bit of radioactivity? I can drive you.'

'No,' Cat insisted. 'You can – but you won't.'

He shrugged.

'Can I ask you something?' she said, shyly.

'Of course,' Django said, clenching his jaw on a yawn.

'Maybe when you're not tired,' Cat wavered, thinking better of it.

'Ask now,' he told her.

'Do you think it's a bit ominous,' she asked, 'that I wasn't really born of Love? That actually, I was the result of Adultery? A brief fling?'

328

Django sipped his tea silently. 'Don't be overly biblical and sanctimonious, Catriona,' he said crossly.

She plucked at the grass and thought about it. 'Sorry,' she said after a while.

'Let me ask *you* something,' Django said. He was feeling supremely tired now, a little nauseous too. 'Should I not expect *you* to love me *more* than Fen or Pip love me?' He let the concept hang. 'You're my daughter after all, aren't you? You're my *real* daughter, my *proper* daughter,' he tapped her quite briskly on the shoulder. 'Don't you think *you* ought to love me the most?'

Cat was simultaneously taken aback by his challenge and humbled by the astuteness of the remark. She felt immediate remorse. She'd so rarely been chastised by Django and neither had Pip or Fen. Their family dynamic had hardly ever necessitated it.

'None of us could love you more,' she proclaimed, relishing the new sense of clarity. Her smile grew from her soul and she could see the positive effect it had on Django. 'I'm ashamed to admit that we tried to love you less – last month,' she revealed, 'but we couldn't do that either.'

VT 05154

An early symptom of Django's cancer was to effectively kill off the anger and hurt that Fen and Pip had each experienced towards him since his birthday. It was as if the diagnosis packed up the past and placed life gently on new ground with a firmer footing. Cancer would define them, all of them. They would become nicer people for it. In the meantime Fen and Pip decreed that whatever had happened BC – before cancer – was largely irrelevant. They would pull together; life was too short, family was everything. Cat did so want to flow with their energy but unconditional love and trust were still in a holding bay, guarded by a self-protective wariness. She found herself both chipping away at it but building it back up too.

For Ben and Matt and Zac it was quite simple, really. Men for the most part are blessed with the ultimate take on the situation. Say less. It's not Neanderthal, it's genius. A variant on the theory that it takes a multitude of muscles to frown, but only three to smile. It was far easier to be nice than to be at loggerheads, it was far nicer to just feel love than argue about the vagaries of it. Love wasn't a matter of equality after all, but of equilibrium.

*

However, though Fen and Pip felt a welcome sense of relief at the warm waves of harmony and support, Cat's feelings of unease and dissatisfaction were contagious and before long a gnawing realization crept in that fundamentals remained untreated, unfixed.

So, though Fen acknowledged her present disinclination to even think about Al or anyone like him was due to her overriding concern for Django, the fact that she *had* been indisputably courting infidelity, could not be explained by Django's cancer. Similarly, though Pip now welcomed Zac's embrace and found great comfort in his calm and level-headed assessment of her uncle's illness, she knew too that joining forces on Django's behalf cleverly waylaid them from tackling the impasse existing in their marriage. As for Cat, if she split her time on a purely practical level between being a nurse and a bookshop manager, if she focused on jazz with Django and cancer with Ben and ISBNs with head office, then she reasoned she would have no time for the needling concerns about her own sense of self.

Mothers, daughters, lovers, liars – who were they? And how might Django's illness shape who they could become? In the clear light of each new day, questions yet to be answered came more and more to the fore. Questions to face head-on and answers not to be flinched from. They were prepared, at last, to question themselves. And at last they felt prepared to seek answers from somebody else too.

'What will Denver be like at this time of year?' Pip asks Cat.

'Hot,' Cat says and she doesn't need to say *Why?* It's of sudden comfort to her that the telepathy gifted amongst sisters obviously extends to half sisters too. She's always had it with Fen and Pip. The more recent discovery of specific DNA wasn't going to alter it. 'Lovely,' she says, 'but hot.'

Fen looks from left hand to right, from Cat to Pip, and lets

331

her gaze rest on her daughter who is grabbing at Pip's rug in a bid to get onto her knees. 'I've never left my baby for more than a few hours,' Fen says quietly, attuned to their thinking.

'Could you leave her for a few days?' Pip asks tentatively, burning a knowing look at her sister.

Fen locks eyes with her. She shrugs. She nods. She shrugs again.

Pip turns to Cat. 'Could the shop spare you for a few days? Do you have any holiday entitlement?'

Cat shrugs and then she nods.

'Django will have an address,' says Pip. 'Who's going to call him?'

'You are,' say Fen and Cat together.

Django isn't surprised by the request. But he won't tell them he is relieved until they're back home again. 'OK. Hold on. It's in my address book. Where's my address book?' The telephone receiver is clattered down as he rummages around for some time. Pip raises her eyebrows to her sisters who listen in and smile. 'Here's my address book,' they can hear him say in the background because he's momentarily forgotten to retrieve his receiver. He picks it up. 'Hullo? Hullo? Are you still there? Ericsson. Here we are. Mrs P. Ericsson. 84 Emerson Street. Lester Falls.'

'Thanks,' says Pip, about to change the subject, as if the intended trip is no big deal.

'Vermont,' Django adds, 'VT 05154.'

Pip's pen hovers, frozen. Fen mouths, *What? What!* 'Pardon?' Pip says.

'It's a zip code. VT 05154.'

'I know it's a zip code,' says Pip, 'but what's it doing in *Vermont*?' Cat and Fen now crowd around the telephone, which irritates her. She's trying to concentrate and figure it out. She brushes them away as if they're children.

'Because your mother lives in Vermont,' they all hear Django clearly say, however, 'she never moved.'

'You said Denver,' Pip objects and Cat backs away now, feeling deflated at possibly more twists to the tale.

'I did not,' Django is saying carefully. 'Your mother ran off with a cowboy from Denver when you were small. But you've never asked where they lived. And they lived in Vermont. Never moved.'

Lester Falls

They didn't expect rain. Nor did they anticipate Lester Falls to be so plain. Pip knew better than to expect the maple trees to be ablaze with fiery foliage in June, but she had hoped for pretty weather-boarded houses, Adirondack chairs on porches, the odd covered bridge or white wooden church; it was thus difficult not to feel hard done by with this incessant drizzle in a rather nondescript town. Especially after an arduous three-hour drive from Boston. For Fen, picture-postcard perfect scenery had been an imperative notion when it had come to packing her suitcase and leaving her eleven-month-old baby; her ache for Cosima was now manifest in the gut-hollow, throat-ripped perpetual threat of tears. Cat found herself resenting her sisters for organizing the trip in the first place and she lagged behind, sulking to herself darkly that it must be easier for them than for her. With Fen close to tears and Cat glowering to herself, it was down to Pip to jostle maps and leaflets and figure out what they should do and where they might stay. Privately, she cursed her mother for not living somewhere more picturesque and she cursed her sisters for standing around gormlessly leaving everything to her. She remembered the quote on the mug Fen had bought her last Christmas which said that an older sister helps one remain half child, half woman; just then, Pip wished her younger sisters would opt for the grown-up identity.

'We should have stayed in Boston,' Cat said sulkily. 'A little retail therapy would probably be far more curative than some misguided fact-finding mission with some woman we don't even know.'

'We shouldn't have come in the first place,' Fen muttered, staring at outdated fashions fastidiously displayed in a shop window. 'What do we hope to achieve anyway? We don't even know what we want to say. We'd have been better off spending time in Derbyshire with Django.'

'For God's sake you two!' Pip snapped. 'We're jet lagged and we're nervous. But we're here. So let's find somewhere to stay – and something to eat. It's lunch-time.' She stomped off with Cat and Fen mooching behind her.

There's little a great cup of coffee can't soothe. Especially when served by a friendly soul in the comfortable surroundings of a genuine diner. Combined with a sturdy plateful of eggs and grits to raise blood sugar levels and stave off tiredness, Cat and Fen felt revived and able to assess their surroundings and consider their options with Pip.

'We don't know where exactly she lives,' Cat said, squinting at the map.

'Or if she's even here,' said Fen.

'Please God let her be out of town,' Cat said. 'Then we can justify a weekend's shopping in Boston.'

'If she isn't here, I might just fly back home, actually,' said Fen, brightening at the possibility.

'I'll ask the waitress if she knows where Emerson Street is,' Pip said.

'Don't mention her name!' Cat rushed.

The waitress, who had 'Betty' embroidered on a pristine pale blue gingham uniform, was sorry to be unable to help, but she asked the short-order chef who scribbled down directions on a paper napkin.

'Is it walkable?' Pip asked.

'Joe – lady here wants to know if it's walkable?'

Joe came right out of the kitchen, appeared to evaluate the age and fitness of the girls and nodded. 'I reckon. About a half-hour. Who you looking for?'

The girls paused.

'Oh, no one, really,' Cat said.

'You guys on vacation?' Joe asked. 'In *Lester*?'

'Just passing through,' Pip said lightly. 'A friend of a friend of a friend lives on Emerson Street – we thought we'd look her up.'

'Who's that?' Joe asked.

'Um. A Mrs Ericsson?'

Joe thought hard. 'Nope. Can't say I know her. You know her, Betty?'

'I'm thinking, I'm thinking – but no, don't think I do. Say, are you from England?' the waitress asked with breathless awe.

'Yes,' the girls told her.

'That is just so nice,' Betty enthused. 'I could listen to you speak all day long.'

Automatically, the girls found they rounded their vowels and used choice adjectives, much to her delight. After more coffee and flattery, Lester Falls seemed less dull and their hostility lessened too.

'Well, thank you so much,' said Pip, 'that was simply super.'

'Indeed!' said Cat. 'Splendid coffee.'

'Have a nice day!' Betty said.

'Cheerio,' said Cat.

They strolled along Main Street. The rain had stopped, revealing the town to be less dreary than first impressions

336

suggested. The shops were old-fashioned but quirky, the façades comfortingly indicative of small-town America, as portrayed in so many of the films the sisters had seen. A promising landscape was now impressively visible beyond the town. The mountains so thickly forested that they appeared to be clothed in thick green bouclé sweaters.

'We're in the lie of the Green Mountains here,' Pip looked up from the guidebook. '*Vert Mont* – Vermont! Do you see?'

'Shall we walk then?' Fen asked tentatively. 'Joe said it would take half an hour.'

'But say she *is* in,' Cat said. 'We don't even know what we're going to say.'

'Let's find somewhere to stay first,' Pip said.

Sitting tightly together on one of the beds in the family room they'd found in a decent guest house on a pretty street a short walk from the centre of town, the McCabe sisters pored over the local phone directory. They'd missed the entry initially, forgetting that Bob was most likely a diminutive of Robert, but had then found the entry for R. Ericsson. The address was the same as that which Django had provided and gave the girls a bizarre sense of triumph, as if they were veritable sleuth-hounds. Pip jotted down the telephone number. Then they stared hard at the entry again, as if utter concentration might suddenly provide fly-on-the-wall privilege, some sort of telepathy or more clues.

Pip looked at her watch. 'Shall we mosey on up there now,' she suggested lightly, 'you know – just in time for tea?'

'We have another three days, remember,' said Cat and Fen felt herself lurching to the verge of tears at the thought of four more days until she'd actually be home. 'We could look around the town and get our bearings.'

'Find somewhere for supper later,' Fen agreed.

'This is not a holiday,' Pip said impatiently. 'We're here

337

on family business. Now come on.' She picked up the car keys and led the way.

Pip crept the car along Emerson Street. The houses, modern but unexceptional, were set spaciously along it, fronted by steeply pitched gardens making the buildings appear more squat than they actually were. Under their breath, the sisters spoke out the house numbers, falling silent when they came upon their mother's home. Though it fitted well with the style and scale of all the other houses they had passed, its blandness took them aback. Fen felt embarrassed that she'd actually thought along the lines of Bates Motel. She realized how, deludedly, she had been expecting something else; presumed that somehow she'd instantly recognize the house where their mother lived. Something more sinister. Something a lot less ordinary. Pip stopped the car at the bottom of the drive and they looked up.

'Doesn't look like there's anyone at home,' said Fen though she could not base this theory on fact.

'Might as well come back later,' Cat said, 'or tomorrow.'

'God almighty, you two,' Pip sighed, 'come *on*.'

They walk up the drive.

They loiter by the front door.

Then they turn on their heels and walk briskly back to the car.

Unseen from an upstairs window, Penny had watched them arrive and now she's watching them leave. And they've gone. She goes downstairs and sits heavily in Bob's chair. What could it possibly mean? It was a sight she has never envisaged, never even thought about, never hoped for, never dreaded. What on earth should she make of this? What on earth is she meant to do? What on earth do they want? Why didn't they ring the bell? Why didn't she open the door anyway? she asks out loud, again and again. But no one answers.

'We could head off to Boston,' Cat suggested, once they were back in the guest house.

'Or we could just go home,' Fen said. 'Do you mind if I do that? You two hit Boston, by all means.'

'We'll call her,' Pip said and Fen glanced with resentment at the phone book still lying in the centre of Pip's bed. 'We can't go without trying a bit harder,' she told her gently. 'We've come this far. And spent a fortune.'

'How about we phone the number at 9 p.m. tonight, and if there's no answer, we pop up there again at 9 a.m. tomorrow and if she still isn't there, we head back to Boston and Fen can make the 9 p.m. flight?' Cat said.

'Cat o' nine tales,' Pip laughed.

'We can send her a postcard, or something,' Fen said quietly, looking from one palm to the other.

'Are you missing Cosima dreadfully?' Cat asked.

Fen nodded. 'You have no idea how much.'

'But Matt's mum said everything was fine when you last phoned home?' Pip said.

Fen nodded and shrugged.

'Weird to think that Cosima's other grandma is just a couple of miles away,' Cat remarked.

'Weirder to think it's our *mother* just a couple of miles away,' said Pip and they stared at the phone book. 'Right, I'm calling her now.'

'What if she answers?' Cat gasped as Pip lifted the receiver. 'What will you say?'

'What if it's an answerphone?' Fen asked. 'Will you leave a message?'

Pip was already dialling. 'Answering machine,' she said, hanging up.

They stared at the phone.

'What did it say?' Fen asked.

'I don't know,' Pip said, 'I hung up on "Hi".'

'Can I listen?' Fen asked. Pip shrugged, phoned the number and passed the receiver over to Fen who glued it against her ear and tried to detect clues from the wording of the message, the timbre of her mother's voice. She hung up in a hurry before the beep.

'I suppose I ought to as well,' said Cat and Pip dialled the number again. Cat listened hard; though she'd heard the voice only once before, it sounded strangely familiar.

Hi. You've reached Penny Ericsson. Can't take your call right now. Leave your message after the tone and I'll call you as soon as I can.

'Hullo – who is this?'

The voice rang through before the anticipated beep. Cat was so taken aback that one hand was paralysed to the receiver, the other frozen in mid-air where it had been hovering over the phone's cradle. The voice filtered out of the receiver, tinny and faint yet filling the room.

'Hullo?'

Fen stared at Cat wide-eyed while Pip mouthed, *Say something Say something* whilst holding out her hand for the receiver.

'Hullo? Who is this?'

Cat cancelled the call.

They sat in silence, staring at the phone with trepidation, as if their mother might suddenly materialize from it, like some wicked genie.

'She was *there*,' Cat whispered, 'she's there right *now*.' She looked at Pip. 'Please don't make us go back up there tonight.' She held her hand out for her sisters to observe how it trembled. Fen took it and held it between hers. Pip sat and wondered what they should do next.

*

It was like a skewed take on Postman's Knock – the resultant addled adrenalin rush caused by the near miss. Derring-do mixed with jet lag and crisp cold beer in a local bar, combined to ensure a lively evening for the McCabe sisters. They picked at peanuts and at the labels on the beer bottles and giggled at the details of the day.

'It's all very Enid Blyton,' Fen said, chinking her beer bottle against her sisters'.

'Woody Allen, more like,' said Cat, with a long drink.

'Let's just hope it doesn't turn Stephen King,' Pip laughed and she put down her bottle and laid her hands on the table as if they symbolized facts. 'Right. We know that she's here but she doesn't know that *we're* here. Do we phone first or just front up?'

'I wonder if she was in all along, this afternoon,' mused Fen, 'spying on *us* stalking *her*.'

'We didn't ring the bell,' Cat said, 'but perhaps she traced our calls. Do they have 1471 in America?' she wondered, hiccing softly.

'The thing is,' said Pip, 'what do we want to say? What is it that we want to hear?'

Tracing the paths of the condensation on their beer bottles, tracing the pattern of the wood grain on the table, making patterns out of peanuts, they could draw no conclusion.

If Pip had been subconsciously looking for any excuse to confront her middle sister, that night it was presented to her on a plate, or rather in a beer bottle, in the guise of four studenty local boys offering to buy them a drink. It wasn't as if the boys loitered with intent. Or made a pass. Or even flirted harmlessly. They didn't ply them with alcohol, just the one friendly round of beers. They weren't suggestive in their conversation; if anything they were refreshingly artless in their questions. After all, three English girls were something of a novelty and buying them a drink bought an evening's entertainment. They asked about the Queen. They asked the girls to say 'squirrel' and 'bath' and 'pasta'. They asked how old were the houses in which they lived. Though Fen's smile and easy chatter was harmless enough, to Pip it seemed otherwise. With her beer goggles on, she computed simple facts into complex danger signs. She fused the tone of Fen's laughter, the slant of her smile and the glint of her eyes, into the image of a trollop warranting chastisement.

'Nice guys,' Fen commented as the boys left the bar.

'You can tell whose daughter you are,' growled Pip.

If this was a saloon in a Spaghetti Western, loaded silence would have met Pip's verbal gauntlet. But in this bar in Lester Falls, time didn't stand still and the din did not abate and Pip's haughty expression was somewhat diffused by the dim lighting. Both Cat and Fen had to squint at her and say, What? because the beer and the bar and the bizarreness of what they thought they'd heard were so distorted.

Pip looked at Cat. 'Why not ask her what babysitters are for?'

Cat looked at Pip, confused. 'What *babysitters* are for?' she asked and Pip nodded gravely. Cat turned to Fen. 'What are babysitters for?' she asked ingenuously, with a conspiring twitch of her face to signify she thought Pip odd.

Fen took a long moment to answer, in which time Pip's point struck her sharply. 'Tell her they're to alleviate the oppressive humdrum a frumpy mum can just occasionally be choked by,' Fen told Cat whilst glaring at Pip.

Cat looked at Pip. 'She says they're to – oh fuck it, did you hear all that? They choke humdrum frumps and stuff.'

Pip folded her arms and levelled a stare at Fen, whilst speaking to Cat. 'Tell her, Oh! Really! I thought that was the function of someone called Al!'

342

It was well below the belt but it winded Fen all the same, a single spasm deep in her diaphragm forcing her breath into her constricted throat. 'Fuck you,' Fen whispered which was easy enough for everyone to lipread.

'What's going on here?' Cat asked, her gaze leaping from one sister to other. 'Have you fallen out? Have I missed something? Who's Al?'

'Al's your sister's bit-on-the-side,' Pip announced.

'That's not true!' Fen protested.

'*Who is Al*?' Cat repeated. 'What's happened?'

With her hands in her lap, Fen looked deeply into her beer bottle as if hoping for a magical kaleidoscope to transport her away, willing the neck of the bottle to widen and reveal Narnia, Wonderland, anywhere. But it didn't. It didn't even say Drink Me any more. Fen pushed the bottle away and slowly she looked up at her sisters with a smile soft and beatific which she hoped might miraculously solve the issue and change the subject. But it didn't.

'Fen!' Cat implored. 'What's going *on*?'

'Leave me alone,' Fen said feebly as she stood heavily from her stool and made to leave the bar. Almost at the door she stopped. What was the point of this? Storming out would only make her look worse. These were her sisters. Really, she needed their support, not animosity. After all, as the only feeling she harboured for Al was regret, there could be no harm in divulging that at all. Her sisters' friendship was imperative; she hadn't been through life without it and just then she could not contemplate going forward without it. As she made it to the door, she was accosted by the memory of a quote on a tea towel Pip had once bought her, which decreed that anyone who didn't know how a woman could both love her sister and also want to strangle her was probably an only child.

'Sorry,' Fen said, with searching eye contact, as she returned to the table and sat back down for her comeuppance.

'What's happened?' Cat pleaded. 'What did you *do*?'

Fen glanced from one hand to the other and then she looked up. 'There is this bloke called Al,' Fen told Cat apologetically and with a clear shrug of confession to Pip, 'but nothing happened really.' She stopped at her words; glancing back over her memory of the time in Al's room and wondering just what defined something or nothing; what precisely was infidelity. Penetration or intent? Wandering hands or simply straying thoughts? She remembered how she'd deludedly hoped a quick dalliance with Al would provide positive memories that would titillate. But there, in the bar in a one-eyed town in Vermont, the thought of what she'd done, what she'd been on the verge of doing had Pip not phoned her that fateful night, sank a leaden spear of shame right to her core. She dragged her gaze to meet her sisters'.

'I almost cheated on Matt,' she confided with a meek nod and a sad shrug.

'What's "almost"?' Cat asked aghast.

'I met some bloke,' Fen admitted, 'a bloke called Al and he was flirty and young and the opposite of Matt. And I was flattered and tempted. More than tempted. And thank God Pip phoned when she did because if she hadn't I probably would have.'

'Would have what?' Cat asked. 'Phoned Pip?'

'Had sex with Al,' Fen admitted. Suddenly, she realized that she could fob off her sisters with this limited version of events, but not herself. It was time, at last, to change tack and face facts. 'I have to admit, I practically did,' she revealed forlornly. 'If we're talking all the other bases, I'd passed Base 3. We were on the home straight when Pip called.'

'You're joking!' Cat laughed, because Fen's terminology seemed so adolescent and the notion seemed so preposterous. *Fen*? Fen being fingered and having her tits groped while she fiddled with the cock of a bloke called Al? Fen who had

344

embraced to the hilt the all-consuming responsibilities of being a mother at the expense of even a night out at the Rag and Thistle? Fen, the conventional, stay-at-home mummy with lovely Matt providing for her and her perfect daughter?

'I'm not,' Fen said, her eyes downcast as she hid behind her fringe.

'Not what?' said Cat.

'Not joking,' Fen declared.

'But you're not allowed to do that!' Cat protested.

'I lost sight of that fact,' Fen admitted, 'but I swear to you, it stares me in the face every time I look in the mirror.'

'Do you no longer love Matt?' Pip asked carefully, her tone more level, her look softer.

'Of course I do,' Fen said, suddenly realizing she couldn't even consider answering the question any other way.

'But who is this Al?' Cat pressed.

'I don't really know,' Fen admitted, 'just someone who wasn't Matt. Someone with whom I could be more than just me.'

As they walked back to the guest house, Cat and Pip wondered why their sister should think there was anything wrong with just being herself. While Fen just thought there must be something wrong with her. None of the other new mums she had met had gadded off with flower-laying toyboys. The only new mum of whom she knew who had behaved in a similar fashion was her own mother. And Fen and her sisters were in agreement that there must have been something very wrong with her. Fen's last thought on the matter, before she was distracted by the flashing red button on the phone in the room, was to pray that her wayward detour had been temporary and to thank God that it hadn't taken her away from her baby.

But had the woman who had taken herself away from her three babies decades ago, now tracked them down?

Cat, Fen and Pip stared at the flashing red light.

'Could be Ben,' said Cat.

'Or Matt,' said Fen.

'Or Zac,' said Pip.

But there was no message. Just a long recorded silence.

Probably one of the boys.

Playing silly buggers.

Cat looked at her watch. 'If it's 10 o'clock here, it must be three tomorrow morning in proper time.'

'Proper time?' laughed Pip, putting an affectionate arm around Cat.

'Check your mobile for messages,' Fen told Pip, who had the only tri-band phone between them. 'Just in case it's for me.'

Pip took her phone from the bedside drawer where she'd placed it on top of their passports and next to the complimentary copy of the bible which was alarmingly covered in lilac suedette.

The envelope icon signified a message.

'It's just a text from Zac,' Pip told them, opening the message.

`Hope all ok. Just 2 say Tom has baby bro!!! Nathan Oliver, 7lbs 13oz. Evryone doing just fine!!! Z xx`

'What does he say?' Cat asked.

'Pip?' said Fen, because her sister's face had dropped.

'What? Oh,' said Pip, 'nothing really.'

'Sweet nothings?' Cat smiled.

'Something like that,' Pip said, switching off the mobile and putting it back by the purple bible.

The girls were exhausted. It had gone three in the morning proper time, and they'd had a day beset by travel, jet lag, strange towns, their mother's front door and their mother's voice. Cat and Fen shared the kingsized bed, falling asleep within seconds of each other, within minutes of clambering in. Pip turned away from them in her queen bed. Hot tears seeped silently from tired sore eyes.

Evryone doing just fine. Evryone doing just fine. Welcome little Nathan. But I'm not fine. I'm not doing just fine at all.

* * *

Those three silent calls. Penny guessed it was them, her daughters. Her three girls, silent for almost three decades. She surprised herself by hoping that it was. They just wanted to listen, didn't they? Who dialled last? Who was it who hung up on 'Hi'? She had traced the call, to put a place to the number. Brook Barn Inn. She knew exactly where that was. It was a decent enough place. She had spent the remainder of the afternoon and all evening meandering around the house, walking in and out of rooms that had seen no person other than her for seven months. She went to bed early but couldn't sleep. Nearing midnight, she dressed and drove into town. Parked her car, switched off the engine and just gazed and gazed at the Old Lester Inn; wondering what she should do.

Plastic Tubing

'Are you awake?'

'Yes.'

'Is Cat awake?'

'Yes I'm awake too.'

'Sodding jet lag. It's not even seven o'clock.'

'I bet that diner will be open by now.'

'What day is it – is it Saturday?'

'Yes. I think so.'

'It *is* Saturday. We arrived in Boston Thursday night – then came up here yesterday morning. So yes, today must be Saturday.'

'Perhaps the diner won't open so early on a Saturday.'

'Only one way to find out.'

The diner was open and Cat, Fen and Pip were greeted by Betty the waitress who, bizarrely, had 'DeeDee' embroidered on her uniform today.

'The English Roses return, Joe!' she called through to the back before fussing around them, wiping an already gleaming table and straightening the napkin dispenser and cruets. 'You take a load off, girls,' she said. 'What'll you have? Did you meet with your friend?'

The sisters exchanged glances; if they couldn't refer to her as their 'mother' they certainly couldn't refer to her as their 'friend'.

'She wasn't in,' said Pip, deciding to gloss over the ambiguity by polishing her vowels. 'Frightful shame.'

'Frightful shame!' the waitress repeated, marvelling at the words, not the matter. 'Well, if you're kicking around today, there's a lot of fun to be had round here. There's the Falls for a start – if you guys like hiking that sure is one pretty place. There's also some quaint villages near by – Hubbardton's Spring and Ridge – just like you see on the postcards, though most of the postcards are taken in the fall so don't go expecting those colours. And if you like to shop, you head over to Manchester – the finest outlet village. Puts New York in the shade, I'll say.'

Cat's glance to her sisters was sufficient to say that she for one rather hoped the house on Emerson would be empty again today. She found herself looking at the waitress's left breast as coffee was replenished. 'I say,' she said plummily, 'I hope you don't think me rude – but yesterday you were Betty, today you're DeeDee.'

The waitress looked at her bosom, as if to check herself who she was. 'You're right!' she said cheerily, and busied away to collect the girls' breakfasts from the grill, piping hot and delicious.

After a leisurely breakfast, though coffee was topped up and more pleasantries were exchanged with the waitress, they were no nearer finding if she was DeeDee or Betty. Fen and Cat called goodbye to Betty, Pip called goodbye to DeeDee, all three said see you tomorrow.

'Bugger Boston,' Cat remarked as they walked up Main Street, 'let's just do a day-trip to Manchester. When Betty said "dickny" do you think she meant "DKNY"?'

'Or do you think *we've* been mispronouncing the brand?' Fen challenged and she and Cat laughed in mortification.

'Ralph Law-rn,' said Cat.

'Ralph L'Ren,' Fen said.

'Sad thing is, I don't possess a single item from Ralph or Donna,' said Pip. 'I'm not what one would call a designer clown.'

'So let's go to Manchester!' Cat said.

'Or we could just catch an earlier—'

'Hi.'

It was Penny.

Right in front of them.

Sunlight bouncing off her glasses and flashing platinum through her short, silvering hair; her slim, wiry frame appearing to fill the sidewalk. Fen glancing sharply behind herself, as if looking for an escape route; Cat staring at her mother's feet, ten toes with neat nails; Pip stepping forward just slightly but able to raise her eyes only as far as her mother's tiger's-eye pendant.

'Hi,' she says again, this time with an awkward shrug. Pip can feel Cat and Fen looking beseechingly at her.

'Hullo,' says Pip.

'Fancy seeing you here,' Penny says with what would have been a wry smile though her nervousness and the intense sunlight make it appear more of a grimace and a squint.

'We've just had breakfast,' Pip says, cringing inwardly. Since planning the trip, she's prepared many a soliloquy and rehearsed varying degrees of acerbic wit and biting truths. Not once has she practised the line 'We've just had breakfast'.

'You have plans for today?' Penny asks, steering clear of the undisputable fact that the girls can only be in Lester Falls on her account.

'We were going to go to Manchester,' Cat says shyly, addressing her mother's feet. 'Shopping.'

'Nice,' said Penny, as if this was reason enough to have Lester Falls as their base.

'Perhaps a walk to the Falls,' Fen says, glancing over her shoulder again though that's the opposite direction to the Falls.

'Real pretty,' Penny says, as if a hike to the Falls could indeed be the sole purpose for crossing the Atlantic to this little town. 'You could come for lunch,' she says, 'if it fits your day?'

The sisters regard each other in silent consultation.

'Could do,' says Pip, noting half a nod from Fen and a small shrug from Cat.

'Good,' says Penny, wondering what they like to eat. She's never been much of a cook. Never attempted the eccentric fusion cuisine of Django McCabe. 'You vegetarian or anything?'

'What – having been brought up by Django?' Fen says to Penny's sandals – she remembers distinctly they are the same she wore that morning in Derbyshire.

Penny surprises herself by smiling easily. 'So, shall we say noon? I live on Emerson Street.' She pauses. 'But you know that.'

The sisters consider their mother's slightly cryptic allusion.

'Hey, Penny!'

A young woman, much their own age, has approached and she's smiling at their mother, regarding them quizzically.

'Oh,' Penny flusters, and Cat can see that her toes curl slightly, 'Juliette. Hi.'

'Haven't seen you for a while,' Juliette says warmly. 'How you doing?'

'Fine,' says Penny, acutely aware that the last time she saw Juliette was when she stormed away from her, 'just fine. Real busy.'

'Oh,' says Juliette, 'cool.'

There follows a pause so pregnant Penny fears she is on the verge of bellowing in discomfort. Juliette is looking from the girls to Penny, and back again. Smiling sweetly, genuinely friendly.

'I'm Juliette,' she says to the sisters, with a childish little wave. 'Hi.'

The sisters respond with awkward hand-raising of their own.

'Pip.'

'Fen.'

'Cat.'

'Well, I gotta go,' Juliette says, with polite reluctance. 'Sure was nice to meet you all,' she smiles at the girls. 'Don't be a stranger,' she says to Penny, touching her hand. 'We miss you.'

And there they stand for a mammoth moment or two longer.

Penny, a woman who feels she has no right to introduce herself as 'mother'.

And the three sisters who can't yet bring themselves to be known as her daughters.

Pip walked a large, aimless loop. Fen and Cat followed.

'Christ, are we sure about all of this?' Fen asked, standing stock still. 'Isn't it just too bizarre to be having lunch with her? Too quick? Too – I don't know – normal? Too friendly, too accepting?' Pip sighed as she thought although Fen didn't wait for an answer. 'I don't know about you two but I don't feel prepared. I've run through so many scenarios in my head these last few days and in all of them, I'm this empowered woman brimming with erudite proclamations and condemnation. But now I feel very, very small.'

Pip looked ahead. 'Look, we all feel weird – her too, no

doubt – but we're here and this is an opportunity and we have to take it, whatever the outcome.' She paused, tying and retying her pony-tail while she thought. 'If we don't – if we blow her out – imagine how you'll feel once you've returned home. Jesus – I've said it before, it's not a holiday. It's not a social engagement. It's necessary. It's a summit.'

'What do we do about Django? Say she asks?' Fen asked. 'Are we going to tell her?' She looked at Cat who appeared lost in thought.

'I think we avoid lies,' Pip said, reflecting on it. 'After so much dishonesty, the plain truth will do. But let's not volunteer information. If she asks directly how he is, then we'll answer directly. Agreed?'

Fen nodded. Pip looked to Cat who was still avoiding eye contact or comment. 'Cat?'

'Whatever,' Cat muttered. 'I'm not hungry,' she said, thinking fast that she could find if there was a flight from somewhere to take her to Boulder.

'That's totally irrelevant and you know it,' Pip snapped.

'But we don't know her at all,' Cat said, cross with Pip for her reaction.

'What we do know is that she ran away with a cowboy from Denver when we were small,' said Pip. 'Here's our chance to find out why.'

In their fantasies, over the years, they'd created an image of their mother that was far from flattering. They'd never quite given her form – a stereotypical warted wicked witch seemed too contrived – but they'd created the world in which she lived. Most damning of all, they'd given her a world with no style. With the cowboy-from-Denver situation always to the fore, they'd positioned their mother in a poor and tacky version of *Dynasty*. An ostentatious driveway in a boring flat land. A preposterous fountain flanked by disparate figures from antiquity, poorly copied and made from resin. Fake Corinthian columns and disproportionate pediments. White leather sofas. Reproduction furniture with ubiquitous claw-and-ball feet. Lots of gilt. Lots of guilt. Uniformed staff, who all secretly hated her, addressing her as 'ma'am'. The cowboy himself, laughably repulsive in a rhinestone-encrusted ten-gallon hat; corpulent, porcine and with a gait dictated by gout.

But how reality can let a daydream down. For a start, they had to relocate their fantasy from a dull and nondescript land-scape to America's lush and hilly smallest state. Then, on entering Penny's house, the girls were immediately shocked and humbled by the utter contrast to their fantasy. Their sense of control of the situation was compromised. Reality was staring them in the face and they had to swallow hard and meet it eye to eye. No stuffed bison heads. No rifles, criss-crossed, above vulgar stone-clad fireplaces. No white leather anywhere. No staff. Most poignantly: no cowboy. But how they could feel his presence, how noticeable this man was by his absence. The house was tidy and clean, the furniture simple with a slightly dated Scandinavian feel; but no amount of messiness or belongings could change the haunting feeling that this was a lonely house; a place, a space, essentially designed and designated for two.

'Shall I show you around?' Penny offered. The four of them had been gathered in the hallway for some time, taking silent interest in each other's footwear whilst practising what to say. 'We built this house in '74.'

It was the same in every room; the house and its contents seemed to be putting on a brave smile, a bit of a show. Crisp linen, pretty curtains, handmade cushion covers and warmly worn rugs were easy on the eye in a futile bid to keep the solitary sadness from view. Everywhere appeared airy and light but a pervasive sense of melancholy cast metaphorical shadows which were long. Following behind Penny, Pip wondered whether this was their mother's home or her purgatory. Fen thought of their childhood house at Farleymoor; the scamper and warmth there, the welcoming dishevelment, the flow of company; the ring of home. The last room Penny took them to was the sitting-room, with its picture windows presenting a painterly and flawless view to a nicely tended garden rolling gently down to a thatch of trees that swathed its way up to the skirts of the hills beyond.

'Take a seat,' Penny said. 'Can I fix you a coffee? Something soft?' and she hurried off to the kitchen to compose herself and gaze quietly out of the window at the hire car of her daughters who were currently making themselves comfortable just across the hallway.

Cat stared at the chair. It was truly monstrous, the clumpy wood lacquered until it looked plasticized, embalmed even. She couldn't help but admit to herself that it was the sort of piece that Django would declare marvellous. She turned her attention to other features: the low table in burr oak laden with three neat piles of large-format coffee-table books; framed photographs on the mantel that would need to be seen up close; a large selection of board games piled on the lowest shelves either side of the fireplace; a chess set on an occasional table, its players standing to attention as if a game was imminent. Cat would have liked to peruse the photographs but a perverse desire to appear in Penny's eyes not remotely interested in her life kept her sitting on the sofa, looking at the chair.

'So,' said Penny breezily as she came into the room with a tray, 'here's your juice. I mixed cranberry and apple. And some cookies.'

Everyone sipped awkwardly and nibbled self-consciously.

'We were looking at the chair,' Fen said at length. 'It's – unusual.'

Penny regarded it for a moment. 'It's revolting,' she colluded, 'but it was Bob's most favourite possession. And though I found it easy enough to give all his clothes to the mission without so much as a sentimental sniff to his shirt collars – the chair, well, I just couldn't do it. I had to keep it.' They all looked at the chair, as if willing it to talk. 'Try it,' Penny said to Fen, 'go ahead.' Fen glanced at her sisters, then balanced her cookies on the rim of her glass and went over to sit down. 'Well?' Penny enquired.

'It's not designed for my shape,' Fen said diplomatically.

'I'm more of an Eames lounger girl,' said Pip, when Penny gestured for her to try. Cat avoided eye contact.

'My mother used to say every pot has its lid,' Penny said, 'so, perhaps every backside has its chair.'

Pip considered this. Then she thought about their maternal grandmother. 'When did she die? Your mother?' she asked.

'When I was fourteen.'

'Your father?' Pip asked.

'When I was very young.'

'Do you have any siblings?' Pip continued to probe.

'No, I have not.'

'Any other children?' Fen asked.

'No,' said Penny, 'I have not.'

'Stepchildren?' Pip asked.

'Nope,' Penny said, seemingly engrossed in massaging her cuticles, 'none. That's it. No family left.'

Pip thought to herself that if this was Hollywood, there'd be soaring violins and group hugs to accompany them proclaiming *Hey! We're your family! We never stopped loving you! Love means never having to say you're sorry! Oh Mom, it feels like we're home!* But the thought held no attraction and she reminded herself that this was not a journey to reconciliation, it was a fact-finding mission.

'I don't know if I was the lid or the pot,' Penny was saying, her thumb playing anxiously over her fingertips, 'but whichever I was, Bob was certainly the other.'

'We thought you lived in Denver,' Cat said, speaking for the first time. 'I lived in Denver for three years. We thought you lived with a cowboy.'

'Bob?' Penny looked incredulous. 'A *cowboy*?' She mused this over. 'I mean, he looked the part, when I first met him, in his blue jeans and his boots and his buckle belts and bootlace ties. And he *was* from Denver. But he wouldn't know one end of a horse from the other. He never got close enough anyway, on account of his asthma.'

'Oh,' said Cat.

'All these years you've been thinking I've been living with John Wayne on a ranch out west?' Penny started to giggle. It was Fen's giggle – Cat and Pip could detect it in an instant and they both glanced automatically from their mother to their sister; intrigued, disturbed. 'Oh my!' Penny continued. 'Would he have loved that.'

'Was it something to do with asthma?' Pip asked. 'How he died?'

'No my dear, he had cancer,' said Penny. The sisters looked at their laps and said sorry. And then they privately hoped that Penny wouldn't ask after Django because they didn't want to say the cancer word out loud. They hated saying the word. It was impossible to say it without a hush. And that seemed to dignify the dreadful disease. And anyway, his results weren't in. They didn't want to jinx Django.

Penny had crossed to the mantelpiece and selected a clutch of photographs. She passed them around. They studied the pictures, looked hard at Bob. He did not look anything like they'd imagined. The photos showed a tall, slim man in sensible V-necked sweaters, with a tidy slate-grey beard, round spectacles, silver glinting hair neatly clipped short beneath a smooth, tanned pate. Smiling. Easy, open, attractive smile. In most pictures, his arm was warmly around Penny. He looked normal and nice and Pip was surprised by how easy it was to tell Penny so. Cat wanted to say that he looked nothing like Django but she didn't. She felt slightly offended that there was no physical similarity at all. Instead, she focused on an old photo, from the seventies perhaps, in which Penny could well have been Pip, the same tilt of the head, the identical sparky smile.

'If he wasn't a cowboy,' Fen said, 'what did he do?'

'We had a business,' Penny said. 'We were very good at it. Tubing.'

'Tubing?' Fen looked disappointed.

'Yes,' Penny confirmed, 'plastic tubing. Bob Ericsson sure was the king of plastic tubes and components! Now would you look at the time – I'm going to fix our lunch.'

For the first time in their lives, Pip, Fen and Cat did not act like sisters; they did not huddle together to confab and support. They didn't even look at each other. They sat in their own heavy spheres, with thoughts spiralling nearly out of control. It was like having nothing to cling on to after a lifetime of clutching at straws which, when looked down, had opened onto a fantasy world of imaginative exaggeration and convoluted details. All of which had been comforting in their negativity. Yet in the space of an hour, the McCabe sisters had had to let the vulgar cowboy go, and the revolting ranch and the obsequious staff and all the rhinestones with him. Plastic tubes now replaced their hollow straws. They had a face to put to a name and the face was friendly. And though they'd been staring at their mother, noting all the details of her face, computing all her mannerisms, what they could see most vividly was her sadness and loneliness. It was all a bit disconcerting. A great love had been lost, and it was this love which defined this woman – not them. It was clear they never had done. The bluntness of this hurt. But the fact that a great love had existed also gave the protagonists qualities that Pip, Fen, Cat and even Django had spent their lives denying them.

Penny had started to sing. They could hear her. They didn't know the tune. But the sound broke their hermetic isolation from one another.

'I've just realized – we've probably never asked Django much about her or her cowboy because our family folklore of "Your mother ran off with a cowboy from Denver when you were small" had served as an answer in its own right,' Pip said. 'And I suppose we've always held her and the evil cowboy as somehow responsible for our father's death – like they caused the heart failure.'

'But there was never a cowboy,' Fen said flatly, 'there was just plastic tubing and now there's just a lonely widow. Who's currently cooking us lunch.'

'I'm not hungry,' said Cat and her voice was hoarse, 'and I no longer want to be here.'

'We'll go after lunch,' Pip said.

'Yeah right,' Cat muttered. 'I want to go now. Not after lunch.'

'Well we can't,' Pip whispered in a hiss.

'Why the fuck not?' Cat whispered back.

'We can't,' Pip said.

'Don't tell me what I can and can't do!' Cat objected. 'You two bloody stay then – I'm not.'

'Cat!' Pip said.

'Fucking hell, Pip,' Cat said, 'just because I can't be as *big* as you or react in your controlled way.'

'Calm down, for goodness' sake,' Fen said.

'It's hard enough dealing with what I do know,' Cat said. 'It's like with Django – you two want to know all about the tests and the treatment and the prognosis. I don't. OK?'

'I know it's difficult,' Pip started.

'Don't patronize me,' Cat said, pointing her finger. 'I'm going for a walk. I'll wait by the car. Or I'll go back to the hotel. I don't know. But I'm not staying *here*.'

And she left.

And when Penny heard the front door shut, she wondered if they'd all gone. She felt almost jubilant to find that two of her three wanted to sit at her table and eat lunch with her.

'Cat's just—' Pip paused.

'It's OK, honey,' Penny said, 'you don't have to explain for her.'

But Pip felt duty-bound to. 'It's sort of hit her the hardest, perhaps,' Pip said, 'on account of her not knowing about – well, her father.'

Fen was suddenly terrified Penny would say, Ah and how is Django? and she didn't want her to so she changed the subject urgently. 'Gorgeous bread!' she exclaimed.

'Bob's favourite,' Penny revealed and from then on she talked only about Bob. She said she'd map out Bob's route to the Falls for them. She asked how the guest house was – because Bob had always said that the town lacked a really good hotel.

'He'd say, "If you build it, they will come",' she reminisced.

It was more exhausting than tedious – Pip felt obliged to nod sympathetically at every mention of this woman's late husband. They'd long finished eating but they remained at the table, which Bob had shipped over from Denmark where he used to do a lot of business, so Penny said.

'Well, we ought to make tracks,' Fen said after a coded glance to Pip.

'Perhaps we'll take Bob's route to the Falls tomorrow,' Pip said, standing, 'if we decide not to take an earlier flight home.' She gave Fen a little smile.

'When you due to fly?' Penny asked.

'Monday evening at the moment,' Fen sighed.

'The red-eye? You know, Bob swore by Melatonin to combat jet lag. Wait – I'm sure I still have some.' Penny disappeared upstairs, leaving Pip and Fen to stare at each other and shrug.

'Thank you for coming,' Penny said, giving Pip a pot of pills. 'It's nice for me to talk about Bob. Feels like I can honour his memory by recalling the minutiae – like I'm bringing him back to life by describing him to folk who never met him.' She paused, consumed by some deeply private thought. 'Too bad you never met him.'

'I'm sorry for your loss,' Pip heard herself say, edging across the hallway towards the door.

'Thank you,' Penny said, opening the door and shivering a little though it was a warm soft breeze which trickled in.

Fen stopped at the threshold. 'How old was he?' she asked. 'And had he been ill for very long?'

'He was seventy,' Penny said, 'and he'd been ill five months.'

'Five *months*!' Fen exclaimed. 'That's *terrible*.' She thought of Django and felt panic.

Love at Long Distance

'Marjorie? It's Dr York's wife – it's Cat. I'm sorry for phoning reverse-charges. I'm in a phone box and I want to speak to my husband.' She began to cry. 'I want to speak to Ben.'

'My dear, he's consulting at the moment. The Saturday evening clinic is very hectic.'

'But I'm phoning long-distance.'

'Are you all right? Is everything OK? Is this an emergency?'

Cat cried silently while Marjorie said Hullo? Hullo? down the phone.

'How long will Ben be? How long will Dr York be – do you think?'

'Is it an emergency, dear? I can call through if it's an emergency.'

Cat thought about this. And she thought about her husband, with some rugby player's prize tendon in his hands. 'It's not an emergency,' she had to sadly admit, 'I'm just lonely. I miss him.'

'Can I take a number for you?'

'This is a pay phone,' Cat said, 'in Vermont. I can't remember the stupid place I'm staying.'

'And when are you coming back?' Marjorie asked in her best soothing voice.

'We fly Monday night.'

'That's lovely and soon,' Marjorie enthused.

'But I miss him now,' Cat stammered, crying again. 'Is he almost finished? Do you think?'

'I'm afraid not,' said Marjorie. 'All these sportsmen with their strains and pains from today's games. Why don't I send him a nice message for you – like that other time.'

Cat brightened a little.

'I could say, "Dr York, your wife says absence is making her heart grow fonder," or something along those lines.'

Cat thought about it. 'Will you tell him I called, Marjorie? Tell him I miss him. Tell him I love him. Tell him it's rubbish here. But tell him I'm fine. Tell him I can't wait to see him.'

'I've written it down,' said Marjorie, 'word for word.'

'And tell him that for me, family means him,' Cat said. 'Tell him I love him.'

When she stepped away from the hood of the pay phone and turned to consult her whereabouts on the edge of town, Cat saw that the hire car with her sisters in the front seats had pulled up and was waiting. As she regarded them, tears still wet on her face, Pip wound down the driver's window.

'Hullo my pretty girl,' she said in a commendable Bill Sykes voice. 'Want to come and see my kittens and puppies?'

Cat was at once helpless not to giggle.

'Get in the car goddammit!' Fen leant across Pip, drawling in a deep American accent, as if they were about to start a cops-and-robbers chase. 'Get in the goddam car god-dammit.'

So Cat got in the car, drying her eyes on the way.

For there is no friend like a sister,
in calm or stormy weather,
to cheer one on the tedious way,
to fetch one if one goes astray,
to lift one if one totters down,
to strengthen whilst one stands.

No-Brainer

Bob's route was certainly scenic and the view from the Falls was postcard wonderful the next morning. Fen stood with her eyes closed, her hands clasped behind her head, breathing deeply, the air feeling thinner, finer, than down in town. Cat murmured that Ben would love it.

Pip thought to herself how Tom would too. 'They look like Hornby model railway hills,' she said, gazing at the spread of tree-clotted hills, 'like great big sponges dipped in green poster paint.' Her voice faltered.

'Are you all right?' Fen asked her, eyes still closed.

'Yes,' Pip said, with some busy blinking, 'I'm just tired. Yesterday is seeming more and more bizarre. I'm fine. Fuck it.' But then she squatted down and took her hands to her face, her shoulders heaving with her tears long before she made a sound.

'Pip!' Fen dropped down beside her and put an arm around her back.

'Pip don't *cry*,' Cat implored, crouching to the other side of Pip.

It was horrible to see Pip cry because she so seldom did. She was, after all, the great Mopper of Tears; a role neither of her sisters felt they could fulfil anywhere near as well. Pip had goose bumps on her forearms. It had been T-shirt weather on the lower part of the hike but the breeze at the top was insistent in its chill. Fen rubbed her sister's arms.

'Don't cry,' Cat continued to plead, as much for her sake as for her sister's. 'What's wrong?'

Pip gave one vigorous sniff, then took the sensible deep breaths she always advocated to others. In through the nose, out through the mouth, in through the nose, out through the mouth. She cleared her throat, stood up with her hands in the small of her back and had a good stretch. 'Fuck it,' she said, her voice now strong and surprisingly indignant, 'fucking *hell*.'

Cat and Fen looked at each other, a little bewildered. Something was coming and they couldn't anticipate what.

'I think she truly believes we've come all this way to offer our condolences on the death of her husband,' Pip laughed caustically. 'Don't you remember, Fen? When she thanked us for coming and said how nice it was for her to talk all about Bob to folk who'd never met him? Do you realize, she never once asked us a single thing about ourselves?' She put her hands on her hips and glared at her sisters. 'She's a self-centred old bag!' Pip rarely spoke ill of anyone, let alone with such a crude insult, and the sound of it was so out of character that Fen burst out laughing. 'It's not fucking funny,' Pip seethed, 'it's fucking sad. The whole thing. Our whole history. The fact that we've spent a small fortune coming out here. What's the prize?' She looked from Cat to Fen. 'Do you feel better? Either of you? Do you think it was a good idea? You were right yesterday, Cat. I should have followed you out instead of sitting politely and being Miss Maturity, Mrs Stupid Fucking Level Head, Mrs Pathetic Giver of the Benefit of the Doubt.' And with that she marched off.

'For fuck's sake, Fen,' Cat said under her breath, 'what are we going to do?'

'Come on,' murmured Fen, automatically stepping into the role as next-eldest and leading the way after Pip.

Pip stomped down from the Falls. 'I'm starving,' her only comment, called over her shoulder. Fen and Cat shot each other worried glances as they tried to keep up. She headed directly for the diner, which had provided their hearty breakfast for hiking a few hours earlier, and slumped down at the table they'd appropriated as their own these past three days. DeeDee, embroidered as Betty again, was delighted to see them so soon, charmed by the flush of their reddened faces.

'Joe – the hikers are back!' she called through. 'My, you girls must have made quick work of our Falls,' she marvelled while cleaning their table unnecessarily, straightening cutlery and presenting the menu though it already stood to attention before them, laminated and clasped between two steel blocks. 'No specials today, on account of it being Sunday, but if you need refuelling, you'll be wanting the burgers. We make them ourselves and the beef is from the Holstein herd just up at Brook Farm.'

'Sounds super,' said Fen, with an anxious look at Pip.

'Super duper,' Cat added, for Betty's pleasure.

'We'll have three, then,' said Fen, 'and a pot of strong tea too, please.'

Cat and Fen sat next to each other. Then leant across the table and took Pip's hands in theirs.

'It's OK,' Fen said to her.

'Pip,' Cat all but pleaded again.

'Fucking *hell*,' Pip growled under her breath. 'The point is – I didn't cross the frigging Atlantic in search of an apology and it may have been a bit hopeful to even expect an explanation. But Christ, to be asked *nothing*?'

Fen wondered what to say. Should she try and calm Pip or bolster her? 'I know,' she said, 'I know. I can see exactly what you mean. I now know all about tubing – but *she* hasn't a clue I have a sodding MA from the Courtauld Institute.'

'I told her I lived in Denver for three years,' Cat said, 'but she didn't ask me a thing about that.'

Pip buried her head in her hands and tugged hard at her hair. 'It's amazing we're as normal as we are,' she said hoarsely, with a burst of hollow laughter. The burgers arrived and she took great snatching bites. 'Christ, this is fucking delicious,' she said. 'Sorry about my language.'

'You swear as much as you fucking like,' Fen encouraged her, anything to restore her sister.

With blood sugar levels raised, stomachs full and nerves settled, they took stock of the situation once more.

'You say we didn't come here for an apology,' Fen said to Pip, 'but you know what, I think we *are* entitled to an explanation.'

'I sort of wish we'd never come,' Cat said quietly, 'but I suppose I'm pleased we are actually here. Thing is, I don't know what I came for – and I'm not really sure what it is I'll be taking home with me.'

She looked at Pip intently, willing her to respond. 'I mean, I'm sorry for her loss,' Pip said in her more usual voice, 'it must be ghastly – but for God's sake I don't even know if she was interested in telling us apart. I tell you something – we're not going home until we've had our say.'

'Are we going back?' Cat whispered. 'To the house on Emerson?'

'Yes,' Pip declared. 'God, don't look so scared, Cat – you're coming too this time, all the way. She's only human. We should use this trip to bury the mystique of her, once and for all.'

From the outside, the house on Emerson Street looked as empty as it had on their first visit. But to the sisters, they sensed it was brimming with information. They rang and they knocked and Penny seemed quite pleased to see them on her doorstep.

'Hi! How were the Falls?' she greeted them. 'Did you take Bob's route?'

All the confrontational power, the burning right to feel cross and cheated which Pip had amassed, simpered away in an instant in the presence of this woman. For the first time in her life she stood on a precarious threshold, wishing her younger sisters were in front of her, and not behind.

'Won't you come in,' Penny asked.

But Pip eyed the open door with suspicion. Bob was in there. This amazing man who looked so nice and who had loved their mother with all of his great big heart. Instinctively, she knew if they went in and sat in the kitchen and said yes to tea or coffee or cranberry and apple, they'd be back in Bob's space where the hurt and the anger that were justifiably theirs would be banned from the home of this widow. Pip reminded herself of her manners, her sense of decorum, both fastidiously instilled by Django.

'Are you OK?' Penny asked her, looking to Fen and Cat who both avoided her gaze. 'Are you OK, all of you?'

Pip was distraught at her emptied mind, her stupid silence. But suddenly Fen was alongside her. 'I have a daughter,' Fen proclaimed with slicing calm. 'Cosima is eleven months old.' Fen locked eyes with Penny. 'I have chosen to leave her for four days and five nights. You chose to leave us full stop.'

Fen observed Penny bristle and though she remained motionless, Fen could detect her pull back. 'It must seem that way,' Penny said, a guarded hostility edging into her voice.

'How did you do it?' Fen asked, genuinely flummoxed, slightly incredulous. 'I just don't know how it is possible, what with all the hormones and the *love*. Christ – the love!

I've never known such love! It's so exquisite it's almost painful. The emotion I feel for my partner is strong and stuff, but the emotion I feel for my child is. Is. God. It's *primal*.'

'You must be a very good mother,' said Penny, an unidentifiable tone to her voice.

'She is,' Cat parried in her sister's defence, 'she's amazing.'

Fen shrugged. 'I'm all right,' she reasoned, 'but I'm nothing special and that's the point. I'm just a normal mum – slightly neurotic, a bit dippy, mostly tired. But you see, I actually don't really care about why you left – it's irrelevant. You ran off with some cowboy from Denver, or the tube man from Vermont – the rest is history. But I've come here – I've left my baby thousands of miles away – because I would like to know *how*. How did you do it?'

Penny did not look discomfited and it irked Fen. In fact, it seemed her mother was thinking about these questions for the first time herself.

'How did I do it? I guess I felt I had no option,' Penny said at length. 'This man was my destiny. Being a mother – glaringly – was not. A man in my situation might have doubted himself to be the real father, on account of not feeling paternal. A man in my situation might have questioned DNA, might have said Are you sure I'm the father. But I couldn't exactly say, Are you sure I'm the mother – though actually, that's how I felt. My body conspired against me. Babies born to the wrong person.'

The sisters were too hurt to respond.

'Did you *ever* think of us?' Pip finally spoke. 'Did you *never* miss us? Did you never waiver? Or wonder?'

'No one ever challenged me,' Penny told them. 'You three were never a challenge – you were, all of you, good as gold. You ate, you slept, you were never ill or fretful. You weren't demanding, you didn't need me. It was easy. Nicholas never tried to stop me. Derek never tried to stop me. No one begged me to stay. It didn't seem to matter to any of you if I stayed or if I went; I wasn't needed. I never felt I made much impact on your lives. But I changed Bob's from the moment he set eyes on me. And that changed me. I found my calling. Does that make sense?'

'So if we'd been colicky nocturnal babies who didn't eat, things might have been different?' Fen posed, thinking of her little daughter's peculiar appetite for all things orange. She remembered how Cosima loved to lie, stomach down, over the boughs made by her mother's arms, like a little leopard in a tree. She recalled her own pure panic when Cosima's temperature rocketed to 104. She thought how, right at this very minute, on the other side of the ocean and the other side of the day, Cosima would be fluffy and fragrant and snuggly in her babygro, ready for bed. 'I don't need to feel needed,' Fen qualified. 'I'm a mother and by definition, that's a sometimes thankless task.' She paused. 'But I don't need to think about the level of love I have for my child. It over-rides all else.'

'The primal love you speak of I felt too,' Penny continued, gently insistent, 'but I felt it for Bob. That was birth in its truest sense for me – I was born anew when he touched my soul.'

'Oh shut up with all the Hollywood bullshit waffle,' Pip snapped. 'Can't you see we haven't come all this way to hear about Bob. We've come for plain, honest answers.'

Penny, visibly affronted by Pip's vitriol, motioned to the house. 'Won't you come inside? Please?'

'No!' Pip said.

Penny sighed. It appeared her daughters had not liked her initial and most honest explanation. In fact, they hadn't believed her. 'It was the sixties,' she tried. 'I was eighteen and I popped you out, 1, 2, 3. It happened so fast, so easily. I don't know. I don't know. Would they call it post-natal depression these days? I don't know.'

'Were any of us conceived out of love?' Cat asked. 'Did you create any of us intentionally – or were we just the inconvenient consequences of some 1960s recklessness?'

'Well—'

But Cat needed to continue. 'Jesus,' she said, 'most of my friends' parents got through the 1960s just fine, with little more than photographic evidence of a dodgy dress sense for proof.'

'I hadn't time,' Penny said slowly, 'or maybe I blocked it out. Who knows. It was such a long time ago. I was so young. So caught up in the shock of the new. I'd never been out of England, let alone on an aeroplane. I filled my every waking hour with Bob.'

'Did you not miss us? Did you *ever* miss us?' Fen challenged her but Penny's face wore no emotion. 'Christ – did you even *think* about us?' she pressed.

Penny thought about it. 'Occasionally,' she said quietly, nodding.

'And?'

'I just occasionally thought about you.' Her voice was quiet.

'You do know our father died of a heart attack quite soon after you left?' Pip declared.

'A *heart attack*?' Penny looked confused.

'Did you ever regret it?' Cat asked. 'Do you have any regrets?' She wanted to ask her if she regretted her fling with Django. But what if she quickly nodded to that too? It would be such a searing indictment of Django. And wouldn't it mean she regretted Cat's birth too? And wouldn't Cat then have to live with the notion that she was never meant to be? So she said nothing. She stared at her mother, hoping to compel the woman to look straight into eyes that were just like Django's.

Penny looked from Cat to Fen to Pip. She looked to the

372

middle distance and her face crumpled a little as she shook her head apologetically. 'No regrets – not as such. Though I am sorry – but I guess that doesn't help.' The sisters stood, staunchly unmoved. 'How can I explain it?' Penny flailed. 'I don't see it as a sacrifice because it never felt like I had a choice to make. The kids round here have an expression they use when something is glaringly obvious. And for me, back then, it was a *no-brainer*. Bob came along and everything made sense. Sure, on paper, my actions appear inexcusably wicked but, I don't know, it made perfect sense to me back then. Even now. I can't explain. I don't expect you to understand.'

Penny took a step back. 'If I was evil,' she said hoarsely, 'if I'd done wrong then surely the natural balance of the world would ensure I wasn't entitled to a smudge of the bliss I was blessed with?' She felt so tired. She wanted to shut the door and sit down and be on her own. 'Perhaps not all women are cut out to be mothers. Maybe I'm just not maternal,' Penny said, starting to close the door. 'Perhaps there's a flaw in my genes; something missing. But anyway, it appears you three have not inherited it. So there you go. You're the lucky ones. Go ahead and hate me if it helps you bury your past and reclaim your lives. I guess we're strangers, you and me. We always were.'

The three sisters stand side by side. Their mother's door has been shut in their faces. Though their limbs are touching, they stand distinct and alone; each constricted by hermetic self-sorrow.

My mummy never loved me.

My mummy never loved me.

My mummy never loved me.

373

Freedom Trail

To be homeward bound the next morning seemed all that mattered. It mattered more than delaying their departure from Vermont with a last breakfast at their little diner. Instead they boarded the first bus to Boston hungry but desperate to be on their way, to turn their backs on Lester Falls and Emerson Street. To head home. But they arrived in Boston with a day to get through and even for Cat, shopping held no allure. In the end, Pip suggested they walk the Freedom Trail, not because she was particularly interested in Paul Revere and John Hancock, but because it gave them a red line to follow and she didn't have to think. They meandered and mooched and didn't really take in the culture or the sights. They were wasting a day but they felt there was little else they could do with it. They idled at Rowes Wharf before taking the water shuttle across to Logan airport, still managing to arrive at the airport with three hours to spare.

Penny, however, had arrived a whole two hours before that. The girls didn't see her but she watched them, waiting until they turned away from the check-in desk, before she approached. She could hear Pip suggesting to the other two that they might as well go through passport control immediately. Penny thought to herself how easy it would be to turn away; they'd be none the wiser. Perhaps it would be for the best to go now because all of a sudden she wasn't entirely sure what had possessed her to make the trip anyway. It wasn't as if she had anything new to say. If she went now, she could catch the bus that would go to Lester direct. And she'd be home at just past her usual supper-time. It made sense. She didn't like cities and she disliked airports more. She'd come on a whim anyway, and perhaps it was common sense to turn on her heels and just go. She observed Cat, Fen and Pip from behind, thought how nicely cut their hairstyles were. Pip's neatly French-braided, Fen's light and loose, Cat's softly cropped. And then it struck her that, regardless of their colour being natural or not, she actually couldn't recall the hues of their childhood locks. Cat had been practically bald when she left anyway. But had Pip always had such beautiful glints of caramel? Had Fen's hair been spun with threads of gold from the start?

Something is catching in Penny's throat. And whatever it is has now transferred to her eyes and charged her tear ducts. Passport control is just yards away. And if she doesn't go now she'll have to say something. But if she goes now, she'll never see them again. Maybe that is for the best. They're fumbling with their tickets and passports. If they drop something, they'll see her. If they don't, they'll be gone from view in the next moment or two.

Pip is moving.

'Wait!' Penny cries.

The sisters turn. They turn and they stare. They weren't expecting to see Penny Ericsson again. Not at the airport. Certainly not with tears running down her face.

'Hi,' she offers them, 'hi.' She dips her head and sobs,

buries her face in her hands and half hopes that when she next looks up, these three girls will have gone.

But they're standing here still.

'I,' Penny falters, 'I took the bus.' It doesn't really mean much at all, but it is a short enough sentence for everyone to cope with. 'I didn't know which flight you were on.' This was true. 'British Airways!' she marvels, as if the airline is indicative of the girls' affluence. 'Very nice.'

'We're early,' Cat says but though she's glanced at Pip, it seems her eldest sister has yet to find her voice.

'Oh,' Penny enthuses, 'it's so good to be early. It's a great idea. You get the good seats, with the leg room. You get to shop and relax. Good for you. Good for you.'

'Actually,' Pip says, 'we just want to be on our way. We just want to go home.'

Penny stops, a little startled. 'I'm sure,' she says, 'I'm sure you do. To your families and your children.'

'I don't have children,' says Cat.

'I have a stepchild,' says Pip, 'he's called Tom. He's nearly ten years old.'

'He's a lucky, lucky boy,' says Penny, with such feeling that some of it seeps over to Pip.

'Thank you,' Pip mumbles. 'I feel I'm the lucky one, though.'

Penny is trembling visibly. 'Anyway, I guess I'd better go,' she says. 'Just wanted to wish you a safe journey, and all.' And she turns and starts to walk away.

'Wait!' Fen calls when Penny is precariously close to being beyond earshot. Penny stops and faces them again; this time they move towards her. Fen's hand baggage feels heavy, cumbersome; reason enough to walk slowly, with stilted gait. 'Why did you come today?' Fen asks, busy with the straps of her bag.

Penny is swiping away tears as if they're as irritating as

midges, she's rubbing at her nose as if something has gotten right up it. 'Oh,' she waves the air dismissively, 'you know.' But the look on Fen's face tells her that no, she doesn't know. Penny considers inventing a pal who works at the airport – but what a lame and crazy thing that would be to say. She falters, then she broadens her shoulders and nods emphatically. 'I guess I just wanted to say I'm glad that you girls have had a good life.'

'All things considered,' Pip says bluntly, 'yes, we have.'

'You've been so well brought up,' Penny compliments them.

'That'll be Django,' Fen says pointedly, 'on account of our father's heart giving out not long after you'd gone.'

Penny frowns. She takes a moment, then she nods. 'Yes, sure,' she says, 'his heart.' She rocks gently on her heels, begins to talk with her hands in lieu of words. 'I came here to find you,' she says, her voice breaking, 'to tell you I lied. I *lied*. I wanted you to know that, actually, I *have* thought about you. I have thought about you over the years, but in deep, dark privacy.'

Her daughters glance at each other and then regard her non-committally.

'I was never made to be a mother and I never told Bob I was one,' she confesses and she lets the huge fact hang, lets it resound in the departures hall; declared out loud and never to be denied. 'I never told Bob,' and she shook her head sadly at herself. 'He never knew I had three daughters.' She can see these three daughters of hers balk at this. 'I met him when we were still living in Battersea – I'll bet you don't remember that house? The wallpaper on the ceiling in your room? Floral – yellowy beige? I hardly ever went beyond Battersea but I had to go to Victoria – there was a clinic there that I'd heard of, I guess now they call such places Well Woman or Family Planning. I wanted the pill. But when I got there I just couldn't face going in. And I walked around and I was hot and upset and I went into a hotel and ordered Earl Grey tea. And Bob was there.' She shrugs, as if it had been the simplest turn of events, as if he'd been waiting there for her all along. 'There was Bob. That was it.'

Pip, Fen and Cat regard her. They don't have words just now.

Penny sighs. 'Your life is the richer for having not had me – I assure you,' she tells them, sounding quietly defiant. 'But my life – my life has been the poorer.' Her voice is now hoarse, as if the honesty has taken all her energy. She takes a moment and continues brightly, bravely. 'Look at you!' she marvels in a whisper that is sandpaper yet silk. 'Look at you! Such very fine women. You beautiful beautiful girls.'

I'm so proud of you. She mouths the words. *So proud of you.*

Again, the sisters stand side by side but in their own closed-off spaces. Penny has no voice now. She presses her fists against her heart. She opens her mouth but no sound comes out. Her lips move and her daughters can read what she says.

My beautiful, beautiful girls.

Then she shrugs and begins to back away. She raises her hand in a small, motionless wave and forces her quivering lips into a semblance of a smile while she watches as Cat cautiously raises her hand too. Fen is gazing at her, tears slicking down her cheeks. Pip's head is downcast but she flickers her eyes up to meet her mother's and though there's wariness, there's no hostility now.

Finally, Penny has to turn. She has to go. The scamper and whirl of an international airport takes her away. She goes without telling them that actually their father died of liver failure because he was a drunk – and not heart failure

378

as they thought. It was her gift to them; to Django too. And it could also be part of her penance. She goes without telling them that she loves them, because she doesn't think they'd believe her and she didn't know herself until that morning when she rushed for the bus to Boston.

Red-Eye

The red-eye flights which leave the east coast of the US in the evening to arrive at the crack of UK dawn, offer a peculiar phenomenon of time travel. The flight isn't a long one but each hour it gains, as it races to catch up with GMT, is an hour lost in the lives of those on board. All around Fen, Cat and Pip, fellow travellers were desperate to sleep, eschewing the in-flight entertainment, the meals, to busy themselves with towelling socks and eye masks and fluorescent plugs of foam which, despite moulding and compacting, soon appeared to ooze uselessly out of their ears. Seats were cranked back to the maximum but still allowed only a paltry degree of recline, and small excuses for pillows were wedged around already cricked necks. With thin, static-creating blankets offering a little privacy, but not much in the way of warmth, passengers prayed for sleep and tried not to think that beyond those curtains boastfully closed at the front of the cabin those who never flew cattle class were prostrate under cotton-covered quilts and already fast asleep.

Though there had been an exasperating two-hour delay, and though it was now midnight in Vermont, or 5 a.m. GMT, the McCabe sisters couldn't sleep. Just then, time wasn't one coast or the other, time wasn't passing in minutes or hours, nor was it night or day, not even yesterday or tomorrow, in this hinterland up in the sky. In a twilight zone of sorts, life seemed suspended at 40,000 feet above the Atlantic Ocean. A little like the sensation of jet travel itself. Allegedly, the plane's ground speed is over 600 miles an hour, yet everything feels quite still. It's the same with the sound of flying; it's a little like a dog whistle, neither noisy nor soundless but there, unmistakably, all the while.

In a dimmed cabin, illuminated sharply here and there with the overhead reading lights, the McCabe sisters sat. After thrashing around with the blanket and the pillow and the freebies that were meant to assist her flight experience, Cat now read Fen's magazine; the eye mask propped atop her head making chaos of her hair. Pip and Fen were doing the *Times* quick crossword, having shared the paper and pored over every page as though it was a link with a country they'd been far from for years.

'*Makes world go round,*' Fen mulled, 'four letters.'

'Axis?' Pip suggested.

'A X I S,' Fen spelt, somewhat unnecessarily, out loud. 'It fits.'

But it didn't. Because 4 down had to be 'pompous' on account of 13 across being 'Israel'.

'Shit,' said Fen, 'something O something something. *Makes world go round.*'

'Pole?' Pip said, her mouth busy with a Murray Mint which, along with the round tin of boiled square sweets dusty with sugary powder, was confectionery she'd never normally choose yet always bought for travel.

'Pole,' Fen mused, 'yes, I see. Like North and South. Well, it fits. I'll put it in lightly.' Her biro scribbled out A I X and she wrote P L E in small, light, neat letters.

'Poles don't make the world go round,' Cat piped up. 'It's

gravity, isn't it? What's a four-letter word for gravity?' They thought hard but had no answer.

'Doesn't the earth rotating have something to do with the *moon*?' asked Fen ingenuously, never much of a scientist or astronomer. 'That's four letters, second letter O.'

'Hang on,' Pip challenged, 'is there a question mark after the clue?' Fen confirmed that there was. 'Ah,' said Pip, 'then it'll be a Funny. You know – not a straight answer.'

They pondered what could make the world go round in only four letters, second letter O, that was amusing.

'Got it!' said Cat. 'Money makes the world go round! D O S H.'

'Don't be stupid,' Pip laughed, while Fen's biro was poised, ready to scribble out and reinsert.

'Let's do 17 down instead,' said Fen, 'and come back to it.'

A few clues later, they were still none the wiser. Something O something something. They gave up, and did a quiz in *Cosmo* instead: 'Apron Strings or Fur-Lined Hand Cuffs – domestic dominatrix, or just dull?' Maybe it was a quirk of altitude to reveal more at 40,000 feet than at ground level, but much to everyone's surprise, it transpired Cat was the most adventurous of the lot, even by *Cosmo* standards.

Pip shared out her powdered sweets. 'Love!' she suddenly proclaimed. 'L O V E. *LOVE* makes the world go round. Second letter O.'

'Genius,' Cat declared, 'love makes the world go round.'

'Love makes the world go round,' Fen nodded, writing in the letters to complete the puzzle. 'It would be nice if it did,' she said thoughtfully. She looked from sister to sister and shrugged sadly.

It was probably that quirk of altitude again, of being neither here nor there in time or space; the opportunity of this strange non-Newtonian moment. 'Do you know what I think?' Cat said, leaning in from her window seat to regard Fen. 'I think that you're a bit too in love with the fantasy of being in love.' Fen looked taken aback. 'Remember that Shakespeare sonnet you read at my wedding? About love not changing?'

'*Let me not to the marriage of true minds admit impediments,*' Fen quoted softly.

'Well, you see old Will may be a genius in some respects – all that iambic pentameter and a zillion plays – but actually, I think he was wrong with the *Love is not love which alters when it alteration finds* bit.' Cat paused as if she was guilty of the most appalling blasphemy. 'People *do* change and love has to change with them; it's logical that the process of love goes through changes too, and we have to adapt.' She stopped to give a little shrug. 'I think you're probably frustrated that you don't feel that heady rush for Matt any more, that the butterflies don't rampage around your stomach every time you look at him or he touches you. That instead of floating around the still point of the turning world you now trip over toys strewn over the floor and argue at midnight over whose turn it is to stack the dishwasher.'

Fen's downcast eyes revealed this was obviously the case.

'But I think you've misread the situation as having fallen out of love with Matt,' Cat defined. 'You just need to put on your glasses and read it a little more carefully. I read somewhere that being in love is just a cocktail of chemicals which course through the body for the first twelve months – natural amphetamines. Which is why the sensation is so addictive.'

Quietly, Pip wondered when her little sister had become so wise, but then she had to consider that Cat was thirty-two years old and married to Ben. And she'd lived abroad, not knowing a soul, for four years, striding out in an alien territory, finding friends and making a happy life for herself. She smiled at her fondly.

'Matt gets on my nerves,' Fen was admitting sadly, drawing Pip's attention back. 'He irritates me. In that stupid, clichéd, lid-off-the-toothpaste kind of way. I think I've always known that Matt is the one, but for a while, one wasn't enough.'

'You're bored,' Pip defined.

'Our life is boring,' Fen agreed. 'I think I'm boring. I'm a woman of no substance. And you're right about the dish-washer, Cat.' It felt safe to talk, as if what was to be said would stay there, in no man's land, in no time, sealed in a bubble of altitude. Fen looked from one palm to the other. Talking out loud verified the situation; but it made her feel both a little disloyal to Matt, yet greedy for support. 'I've gone off sex with him,' she admitted, 'it's so predictable. I have to shut my eyes and fantasize. But that stupid thing with Al – it wasn't about sex, it was about me being bored and feeling hard done by because of it.'

'I think we have too high expectations of sex,' Pip suggested. 'Our society is over-sexualized. Something essentially private has become so public – all those sex scandals to read about, from politicians to pop stars, emblazoned everywhere, from the red-tops to the broadsheets, from *Heat* magazine to *Marie-Claire*. What was seedy and underworld has become everyday. Sex shops on the high street. Pole dancing and Pilates sharing gym space. Porn now a middle-class pastime. *Desperate Housewives. Footballers' Wives.*' She gave a shrug. 'It's easy to think everyone's having more sex, better sex, than you.'

'Well I still fancy Ben,' Cat confided, making it personal, 'but I constantly fantasize. God, if I open my eyes when we're having sex, I'm quite surprised to see *him*, my *husband*, not Johnny Depp. Or a Viking. Quite disappointed, actually.'

'A *Viking*?' Fen shrieked.

'Sometimes I leap forward a few centuries and allow Henry the Eighth to overpower me in the maze at Hampton Court,'

Cat admitted and she was absolutely serious, 'codpieces, serving wenches – the lot.'

'Bloody hell, Cat!' Pip marvelled.

'Don't tell Ben.'

'So you're advising me not to close my eyes and think of England,' Fen mused, 'but of Nordic pillagers and fat dead monarchs?'

'Whatever takes your fancy,' Cat nodded with a wink. 'Actually, what I'm saying is you have the power to improve your sex life.'

'Is that a quote from *Cosmo*?' Pip asked. Cat stuck out her tongue. Pip raised her eyebrows and turned again to Fen. 'And on a purely practical level, your life simply *can't* be the same as it once was, not now there's a baby added to the equation.' Fen looked at her sharply. 'Because you're a perfectionist, Fen, it follows that you're not very tolerant,' Pip defined diplomatically. 'I mean, in some respects it's great to have such high standards, but in others it's your biggest hindrance.'

Cat nodded. 'You're a brilliant mother and Cosima is a credit to you, but if Pip, or I, or Matt don't dress her or feed her or play with her or put her down quite like you do, it doesn't mean we're doing it *wrong* – just differently. And your way probably is better – but that doesn't mean we're doing it *badly*—'

'And Cosima doesn't seem to mind,' Pip added, 'as long as she's dry, fed and cuddled.'

Fen, sitting between them, momentarily felt persecuted. But she couldn't flounce off because there wasn't the leg room. And she couldn't block her ears with the foamy plugs because she'd already dropped them on the floor. She'd just have to sit still and work out how to lessen her discomfort. A little shift, here and there. 'Deep down, I know,' she said at length. 'Deep down I think it's a matter of identity and how mine has changed – beyond my belief and beyond my control. An identity crisis, if you like. Suddenly, I'm a stay-at-home mum.' She stopped abruptly and stared at the clasp on the drop-down tray. 'I don't think it suits me,' she said quietly. Her sudden honesty, her clarity of her situation, surprised Cat and Pip. 'I was never a thrustingly ambitious career woman,' Fen said, a little wistfully, 'but I did love work, and my role, and my world in which I excelled. God, I used to be asked to lecture at the Tate Frigging Gallery! I've had papers published! I have a double distinction at Masters level from the Courtauld Institute!' She stopped abruptly. 'How can I say all this – with such longing?' she whispered aghast. 'It's a terrible insult to my little baby.'

'No it *isn't*,' Pip said cautiously, 'it's about *you* – not Cosima. Not Matt. You only think Matt is boring because actually you find your life now a little dull in comparison to how it was. And because you perceive that to be a loaded thing to admit, so you pass the buck and shift the blame.' Pip could see from the wince on Fen's face that the nail had been hit square on the head. 'But a fling is not the answer,' she continued sternly. 'It'll only make you feel worse. You need a deeper embrace – and to feel it, you need to embrace what you do have.'

'I know, I know. God, I can't believe I tried to liven it up by fooling around with that idiot, Al,' Fen said darkly.

'Don't call Al an idiot,' Cat now joined in, 'it's not his fault. He didn't know. It was about *you*. He was just the antithesis of Matt. That was the initial attraction for you – and ultimately, his downfall too. Thank God.'

Fen dropped her head at the weight of the truth. She nodded sadly. 'It wasn't so much that I felt bad about myself, more that I've lost sight of who I am. I wanted to feel more than just Cosima's mother. No one looks at me any more – when I open the door to you, or Matt – whoever – you don't even look at me; attention is focused downwards, to where Cosima is. I don't want attention taken from her, my God she's so amazing she's worthy of day-long marvelling – but I feel I've ceased to exist beyond being her mummy. And after that, I'm Matt's long-term partner. So where's Fen gone?' She stopped, as if about to physically search. 'Can she still hold her own? I suppose that's what I went looking for with Al. A little excitement that came not from Matt, not from Cosima. Something naughty but essentially harmless that would make me feel good.'

'Chocolate makes you feel good,' Pip mused, 'but that doesn't necessarily mean it's good for you.'

'Did you know that those loved-up hormones I was talking about are the same as those released during high-risk sports and eating chocolate?' Cat revealed. 'That's why it's all so addictive.'

'Cat,' Pip digressed, 'how do you *know* all this stuff?'

'My husband is a doctor,' Cat said. She grinned. 'And I have subscriptions to *Marie Claire* and *Cosmo*!'

'You know how you can feel like a fat lump after a chocolate binge?' Fen said. 'Well, after Al, I felt like a stupid old slag.' She looked miserable. 'You could say I've totally gone off chocolate.' She still looked miserable. 'You could say, I've learnt my lesson. I've had my fill.' She glanced at her sisters for approval. 'I *have* learnt my lesson, you know.'

'Why don't you go back to work?' Cat suggested brightly. 'It gives you a buzz and you love it. It's your world and you're brilliant at it.'

'But what sort of mother will that make me?' Fen protested, defensive and distressed.

'A working mum?' Pip said. Fen shook her head vehemently. 'Cosima is a credit to you,' Pip said kindly. 'That baby is a sweet, easygoing, gorgeous and secure little person. She's not going to feel abandoned.'

'In fact, she'll probably love being socialized,' Cat said. 'She won't notice that you've gone.' But Fen's glare said that, at 40,000 feet, this was the wrong thing to say to a woman who hadn't seen her child for four days and five nights.

'Maybe I just need to learn to fall in love with Matt again,' Fen said sadly, 'but it seems very contrived. And I'm not sure how to go about it.'

'He's just a little older, a little more squidgy than when you first met,' said Cat, 'but that's all. It's not just Shakespeare who got it wrong, Ali McGraw was full of crap too – all that *love means never having to say you're sorry* bullshit,' Cat said, echoing her mother's sentiments about that film, not that she was remotely aware of this fact. 'It's a prerequisite of love that we do humble ourselves when we're wrong, when we've been mean; that we say sorry to those we love – because often it's those we love most who are the easiest for us to hurt. Bizarrely.'

The sisters sat and thought. 'I tell you something,' Fen said, 'and I can't believe I feel this – but I actually envy our mother a little.' Cat and Pip looked unsettled. 'No! Not that she buggered off and abandoned her children,' Fen hastened. 'I envy her the scale of the love she had. It was omnipotent. Call me a daft romantic or a deluded fantasist or whatever, but I wish I could have that.'

'I know what you mean,' Cat said quietly. 'I want to detest her but I have to admit, hers is an awesome and tragic love story. And I can't believe I can say I feel for her – but I do.'

'She has no happy ever after,' Pip said pensively. 'Love is nothing without honesty,' she continued, 'and she never told Bob about us. Fucking hell – can you believe that? I'm still reeling from that one. She was hardly who even *he* thought she was. God, we all have little secrets from our partners, elements of our privacy we don't want to reveal. But not telling him about three daughters is slightly more shameful, more loathsome, than going to base three with some studenty type.'

Fen looked at Pip with gratitude for making light of her transgression, for placing it far down the scale of iniquity in comparison to their mother. 'You didn't buy anything for Tom, did you?' she changed the subject.

'I don't know what to do,' said Pip.

'Buy something from the airline mag,' said Cat, leafing through it.

'No,' said Pip, 'no – I mean I don't know what to do. With Zac.'

Cat looked horrified and Fen looked dumbstruck. Their sister looked distraught.

'We're at the most almighty impasse,' she told them, 'and to be honest I'm starting to worry that we won't get through it.'

'What's happened?' Cat gasped.

'What's happened?' Fen asked Pip tenderly, her hand on her sister's arm.

'He doesn't want children – and I do,' Pip shrugged.

'You want children? Since when?' Fen asked, stunned.

'A few months,' Pip said. 'It surprised me too. I don't know if it's the tock of my biological clock, or a surge of hormones, but yes, absolutely, I want a child.' She paused. 'But Zac just laughs at me and says, No you don't.'

Fen was astonished. 'Zac?'

'Oh, and I found out, on Friday, that June has had the baby.'

'While we were here – there?' Cat asked. 'Why didn't you say? Wow that's wonderful!'

'In theory, yes,' said Pip, 'but it's killing me.'

'What did she have?' asked Fen.

'A boy,' Pip said, 'seven pounds something. Nathan. A baby brother for lucky, lucky Tom. And yet I feel hollow –

hungry – all I can think is it should have been me.' She stopped. 'I want a family. I'm in my mid-thirties. I have to ask myself, why does Zac not want one with me?'

'Why doesn't he?' Cat asked. 'What does he say?'

'Say?' said Pip.

'About not wanting to have a family with you?' Fen asked.

'When I say I want a baby he just laughs and says no I don't,' Pip said.

'But when you've asked him, specifically, why he doesn't want a family with you,' Cat paraphrased, 'what on earth are his reasons?'

Pip stopped. 'I haven't exactly asked him that – in so many words, precisely.'

Fen and Cat looked at each other. 'Why *not*?'

Pip thought about it. 'He'll just laugh it off.'

'That's what you think,' Cat said, glancing from one sister to the other. 'Bloody hell you two, after a lifetime of taking your advice and respecting your pretty astute theories, can I now just tell you both to practise what you bloody preach? You have an aversion to confrontation, Pip – that's why you always immerse yourself in being the Great Looker-Afterer – because if you busy yourself helping others with their problems, you needn't consider your own. But you have to confront Zac – he's your husband after all. It's your *duty*.'

It felt odd yet strangely comforting to Pip to be told what to do, especially by her little sister. 'I'm worried he'll say no,' Pip admitted, 'and then I'll be stuck, with no options. Because I *do* want children.'

'With Zac?' Fen asked.

'Ideally,' said Pip.

'Breakfast!' the air hostess announced.

'Breakfast?' the girls were disorientated.

'We'll be landing in an hour and a half,' the hostess said helpfully. 'Lovely tail wind.'

'I can't believe we've talked this entire flight,' Fen bemoaned, wondering how a bread roll could be so cold without actually being frozen. 'I ought to have slept. I'll be useless in a few hours.'

'Well, we have Bob Ericsson's Melatonin, remember,' Pip said, unable to spread the pebble-hard pat of butter. 'It's in my hand luggage.'

'What did you get from the USA?' Cat jested, putting on an accent. 'Oh just some jet-lag pills from my absentee mother's late husband.'

'She doesn't have a happy-ever-after,' Fen said. 'Amor did not vincit omnia for Penny.'

'So let's make sure it does for us,' said Cat, with a nudge.

The reality was that the sisters didn't actually know or remember the grown-ups as they were thirty years ago. The muddle was of their making and ultimately one of them had run away, two had died and one had kept huge secrets because he thought it was the right thing to do for the girls themselves.

The cabin lights are on, the window blinds are up, the day blazes outside the jet windows. It is morning, unmistakably. Britain will be off to work. Their mother will be sound asleep. Django will be making porridge. Matt will be kissing Cosima and rushing out the door. Zac will be telling Tom to get a move on. Ben will be oversleeping because there is no alarm clock as good as Cat.

They are back on terra firma, on home ground, in the here and now, and they must go their separate ways.

'Everyone will want to know everything,' Cat rues, 'but I don't really feel like revealing much. It feels private.' She turns to Pip. 'But what if Django asks?'

'Direct question, direct answer,' Pip shrugs, 'but it may be prudent to be economical with details.'

'I wonder if his results are through,' Fen says. 'No one's said anything to us on the phone.'

'It's been a mad, extraordinary time, of late,' says Cat.

'It's been life-changing,' Fen qualifies.

'Everything will be fine,' Pip tells them.

And they believe her.

'Everything will be fine,' Pip says again.

'Will it?' Fen asks her. 'Will I?'

'Django too?' asked Cat. 'And you?'

The McCabe line-up is back on its more usual footing.

'Everything,' said Pip. 'We'll all be fine.'

Return of the Natives

Fen adored Matt's mother, Susan Holden; a sparky yet maternal woman, energetic and independent but also warm and calm, who had been widowed before Fen met her. She was perhaps the only person from whom Fen was happy to take advice on child-rearing; but Susan also seemed only ever charmed by Fen's zealous love of Cosima. Fen never had any criticism of Susan's techniques – they were as good as her own. Almost. Susan instinctively unfurled the frill from the elasticated legs of the disposable nappies and Fen felt no need to double-check this, as she still did when anyone else changed her baby. Susan knew exactly how long to immerse a bottle in a Pyrex jug of boiling water and though the temperature of the milk was always spot on, still she verified it with a dab to her wrist. She wouldn't dream of saying, Why don't you get a microwave, it takes six seconds to warm a bottle. Susan never said 'Shh!' to the baby – a sound Fen herself could not abide – but used the more soothing hush and coo to far greater and more expedient effect. And if she watched her son, sweetly cack-handed, feed the baby yoghurt with the wrong kind of spoon and no wipes to hand, she'd throw Fen a conniving look which said *Men! Aren't they useless, the silly sods!* She was unstinting in her praise for Fen. But there again, Susan had always longed for a daughter. Now she had a granddaughter too. She felt that, between her and Django, Cosima would have a colourful yet balanced experience of grandparenting. And she liked the way that Fen ensured every weekend in Derbyshire was balanced with a weekend in Gloucestershire with her. Susan thus appreciated how important it was that Fen's homecoming was just right. The house was spotless and so was Cosima and when Fen came in, Susan diplomatically disappeared to boil the kettle, allowing Fen and Cosima to reunite in utter privacy.

'She missed you,' Susan stressed to Fen, who had eventually appeared in the kitchen clinging to her baby almost as much as the infant snuggled against her. 'She missed you very much. You could tell. She didn't pine – she was happy enough – but look how happy she is to have you home.'

Fen's eyes were wet and her heart swelled. 'Has everything been OK? Did she eat OK? Sleep through? Nappies nice and regular? Afternoon naps?'

'Everything like clockwork,' Susan assured her. 'Look, I jotted down a little résumé of each day so you can catch up on all the intricacies.'

'You are a brick, Susan,' Fen said sincerely.

'Now there's a term I haven't heard for a while,' Susan laughed.

'It's a Django-ism,' Fen said. 'Is there any news, do you know? Results?'

'Not as far as I'm aware,' said Susan.

'Any day now,' said Fen solemnly.

'Well, you're all going to Derbyshire this weekend, aren't you?' said Susan.

'Cosima's first birthday,' Fen smiled. 'Are you sure you can't change your Ladies' Guild thing and be with us?'

'I can't, my dear,' Susan apologized. 'Normally I wouldn't

think twice – only it's our annual dinner and it is for charity. And I can't be doing with being the butt of consternation or gossip – not at my age, and not in a village as small as mine.'

'OK,' said Fen. 'Perhaps we'll come to you the following weekend, then?'

'Lovely. I think all women should be entitled to prolong their birthday celebrations – I'm glad to see you're priming Cosima already,' Susan said.

Suddenly Fen realized she had no idea when her mother's birthday was. Nor was she sure of her precise age. And she felt she'd really quite like to know the day, that she ought to know the day – not to send cards, but just so that she could acknowledge, at some point, *Today is my mother's birthday*. Just so she'd be able to say with authority, *My mother is fifty-something*.

'And how was Cosima's other grandmother?' Susan was asking, astutely casual.

Momentarily, Fen was confused. But Susan was quite right; on paper Cosima had two grandmothers, on paper Penny was a mother and a grandmother. 'She was –' Fen paused. What was she exactly, this Penny Ericsson? 'She was – *there*,' Fen said thoughtfully and Susan sensed this was information enough at this juncture.

'Matt missed you,' Susan told her.

Fen felt her face being scanned for a response. 'He probably didn't notice me gone,' she said and she was surprised to hear by her tone that she alluded more to her own inconsequence, than any derogation towards Matt.

'Oh, he did,' Susan assured her. 'I think it did him good.'

Fen pressed her lips against Cosima's fat cheeks. 'I missed him,' she said quietly. 'It did me good too. I can't wait to see him.'

'If you can stay awake,' Susan remarked. 'Go and have a

power nap – just an hour or two of restorative oblivion. Cosima can take me to feed the ducks.'

'Are you sure?' Fen asked.

'Of course I'm sure,' Susan said. 'She's no trouble at all. She's an absolute pleasure to look after.'

'Thank you,' said Fen.

'Say, *See you later, Mummy*. Say, *Sweet dreams*,' Susan cooed on Cosima's behalf.

'See you later, little baby,' Fen said, with a little wave. Then she turned and went upstairs to bed with her share of the Melatonin.

Pip felt slightly insulted by Tom's clothes, strewn around her home in the most unlikely of places. She wondered if she'd been deluded or just unreasonable to hope that her husband and her stepson might at least have tidied the place for her return, even if a bunch of flowers or just a welcome-home note were beyond their imagination. She loaded the washing machine, checked the fridge and wrote a shopping list, made the bed and tidied wet towels from the bathroom floor. If she went to Sainsbury's now, the washing would be ready to hang out by the time she was home. She could then put another load in and take a quick nap before collecting Tom from school. Was Tom staying over that night too? Was June back home now? She could phone Zac and enquire. There again, she could phone June. Or she could just ask Tom when she saw him. But Pip's mind was too befuddled by travel and tiredness to make a decision. And anyway, she didn't need to know just yet.

In the supermarket, perusing the aisles a little absent-mindedly, a peculiar selection of items in her trolley, Pip stopped and stared. It struck her that there was an almost charming paradox about condoms being placed next to home ovulation kits, pregnancy tests sharing shelf space with tampons, KY jelly and cracked-nipple balm tube by tube. It brought to Pip's mind those adverts for pregnancy tests – they never showed the result on the dipstick that was causing the beautiful couple to hug each other in such joy. Were they pleased it was a false alarm after an unprotected shag? Or were they celebrating the outcome of careful planning for a family? She picked up the ovulation kit and wondered, very privately, about buying it, about getting to know her biorhythms and her hormonal peaks and troughs. But she put the pack back hurriedly and rushed away from the section, as if her not lingering a moment longer could somehow banish the thought of tricking Zac and absolve her of momentary, improper intent.

As June lived in Swiss Cottage, just a stone's throw from Sainsbury's at the O_2 Centre, and as Pip didn't feel quite so tired any more, she decided that she might as well take a circuitous route home.

June's mother answered the door. 'Pip – how lovely. Is Tom with you?'

'No – he's still at school,' Pip told her, suddenly wondering if her timing was off kilter. She checked her watch. Almost 2 o'clock *proper time*, as Cat would say. 'I've just been to Sainsbury's. Just thought I'd pop by. Just got off the plane, actually.'

June's mother smiled benevolently. 'They're sleeping,' she apologized. 'I don't want to wake them – but June will be so sorry to have missed you. You will come in later, won't you, when you bring Tom back?'

'Of course,' Pip said, not quite knowing if she was disappointed not to be having Tom at her place that night, or whether she was apprehensive about having Zac to herself. 'Can't wait.'

'He's absolutely gorgeous, the little mite,' June's mother said proudly.

Pip drove back with tears streaming down her face. 'It's just jet lag,' she berated herself.

She hadn't seen the note but once she sat down with a cup of tea having put away the shopping, hung out the washing and put the next load in, she found it pride of place on the coffee table.

> *Welcome home, Mrs.*
> *Would you mind doing the school run – and taking*
> *Tom back to June & Rob's?*
> *See you later. Sainsbury's delivering 5–7pm.*
> *I'll cook.*
> *Missed you.*
> *Z xx*

Pip sipped her tea and traced the marks of Zac's kisses. And then suddenly she was waking with a start and thinking Christ almighty, I zonked out for two hours and I'm going to be late for Tom.

'He blows bubbles, my baby brother,' Tom tells her.

'Is he gorgeous?'

'He has yellow runny poo,' Tom marvels.

'How's your mum?'

'She says she has udders,' Tom reveals, 'and there's a milking machine she's borrowed from the hospital. No one is allowed in the room when it's on.'

'It's so exciting for you all,' Pip says, glancing in the rear-view mirror at Tom who is gazing proudly out of the window with a great big grin on his face.

'My baby doesn't half burp,' Tom says.

The first thing Pip thought was that June looked as tired, as disoriented, as she felt. The second thing Pip thought was that baby Nathan Oliver was more tiny, more perfect than she could possibly have imagined. Just then he appeared to be the most beautiful newborn baby in the world.

'Do you want a cuddle?' June asked her.

Pip smiled and put her arms around her.

'Not with me, you daft cow, with the baby!' June laughed.

Pip cradled Nathan. She remembered this feel from Cosima – that the bundle could be so tiny and yet feel so heavy, so full of life, so enormously and wondrously and terrifyingly precious. She brushed her lips along the crown of the baby's head, the feel of peach fuzz hair mingling with the incomparable fragrance of a newborn accosting all five of her senses at once. She looked at June, her smile spreading. 'He's absolutely gorgeous,' she said.

'Hug him some more,' June said. 'I'm sure I told you there's some tribe somewhere that hug each other's babies the whole time – apparently it increases fertility like you wouldn't believe.'

Pip thought about ovulation kits; about surreptitious enhancement of fertility. But this wasn't the same. Zac would expect her to be cuddling the baby. After all, he'd probably already cuddled Nathan too.

June nudged her. 'Seen Zac yet?'

Pip shook her head.

'Here,' said June, 'have another cuddle with Nathan before you go.'

There were two messages on the home phone when Cat arrived back. One was from Ben, saying he'd left a message on her mobile too, to say he'd forgotten about a talk he was to give to a local hockey team and he'd be back late. The other was from her assistant manager at Dovidels, apologizing profusely, knowing she'd be jet lagged, but they were short staffed and Lorna Craven was visiting the store and was there any chance Cat could come in. She phoned both back and told them not to worry, she'd see them later.

Lorna Craven was high up in head office but subscribed to a hands-on approach across all the stores and was popular with the staff because of it.

'They tell me you're just back from the US?' she said to Cat, having praised her for the commendable figures last month.

'That's right,' Cat said, 'family business. I took it as holiday, though. And I don't have any other plans for time off for the foreseeable future.'

'Everyone needs a break,' Lorna reassured her, 'though family business can seldom be classified as a holiday.'

Cat raised her eyebrow in agreement.

'I thought your family were in the North somewhere?' Lorna commented.

'They are,' Cat said. She paused. 'They are.' It was on the tip of her tongue. She could bite it back, or she could let it tumble. 'My mother lives in Vermont now,' she said, surprising herself how easy that had been.

'I see,' said Lorna. She tipped her head and regarded Cat. 'You're doing a great job here, well done.'

'Thanks!' beamed Cat.

'We're opening a store in Sheffield – at Meadowhall – do you know it?'

'Of course I know Meadowhall,' Cat laughed. 'I grew up in Chesterfield – Meadowhall was the closest thing to paradise and teenage bankruptcy for me and my sisters.'

Lorna laughed. 'Do you still have family in Chesterfield?'

'Yes,' Cat said, 'I do.' And for the first time she wondered how to refer to Django. Everyone who'd ever known her knew him simply as Django; he'd needed no further clarification.

But Lorna didn't know anything about Cat, really. 'Our father lives there,' Cat told her because it felt right and sounded good and, in essence if not on paper, Django would always be as much Fen and Pip's father as her own.

'You wouldn't have plans to move back to the area, would you?' Lorna asked and before Cat could say, God no, my sights are set on Tufnell Park, Lorna added, 'Because I would give serious consideration to you running the Meadowhall store. It's going to be our flagship. Coffee shop, events hot spot – the lot.'

Cat stood and stared. She wondered if she'd heard right or whether jet lag was now playing tricks on her. She wondered, for one ghastly moment, whether the foam ear plugs were still protruding like fluorescent slugs, from her ears.

'Think about it!' Lorna said cheerily. 'Now let's go through the next month's forecast. Then you ought to go home – you must be exhausted.'

'My mother gave us some Melatonin,' Cat said, clicking the computer into action.

Fen McCabe and Matt Holden

If only Matt and Fen could have known each was as apprehensive about their reunion as the other. If only they could have been privy to the information that they both had tampered with the parameters of fidelity but regretted it deeply. And then have such information magically erased from their memories. It is easy to forgive, not so easy to forget. But in some ways, to live with the guilt, to stomach it and suffer it, to learn from it, guards against further transgression. They'd had five days and five nights apart, they'd been separated by a seven-hour flight and several time zones, but in their souls it now felt that they'd made it across a sea far darker and more inclement to be back home together again.

'Welcome back, cowgirl.'

'Howdy, partner.'

What on earth possessed me? each thought as they kissed hullo and hugged that it was good to see you. *What on earth possessed me to turn away from the love of my life?*

In their eyes, each other was staggeringly incomparable to the dalliances of their momentarily misplaced desire. *What on earth possessed me? I won't be doing that again. Christ, I almost lost my mate.*

'You need to keep her awake,' Susan said. 'She needs to stay up until her proper bedtime or her sleep pattern will be disrupted for days.'

'It is her proper bedtime,' Fen said. 'I was just boiling the kettle to warm her bottle.'

'I wasn't talking about Cosima,' Susan said, 'I was talking about you. And I was talking, actually, to Matt.' She turned to her son. 'Take Fen out for a nice spicy curry. I'll babysit.' Both Fen and Matt sensed that his mother was choreographing the situation, that she had some innate sense that they needed a little time and space to slot back in together, that she sensed their separation had lasted longer than five days and five nights. To be a mother is to be granted a sixth sense. To be a good mother is to use that gift wisely. To use that gift wisely is to have the child's best interests at heart, however old the child. As Fen gave Cosima her bedtime bottle, she thought that perhaps her mother hadn't been granted that sixth sense. As she said goodnight to her dozy baby, she wondered whether her own mother had simply been not a very good one. As she put on a little make-up to mask the jet lag, she wondered if, in fact, her own mother did have a sixth sense and had somehow known intuitively that her daughters' best interests did not feature her. Maybe she had been a good mother in that respect. But spiralling theories could not produce definitive answers and, actually, it didn't really matter. It didn't matter at all, really, any more. Because Fen knew that her own little family was in the safest of hands.

Fen slips her hand into Matt's as they meander back home. Usually, a curry means heads down and eat. Tonight, though, they ate only at opportune pauses in the conversation.

'Can you believe our little girl is going to be one year old?' Matt marvels.

'I hope we have Django's results by then,' Fen says. 'Then it can be a double celebration.'

'Hear, hear,' Matt says. 'I wonder if he'll want to know all about your trip. All in all, was it a good trip, Fen?'

'It was,' she says. 'I feel I have answers now, whether or not they were given directly.'

'Do you think you'll see her again?' he asks. 'Keep in touch even?'

'I don't know,' Fen thinks about it, 'I don't know. At the moment, I can't answer that. I'm still not quite sure what I feel or what I want. We all reacted so differently. I think Cat, ultimately, probably accepted her more. Pip, though, still feels pretty raw. And me? I don't know, Matt. I feel a bit indifferent.'

Matt nods thoughtfully.

She takes her hand from his and puts it around his waist, slowing her pace. 'I think what the trip did for me was finely tune my desire to provide the best for my own little family. For Cosima,' she stops. 'For you, Matt.'

He kisses her forehead. 'That's nice to hear,' he said.

She hangs her head. 'I haven't been very nice, have I? For a while.' Her voice quiet but audible.

Matt is about to protest, but he decides not to. 'I don't think I have either,' he says instead. 'I didn't know it was going to be so tough – so baffling.'

'And I didn't know it was going to be so all-consuming, so exhausting,' Fen says.

Matt gives her pony-tail a gentle tug. 'We'd be pretty daft if we were to let the best thing that's happened to us – as individuals – cause discord for us as a couple. It's not about choosing the one we love, it's about then loving the one we've chosen.'

Fen nods. 'You're so right.'

'We're publishing an article to tie in with the Picasso/ Braque exhibition,' Matt says. 'It's a good piece. One thing struck me so deeply – Braque said it about Picasso.'

'He said, "We were like two mountaineers, roped together" – that's what you're going to say!' Fen interrupts.

Matt looks at her, impressed. Then his expression softens and he regards her more quizzically. 'That's us, Fen,' he says, 'you and me. We're in this together. There's nothing we can't surmount. As for the view from the top – I only ever want to share it with you.'

'I was starting to fall,' Fen's voice wavers, 'I was dragging you down with me.' She turns to Matt and folds her arms around him. 'I'm so sorry. But it was never my heart that grew cold – just my feet. For an unfathomable moment.'

'Me too,' he says to the top of her head, 'me too.'

There they stand, locked in an embrace in the middle of the pavement blocking the way like a couple of teenagers. Passers-by must drop down from the kerb to pass them, but they can't help but smile as they do so. Fen and Matt make a lovely sight.

They walk on, holding hands and swinging their arms, feeling so much lighter for love flowing between them. Fen stops. Matt turns to face her. She looks upset. 'How do you feel about me perhaps going back to work?' she asks.

Matt regards the lines and the squares of the pavement and the furrows of Fen's brow. 'I think it might be a really good idea,' he says measuredly. 'Not because of the money,' he hastens, 'but for you. Cosima will be fine, you know.'

'I know that now,' Fen tells him, 'but more importantly, I now know I'll be fine too.'

'Course you will,' Matt encourages her. 'You'll be more than fine.'

'I suppose until quite recently – well, until right now – I still felt that we're umbilically attached. My little girl and I. You could say it's actually been *me* with the separation anxieties, not the baby.'

405

'Yes, that's a very valid point,' says Matt sweetly, 'but don't misinterpret your maternal qualities, Fen. Don't do yourself a disservice.'

'I would like to go back to work,' Fen says, 'for *me*. I suppose I romanticized the image of me as a full-time mum. But actually, I think I *need* to work.'

'I think you'd be a happier bunny for it,' says Matt, 'and anyway, you couldn't be a better mummy. Do it for you.'

Fen's eyes are downcast. 'Have I been awful?' she asks him.

'Not awful,' he says, 'not really.'

'Not really?' Fen pursues. 'Or not really awful?'

Matt laughs and pokes her. 'Not really awful,' he clarifies and kisses her on the forehead.

'Becoming a mother has been so monumental. I'm different now from the woman who didn't have a child.' She pauses. She looks at Matt intently. The father of her child – beautiful man. 'I'm worried. Am I as nice as that carefree girl you fell in love with?'

He tips his head and regards her quizzically. 'I see only the girl I am in love with,' he says. 'I have eyes only for you.' He kisses her tenderly and Fen's eyes close in gratitude and relief and happiness. 'Come on,' he says, slipping his hand into the back pocket of her jeans, giving her bottom a friendly and affectionate squeeze, 'let's go home.'

'I was thinking of asking Pip if she'd look after Cosima on the days I go to work,' Fen says.

Matt thinks about it. 'I don't know,' he says. 'The occasional day now and then is one thing – but she has her life too.'

'But she loves babies.'

'So she might then have her own, soon enough.'

Fen glances at him, wonders whether to confide but decides she should honour her sister and moves away from the topic.

'Perhaps you could ask around the other mums,' Matt says, 'nanny-shares and the like?'

Fen considers this. 'I will,' she says. 'Good idea.'

Fen is wide awake at three in the morning. She lies in bed, aware of Matt sleeping peacefully beside her. She spoons up against him. The smell of him, the feel of him, so familiar.

I suppose, for a while, stupidly, I saw monogamy – and domesticity – as suffocating my ability to fly and be colourful and carefree. I feared it would sap me of my individuality. But the truth is I'm not carefree, I have huge responsibilities and commitments and whereas momentarily I wanted to shirk them, actually I want to embrace them, venerate them – and never abuse them again. Life is too short, families are too fragile. You are my One. Crappy pop songs and bad poetry hail love to mean two become one. But look at what you and I did, look what our love did – we two became three.

'Matt?' He doesn't wake. He smells so nice. He feels so good. Fen's arm is around him, it's as if he's sitting on her lap and it's nice to have him there. 'I'm sorry.' She thinks about why she is so sorry. 'I probably gave you leave to doubt my love for you,' she says. She nustles against his hair. She kisses the back of his neck. 'Madness,' she says. 'I love you.'

Matt continues to pretend to be asleep.

Pip and Zac Holmes

Pip was apprchensive about seeing Zac. It had taken her sisters to make her see that she'd need to broach the subject because her husband didn't realize the enormity of it for her. However, he was running late and she was starting to feel very tired and rather emotional. She had been taken aback by how hard she found it to take her leave of Tom at his mother's house. It had been a lonely drive back up Fitzjohn's Avenue and once she was home how she craved the happy distraction of Tom rambling on about the personal hygiene of his teachers, the vomtasticness of school dinners and the outrage of so much homework. There was nothing to do. No one to talk to. Just an awful lot to think about. Pip was immensely fond of June and she'd loved cradling baby Nathan but just now she deeply resented June the apparently effortless perfection of her family and she loathed herself for feeling this. She was appalled that she should think June had more than her fair share.

Zac's dilemma was whether to wake his wife or let her sleep. He stood and looked at her, curled up on the sofa, the remote control tucked under her chin, her lips parted and slightly squashed by the conked-out angle in which she'd fallen asleep. She looked young, childlike almost; peaceful. Perhaps he should leave her be. But he knew her theory on jet-lag management and, though she might be temporarily grumpy with him in her grogginess, he reckoned she'd ultimately thank him for waking her. He tried as gently as he could, by tucking her hair behind her ear, by laying his hand on her shoulder and giving it a little shake. Then he whispered her name and gave her buttock a friendly tap. But still she slept. He decided to start cooking but not even wafts of garlic or the clatter of pans roused her. He watched a little television, laying her bare feet in his lap and lightly fiddling with her toes, but she didn't stir. So, with the supper simmering and the wife slumbering, he cranked up his laptop and did a little work.

'Something's burning!' are Pip's first words to him.

'Fuck!' is his back to her.

The pan is such a mess and Zac looks such a hungry, sorry sight, that Pip can't help but laugh a little.

'I'm starving!' he protests. 'I can't believe I find spreadsheets so fascinating to the exclusion of everything else including my house burning down. I'm a sad fuck,' he rues. He peers in the pan. 'A hungry sad fuck.'

'No, you're not,' says Pip, about to surprise herself, 'you're lovely.'

Zac is quite startled by this; he's become quite used to Pip guarding the affectionate, demonstrative side of her nature. 'Thank you,' he says, coming back through to the sitting area. 'You're not too bad yourself.'

They look at each other, waiting to see who will smile first, who will talk next.

Pip does both. 'We had a mad trip,' she says, 'but it was a good thing to do – though it didn't feel as such when we were in the thick of it.'

'What's she like?' Zac asks. 'And would you like me to refer to her as your mother or by her name?'

'Let's call her Penny,' Pip says.

'What's Penny like?' Zac asks.

'She's all right,' Pip says. 'I sort of wanted her to be evil incarnate, but she's not. She's not actually a *bad* person. I can now allow her that fact.'

'That's good,' Zac says, 'that's closure, I suppose.'

'Actually, it feels like the opposite,' Pip says, 'which is why I still feel so unnerved, I suppose. There's an opening now. I don't know how much contact we'll have. But she really is at the end of the phone or just a plane journey away. I can put a face to her. I will see her again – I don't know when. But there will be a time. And I don't think I mind.'

'That's very noble,' Zac says, with genuine admiration that flatters Pip.

'More importantly, is there any news of Django?' Pip asks.

'Not as far as I'm aware,' Zac says, 'but we're up there this weekend, aren't we – for Cosima's birthday? Talking of news and birthdays – did you get my text, about the baby?'

'I did,' Pip says, 'thanks.'

'He's adorable,' Zac says.

'I know,' says Pip, 'I saw him this afternoon – when I took Tom back.'

'Oh,' says Zac, following it with a little awkward nodding.

'Yes,' says Pip, busy with her lips, glancing all around her.

'He's adorable,' Zac repeats, 'isn't he?'

'Absolutely adorable,' Pip says, 'and Tom is made up.'

'Isn't he just,' says Zac.

Go on, Pip! Go on! The scene is primed for a heart-to-heart. You're calm and Zac seems amenable. Say something!

But Pip is now flipping through the *Evening Standard* and she can't see that Zac is staring at her, hoping to catch her eye. 'Nothing on the box,' she says, having spent an inordinate amount of time scouring the TV listings.

'And nothing to eat,' says Zac.

'What shall we do?' Pip asks, happy for Zac to suggest a takeaway and a DVD.

'We could get a takeaway, watch a DVD,' he says.

'OK,' Pip responds.

'Or,' Zac says, sitting on the edge of the coffee table and cupping her face in his hands, 'or we could just go to bed and make a baby.'

Pip's immediate reaction is that it can't possibly be as easy as this. Surely the wrought confrontation she's been planning, dreading, needs to be played-out. There needs to be some level of workshopping, surely, at the very least. Angst. Tears. Proclamations. Soul-baring. Heart-beating. A fight. Should she say, Are you sure? Should she say, You don't really mean it, what's changed your mind? I thought you thought I was joking? But you said your family is complete with Tom? You're just saying this to keep me happy/ keep me quiet?

But luckily for Zac, and ultimately for Pip too, she's a bit too zonked by all the travel and the enormity of the last few days to decide which sentence to deliver. So, she just sits and gawps and Zac swells more at this sight than when she sat and gawped at the Tiffany box with the platinum-set princess-cut engagement ring four years ago.

'Have you gone all broody on me?' she asks wryly.

'Yes, I suppose I have,' Zac nods. 'I want a baby with you.'

'No you don't,' Pip says, trying not to grin, but Zac knows she's teasing him.

'Yes I bloody do,' he tells her.

'Was it hugging little Nathan?' Pip asks.

'Oh God, June's been on at you with her tribal fertility theories,' Zac laughs. 'To be honest, while you've been away, I just had a long think about it all.'

'Zac,' Pip whispers, her hand on his cheek, loving him so much.

'I wish I'd realized you were serious earlier,' Zac says. 'We've missed out on a lot of mating opportunity.'

Cat and Ben York

Cat was watching *ER* when Ben arrived home. She wasn't so much watching it, as staring at the television with a slightly glazed expression.

'You're still up,' he remarked. 'Aren't you knackered?'

'Is Melatonin safe?' Cat asked him.

'Yes – it's just not licensed here,' Ben told her, 'though I'd argue it's better for you than Temazapan or Valium. Did you buy some in the States?'

'Penny gave us Bob's,' Cat told him.

'Penny gave you Bob's?' Ben repeats, raising an eyebrow. 'Did she give you anything else? Say – an explanation for why she buggered off with the cowboy in the first place?'

'He wasn't a cowboy,' Cat said, 'he was the king of plastic tubing. And she did, actually – she did give an explanation of sorts. She wasn't nearly as scary as I expected. Just sad, really.'

'Do you mind if we switch this off?' Ben said, glancing at the television. 'It's too much like work – but my hospital is not nearly as exciting and my staff are nowhere near as good-looking. I find it a bit depressing.'

Cat laughed. And then bit her lip and tipped her head to

her shoulder which Ben knew to herald a request of some sort.

'What is it?' he teased. 'What do you want? Oh Christ – how much did you put on the credit card?'

'Nothing,' Cat protested, 'it doesn't matter. *Nothing.*'

'Nothing on the credit card?' Ben was aghast. '*You?*'

Cat nodded. 'Honestly,' she told him earnestly, 'we didn't shop, we didn't have time.'

'So what were you going to say?' Ben probed.

Cat thought about it. And then she reckoned that it was such an unexpected and probably daft, impractical and altogether bizarre thought, that she'd be wise to say no more. It was probably just the jet lag speaking anyway. Or Lorna Craven.

'How are you, babe?' he asked her. 'So it was a good trip to make?'

'Yes, it was,' she said. 'I feel a lot more settled. The trip quashed the drama, the mystique. I used to think it was something to fear, to be ashamed of, to run from and yet, I suppose, to be slave to as well. But actually, I had nothing to do with anything. It's just a bit of a sad story, really, but it's a story in which I now realize I actually played no part.'

'I'm so pleased for you,' Ben said tenderly.

'Pip seemed to have the hardest time, but there again, she's always taken on the role as mother so I suppose meeting the real one was a little like coming face to face with her nemesis,' Cat said thoughtfully. 'I had a bit of a hissy fit on one day but after that passed I felt a lot more rational. Fen came out with some cracking one-liners – becoming a mother has made her so much more powerful than she gives herself credit for.'

'Do you think she looks like you?' Ben asked.

'I can see Pip in her,' said Cat, 'or her in Pip.' She paused. 'Anyway, I have Django's eyes, remember. Is there any news, Ben, with his tests?'

Ben shook his head. 'I'm sure there will be by the weekend, though. We'll all be there together.'

Cat was pensive. 'Ben. It's just.' She floundered for words. 'I don't want to know – if it's bad, the news. I've thought about it. My feelings for Django are so fragile, so new, so promising. I don't want that to be taken away. I've only recently found him. I can't cope with even the thought that I won't have him for ever. It sounds pompous but this trip to the States, it was about my identity. Not just mine – my sisters' too. But I see myself for who I am – a young woman with my life ahead of me. I want to live it to the full. I want happy times to outweigh sad times. Those around me – my mother, my father – there's been such sadness and weird stuff. I sort of feel sorry for Penny, for my mother. The time I spend with Django I want to be happy, quality time. Does that sound naive? Does that sound deluded? I don't want dark clouds looming when I'm with him, I want only sunshine.'

Ben took a moment and then nodded. 'I understand,' he said, 'but you know he wants me to know all the details, the facts and the figures?' Cat nodded and shrugged. 'I respect your wishes. And I respect his.'

'Thank you, Ben,' she said. 'It's funny – my family is certainly unconventional. But it's such a relief to finally feel that I don't come from bad stock or from damaged genes.'

'So if there are no hereditary implications,' Ben said, 'are you ready to make babies?'

Cat laughed. 'Dr York, is that as good as your bedside manner gets?'

'OK,' Ben said, 'OK. But I'm actually serious here. You can't deny male broodiness. It exists. It's medically proven. I should know. I'm the frigging doctor – and a broody one. Would you like to have a baby? With me?'

Cat didn't laugh, but she did smile at her husband. 'A

family is a very nice idea,' she announced, which was good news to her as well as to Ben, 'but can we wait a year or two? I only want to have a family with you – but I'd like a year or two to get my career under way first.'

Ben considered this quietly. 'I won't tamper with your pill, then, not for the next year or so,' he said, with a theatrical sigh. She kissed his chin, his lips. 'Now go to bed,' he told her. 'You look absolutely washed out.'

At 3.15 the following morning, the three McCabe sisters are wide awake. When Matt perceives Fen to have finished her declarations, he pretends to wake from a deep sleep and finds her very keen to seal her words with slow and exquisite love-making. Zac and Pip substitute the familiarity of rampant sex for the fascinating business of procreation and fall asleep in each other's arms, sticky but hopeful.

In Clapham, Cat lies in bed, awake, and thinks about sex. Sex, she thinks, is about more than just making babies. It's about happiness. About communication on a higher level than language. It's about love.

It's about lust!

She turns on her side and gazes at her husband sleeping. She feels horny. She touches his lip lightly with her fingertip and he gruffles and turns away from her. The sweep of his beautiful back. Slowly she takes her lips to the gentle slope of his shoulder-blade and presses against it. Then she licks her lips and takes her mouth to his skin again. She runs her hand along his arm, his muscles, his strength. She finds his hand, his fingers are sleep soft but she feels along the length of each one. She takes her hand back up to his chest, strokes him and hovers her hand lightly over the little smattering of hair he has there. Carefully, she feels down his stomach. Then along his thigh, as low as she can reach. Does she want him to wake? She's not sure. She's enjoying having him all to herself. She kisses his neck and flicks her tongue over the soft bud of his ear lobe. She feels his arm again, his chest. Down to his stomach. His fingers – still limp. And she takes her hand down lower. And finds his cock straining and erect. *Fascinating*, she thinks to herself, *it has a life of its own. Women often chide a man for thinking with his cock – but I rather think a man's cock thinks for him.*

She encircles his penis and tugs it gently. Still Ben sleeps soundly. She goes beneath the covers and very carefully takes the entire length of him in her mouth. She doesn't know whether to feel a little insulted that not even a surprise blow-job can rouse him. Though he is certainly aroused. She comes back up and spoons against him, her hand loosely around his erection. She lies there, in the stillness and the silence, loving him.

'Is that it?' Ben suddenly says.

And now he's turning onto his back and plugging her mouth with his tongue before she can say, You sod, you were awake the whole time. His hands are everywhere. He pinches her nipple lustily and she gasps. He burrows between the lips of her sex to find her oozing with expectation and desire for him. He fingers her, nudges at her hardening clitoris and she moans and she could come there and then but suddenly his hand is away and he's brought it up to her mouth where her tongue and his lick her juice from his fingers.

'I am going to fuck your brains out now,' Ben murmurs and Cat is too turned on to answer him back, to use her voice for anything other than panting. Hot and sweaty, they giggle and grunt their way through a rude shag.

To *the* Bone

After Ben's phone call at lunch-time, Matt and Zac spent the rest of the day saying 'Shit' and 'Fuck' at regular intervals until it was time to meet at the Mariners.

'Glorious day,' the landlord enthused.

'Was it?' Matt remarked, realizing he'd taken no notice of the weather, no notice of much else at all.

'It's a shit day,' Zac sighed as they took their pints and awaited Ben, 'just awful.'

Ben arrived soon after, draining his pint to quench his thirst and prepare his voice.

'As you know, Django has requested that I am fully briefed by his doctors,' he started, 'and today we have been told that the grade of cancer in Django's prostate is high: 8–10 and the stage of the cancer is T4. It's not good. There's secondary cancer in the bone – as was feared. It is anticipated that it will spread to the lymph nodes too.' He rubbed the bridge of his nose and winced audibly. 'It's not good. Not good at all. We have nothing we hoped for – nothing that we told him, or the girls, to stay positive for.'

'No treatment?' Zac asked.

'There is treatment,' Ben said, 'but no cure. He'll be offered radiotherapy – as a palliative treatment. It's very effective at alleviating symptoms like pain, especially in the bone. There's some discussion of hormone therapy – reducing his testosterone levels can slow down the growth of cancer cells and can even shrink the tumour and minimize the spread but they need to know more about the spread of the cancer to decide whether treatment is viable.'

'More tests?' Zac said.

'Scans, mainly,' Ben explained. 'They could operate and remove all or part of the testicles – but I doubt they'd do that for Django considering his age and the stage and grade. Then there are drugs given as injections or pellets under the skin of the abdomen, or as liquid injected into the muscle every month or so. Or there are hormone therapy drugs in tablet form.'

'Those sound better,' Matt said. 'He'll find a way to integrate them into some recipe or other.'

Ben smiled only briefly. 'There are awful side effects,' he said. 'Sexual impotence, loss of desire, hot flushes, weight gain, tiredness. Even breast swelling and tenderness.'

'Christ almighty,' Zac said angrily, 'if the poor bugger hasn't suffered enough indignity, enough worry and enough discomfort already.'

Matt spread his hands on the table. 'Look, whatever treatment he goes for, this thing is going to kill him – is that what you're saying?'

'In a hard, hard nutshell, yes,' Ben sighed.

'Django McCabe has terminal cancer,' Matt said, to make quite sure he had the facts. 'And there's nothing that can be done apart from alleviate the symptoms? How the hell am I going to tell Fen?'

'It's for Django to,' Ben said, 'though I know for a fact that Cat won't want to know specifics. Will Fen? Will Pip?'

'You know Pip,' Zac said softly.

'Look,' Ben said, 'when we go up tomorrow, we'll see how he's taking it and perhaps we, as a family, can gauge how to proceed.'

Hard Facts and White Lies

Fen had bought a book for Cosima's first birthday. She'd bought her many other gifts too, predictably, but she felt the book was the central present. She bought it because she liked it though it was arguably beyond the intellect of a one-year-old. Even for a bona fide art historian with a double distinction from the Courtauld Institute, the illustrations were beautiful and accomplished: exquisitely gentle, unwhimsical and somewhat melancholy. Coupled with this, Fen found the tale simultaneously heart-rending yet uplifting – the lonely little beaver who thinks the echo of his own crying is the sorrow of another and sets off across the great lake to see, befriending a clutch of other lonely souls en route. Something about the book struck a chord with Fen and she made Matt read it, cover to cover, who said, Very nice, dear, and returned to his issue of GQ.

There was something of the little beaver in each of the McCabe sisters; something of the echo in those who loved them.

When you are sad, the Echo is sad ... When you are happy the Echo is happy too.

Thus, when they tumbled out of their convoy on a clammy Saturday morning in July, and bounded over to Django like excitable puppies, what could the man do but allow his depleted cells to become bolstered by their happiness.

'Do they know?' Django asked Ben, out of earshot of the others.

'We haven't told them yet,' Ben said.

'But you have told the menfolk, like I asked?'

'Yes,' said Ben, 'I did. Everything is your call, Django. We're here for you. Here to help.'

Django thought about it. 'Let's see how things progress. There's a birthday to celebrate. And tales from their trip to be heard. And why would I want to risk losing their laughter, those expansive smiles, all this happy love by imparting gory details and gloom?'

'How are you feeling?' Ben asked.

'No worse. No better. A little tired, perhaps – but I do find this heat rather enervating. I ache and I creak and I wake up on the dot of 5.15 each morning.' Django paused, then he slapped Ben on the shoulder. 'But other than that, not too bad for a cancerous old septuagenarian. Now come along. I've made Pimm's. I had no mint but there was parsley in the garden so I've used that instead. Let's gather the troops.'

Quite conversationally, after the hors d'oeuvres and whilst serving the main course, Django dished out details of his illness whilst spooning out the fisherman's pie which also had kidney beans added for their gorgeous colour, plus a little chicken for extra protein. 'Good news, the radiotherapy will put paid to the aches and pains. Potatoes, Cat? It's just a bit of a bugger about the other bit – but as Ben said, it's quite possible to live a normal life, to enjoy just as long an innings, in spite of it.'

The McCabe sisters looked from Django to Ben. Ben read

the situation in an instant: he knew that Django was tinkering with the truth just as he tinkered with recipes – all the essential items were used, but in quantities Django had decided were best, with one or two added ingredients to make the flavour uniquely his own. Django's way with cancer was going to be like his way with food. Django would justify to himself that it was a little like jazz, a collection of notes to make into a scale for which he had the freedom, the right, to tinker with the emphasis and the order.

But though the girls had an ear for jazz, medical information was clangorous to their ears. They didn't quite understand what they were hearing, nor whether they should turn to Ben or Django for further information.

'Do you have the results?' Pip asked.

'When did they come?' asked Fen.

Cat said nothing. She couldn't. Her heart pounded in her throat. *Don't let him have results yet. I don't want facts. I just want to have hope.*

Django peered at the potatoes, as if making his selection required utter concentration. He spooned them onto his plate, added a dollop of HP Sauce, motioned to Matt to replenish his glass with Pimm's and then he turned to the girls as if he'd forgotten what they'd asked. 'Oh,' he said vaguely, 'that they can treat my old bones with radiotherapy which will very much help with the discomfort I sometimes experience.'

'Has it spread?' Pip asked. 'Is it not just prostate cancer – is it in your bones too?'

'It's spread a little,' Django said.

'What's the buggery bit – about the prostate?' Pip persisted.

'The buggery bit about the prostate?' Django said, as if trying to recall. 'Oh – that. Yes, my prostate's in a sorry state. But it's a bit like your appendix. Or the Monarchy. Not really needed.'

'Can they treat it?' Pip urged.

'As Ben said,' Django said diplomatically, with the swiftest of conniving glances to the doctor, 'sometimes it's not worth it – the treatments and the side effects are worse than the symptoms of the cancer. And the cancer mightn't impinge on my lifespan anyway. Now come on, Fen, Cat – you haven't touched your celeriac. I mashed it with cottage cheese, the pineapple-y variety – is it not nice?'

Ben follows Django through to the kitchen, under the pretext of carrying the pile of plates and empty bowls, all of which have been scraped pleasingly clean. Django is rummaging in cupboards and drawers, muttering. Ben puts his hand on the man's shoulder. 'Are you all right?' he asks.

'Yes, yes,' Django says, a little irritated. 'Ah, here are the little sods.' He brandishes the jar of morello cherries.

'OK,' says Ben. But his hand is staying put. 'You sure?'

Django thinks about this. 'I'm choosing not to use the word *terminal*. When the girls are sad, I am sad. When they worry, I worry. More importantly, when they are happy, I am happy. And however long I *do* have, I may as well have a gay old time of it.' He pauses, tips his head and regards Ben. Echoing the affection of his son-in-law, Django places his hand on Ben's shoulder. 'But thank you, Ben,' he says. 'The girls – they all seem different. Not just happy and effervescent and back to their old selves – but as if they are proud to be in *new* selves too. It must have been a good trip to the States. It must have been a good thing to do. It would be most fitting if good is what ultimately comes out of it all. My lot screwed it up – but Cat, Fen and Pip are ironing out the creases very nicely. Could you fetch the ice cream from the freezer?'

But before Ben can do this, Django puts his hand on his shoulder again. 'Ben – have I in some way contributed to my condition? I don't mean to sound bonkers or melodramatic but if health is not just about what we put into our bodies but what we do with them, if health is a state of mind—' He trails off to clatter around the cutlery drawer. 'Just deserts,' he murmurs.

'Teaspoons will do fine,' Ben says helpfully.

'No – not *desserts,*' Django smiles. 'I'm wondering whether my deeds and my actions have somehow contributed to my downfall.'

Ben puts the ice cream down on the counter firmly. 'Django,' he says, 'cancer is cancer. It's an insidious, revolting affliction. It's rogue cells. Bastard things. They have no conscience. They certainly don't differentiate between victims. There's no proof that reprobates are struck down more than the virtuous. And my God you have far more bloody virtues than you have sodding faults. There's nothing you could or could not have done. It's not your fault. It's just fucking bad luck, Django.'

Django's eyes are tear stung. 'You do swear a lot,' he tells Ben with a fond cuff to his ear.

*   *   *

Cosima spent her first birthday picnicking in the grounds of Chatsworth House. Her father and her Uncle Zac spent her first birthday urging her to walk.

'Her knees are too fat,' Ben laughed warmly. 'Look at them – they look like scones. And look at those rolls of flesh around her thighs. A mini sumo wrestler!'

'Fuck off, Ben!' Fen protested, firing cornichons at him.

'Language, Fenella,' said Django.

'I'm teasing,' Ben said. 'She's glorious. Absolutely glorious. She's a credit to you. Skinny babies don't bear thinking about.'

'Talking of babies,' Django said, 'how is Tom – what news of his little brother?'

'He's so gorgeous!' Pip drooled, her accent becoming

alarmingly like Tweetie Pie. 'His weeny teeny toes!'

Django flung Zac a very obvious look of sympathy.

'Pip is currently stuffing herself with alkaline foods and God knows what because she's decided she wants a girl.' Zac paused. 'I'd quite like a girl too,' he said wryly. 'I wonder if cousins warrant a discount from South Hampstead High School for Girls.'

'But we haven't put Cosima's name down!' said Fen, after a pregnant pause and a jubilant wink to Pip.

'Are you trying for a family?' Django's eyes danced from Pip to Zac.

'Absolutely,' Zac told him and the pleasure which criss-crossed Django's face was priceless.

All eyes, with eyebrows raised, were suddenly volleying between Cat and Ben. Ben just grinned but Cat lobbed asunder whatever foodstuffs were still on her plate.

'Leave me alone!' she protested, sticking out her tongue. 'I'm younger than you lot! I assure you Ben and I will pop them out – when we're ready. But I want to give my career a chance, I really do.'

'I'm hoping to go back to work,' Fen announced casually, plucking at grass while a flickering across her face belied an immediate need for approval, 'in the autumn, perhaps.'

'That's wonderful!' Pip said.

'Good for you,' said Cat.

'Part-time,' Fen quantified.

'Well done darling,' Django said, 'it'll suit you.'

'I know,' Fen said, 'I see that. So keep your ears open for a good nanny, everyone.'

'I'll ask June,' said Zac.

'Someone at work is bound to know,' Cat told her.

'I could always help out in the interim,' Pip offered.

'Thanks,' said Fen, having a surreptitious glance from palm to palm, 'thanks, you lot.'

426

'Hey – did you know they're opening the flagship branch of Dovidels at Meadowhall?' Cat said to no one in particular. 'Lorna Craven from head office told me.'

'Meadowhall, hey,' Django said. 'I remember when Meadowhall was just that – all fields.'

'Django!' Pip and Fen groaned.

Ben observed his wife looking pensive and with an awkward blush.

'Excellent hospitals in and around Sheffield. And the outlying area,' Ben said casually, to no one in particular.

* * *

'It's weird, isn't it,' Zac says to Ben and Matt, sharing more Pimm's, this time with courgette in lieu of cucumber, 'it's a fucking awful time, really, shit news, horrible things to come – but it's been a blazing weekend. Really happy. All of us.'

'I know exactly what you mean,' Matt concurs. 'This will probably sound trite but I just want to say, Aren't families *great*.'

Ben chinks glasses with them. 'It's been a good weekend,' he agrees, 'but more than a weekend. I don't know – it feels like we're approaching this truly privileged time. Many families aren't granted this – loved ones are taken suddenly, violently, by cars or heart failure. Or worse. But we have hindsight before the event has happened – we know from the tragedy of others not to let this man go before we say goodbye. That he'll never wonder how much he was loved. That we – the girls – his friends – will never rue not saying all there was to be said. Managed well – and advances in medicine mean it can be managed well – Django can have a good death. When that time comes.'

'When will it come, Ben?' Zac asks.

'Level with us,' says Matt.

'I don't know,' Ben says. 'I'm not just saying this – truly, I don't know. I don't think it will be a sudden, steep deterioration. But the process has started. We'll have to see. He'll make this Christmas,' he pauses sadly, 'but perhaps not the following one. There's a general reluctance to specify possible time remaining, because it can only sound like a death sentence – *when* you'll die, instead of how much life you can still live.' Ben pauses. 'I think Django's take on it is robust – and I think he's kept our girls firmly in his heart by plying them with ambiguity.'

'You don't feel we're pulling the wool over their eyes?' Matt wonders.

Ben shakes his head. 'No, I think we follow Django's lead.'

'Pip will read up on it,' Zac says. 'If she wants to – can she speak to you?'

Ben nods. 'It seems what Django wants them to know is that though there's no cure, it's quite possible to live a normal lifespan in spite of it.'

'I tell you,' says Zac, 'if ever a man will truly live until he dies, it'll be Django McCabe.'

'Hear, hear,' says Ben.

'To Django McCabe,' Matt toasts. 'Long may he live.' And they chink their mugs of Pimm's together.

Sundae

'Maybe I'll just sell the house and move to a nice condo in Florida. Somewhere near Marcia's place. Buy new things. Have a yard sale before I go. Give *you* away for free,' Penny Ericsson says to her late husband's chair. She crosses to the mantelpiece, but instead of looking at the photos, she raises her eyebrow at her reflection in the mirror.

'Or maybe I'll just stop talking to myself, stop it with the pie-in-the sky planning and just go into town and do my grocery shopping.'

It was the hottest July on record. It was a day for ice cream. It was the day that Penny felt able to return to Fountains ice-cream parlour. Juliette welcomed her as if she'd only been in the day before.

'Hey Penny,' she said, 'take a seat. I'll be right there.'

Penny perused the menu. There were new additions but she fancied old favourites. 'I'll have a scoop of Banudge-nudge, a scoop of Chippy Chippy Bang Bang and a scoop of Fudge Fantasia.' She stopped, not because she was deliberating over toppings, but because she was suddenly thinking of Derek McCabe and his imaginative take on food.

'Excellent choice,' Juliette said. 'Toppings?'

'Hot chocolate,' said Penny, 'and Lucky Charms.'

'Coming right up.'

Penny sat and gazed down the street, the heat haze wavering the vista.

Juliette returned soon, presenting the sundae with a triumphant smile. 'Enjoy!'

'Thank you, my dear,' Penny said. She paused. 'It's nice to see you again, you look very well.' She unfurled the long-handled spoon from the paper napkin and toyed with the ooze of toppings.

She was aware that Juliette was about to speak. 'I'm getting married!' Juliette announced.

Penny looked up. 'That is just so nice,' she said with genuine warmth. 'Congratulations, my dear.'

Juliette took this as an invitation to sit down and tell Penny all about the proposal and to sketch out her ideas for frocks on the paper napkin. Meanwhile, Penny made headway into her ice cream, feeling obliged to take small, polite mouthfuls though it was so delicious she wanted to wolf it down. She'd started doing that at home, on her own. Sometimes, when she was very hungry, she'd scoff directly from the tub or container or foil tray. Sometimes, her supper was so hot, she'd have to stand there with her mouth agape, fanning her hand at the food scalding her tongue. Occasionally she'd even given out a great appreciative burp. She had no audience, after all. Now that her appetite had returned, she realized how hungry she had been feeling.

'Last time I saw you,' Juliette said, 'I wasn't engaged.'

'That's lovely,' said Penny, thinking that Chippy Chippy Bang Bang was possibly the closest thing to ambrosia she'd ever tasted.

'You were with the three girls,' Juliette continued.

Penny stopped mid-mouthful, a glob of ice cream electrifying her sensitive gums.

'Were they your daughters?' Juliette asked shyly.

Penny waited, using her tongue energetically to calm the flare from her teeth. She nodded. 'Yes, they were my girls.'

Juliette beamed. 'How neat that they came over.' She touched Penny's forearm. 'Did you talk it all through? Did you make amends? All that crap about you being a bad mother,' Juliette chided gently. 'I knew you were nice. I told you so.'

'You're very sweet,' Penny said, feeling very uncomfortable.

'Bet your phone bill is mighty big, what with all those long-distance calls,' Juliette laughed.

It occurred to Penny that she didn't have any contact numbers for her daughters. She did have Django's number. But actually, was there any point in phoning him? And if she did find out her daughters' numbers, whom would she phone first? More to the point, what would she say? What would they say? Reluctantly, she had to admit to herself that she'd already said everything, really, that day at Logan airport. And she knew that she'd relinquished any right to contact when she'd left them all those years ago. It was quite possible that she would never see them again.

Moving On

Ben glanced at Cat who was spooning through her cornflakes as if searching for a more tasty one elsewhere in the bowl.

'Are you OK?' he asked.

'Hmm?' She looked up. 'Pardon?'

'Are you OK?' Ben repeated. 'You seem miles away.'

'Oh, I'm fine,' said Cat, 'just thinking about work and Django and Django and work.'

Ben gave Cat a kiss and headed for the door. He paused and returned to her.

'Pinch, punch,' he said, doing precisely that. 'August 1st?'

'Oh,' said Cat, rubbing her arm. 'Ouch.'

'You're meant to give me a slap and a kick for being so quick,' Ben told her, 'or at the very least, a poke in the eye for being so sly.'

'Ben,' said Cat, who did usually biff and bash him on the first of each month, 'do you think someone ought to be with Django when he has his first radiotherapy next week?'

'Well, what does he say?' Ben asked though he knew what Django had said, having spoken to him about precisely that the day before.

'He says no,' said Cat.

'Let's go up a couple of days after that, at the weekend,' Ben said. 'We'll probably be of more practical use to him then.'

Cat brightened.

'The sales will be on at Meadowhall,' Ben told her, with a wink.

Ben thought about it again all that day. And the next. And he thought about it intermittently throughout the following week, even talked to colleagues and superiors, all of whom listened intently. He thought about it as he drove up to Derbyshire, two days after Django's first session of pallia-tive radiotherapy. But it was only when Cat dragged him around Meadowhall that he knew he had thought about it thoroughly and enough.

All angles. Pros and cons. For and against. On the one hand, and on the other. He'd considered everything to arrive at an informed decision about which he was more than content, he was actually fairly excited.

He'd choose his moment.

'This is where Dovidels' flagship store is going to be,' Cat told him as she tried to peer through some unremarkable boarding.

This was his moment.

'I've been thinking,' said Ben, peering through the gap as well, 'about leaving St John's.'

Cat looked at him, alarmed. 'Why?'

'Because I fancy a change—' Ben started.

'A change? But what would you do? You're a doctor – you're a specialist!' Cat exclaimed, aghast.

'A change of scene,' Ben said. 'Same job – well almost – different hospital.'

'But why?' she pressed. 'You like St John's, don't you? The department? The staff? Your colleagues?'

'I do,' Ben said, 'but an interesting opportunity has been put my way to do something similar elsewhere.'

'Where?'

'Sheffield.'

'*Sheffield?*'

Ben shrugged. 'Makes sense,' he said, 'in terms of *my* career. But of course, you have to feel happy with it.'

'It makes perfect sense in *my* career too!' Cat enthused artlessly. 'Lorna Craven from head office as good as offered me this very store as my own.' And she began to pat the boarding affectionately. 'Best of all, we could be nearer to Django,' she declared, 'nearer home.'

'You won't hanker after Tufnell Park, then?' Ben teased her.

'I tell you something, Dr York, we can multiply our Tufnell Park pounds by three round these parts.' Cat took a step back, crossed her arms and narrowed her eyes, as if envisaging what the Dovidels shop front could look like. 'What a coincidence,' she marvelled guilelessly, 'how very serendipitous.'

Not really, thought Ben, for whom Cat had long been an open book. And his best ever, all-time favourite read at that.

Christmas

'Bugger the brandy butter,' Django said as his family gathered around on Christmas Eve. 'This year we're having good old tomato ketchup with *everything*.'

Tom wrinkled his nose in delight at the deliciously revolting thought of ketchup and Christmas pud or, better still, ice cream and ketchup.

'Did you forget the Bisto?' Pip asked.

'Bugger the Bisto!' Django declared. 'When did you ever, *ever*, know me not to make my gravy from scratch. Bisto, she says, *Bisto*!'

'She has a thing about Bisto,' Tom said darkly. 'It's a mad pregnant-woman thing.'

'She makes it up in a mug and drinks it like tea,' Zac colluded with his son, 'by the gallon.'

'It's just a craving,' Pip shrugged, 'it's only natural.'

'She even drinks it at *breakfast*,' Tom said, with a lively repertoire of throwing-up faces for emphasis. 'That's *so* not natural.'

'Anyway, I've brought my own Bisto,' Pip told them, 'so what's with the ketchup, Django?'

'Lycopene!' Django announced. 'A wonderful antioxidant

to be found in the humble tomato but the potency, the *bioavailability* increases when cooked. So, it's out with the HP and in with the ketchup – I have it with everything now. Ben, I read that Lycopene is twice as potent as the better-known anti-cancer betacarotenes, and one hundred per cent more bioavailable.'

'It sounds about right,' Ben confirmed.

'Ketchup it is then,' Django declared.

'Will ketchup make you better then, Django Gramps?' asked Tom.

Django gave the boy a smile and ruffled his hair. 'It makes me *feel* better,' he told him, employing the gentle ambiguity which his friends and his family had come to respect as his right over the last few months.

'Can I help?' Cat asked. 'Anything I can do? Squirt the ketchup, or something?'

'Everything bubbles and simmers,' Django told her. 'Everyone relax and enjoy. Christmas is coming and the family is here. Supper will be in an hour or so. Don't chew that, Cosima – it's very old. Django Gramps found it in Alaska. In 1965.'

'I'm lucky, aren't I?' Tom announces to Pip who has brought him up a glass of water and a torch, at bedtime.

'Are you? In what way?'

'Some people – actually, what I mean is some *children* – have rubbish families. Like Tom B in my class – he's having a divorce. And Alex doesn't see his dad at all, hardly, now he lives not in London with a new baby.'

Pip tips her head to one side. 'We are lucky, aren't we?' she says warmly.

'But isn't it strange, then, that here's you and your sisters with that mum who ran away with the cowboy, and here's me with two lots of dads and mums – but we're all the happiest bunch I've ever known in my whole life.' Pip smiles and Tom welcomes her ruffling of his hair. 'Because did you know something? Ed's parents have done a divorce too and Ed told me that they try and out-present each other. At first I thought, Wow cool. But then he was really upset and actually told me he *hates* it. He even hates the stuff they buy him, he says. Can you believe that? Even hates his *bike*.' Pip makes sure she looks suitably stunned. 'Ed says all those gifts are like *bribes*. He said they're called guilt-trips. He says "Can't buy me love".'

'That's a song,' Pip tells him, 'do you know it? It's by the Beatles.'

'The Beatles are cool,' Tom tells her, 'everyone knows that.'

'Did you know Django actually worked with them for a short while?'

'No way!' Tom exclaims.

'Yes way,' Pip laughs, 'you can ask him all about it tomorrow.' She kisses him. 'Night night, Tomtom.'

'Night, Pippity.'

Pip hovers in the doorway. 'If I said "I love you" would you squirm and puke?'

Tom takes a moment. 'Nah. You can say it, if you like.'

'I *love* you,' says Pip.

'And I "*el*" you,' says Tom.

Fen snuggled up to Matt later that night. She knew if he kissed her forehead and then kissed the bridge of her nose immediately after, he was feeling horny. If he kissed her forehead twice in succession, he was tired. If he kissed it once, and kissed nowhere else, there was something on his mind. Two kisses it was: one to her forehead and one to the bridge of her nose.

'Wait!' she giggled a whisper and slipped out of bed, tiptoeing from the room which, in an old creaky house like

437

that on Farleymoor, was a pointless exercise really, laughably futile actually. Matt grinned in the dark. What on earth was she up to? He was full – dear God don't let her be raiding the fridge for whipping cream. Or ketchup. Fen returned and padded back to the bed. She ripped back the quilt and straddled Matt, his hands on her hips as he attempted to lever her into position.

'Oh no you don't!' she chided, twisting her body away from him. The room was extremely dark, there was no moon, no street lamps, no night lights. 'Merry Christmas, big boy,' Fen whispered coyly and Matt could feel something caressing his balls, tickling up and down the shaft of his cock. His pelvis rocked in response to his desire. What was it? A feather? Some as yet unidentifiable foodstuff? Something from under the Christmas tree?

'Ouch!' That didn't feel so nice, it felt as though his prick had been pronged, something scratching his balls. 'What the fuck *is* that?' he asked.

'Mistletoe, silly,' Fen giggled, 'it's Christmas.'

'How do you feel?' Zac asked Pip, who was sitting bolt upright in bed, staring straight ahead, while he wrapped Tom's presents on the end of the bed.

'A bit indigestiony,' Pip admitted.

'Nothing that a nice mug of Bisto couldn't cure?' Zac asked. 'Would you like me to make you a mug? I have to go downstairs to nibble the biscuits Tom left for Father Christmas.'

'Oh Zac, would you?' Pip said gratefully. 'You won't mind it stinking the room out?'

'How can I mind,' Zac said, 'when Santa's bought me a Rolex Oyster?'

'But Santa hasn't bought you a Rolex Oyster,' Pip told him sadly.

'I'm teasing,' Zac said. 'I don't believe in Santa. But do you think you could make your next craving camomile tea or something?'

Pip sipped her gravy and Zac wrapped presents. Pip marvelled how someone so precise with figures and percentages could make such a hash of papering a parcel. 'Zac,' she said, 'fold in, fold in, turn up. Here, hold my gravy, I'll do it.'

'Can you believe this time next year a little person will be celebrating Christmas with us?' Zac mused.

Pip smiled. And then she felt very sad. 'I pray that we'll *all* be here, *all* of us.'

Zac took her hand. 'He looks well, I thought. No different to when we were here a month ago.'

'He seems tired, though, don't you think?'

'Christmas is a tiring business,' Zac levelled, 'when you're making it for a big family. He seems very happy, to me.'

Tom and Cosima were sharing Cat's old bedroom. Cat and Ben weren't staying at the house at Farleymoor. They now had their own little house in Darley Dale, just twenty minutes away. But they would be back in time for breakfast with the family the next morning.

'Funny isn't it?' Cat says, jolting Ben from the verge of slumber.

'Hysterical,' he murmurs sleepily, hoping if he agrees she'll say no more and let him drift off to sleep.

'What's hysterical?' Cat asks and with all the movement on the mattress and rearrangement of the duvet, Ben can sense she's propped herself up and is staring hard at the back of his head.

He rolls onto his back with a sigh. Then he turns towards her. 'Are you about to put the light on?'

'Yes,' says Cat, doing just that. 'What's hysterical?'

'What's funny?' Ben counters.

Cat is diverted. 'Oh. I just meant it's funny how everyone is up at the house, and you and I are snuggled up here. Yet this – more than any place I've ever known – this is home. This is my home.'

Ben wonders why this is funny. But he swiftly decides not to ask.

'It's also funny how I thought I had everything meticulously planned – and this time last year Darley Dale was way off my map,' Cat says, beguilingly incredulous. 'Isn't it funny how a year of chaos can actually organize itself into the life that's right? Totally be beyond one's control.' She pauses and then smiles, her eyes closing with the surge of emotion. 'I love this place,' Cat enthuses. 'I *love* this place, Ben. I know it's higgledy-piggledy and the water is sometimes brown and there's that damp problem in the sitting-room and you clonk your head on the beam in the hallway and this bedroom is barely big enough to take our bed – but I love this place passionately. I can't believe anyone other than us has ever lived here. It's our *home*.'

'I don't mind that beam,' Ben says, 'and we do have a preposterously large bed.'

'It's about full circles, I suppose,' Cat muses, hovering the palm of her hand lightly over the surface of his cropped, silver-flecked hair to get that velvety feel. 'Because you see it's only now that I know I could never have settled here – less than five miles from my childhood home – unless I'd done the London thing as a single girl and then had a stint out in Colorado as a newly-wed and then returned to the UK all blasé about what was best for us. And the whole time I was destined to be here. It's *here* that I feel my most centred.'

Ben smiles at her. 'Welcome home,' he says lovingly.

'I suppose it's a similar thing with Django,' Cat muses, to herself as much as to her husband. 'I couldn't love him as

440

unconditionally as I do now – had I not had that dreadful period of absolutely loathing him.'

Ben is pleased finally to have the opportunity to elaborate. He's waited for this opening since the day after Django's party. 'And perhaps you couldn't have come this far in accepting the woman on your birth certificate had you not gone out to find her, stood right there in her territory and felt OK about her and, most importantly, felt good about yourself,' Ben says. 'Our parents do define us. And if we like ourselves, then it means that they're not so bad after all.'

Cat is thoughtful. 'You're so wise,' she says and she gazes at him with dreamy affection.

'And hunky,' Ben adds with a frown.

Cat biffs him with a pillow. She wriggles back down and settles her head into her pillow with a tired, happy sigh. 'Merry Christmas, Dr York,' she says and she touches his cheek.

'Merry Christmas, babe,' he says.

*　　*　　*

'Boys,' Django said late morning after the mountain of ripped wrapping paper and redundant packaging had been cleared away, the presents stacked into individual piles at well-spaced positions around the room, 'why don't you go for a blow-through. The girls are going to help me with the lunch. Cosima, you can be an honorary boy.'

'Turtle,' Cosima cooed, which had been her first word and remained her favourite.

'You can be an honorary turtle then, poppet,' Django said. 'Tom, you can lead the expedition. You can take my gnarled old cane – no, not that one. That one is from Selfridges. The other one – it was given to me when I was trekking in Tibet. If anyone can unearth its mystical powers, it's you.'

441

They stood on the flagstone doorstep, Django and his girls, and waved the party on their way; Tom stomping off at a good pace, the men following behind, Cosima sitting proud on her Uncle Zac's shoulders while Ben picked up one pink welly and Matt the other.

'Shall I lay the table?' Pip said.

'I usually do that,' said Fen.

'We'll do the table later, I need you three in the kitchen with me.'

They are in the kitchen, humming to a CD of Christmas carols that Fen bought from the motorway services. There is food on every available surface, including the window sill and the top of the fridge, and the *Times Atlas of the World* is lain across an opened drawer to provide another surface still.

'Now I want you to know, that the thing to remember about parsnips is they're plain. They even look plain. If you enliven something plain, you forget it was plain in the first place. Like Plain Jane at school – pop a lovely hair band on her *et voilà*.' The girls give each other their secret *he's-nuts* look that they've honed over the years to being all but imperceptible to anyone else. 'And so it is with parsnips,' Django continues. 'Ginger is the key. I always add a little ginger to parsnips. Ginger root, mind you, not that powdered excuse.'

'God, I quite feel like chewing ginger root,' Pip murmurs.

'Well, if there's any left, you can,' says Django. 'And I always like to use this knife for the parsnips. And I find this angle works best. You try, Cat. Now you, Fen. Pip – your turn. Good stuff.'

The girls break into a pseudo-operatic chorus of fa-la-las for 'Ding Dong Merrily on High' and Django conducts them momentarily with the soup ladle before noticing the time. 'Carrots and broccoli,' he says. 'There's a secret here and it's

442

to do with texture. Broccoli can be alarmingly woolly – but I find if you add a little lemon juice to the water in which you steam it, *pas de problemo*!'

The girls nod earnestly and then sing along with 'Good King Wenceslas'.

'Carrots!' Django declares above their din. 'Brown sugar elevates this humble but highly hued vegetable above its common status as horse fodder.' The girls keep singing but they give him the thumbs up.

'Have you a secret for sprouts that stops them smelling like farts?' Cat giggles.

'Catriona!' Django objects. 'We don't do sprouts in this family.' The girls consider this. It was true. 'I think I'll sit down for a moment,' Django says and makes his way, a little falteringly, to the chair.

The girls hurry round.

'Are you OK?'

'What's the matter?'

'What can we do?'

'I'm fine,' says Django, 'it's just the excitement.'

'But you look in pain,' Pip says.

'Just a few aches and gripes,' Django says. 'Don't read into it – I *am* seventy-five. What did I want to say? Ah yes, roast potatoes. Roast potatoes.'

And it suddenly strikes the girls hard in their hearts that, actually, they're not helping Django prepare Christmas dinner. This isn't a cookery lesson. This is not about this Christmas or past Christmases, this is about Christmases yet to come. This is the passing down of family recipes, the imparting of knowledge, the handing over of experience and quirks, the conveying of preference and methods in the sincerest hope that family traditions will continue. The room rings far louder with the resonance of this, the solemnity of such responsibility, than it does with 'Silent Night'.

443

'Don't cry,' Pip whispers to Django who is dabbing his eyes furiously.

'I'm not crying, darling,' he says, 'it's just the onions. It's just the onions. The buggers. When it comes to onions, my advice is to suck a spoon and chop them in water.'

With the children sound asleep upstairs, their new favourite toys propped up on the bedside tables so that they can be viewed and adored on waking, downstairs it is time for the McCabe yuletide tradition of The Great Ring Round. This is the one occasion in the calendar when Django McCabe cannot be prised off the telephone and it is the one day when the telephone company realizes he is a viable customer after all. Bibi is phoned in Paris, Toni is phoned on the shores of Squam Lake, Rayner is rung in Sausalito. They call Babs Chorlton down the road and then Jim McKenzie up in Glasgow. Django bestows Christmas cheer and chatter before passing the caller to Pip, Fen and Cat; going through the ages, over the years. Gregor and Ferdy stay on the phone for over half an hour. The Merifields laugh and say, Why are you phoning us, McCabe, we'll see you tomorrow for Boxing Day drinks. Django shouts down the phone to make himself heard to Vauxhall Vinnie who is now rather deaf. This year, sadly, there are no Bebop Boys left to phone. Joe and Jack go through their own tradition of asking the McCabe girls to tell them about each and every present and what exactly it does. Everyone adds the word 'healthy' in wishing Django a happy new year.

'I'm all talked out,' says Cat, popping an After Eight into her mouth.

'I don't think Joe and Jack quite got what an iPod is all about,' says Pip, 'though personally, I thought I explained it pretty well.'

'It was so nice to speak to Bibi,' says Fen. 'I don't think I've spoken to her since your birthday.'

'Just one more phone call,' Django declares, to groans all round, 'then I promise you, I'll put the thing in the broom cupboard.'

'But we've done everyone,' Pip declares.

'I thought we might phone your mother, actually,' says Django. The girls fall silent. It's one thing to honour the requests of a dying man, to learn his way with roasting potatoes, it's another to agree to a potentially bad idea. But Django reads their minds. 'It's not a bad idea,' he says quite firmly, 'it's the right thing to do.'

Penny had refused Marcia's invitation to Christmas lunch; it was her first on her own and she wanted to spend it at home, not for any maudlin self-indulgence, but because she and Bob had never made a big fuss about Christmas anyway.

She is eating her lunch, direct from the foil container, when the phone rings.

'That'll be Marcia,' Penny murmurs, 'hoping to change my mind. Well I've eaten now – but perhaps I will join them for cards this evening.' She walks over to the phone.

'Hullo?'

'Penny? It's Django.'

'Django?'

'In England. United Kingdom. Derek McCabe.'

'No – no, Django is fine. Django is good. My *goodness*.'

'I'm phoning long-distance – can you hear me?'

'Yes, I can hear you. I can hear you just fine.'

'We're all here, all of us, in Derbyshire, as per usual. We thought we'd give you a tinkle. To wish you a merry Christmas and a happy new year.'

Penny is speechless. But being speechless scares her because she knows Django hates telephones and he might misconstrue it as a fault on the transatlantic line. She must speak. She must. 'My,' she says, 'my. That's very nice of you. I wish you a merry Christmas too. You – plural.'

'This line is very clear, isn't it?' Django marvels.

'Yes it is,' Penny agrees.

'And how are you?' Django asks. 'This time of year – I imagine it can't be easy.'

'Thank you,' Penny says, 'but you know it's OK – it's better than I thought. I've just had my lunch. It was tasty. And I'm going to play cards with friends tonight.'

'You are on your own?' Django queries.

'Yes,' Penny says, 'I am.'

'That's not right, not on Christmas,' Django says. 'Well I'm jolly glad we phoned now, I most certainly am.'

'I'm OK, Dango,' Penny says and she cringes because although she wanted to say Django she started saying Derek instead. 'And how are you?' There's a pause. 'Hullo?'

'Still here,' says Django, 'I'm still here. I've had a spot of bother, but I'm still here.'

'Are you OK?' Penny asks.

'I feel fine,' Django assures her. 'I've had a very happy day. I'm passing you over – we have a tradition on the McCabe Great Ring Round, we go through the ages – so you'll have Pip, followed by Fen, followed by Cat.'

'Hullo?' says Pip.

'Hullo Philippa.'

'Merry Christmas.'

'And to you. How are you?'

'I'm pregnant!'

'Oh! Oh! That's just wonderful news. When are you due?'

'Late June – a week before Fen's daughter turns two.' A pause. 'How are you?'

'I'm great, thank you.'

'Would you like to speak to Fen?'

'I'd like to speak to you a little longer,' Penny says, 'if I may.'

'Oh, OK.' A pause. 'How are you, then?'

'I'm great. I'm great. How nice to hear from you.'

'Yes. And you too. Merry Christmas – I hope you have a happier year ahead.'

'That's kind. Will you – well, will you let me know about the baby?'

'Yes,' says Pip, 'of course I will. I'm passing you on to Fen now. Bye bye.'

'Goodbye, Pip.'

'Hullo,' says Fen.

'Merry Christmas, Fenella.'

'And to you – and a happy new year. I hope it's a good one.'

'Thank you. And how are you?'

'I'm fine. Cosima is eighteen months old. She speaks a little. She says "turtle" quite a lot, actually.'

'How extraordinary! How endearing. Your first word was "apple". Pip's was "goody" and I'm afraid I don't know what Catriona's was.'

'Oh. Quite.' A pause. 'How is the weather?'

'We have snow, we have a white Christmas. It's picture perfect. And how is it with you?'

'It's a little overcast. But quite mild, actually.' A pause. 'Would you like me to pass you on to Cat, now?'

'I'd like to speak to you a little longer,' Penny says, 'if I may.'

'Oh yes. Of course.'

'What have you been up to?'

'I've gone back to work, part-time, I'm enjoying it immensely.'

'Good for you. That's great.'

'Thanks. And you?'

'Oh, I've been painting the house. And hiking. And I went to Florida with my friend Marcia – she has a condo there. Boy was it hot.'

'That sounds good,' says Fen. 'I'm going to pass you on to Cat now. Have a very merry Christmas – and a lovely year to come.'

'Thank you, Fen, thank you,' says Penny.

'Hullo,' says Cat, 'Merry Christmas and a happy new year.'

'Well thank you, Catriona – and I wish you the same. How are you?'

'Great – busy. Ben and I moved to Darley Dale. I'm heading up a new flagship bookshop near Sheffield and Ben is Dr Big in sports medicine at the local hospital.'

'My, you girls – you have so much to be proud of. What achievements. It's wonderful.'

'Thank you.' A pause. 'It's nice to be nearer to Django.'

'Is he unwell? I get the feeling he is.'

'He is.'

'I'm so sorry,' Penny trails off. She doesn't want to hear that it's cancer. But she suspects it is. She feels her instincts are heightened, having lived through Bob's cancer. 'What have you done today – what is Christmas Day like for you?'

'Oh, we've cooked and eaten and unwrapped an obscene amount of presents.'

'Good for you!'

'And phoned all our friends,' Cat thinks for a moment, 'and family.'

'Is Django still there?' Penny asks.

'Yes – do you want a word?'

'A word is exactly what I want,' Penny tells her. 'Goodbye, Cat. And merry Christmas. To you all.'

'Hullo?' says Django.

'Hullo Django,' says Penny. 'I just wondered – I don't know why I just wondered.' She pauses. She laughs a little. 'But I just wondered if perhaps you remembered what Cat's first word was?'

Django pauses. 'Garden.'

'Garden,' Penny marvels, 'that's lovely. Well I guess I ought to let you go.'

'OK.'

'Thank you so much for calling me. I'm quite – I'm quite. I'm overwhelmed.'

Django looks around the room. All eyes are on him. 'Maybe next year we can entice you over,' he says.

Penny is speechless but again she fears Django might presume the line to be dead.

'Oh my,' she says quietly, 'well. That is some invitation.'

'Good!' Django declares as he smiles at his girls. 'That's settled then.'

In loving memory
Liz Berney
12.2.1968–24.12.2005

Acknowledgements

No matter how deeply I love my characters and believe in them, I must reluctantly admit to spending most of my working life with people who don't actually exist. However, behind the scenes, I am blessed with a dynamic and crucial support network helping to bring my books to life. Sincerest thanks go to my team at HarperCollins – especially my esteemed editor Lynne Drew. My agent, the inimitable Jonathan Lloyd, thank you – your percentage is my pleasure. Dawn Gobourne (and Hilary, Germaine and Ana) at Haringey Library Services – thanks for making my working days so happy and cosy. Mary Chamberlain, my eagle-eyed copy-editor, and Sophie Ransom, my tireless publicist – thank you both for your patience and your attention to detail. I'd also like to extend my gratitude to Bex Lane, Jerney de Vries, Naina Patel, Sue McMillan, Souki Hartigan, Sue McCormack and Sarah Henderson for enabling me, in so many ways, to write this book.

The Holistic Cancer Care Centre, James Cook University Hospital, Middlesbrough (*in memory of David Sutcliffe 1937–2005*).

Love Rules

Freya North

Love or lust, passion or promises?

Thea Luckmore loves romance and lives for the magic of true love. She's determined only ever to fall head over heels, or rather, heart over head.

Alice Heggarty, her best friend, has always loved lust – but she's fed up with dashing rogues. Now she's set her sights on good, sensible husband material. And she's found him.

For Thea, a chance encounter on Primrose Hill ignites that elusive spark. Saul Mundy appears to be the perfect fit and Thea's heart is snapped up fast.

However, newly-wed Alice finds that she's not as keen as she thought on playing by the rules and she starts to break them left, right and centre. At the same time, a shocking discovery shatters Thea's belief in everlasting love.

When it comes to love, should you listen to your head, your heart, or your best friend?

'An emotive novel that deals with the darker side of love – these are real women, with real feelings.'   *She*

'Tantrums, tarts, tears and text-sex… what's not to love about this cautionary tale for new romantics?'   *Heat*

'It's an addictive read that encompasses the stuff life is made of: love, sex, fidelity and, above all, friendship.'   *Glamour*

ISBN 0 00 718036 5

Innocence

Kathleen Tessaro

Love. The greatest temptation of all.

It's a long way from Eden, Ohio to London. Eighteen-year-old Evie leaves her hometown for the first time to come to England and follow her dream of being an actress. With fellow students Imogene and Robbie, she studies drama – and life. Her friendship with the bohemian, outrageous Robbie illuminates her new world. Together, anything is possible.

But then life, and love – in the shape of struggling rock musician Jake Albery – intervene, and everything changes.

Fifteen years later, Evie is a single mother, teaching drama and living with the eccentric Bunny in her house of artistic lodgers. Robbie's gone. And Evie is trying to forget the past and dreams they once shared.

Then an old friendship comes to haunt her – literally. And suddenly everything is possible again …

'This is the 30-plus equivalent of the coming-of-age novel: a coming-awake novel for women who have wasted their 20s on cheap men and rough wine.'   *Guardian*

'A warm tale of love, friendship and following your dreams.'
                                                                 Cosmopolitan

ISBN 0 00 715145 4